More
than
Friends

Also by Tracy Culleton

Looking Good
Loving Lucy

More than Friends

TRACY CULLETON

POOLBEG

Published 2005
by Poolbeg Press Ltd
123 Grange Hill, Baldoyle
Dublin 13, Ireland
E-mail: poolbeg@poolbeg.com

13 5 7 9 10 8 6 4 2

A catalogue record for this book is available from the British Library.

ISBN 1-84223-200-2

Typeset by Patricia Hope in Palatino 10/13.5
Printed by Litografia Rosés, S.A, Spain

www.poolbeg.com

About the Author

Tracy Culleton lives in County Carlow with her husband and nine-year-old son. She invites you to visit her website **www.tracyculleton.com**, or to e-mail her at **tracy@tracyculleton.com**. Tracy loves hearing from her readers!

Acknowledgements

First of all, thanks must go to Jacintha, who gave me the inspiration for this story.

Secondly I'd like to thank editor *extraordinaire*, Gaye Shortland. She always does a brilliant job, but she outdid herself this time. If you enjoy this book, please spare a thought for Gaye because it wouldn't be half the book it is without her.

Thanks must also go to Peter, who kept the home fires burning, and Tadhg who didn't interrupt me too much (and thanks also to Peter and Tadhg for the sheer joy and richness they bring into my life).

Thanks again to the Irish Girls – fellow women writers who have so welcomed me into their group, and with whom I can share the joys and tribulations and challenges and fun of being a writer.

Thanks to all the members of the **www.writeon-irishgirls.com** website – a place where writers and readers can meet and mingle. It's been great fun.

And, of course, thanks to you, the reader, without whom there would be no point in doing any of this. Thanks for the feedback for my previous novels, and your continued support. I hope you enjoy reading *More than Friends* as much as I enjoyed writing it.

For Frances,
sister *extraordinaire*

Chapter 1

"It's a truth universally acknowledged," I pronounced glumly, idly whirling my spoon around in the *Café-Café* signature royal-blue mug, "that a woman in possession of a loudly ticking biological clock must be in search of a husband."

"What?" demanded Gaby, daintily nibbling at the fluffy pink marshmallow from the top of her creamy hot chocolate, "and would you ever stop stirring that coffee? It's very annoying."

I complied, placing the spoon down onto the faux-marble table.

All around us in the brightly coloured café other people were engaged in cheerful conversation, and the sound reverberated around our heads.

"So, what were you saying?" Gaby asked as she sipped from her mug.

"I was paraphrasing Jane Austen," I told her loftily. "If I'm stuck on the proverbial shelf, I might as well be cultured about it. And I'm beginning to think that I *am* on that shelf, and it's not very comfortable, and the view is dull."

To give Gaby her due, she made a huge effort – albeit not an entirely successful one – to look modest. Since the advent of Bridget Jones I'd noticed that all my married friends were seriously risking hernias trying not to appear self-satisfied about their marital status. Partly genuine kindness, I thought, and partly the desire to avoid accusations of Smug Married-ness.

But to be fair, it was tough for them. It had to be hard *not* to be smug when you had achieved the prize of the marriage ceremony. Or at least the joint-mortgage ceremony. Obviously, it was difficult not to be complacent, and even the tiniest little bit condescending, when you, from the safe harbours of married life, viewed the stormy waters and choppy seas of single life . . . I hope I'm not overdoing metaphors here – I suspect I might be.

But it was truly how I saw them: safe in happy coupledom, secure in having found The One, in knowing that they had been selected from all the people in the world to be the chosen spouse, and that there was now, and always would be, a place where they belonged. I desperately envied that and wanted it for myself.

And yes, rationally, I knew that marriage didn't always, or even often, provide that safe harbour – that there were affairs and divorces and rows and disappointments and bitterness and disillusionment. Still I was hoping and yearning to avoid all that, to have the fairy-tale romance in which I would, against all odds, live happily ever after.

I have to reluctantly confess that my keenness, or perhaps *desperation* is a better word, to find a mate made Bridget Jones' anxiety look like mild concern in comparison. I was thirty-two, and the calendar was tracking the countdown to thirty-three with dizzying rapidity. Time was running out.

"But, Sally, I thought," said Gaby, picking her words delicately, "that you had sworn off men. After your experience with Shay –"

"Yes, I know, I know," I abruptly cut her off. That's the trouble with lifelong friends. They quote your own proclamations back at you. "But I've got to give them one last chance, Gaby. They can't *all* be commitment-phobic like Shay, may he be forever accursed for taking three years of my life before telling me he wasn't ready to settle down."

She gave a short snort of sympathetic laughter.

"And they surely can't *all* be football-obsessed immature eejits like Fintan, God bless him, but he'll be a fine man if he ever grows up."

"Too true."

"They can't *all* be self-satisfied thirty-going-on-sixty gits like Simon with his pension plans and his inviolate routines. There must be *some* nice men out there and, after all, I only want one. That's all it'll take. I'm tired of being single. I want to settle down, and I want a baby, therefore I need a man."

"You don't need a man to have a baby," she pointed out. "There's ways and means, you know. There's even a website which delivers donated sperm direct to your door. I read about it the other day." She shook her head,

3

half in disbelief and half in admiration – that woman who gets her sperm delivered the traditional way, and regularly and exuberantly if she's to be believed. "Sounds to me like the ultimate male order!" she deadpanned and then collapsed at her own wit.

"Ha, ha," I said politely, and then went on, "but I want a *man*. I want the whole package: the joint mortgage, the romance and love, the your-parents-or-mine row at Christmas, the warm back against which to thaw cold feet, the never *having* to organise activities for Saturday night, the staying in being as much a valid lifestyle choice as going out."

"There's more to it than that," she ventured.

"I know there is. I want it all. I want a settled life with my own man and a baby on the way, a baby conceived the natural way, with a doting father and partner being an essential part of the picture. Is this really too much to ask?" I queried, a little loudly I grant you.

"No, no, it's not," she hastened to reassure me, sending anxious glances around the café in case people were looking at me. "No, Sally, it's not too much to ask at all. It really isn't."

I continued with my speech. It just rolled out of me. Well, I had given a lot of time to thinking about this stuff.

"I think that actually it might well be too much to ask. I think all the good men have been snapped up long ago. Snapped up by women like yourself, Gaby, who had way more sense than I did, who realised that although theoretically there was a man for every

4

woman, there wasn't necessarily a *good* man for every woman."

She was carefully not looking smug again.

I continued, "Taken by women who realised that it's far better to get the pick of the crop than have only the choice of everybody else's rejects and the commitment-phobes. Women who realised that partying away your twenties believing that thirty was time enough to get married was very, very, short-term thinking. As well as being totally erroneous." Then I finished by telling her, and not for the first time, "You're so lucky, you know."

"I am. I know it," she said seriously, and I knew that she did.

She and Peter had been inseparable since they met and Peter had this half-dazed expression on his face at times, as though he was still trying to come to terms with his good luck that Gaby had consented to be his wife. He would do anything for her, not because he was a wimp, because he certainly wasn't that. No, he would do anything for her simply because he adored her so much he was constantly trying to give her the sun, moon and stars, or failing that, everything else. As she said herself, she had to be careful of the most innocuous statement. Casual comments such as, 'That's a nice song,' could result in that singer's every album turning up on her pillow a couple of days later.

I sighed and took a contemplative sip of my tea as I thought about it. It had set the bar very high for the rest of us. Because, you see, I didn't *just* want a husband/partner/significant other and baby(ies). I wanted that *and* I wanted to be adored as Gaby was.

Yes, yes, I said to myself, and a Lotto win while I'm at it, and another four inches of height, and longer thicker hair – might as well dream here as in bed, as they say.

But still, I'd seen Gaby experiencing this and so I knew that it existed. And surely I was as wonderful as Gaby? Well, nearly. Wonderful enough to merit being adored anyway. At least for a little while. Peter's adoration of Gaby showed no sign of abating, but I'd be happy to be adored like that even temporarily during the first flush of romance.

"I *am* lucky," she repeated now, "but I'm sure that you'll be lucky too. Speaking of which, I thought there might be something going on, or about to go on, between you and that man in the gym. What was his name again?"

"David," I said, "David Corrigan." He was co-owner, with his friend Darius, and part-time training instructor of *Svelte,* the gym I frequented.

"That was it – David. You've mentioned him a lot recently, and I was wondering if there was something going on there?"

"Well, there wasn't. There isn't," I said shortly. "Turns out he's gay." I drained my cup, and poured some more tea from the teapot.

"Oh dear," she said sympathetically, "that's an awful pity."

"Yes, it is," I agreed, carefully adding milk to my newly poured tea. "And I felt awfully stupid when I found out, because I hadn't realised. But really, did I expect all gay men to go mincing around the place with one hand on their hip ad the other fluttering airily? How appallingly prejudiced of me!" Gaby laughed as I continued, "But it's okay. We're still friends anyway, and that's the main thing."

"Indeed . . ." she said, looking ever so slightly amused. "Back to the drawing board then! So, you want a man, why don't you do something proactive about getting one?"

I glared at her. "Gaby, I know that you have read *Men Are From Mars, Women Are From Venus.*"

"Of course, I have. Hasn't everybody? What of it?"

"Then you should know that it's only insensitive blundering men who insist on offering solutions. We wonderful, understanding women offer sympathy, empathising by saying things like, 'poor you, it sounds dreadful'."

It was her turn to glare. "I don't remember the book being *quite* so judgemental," she said with just a soupçon of sarcasm, "about men offering solutions, nor quite so congratulatory about women being empathetic."

"Well, no . . ." I admitted.

"And even if women do *tend* to offer sympathy rather than solutions, that doesn't mean that a woman can *never* offer a solution, especially not when her friend is being all self-pitying and whingeing and really does need a kick up the backside and is lucky to be getting away with mere solution-offering," she finished robustly.

I grunted, but given that she was right it was a conciliatory grunt rather than an argumentative grunt, and she knew me well enough to correctly interpret it.

And so she continued: "Let's see . . . what can you do to get a man? Why don't you go out more?"

"Come on! You know I go out quite a lot! But it's a waste of time. I've told you! Clubs and things are like a meat-market. Most of the men seem more interested in their pints than in women for most of the evening and then when they do approach you at the end of the night they're breathing alcohol fumes all over you and are just after a quick shag. And not even a mutually pleasurable shag – they're way too pissed for that kind of finesse. More a scratching-their-itch shag." I caught her half-horrified, half-amused expression. "Seriously, Gaby, it's what men themselves have told me as they spray their conversation all over me. They're too pissed, usually, even for guile. 'Any chance I can come home with you,' they say. 'I'll be quick and be gone before you know it'."

She laughed through her amazement. "I'm so out of touch. I really am!"

"That's because I usually spare you the worst details – but you're better off," I told her dourly. "And then there are those you just *know* are married. They even have white missing-tan marks on their ring fingers, and it never seems to occur to them that we might notice!"

"How stupid!"

"Tell me about it! Besides," I emptied the remainder of the teapot's contents into my cup, "most of my friends are married now – you're all copping out." I laughed ruefully. "So it's harder to get friends who are even interested in going out on the town. And if any of them do, they just want to stick together and have a laugh – they obviously don't want to chat up men."

"Right. I can see that that's not ideal," she conceded. "Okay – so what about night-classes? Car maintenance or something like that?"

I gave her such a withering look that she caved in immediately on that one.

"I know," she suggested brightly, sitting up straighter in her enthusiasm. "Why don't you join a dating agency? There's quite a few on the internet. Or try that new speed-dating."

"A *dating* agency? *Speed-dating*?" I echoed, appalled.

"Sure. Why not? They're the new bumping-into-each-other – I read that somewhere."

I looked sharply at her, unsure as to whether she really had read it somewhere, or whether she had just made it up. She looked back at me, blue eyes wide open, the very picture of innocence. I decided that it didn't really matter who had made it up: Gaby, or some hack under pressure from a deadline. Either way, it was stupid.

"I'm not joining a dating agency," I told her firmly. "Or going speed-dating." I placed my now-empty mug down on the table for emphasis.

"Okay," she shrugged. "It's up to you. But I'm out of suggestions, I really am. Either do something to meet somebody, or stop whingeing about it. I'm surprised that you find it so difficult, though," she said looking at me consideringly. "It's not as if you're ugly, after all."

"Thanks," I laughed a little wryly. Damned by faint praise. No, I wasn't ugly, but I wasn't God's gift either.

I'm medium height, with a medium build which stays that way only through a lot of effort at the gym and restraint at the table. At that time, my hair was shoulder-length and, though naturally brown, was resolutely blonde through judicious applications of that magic stuff from a bottle. I have fine delicate features (I prefer the words 'fine' and 'delicate' to sharp) with deep-green long-lashed eyes – definitely my best feature. So no, not ugly. And I scrubbed up well though I say so myself. I put a lot of effort into looking my best – I got my hair styled regularly, was at all times elegantly made-up (even when I was working out – seriously), and I always wore stylish well-looked-after clothes.

But I'd thought about this question of good looks a *lot* recently, and I wasn't entirely sure that it had that much to do with whether you got married or not. Have you ever noticed how many ugly people are married? Loads, that's how many.

A case in point: Gaby. Not that she was ugly, far from it. But she was definitely on the plump side of curvy. She was the sort of person who gives being overweight a good name. She freely admitted that she had always been at least a size sixteen and that she fluctuated between that and size twenty. And she had never, ever cared.

And because she didn't care, nobody else ever cared either – at least, that was my theory. As long as I'd known her she'd never been short of male attention. She'd always had the most beautiful porcelain skin and plenty of it, with abundant curving shoulders and a generous cleavage. Her plump face was pretty rather than classically beautiful, but *extremely* attractive and appealing, and her head of auburn curls, infectious laugh, and warm, tranquil, kind and approachable personality made her irresistible.

I had also come to the conclusion that a huge part of her secret was that she was so completely relaxed and comfortable in her skin. It had simply never occurred to her that anybody might think less of her because she didn't conform to our culture's fashionable figure . . . and so nobody did think less of her.

I often envied her certainty and self-confidence. As I was sweating on the treadmill at the gym, or straining to do just one more length of the pool, I often wished I could be more relaxed about my appearance.

But the reality was that I *didn't* have her confidence, so I continued to make sure I presented myself at my best. For all the good it did me.

Gaby was right, though. I really should put up or shut up. For now I chose to shut up.

"How are Haley and Jack?" I asked, and her face lit up.

"Oh, they're great! Oh, wait till I tell you what Haley said yesterday!" and she shared with me the latest gem from her daughter.

I listened, fascinated. That was one thing Gaby loved about me – that I'd listen for ages to anecdotes about her children. I adored them both so it was no hardship, but a deep part of me was also aware of the huge credit I was storing up for talking about *my* baby when I finally had one. Which I would. I was determined upon it.

Chapter 2

I laughed to myself on the way home. A dating agency indeed! I was keen for a man, not desperate after all, I told myself, quite forgetting my realisation that I made Bridget Jones look mildly concerned. Going to a dating agency was the last resort of the pathetic. Of those who couldn't get a man by normal means.

Like me, a little voice in my head contributed helpfully.

That doesn't mean I'm pathetic, I told it brusquely, *just unlucky*.

Maybe those who use dating agencies are also unlucky rather than pathetic, it suggested.

Hmm, maybe, I conceded.

I began thinking about it in my odd moments – falling asleep, waiting for the next LUAS tram, that sort of thing. The meeting-by-chance method of finding a spouse wasn't, after all, the method of choice for most humans for most of history. Look at arranged marriages . . . they had an honourable history and were still popular in some cultures, and by all accounts their hit rate for successful marriages was as good as, or better than, the falling-in-love method.

I didn't even have to look to foreign cultures for evidence of this, actually. Didn't we in Ireland have a long and distinguished tradition of the matchmaker? Would it be possible to view dating agencies as simply a modern version of that? Nothing to be ashamed of at all.

Really, the more I thought about it objectively, it was ludicrous leaving to chance something as important as finding your mate.

You wouldn't look for a job that way. Of course you wouldn't. You wouldn't just go around in your daily life hoping that somebody, somewhere, would end up saying that such-and-such a company was looking for a new financial advisor.

No, indeed not. If you wanted a new job you scanned the ads, you registered with an employment agency, you wrote to companies you would like to work with. None of that meant that you were unemployable, did it? None of that meant that you were desperate and running out of time and frantic for any sort of job. No, you still kept your standards high.

In fact, I thought, warming to my theme, it meant that your standards could be even higher! The more potential jobs you were aware of, the more options you had, and the pickier you could be about your choice.

Of course, the same thing applied to dating agencies! They weren't for the desperate at all! They were for people with such fulfilling satisfying lives in other areas that they hadn't time to mess around hoping that chance would bring them a mate. They were for people who respected themselves so much that they set about getting themselves the best that was on offer.

And in this manner, in moments and increments of thought, I brought myself around to the idea of using a dating agency. And as so often happens, once I was thinking of such things, I was aware of them everywhere. The small ads at the back of newspapers. An article in a magazine about four blissful-looking couples telling how they met through various dating agencies. This article even gave the contact details of the relevant organisations.

I'm only being curious, I told myself as I logged on one evening to the website www.morethanfriends.ie.

I soon realised that I could browse the site without registering, without committing myself in any way or declaring my interest. So I did that very thing. I perused their selection of heterosexual men between thirty and thirty-five. Within seconds I was looking at a long list. Against each name there were a few details such as age, geographic area and occupation.

I quickly learned that I had the option of clicking on each name to bring up the full profile. About half the men had also chosen to include a photograph

This is amazing, I told myself. It's like the ultimate shopping spree! And I'm window-shopping! I looked in detail at some of the entries. Average people, I realised. Not film-star handsome, but not Quasimodo-ugly either. Just ordinary people looking to connect with other people.

This mightn't be as bad as I had thought. There were

several men who sounded interesting, whom I wouldn't mind at least contacting.

What! *What* am I thinking of? I quickly logged off and glared at my computer as if it were to blame.

I couldn't really be serious about this. Could I?

Why not? I asked myself then. All the arguments I had already used came back to me: far from being for losers it was the option for winners. There was nothing to be ashamed of, long and honourable history and so on.

I've always been very good at finding justification to do things I want to do. So it didn't take me too long to convince myself that it was okay to join this dating agency. More than okay, it was *essential*.

I logged onto the website once more. Okay, here goes, I told myself nervously, feeling as if I were about to launch myself onto a black run in the Alps without ever even having attempted the nursery slopes.

I took a deep breath and clicked on the button to register. Once I had given my credit-card details I was able to move onto the next screen in order to complete my profile. There was a series of questions which were a mixture of multiple-choice and free text.

The early questions were easy to answer:

Name: *Sally Cronin.*

Age: *32.*

Marital status: *single*. Did that make me look very sad, I wondered? Would it make me look as if nobody anywhere had wanted me? Ever. Maybe, I desperately tried to convince myself, it would make me look as if I had very high standards.

Children: Yes, please. Oh, they wanted to know if I already *had* children. Well then, *No*.

Hair colour: *Blonde*. Well, it *was* blonde. So what if I needed assistance to get it that way?

Figure: *Medium build.*

Height: 5'4" (160cm).

Eye colour: *green.*

Ethnic group: *Caucasian.*

Star sign: *Sagittarius*. Did anybody really make decisions on who to contact based on their star sign? I supposed they must do, since the website owners thought it worth including. Think of all the wonderful relationships which could have been, but never were, because somebody was the wrong star sign and so the other person hadn't even contacted them.

Or, if there was anything to the whole theory, think of all the misery that had been saved. Hmm. I didn't even know which star signs were supposed to be compatible with mine, so I just wouldn't factor it into my selections.

Educational level: *Third level degree.*

Occupation: *Financial advisor.*

Income: That was a bit personal at this stage, surely? But then I realised that there was an option of '*Tell you later*', so I picked that. Not that I was planning to tell anybody later, but the system didn't include the option of '*Mind your own business*'.

Smoker: *No.*

Drinker: *Social drinker*. The choices were: *non-drinker*, *very occasionally*, *social drinker* and *regular drinker*, and I had to wonder if anybody ever admitted to being a regular drinker, which seemed to be a euphemism for *raging alcoholic.*

Religion: Again, I'd tell them later (or not).

Then there was a list of attributes on which we had to grade ourselves on a scale of one (not at all) to ten (totally). I had never asked these questions of myself, so it was quite challenging.

The first question was: how emotional was I? Pretty emotional, I'd have said. Not a ten . . . I can be pretty cool if I need to be, and I can be very logical too . . . have to be, really, with my job. Perhaps an eight.

But I'd better not put an eight, I thought. Men hate emotional women, don't they?

But there was no point putting down a two or three. It would be too hard to live up to. I could picture myself sitting in a coffee-bar somewhere and being told about some world disaster or starving kitten, and instead of nonchalantly saying, "Oh, really?" (in bored tones, of course) I'd be dribbling tears and blubbing profusely.

Plus, another thought occurred to me: men don't like women to be *too* emotional but they do want *some* emotion so they can be loved and adored. So, far better to stick to within shouting distance of the truth. I settled on saying that I was a seven.

The next question asked how much of a risk-taker I was. Well, I hope I'm pretty adventurous without being stupid. That would make me a six or a seven. So I put down that I was an eight, in the vague, barely articulated hope that it would subliminally suggest I was a bit Lara Croft-ish.

'I have lots of friends,' was the next statement I had to

grade myself on. My immediate reaction was to put a ten. *Of course*, I had lots of friends. Who did they think I was? Some sad pathetic lonely eejit? But . . . if I had so many friends, what was I doing getting involved in computer dating? A score of ten wouldn't ring true at all.

And, I thought glumly as I rested my chin on my hands and thought about it, how was I doing on the friends thing anyway?

I had Gaby and Peter, that went without saying. But Majella had gone to New Zealand and wouldn't be back for a number of years, if ever. And Jan was in London now and I only saw her when she came back for Christmas, and on my bi-annual trip over to see her.

And now that I thought about it, I hadn't heard from Sandra in a while. We seemed to be drifting apart since she had got married. And Carla had the twins now and was so busy I never saw her – we did talk on the phone regularly but . . . actually, come to think of it, we hadn't spoken in quite a while.

In this fashion I went through the inventory of my friends and found it sadly depleted. Not that these people were any less a friend than they ever were . . . well, it depends on how you define *friend*, doesn't it? Was there a certain number of times a year you had to see somebody before you could call them a friend?

And what about my colleagues? I wondered. Could I call them my friends? I smiled as I thought of them: motherly Kathleen, not content with her own three grandchildren but she had to mother us too; Marc, freshly out of college and bright and exuberant; Mary

Kwamba, originally from Nigeria, bright and lively with her dramatic colouring, strong features and vivid ethnic clothing setting off her humorous and engaging personality. We all worked well together, and laughed together and never had rows. Well, hardly ever. And we did socialise together, twice or three times a year. Did that qualify us as friends?

And, of course, there was the gay David. Could I really call him a friend though? I only ever saw him at the gym.

Eventually, anyway, after much further thought, I decided I could ethically give myself a score of eight for the statement, *'I have lots of friends'*.

God, this was tough, and I was only a little bit of the way through.

The next question was easier, however. It asked about my level of fitness, and thanks to all that work in the gym I could put down a nine with a clear conscience.

Then it got difficult again. The next question was free-text and it concerned my hobbies.

What on earth was I going to put for my hobbies?

Well, what did I actually do?

I went to *Svelte* faithfully five times a week – working out three of those days and swimming forty lengths two other days. That should impress them both with my tenacity and also the figure they might assume I was getting out of it.

Apart from that I socialised with my friends. When they were around and available. And I went to the cinema occasionally. Is going to the cinema even considered a hobby?

I wrote – that was another hobby!

Well . . . I *thought* about writing. I had vague dreams of writing a novel one day. Yeah, that'd really impress them. Me and 90% of the population. And like most of that 90% I haven't actually done anything about it to date, hardly. So I couldn't even hope to talk intelligently about it.

But still, I put writing down as a hobby even though, if I'm to be perfectly honest, it's the sort of dream you have when you think you should have a dream. Something to share when people turn to talking about their dreams.

So: gym, socialising and writing.

Could I put down something exciting? Something like . . . like say, scuba-diving?

It wouldn't be totally untrue – I had been scuba-diving once when I was on holiday in the Canaries. I had done a buddy-dive with an instructor. It lasted about half an hour. I ended up with sore ears which refused to 'pop', and I'm sure I had decompression sickness no matter how much they said you couldn't get it in twenty feet of water, but I was very ill for a couple of days afterwards and what else could it have been, I ask you? So I didn't really enjoy it and never did it again.

Therefore *strictly* speaking it wasn't actually a hobby. But it would sound good to say it was. It would make me sound like somebody who did exciting things. The sort of person you'd like to know. And then when they asked me about my scuba-diving I could tell them the full story and get brownie points for honesty and self-deprecating humour all at once. So I added that.

That was enough for hobbies, getting that far had stressed me enough.

Then it got harder still. I had to complete the sentence, *"I would describe myself as . . ."* and there was *no* multiple choice – it all had to be in free text.

After lots of deletions and amendments I eventually came up with: *"I would describe myself as honest, fun, sexy, as having a good sense of humour, chatty and easy to get on with. I'm pretty straightforward, what you see is what you get . . . but that's lots! I've oodles of love to give and masses of hugs to share."*

I hesitated over it. Did it sound too arrogant? But there were a *lot* of entries on this website, so I had to make myself stand out. I quickly checked out other people's profiles, and there didn't seem to be any false modesty going on. Indeed, my own was altogether diffident compared to many. I'd go with it.

Nearly finished now! The last section was to complete: *"My ideal partner would be. . ."*

"Tall, dark, handsome, millionaire, good sense of humour, laid-back, easy-going, generous, owns at least one holiday home abroad." Only joking.

In the end I wrote, *"My ideal partner would be an equal partner with me as we went through life together supporting and encouraging each other, somebody honest and ethical who believed he was as lucky to have me in his life as I knew I was lucky to have him."*

A bit cheesy, a bit cringe-making . . . but the best I could do, and I hoped the implied flattery in it might work to my advantage.

One last question: *What are you looking for?* Again it was multiple-choice, and I had the options of choosing from: *a date, friendship, friendship and possibly more, a good time with no strings, long-term relationship*.

Again, I wondered, did anybody say straight out they were looking for a long-term relationship? If so, did the men run for the hills?

I went back to the men's profiles and looked at the answer to that question. A disappointingly high number of them were only looking for a good time with no strings. And not surprisingly, I discovered when I checked the women's profiles that most of them were looking for a long-term relationship.

No matter how modern our ways of doing things, it seems that men and women still have diametrically opposite definitions of the word *relationship*. It's hard not to feel despondent sometimes. I do hope God enjoys the joke He created.

Anyway, I decided that I would admit to wanting friendship and possibly more. It seemed to cover all eventualities.

Would I include a photo? In the end I decided I would. If I didn't they might think I was too dreadful for words and not take the risk of contacting me. Also, as I've said, I scrub up pretty well and I had some nice photos of myself. What I looked like first thing in the morning was a different story, but they wouldn't get to see that for a long time, if ever.

As I pressed the *send* button I felt a qualm of nervousness. This was *real*. I, Sally Cronin, really was joining an internet dating agency. But along with the nervousness there was also a measure of excitement, of *what if?* Of possibilities.

And then it hit me, just too late to change my mind about sending in my profile: what if *nobody* responded? What if everybody walked through the virtual supermarket aisles of prospective partners and nobody – *nobody* – picked me.

Left me on the shelf, so to speak.

Oh God, the shame! If even the losers who join dating agencies didn't pick me, what hope in the world was there for me?

It won't have escaped your notice that I was back to calling people who joined dating agencies 'losers'. It didn't escape my own attention either, and that was twice as bad because then, by definition, I also was a loser.

What's more, I was going to be such a huge loser that even fellow-losers wouldn't want to know me. If I didn't get any dates from this I would just resign myself to the realisation that I was never going to find a man, never *ever*, and start getting cats by the dozen and live all alone and die a sad lonely death.

A tiny sane part of me protested that I was engaging in some fairly extremist and totally unjustified thinking, but the gloomy depressive side of me managed easily to ignore that bit as I continued . . . and when I died that sad and lonely death my body wouldn't be found for ages, not until the neighbours – those knife-wielding drug-dealing thugs beside whom I was forced to live – complained about the smell, not until then would they find me, and nobody would be at my funeral and . . .

Luckily, just then the phone rang.

"Hi, Sally, it's me," said Gaby's cheerful voice.

"Peter's just going out for an Indian takeaway and a video. Would you like to come around? You can tell him what food you want, but he says on no account are you to suggest a video because it takes him long enough to pick one out without having to take your tastes into account – or indeed mine – I'm under the same restriction!"

"I'd love to!"

Maybe, I thought to myself as I drove around to Gaby's place, maybe I wouldn't die a lonely death, not as long as Gaby was around to be my friend.

Good friends we might be, but I wouldn't tell her that I had taken her advice and joined a dating agency. It would be just too, too, humiliating to admit, when she asked me about it later, that nobody had contacted me.

* * *

But I needn't have worried.

Needn't have worried about not getting any replies, at any rate. Pretty soon e-mails started popping into my inbox.

Hi, I'm George, read one, *I saw your post and I liked what you wrote. You sound like fun! I'm an engineer, 35, separated with one child, a boy. My ex-wife and I share custody, so anybody I go out with would need to be very child-friendly as my son will be sharing my life as much as possible and any prospective date would have to be aware of this. If you think you could be the woman for me and my son, please drop me a line. Forgive me being so abrupt but as I'm sure you can imagine I don't want to confuse my son by bringing lots of unsuitable women into his life so please be sure you want this before writing.*

Perhaps not. I did want children, but my own, not 'here's one I made earlier'.

Or, *Hello, Sally, I'm replying to your post on MoreThanFriends. I too, am looking for friendship and possibly more . . . see where it leads without assuming anything. I think people assume too much about others. Women are especially bad at this, and this is why I haven't managed a long-term relationship so far . . . I can't cope if women start trying to assume things, like just because we've been together for six months they assume I want to start meeting their friends. That really drives me up the walls. You sound like a sensible sort of woman and if you can guarantee not to pressure me with assumptions I'd love to meet you.*

Thanks but no thanks.

Hi, Sally, I decided to contact you when I saw your photo . . . you know, you remind me so much of my twelve-year-old niece. Do you ever wear school uniform?

Words failed me.

Not all of them were creeps. I had nice correspondence with some guys, met a certain proportion of those, but none of them came to anything. There were various reasons for this: either we just didn't have the chemistry, or they had some awful characteristics such as chauvinism or racism, or they were just not attractive enough (hint: washing's a great idea; the chicks really dig it).

* * *

I admitted it all to Gaby one day when we were having coffee at her big Georgian house.

25

"Gaby, do you remember you suggested I join a dating agency?"

"I do," she said, intrigued.

I didn't disappoint her. "Well, I've done it," I told her. "Three weeks ago."

"Well done!" she said. "And is it going well for you?"

I shrugged. "I've had quite a few e-mails from men I wouldn't let my worst enemy go out with. And I've had one or two meetings with men who, while they weren't dangerously weird, were sad and strange. It's not surprising they couldn't get a partner the normal way. What has happened to all the normal but just unlucky people?"

"Like you, you mean?"

"Like me," I confirmed, "but the male variant thereof."

"I'm sure there are plenty of normal but just unlucky people out there," she told me, laughing and really, really, not being in the *slightest* bit complacent and condescending. "You just have to play the averages."

"Yes," I said glumly, "play the averages. Right. Tell you what, I'll give it another couple of weeks and that's it. I'm giving up on that idea. Just to the twenty-first, that's the summer solstice, seems like as good a day as any to knock this idea on the head."

"That's only a couple of weeks away. But no matter. I predict," she said confidently, like some classically rotund fairy godmother, lacking only the wand, "that something – or somebody! – amazing is going to happen to you before that time is up."

Chapter 3

Maybe her words had more power than I realised because one fateful Tuesday just before my self-imposed deadline, I logged onto the internet and Chris's e-mail popped into my inbox.

Hello, Sally, it read, *I read your post on* MoreThanFriends *and I just had to write to you. Something about your post really resonated with me. I hope that doesn't sound too airy-fairy, but it's the truth. I would love to meet you for a coffee.*

But first, silly me, how do you know you want to meet with me? My name's Chris Malley, and I'm 34 years old. I'm single, and I've just got over the break-up of a serious relationship.

I live in south Dublin, and I'm a self-employed IT security consultant and am reasonably solvent . . . although, of course, I'm sure that financial considerations wouldn't sway you.

My friends tell me I'm not repulsively ugly although you'll have to take into consideration that they're a little biased!

My hobbies include tennis and golf and I enjoy socialising with good friends, good food and good wine. I love travel – new experiences, new people, new cultures – and try to get away two or three times a year. I travel for my business sometimes and so I try to combine that with leisure travel.

What I'm looking for in a woman is honesty and integrity above all. That's very, very important to me. I want somebody with a sense of humour who treats as important the things which are important but who isn't serious all the time either. Somebody with a bit of sense of adventure, who wants to live before she dies, but who understands that the slow quiet times are essential too. Somebody kind and gentle. Hopefully somebody with a bit of patience as I can tend to get a bit carried away with enthusiasms sometimes and I need somebody to keep my feet on the ground!

So what do you think? Are you intrigued? I certainly hope so. If so, would you make a man happy and agree to meet for coffee some time? E-mail me back with a time and place and I'll be there.

Best wishes, Chris.

I read over the e-mail again, definitely intrigued as he had hoped. He sounded *wonderful*. And I was extremely flattered, naturally, that he had found that my profile had stood out for him. Reasonably solvent . . . not repulsively ugly. That sounded like understatements for filthy rich and divinely handsome and modest too. Not, of course, as he had said, that that would influence my decision at all.

He was single, but he was just out of a long-term relationship so he probably wasn't so odd that he couldn't relate to people.

28

I wondered why his relationship finished? I'd have to find out. Mind you, I thought, relationships finish all the time after all. There doesn't have to be a sinister reason. People just drift apart, want different things, find they're arguing all the time and are better off without each other. It's an old story.

He lived on the south side of the city . . . so did I, in a one-bedroomed flat in Dundrum. A tiny, tiny one-bedroomed flat.

It was only rented – I had been saving the deposit to buy my own place but as quickly as I saved the house prices increased, rendering my savings inadequate. The lament of many the single person, and indeed many couples, in modern house-price-boom Dublin.

And I have to admit that once I realised the futility of saving, the capital kept getting eroded . . . new car here, holiday there. It's easily done.

But anyway . . . I wondered did he live anywhere near me? Mind you, even now Dublin's still a small enough city – he couldn't live that far away from me as the crow flies. As the traffic crawls . . . that's different.

But he sounded nice. And I *was* intrigued.

I logged onto the *MoreThanFriends* website and checked out his profile. A lot of it matched information he had already given me, but there was other interesting data too.

Name: *Chris*.
Age: *34*.
Marital status: *single*.
Children: *no*.
Hair colour: *black*.

Figure: *medium build.*
Height: *6'1" (180cm).*
Eye colour: *blue.*
Ethnic group: *Caucasian.*
Star sign: *Scorpio.*
Educational level: *third level.*
Occupation: *IT Security Consultant.*
Income: *Between €50,000 and €100,000.*
Smoker: *no.*
Drinker: *Social drinker.*
Religion: *Tell you later.*
Hobbies: *Driving, Travel, Cooking, Film and Theatre.*

He had given himself a score of six with regard to being emotional, a full nine about being a risk-taker and only a four with regard to the statement about having a lot of friends, although he explained that next.

I would describe myself as an intensely private person, who chooses his friends carefully and makes room for only special people in his life. But I'm somebody who has a lot to give and share with the right person. I'm fun and good-humoured and ambitious. I work hard and I play hard.

My ideal partner would be outgoing and cheerful, somebody easy-going with a good sense of humour. Intelligent and genuine, honest and ethical.

Well, I was all of those!

I studied his photograph carefully. It was a head-and-shoulders shot, obviously taken in a bar somewhere as he held up a pint in salute to whoever was taking the picture. My God, but he was gorgeous! He literally looked like a film star . . . thick black hair swept back from his perfectly proportioned face. His bare arms –

30

what I could see of them – were flawlessly muscled, and he was wearing a wide charismatic smile.

I opened up my in-box and quickly typed an e-mail back to him.

Hi, Chris, it was great to hear from you! I'd love to meet with you for a coffee some afternoon. What are you doing next Saturday? Say three o'clock in Silver's? Please advise if that suits you. Best wishes, Sally.

I pressed *send* and the e-mail flew to my outbox. I looked at it as it sat there. Would I log on and send it immediately, or play it cool. I looked at the time – he had sent his own e-mail last night, so it wouldn't be looking too keen to reply this morning. Ahh, the games we play, I sighed, as I decided to send it then and there.

He didn't respond that evening

In the event, it was only after I got home around seven the next evening (after doing my stint at the gym) checked my e-mail that I got his reply.

Hi, Sally, great to hear back from you! I have to tell you I was so nervous waiting to see if you replied. I'm so glad you did. Saturday at three sounds great . . . I look forward to seeing you then.

In the meantime I'd love to hear a little more about you. Let's leave the boring where-do-you-work-where-are-you-from stuff until we meet . . . for now I'd love to know other things about you.

In that moment I thought, oh, please, no. He's not going to ask what my favourite underwear is, surely, or my preferred sexual position. But no, I was relieved to learn as I read on, it was all innocuous stuff.

What's your favourite colour? And why? What was your

earliest memory? Fair exchange is no robbery as they say, so here's my own answers to these questions. My favourite colour is green, and I think that's because it's the colour of nature. I love being outdoors and surrounded by green.

My earliest memory is of running into my house calling for my mother to tell her that my little sister Sheila had fallen and hurt herself. She was only a toddler so I must have been about two and a half or three. I can't remember what happened afterwards, the memory is a snapshot. But my sister's well and healthy now so it must have ended okay!

Look forward to hearing from you.

All best, Chris.

I grinned to myself as I read. He likes nature, does he? Sounds good. I could take nature or leave it, myself, but it reflects well on a man to like it, I always think. And the story of him coming to get help for his injured sister was sweet. I wondered what she was like. Would we be friends?

Stop it, I told myself firmly. You've never even met Chris yet. It's a bit early to be fantasising about being Very Best Friends with his sister!

I sat down and began to type.

Hi, Chris.

Yellow: bright and cheerful and optimistic. My earliest memory is my grandmother's funeral. I was about four and I remember the shock of seeing her dead and asking over and over why she was lying so still and wouldn't answer me. Like with your situation, it's a very brief memory. I don't remember anything else about the day at all.

Until Saturday.

Sally.

I felt quite down and sad for some reason after I sent that e-mail, but I couldn't identify why. And then it came to me. Thinking about GanGan's death brought back the grief and desolation and sense of abandonment I experienced then. I had adored her, and she had adored me, and it was devastating to lose her when I was so young. She was young too – she wasn't even sixty, no matter how old she seemed to me at the time.

I missed her for herself: the astringent scent of her, the feeling of her soft face against my own, the way her chins wobbled as she laughed at my childish antics, the soft cradling abundance of her lap. But I had also missed – and it was only in the last two or three years I had even articulated this to myself – the mirror of myself she had held up to me. I had missed being so important and treasured and special and adored.

Anyway. I pulled myself together. That was long ago and far away. No point dwelling on it. With an effort of will I pushed away the grief and began to cook my dinner.

When I got home from work on Wednesday there was another e-mail waiting for me.

Hi, Sally, do you like sushi? Chris.

I e-mailed back: *Can't stand it.*

An hour later I got: *Good, neither do I.*

I had to ask: *Well then, why did you ask?*

Although I responded straight away he didn't answer immediately. I checked my mail about every twenty minutes that evening, but there was no response from him. So it wasn't until the following evening that I got his reply: *Re Sushi: Just trying to build up a composite picture. These things are important. Have you any brothers or sisters?*

I was disconcerted, as always happened when I was asked that question. I never really knew how to answer it. Eventually I just responded: *Four. Two of each. What about you? Have you any apart from your sister?*

Again there was no answer that evening, but about eight o'clock on Friday his reply popped into my inbox: *No, just the one sister. But we're very close. Look forward to seeing you tomorrow. I'll be the one with the eager expression on my face! XX C.*

I typed back: *Great! See you then.*

* * *

It took ages to get to sleep that night. I was churning with excitement and expectation. And when I awoke the next morning I was immediately aware of both excitement and nervousness. Never mind butterflies fluttering, this was huge tiger moths marching around in my stomach.

I was going to meet Chris today!

I lay in my cosy bed and considered. It could, of course, turn out to be a non-event. All the other dates had come to nothing, after all, yielding nothing but a funny story to tell in years to come once the embarrassment factor had faded.

But somehow I knew this would be different. Our e-mail exchanges had already indicated that we could have a laugh together. We should have fun this afternoon at the very least. And who knew how much more than that?

I wasn't so naïve, I told myself, as to think that he might be The One. But hopefully somebody would be, and why not him?

I wondered what his voice was like. Knowing my luck it would be a tinny high-pitched squeak.

I enthusiastically threw back the covers (why-oh-why could it not be this easy to get up during the week?) and threw on a pair of leggings and a sweatshirt before heading into the kitchen for breakfast. After that I did some chores around the house which helped to pass the hours until it was time to get ready to meet Chris.

I had a long luxurious shower, lavishly using my saved-for-best shower gel. Once I dried myself I spent ages sensuously massaging in the matching body lotion. Not that Chris was going to be getting his hands on my body, but it was nice to feel good about myself. I knew that I'd be good to touch if he should be so lucky, and it gave me confidence.

By the same token I put on matching underwear – a flesh-toned lacy bra and knickers. I hovered then in front of the wardrobe before selecting a pale green summery skirt – he liked green, after all – and a knitted cream cotton top. I then dried my blonde hair carefully and when I gave my head an experimental jerk my hair swung satisfactorily and settled well.

I completed the effect with careful make-up – the kind of make-up which takes ages to do before looking as if you aren't wearing much at all, but just happen to have been blessed with porcelain skin.

Finally I completed the ensemble with silver

teardrop earrings and a matching necklace, and perused my image in the mirror. I studied myself critically. Not bad, I decided. Not great, of course, that goes without saying. But certainly I was looking my best. I could do no more.

What'll he think of me, I wondered. Will I be enough? Attractive enough? Sparkling enough? Intelligent-sounding enough? Educated enough? Everything enough, basically. What will he see when he looks at me, and will he find me pleasing?

That's when I acknowledged how keen I was for this to work. When I had been going on dates with the other men I had been only concerned with whether *I* would like *them*.

Only one way to find out if I would be good enough for Chris. I grabbed my bag and left the apartment. I walked the short distance into the centre of Dundrum and waited at the LUAS stop. The tram came after a couple of minutes and I was on my way to meet my future. I didn't yet know if that future was to be an hour long, a lifetime long, or anything in between. And I certainly no idea of what that future would consist of. But I was going to meet it anyway.

Chapter 4

I arrived at Silver's a well-calculated two or three minutes late, and I stopped a short distance from its door. This was it . . . I was about to meet Chris!

All my original anticipation had evaporated. Either that or it was hidden beneath the layers of apprehension that I was now experiencing. I was conscious of my heart pounding uncomfortably in my chest and a knot in my stomach. And my palms were slightly sweaty – that was going to make a good first impression. Not.

I took a tissue out of my handbag and wiped my hands, and as I did so I debated the option of turning around and walking away. I could do it. I really could.

But, I reasoned as I stood there on that bright summery street, what's the worst that can happen? He's hardly likely to be a maniacal axe-murderer, after all! I laughed at my silliness, took a deep breath and strode towards the restaurant door.

As I walked into the gleaming chrome interior, upon

whose surfaces I never dared breathe for fear of marking them, I looked around me. Immediately I caught sight of a man raising himself to his feet and looking at me enquiringly.

"Sally?" he was saying, in a pleasantly deep and melodious voice. "You look even nicer than your photo."

I walked the short distance towards him, totally congratulating my luck – this man was *gorgeous!* And he was here to meet *me!* I could peripherally see women covertly looking him over, and looking at me to see if I was good enough for such a man. Maybe not, I thought, as I reached him and clasped his outstretched hand, but I'm here!

He wasn't especially tall, perhaps about 5'10 or 5'11, no matter that his profile had said he was 6'1". But we're all allowed a little exaggeration, after all, and he was still taller than I was, so that was okay.

But his body! His face! He was such feast for the eyes that I didn't know where to look first. His build was slim rather than bulky, but his shoulders were broad and his body tapered in the classical upside-down triangle shape. His sleeves were pushed up and I could see smooth, light-brown well-muscled forearms, which boded well for the rest of him.

As for his features – if you were very, very, spiteful and cruel you could call them sharp, but if you had an ounce of poetry in you, you'd call them chiselled. He had a broad forehead and high cheekbones, rather hooded blue eyes which were crinkled now in a smile, a thinnish nose under which were incongruously full and sensuous lips – also smiling and welcoming to me

– and a strong narrow chin. His fine black hair was sharply cut, and he was immaculately presented in a clean, sharp-pressed denim shirt and an equally clean pair of jeans.

All this I realised and noted in an instant, even as we were shaking hands and speaking over each other's 'Good to see you', 'Glad you could make it, sit down. Sit down', 'Were you waiting long?' and so on. His touch was warm and firm and somehow intimate. No matter that it was such a prosaic gesture, it sent a surge a of excitement through me. The chemistry was definitely there. On my side at least.

We sat down on opposite sides of the small table and appraised each other.

"Hi," he said then, with a heart-stopping smile. You know Tom Cruise's smile? Well, this smile made Tom Cruise's smile look like an indifferent grin.

My chest felt as if my heart were literally turning over and I thought to myself, *I could be putty in this man's hands. I really could.* My skin tingled at the thought of my body being putty in his hands and I had to metaphorically slap myself around the face to stop myself slobbering.

"Hi," I said back to him, as coolly as I could. Which probably wasn't very.

"Nice place here," he said, "good choice. Do you come here often? Oh God," he groaned and put his head in his hands, "I can't believe I just said that! What a cliché. What a stupid thing to say!" He lifted his head then and grinned ruefully to me, "Sorry! Put it down to my being nervous."

"It's fine!" I laughed back at him, relaxing hugely at his admission of nerves. "As long as you excuse me whatever stupid thing I say because I'm nervous too. At least you've got your silly comment out of the way!"

It was all going to be okay . . . we could be honest about how we felt, about how we met.

A waitress came up to us then and we both ordered a fancy coffee. After she had gone we turned to look at each other again. I thought to myself that I would never, ever tire of looking at him – assuming I got the chance to be so lucky, of course.

"Have you been a member of *MoreThanFriends* for long?" he asked, and I cringed. Okay, we could be honest about how we met, but I was now learning that my comfort levels with discussing it weren't going *quite* this deep.

"Not long," I said quickly. Well, it was true, three weeks wasn't long. "What about yourself?"

"About five days," he said, grinning his wide smile at me. "I only joined so I could contact you."

"What?" I was totally bemused.

He laughed a little at my confusion, but kindly. "I know that sounds strange! What happened is this. I'm just over the break-up a serious relationship, I think I mentioned that, and began to feel up to dating again."

I nodded encouragingly.

"A mate of mine recently met a lovely woman through *MoreThanFriends*, and he suggested I give it a try. I wasn't going to, but . . ." he shrugged, "something made me log on last Tuesday. And then I found your profile. And as I said, it just resonated with me – if that

40

doesn't sound too weird," he said disarmingly, "and I thought I'd like to contact you. So I joined for the express purpose of doing that. And I'm glad I did."

"I'm glad you did too," I told him, and we smiled at each other, a smile of some sort of undefined promise.

Our coffees arrived just then, and after the waitress left we resumed our conversation.

"So what do you do for a living?" he asked me.

"I'm a financial advisor," I told him. "People come to me looking for financial advice about the best mortgage for them, the right amount of insurance and so on."

"Do you like it?"

"I do! I enjoy the job. It's very satisfying helping people sort out their finances – it's such an essential part of life, after all – and my colleagues are great fun. It's well-paid, good perks, and so on. What's not to like?"

"But is it your life's dream?" he asked

"What do you mean?"

"Is it your life's dream?" he repeated. "If you won the Lotto, for argument's sake, would you still do it?"

"Well . . ." I hesitated, a little taken aback, "I suppose that no, I wouldn't still do it if I won the Lotto. It's a job, a means to an end, and if I didn't have to earn a living then I probably wouldn't keep doing it. But as jobs go, it's great."

"And what would you do," he persisted, "if you were financially independent?"

"I haven't really thought about it," I said, "not really." I wasn't being precisely honest – what about my half-formed dream of writing a novel?

He smiled at me, saying nothing, and I experienced

41

the urge to please him, to fulfil his obvious expectations. Oh what the heck, I thought, why not tell him?

"Well, I suppose I do have a dream. I'd write a novel. It's something I've always wanted to do."

"A novel – what an interesting plan! I always envy and admire people who can do creative things. I'm so left-brain it's nearly a joke."

"That's right," I said. "You're something to do with IT, aren't you?"

"I am," he confirmed. "I'm an IT security consultant, and I'm lucky enough to be able to say that even if I did win the Lotto, I'd keep doing the same thing."

"What exactly does it involve?" I asked politely. I hoped he wasn't going to get too technical, and force me to portray interest when I couldn't understand more than one word in three.

"I help companies with all their technical security needs. For example, I show them how to block holes in their networks. Stop competitors hacking into their systems, that sort of thing."

"Does that sort of thing really happen?" I asked, leaning forward towards him.

"You'd be surprised! Industrial espionage is alive and well. It has just gone high-tech. I was a hacker myself – I never did anything criminal," he stressed, "but I was good at it. And when it became time to set up a business, this was perfect. I'm a poacher-turned-gamekeeper! Though I say so myself I'm one of the best in Europe, and I'm getting business in Asia too."

"That's incredible!" I said, gazing at him in awe. "It makes my own job look so pedestrian."

"Well . . ." he shrugged modestly, "it's a necessary evil. Still," he sighed, "I often wish, as I said, that I could do something creative like writing. Or painting. Anything really. I envy you so much."

"Your job sounds pretty creative to me," I told him. "Finding these solutions surely has a creative component."

He thought about it for a moment. "Hmm . . . I never thought about it like that before. But you may well be right. Maybe I can think of myself as creative after all! Thanks for that, Sally – you're only with me twenty minutes and you're already showing me a better image of myself!"

"No problem," I told him solemnly. "Giving new perceptions are a speciality of mine. I do it all the time," and then we both laughed at the absurdity of it.

"Still and all," he said, finishing his coffee and signalling the waitress, "even if what I do is creative, it's hardly as creative as writing a novel. That would be amazing. What brings you to that particular pursuit?"

"I've always loved writing," I told him, "and it just seems like something I'd like to do if I had the time."

"Lots of people write novels as well as the day job," he pointed out.

"True," I acknowledged reluctantly. "I suppose I must not want it enough to sacrifice my free time, which is why I said I'd do it if I won the Lotto."

"You don't want to sacrifice your free time," he echoed. "That would be the free time in which you pursue your other hobbies?"

"Well, yes," I said hesitantly. There seemed to be

something in his tone as he said that, something knowledgeable, something teasing.

"Hobbies like scuba-diving?" he asked mischieveously.

"Like scuba-diving," I said faintly, and then more robustly, "and socialising with my friends, and going to the gym, and the cinema and – and – stuff like that," I finished with less of a bang and more of a whimper.

"I was intrigued by you saying you do scuba-diving," he said. "It's something I've done a bit of myself. I've even got my PADI certificate!" he said proudly. That was obviously a good thing to have. "How much diving have you done? What's your favourite dive site?"

And so, way sooner than I had thought possible, I had to confess.

"I did one buddy-dive on holidays once," I admitted, "and that was it. I shouldn't have put it down on my list of hobbies but I wanted to appear interesting."

"Oh," he assured me, "you needn't worry about that. You are *very* interesting. At least, I certainly find you very interesting."

"Thank you," I told him, ducking my head a little in embarrassment, in that awkward way I usually find myself acknowledging compliments. Not that I get that many of them. Perhaps if I got more I'd be more practised in receiving them.

Our second coffees arrived then. I observed the waitress give Chris a long, speculative look as she placed them on the table. In doing so, she leaned over far more than was necessary in my opinion, until his head was practically jammed down the front of her blouse. Okay, maybe I exaggerate, but she wasn't exactly being subtle.

When she finally, reluctantly, left, Chris said abashedly, "I think I'm in there if I wanted!"

"She wasn't very subtle, was she?" I agreed.

"Anyway," he said, dismissing her and returning his concentration to me, "you said you liked cinema. What was the last film you saw?"

So we drank our second cup of coffee and chatted some more.

"Whereabouts do you live?" I asked him.

"Ballsbridge."

"Very nice," I told him, Ballsbridge being one of the most attractive areas of Dublin, still retaining its character from the days – long gone – when it was a village outside the city. It was cosmopolitan and lively, within reasonable walking distance of the city centre. He must be more than the 'reasonably solvent' he had claimed.

"Where do you live yourself?" he asked me, in the standard back-and-forwards of conversation, and I told him about my little flat in Dundrum.

"That's not so far from Ballsbridge," he pointed out.

"Not too far, no," I agreed, and the atmosphere was thick with possibilities and maybes.

We chatted on for a little while, until we finished our coffee. He called for the bill and paid it, brushing aside my offers to pay my share. Once outside the coffee-shop we hovered uncertainly. What now? Would we meet again? Would he suggest it? Would I? I knew I wanted to meet him again . . . but did he feel the same? Was he even now looking for a way to ease away gracefully.

He cleared his throat and shuffled a little and I thought, *Here it comes now*.

He said hesitantly, "Sally . . . it's a lovely afternoon. Would you like to go for a walk? In Stephen's Green maybe?"

"I'd love to!" I said, and my heart exulted. He did like me! He did! We turned and strolled together along Grafton Street towards Stephen's Green, chatting still.

As usual Grafton Street was hopping with people as Dubliners enjoyed the leisure of a bright Saturday afternoon – shopping, chatting, coming from lunch or going for a snack. Snatches of animated conversation came to us as we passed by. The sound of laughter and buskers' music filled the air.

As we walked I began to notice something interesting. Everybody walking in the opposite direction invariably ceded right of way to us. Instead of my usual zig-zag find-a-gap-and-take-it method of getting through crowds, we were walking in a straight line, and the crowds were parting before us.

I glanced at Chris beside me and saw that he was striding confidently forward, almost as if he owned the street. I remembered reading somewhere that when people are heading on a collision course towards each other, all sorts of subtle body-language negotiation is going on regarding which party will give way. It became clear to me that Chris was so self-assured that people were picking up on it, and yielding to him in his passage. And I was benefiting from this. As I walked beside him I envied him so much his poise and self-assurance.

As we walked he said to me, "I'm surprised – delighted, of course, but surprised – that you're single, a gorgeous woman like you."

"I have very high standards," I told him. "Besides, I just never yet met the right man. I could say the same about you, though. I'm surprised that you're single," I told him, keen to change subject away from what I perceived as the shame of my single status.

"Well," he said sombrely, "I'm just over a serious relationship – I think I mentioned that. I don't really want to say too much about it because I don't want to talk about Angela – my ex – behind her back. Suffice it to say that she was a damaged, troubled person, and I've realised that no matter how much you try, or how much effort you put in, sometimes people just can't be helped. It took me ages to realise that, and it was tough, and the break-up was difficult, to say the least." He sighed deeply, "But it's over now and it's time to move on with my life."

We paused then at the pedestrian crossing leading to the park, and he looked down at me and smiled, and maybe it was my imagination but I thought that maybe, possibly, that smile said that he would like me to feature in the moving-on bit of his life.

I grinned to myself as we walked along towards the duck pond. By tacit consent we moved on then – for the moment at least – from personal conversation, and we began talking about the people and images we saw around us, stopping with the rest of a delighted crowd to enjoy the antics of a colourful street performer as he juggled red and yellow skittles.

And always I was so aware of Chris's presence. His shoulder at my eye level, his fun expression and cheerful grin as he looked down at me as we chatted, the male clean smell of him which enticed me to move closer and nuzzle – but with an effort I restrained myself. It might have ruined the image no end if I were to launch myself at him in the middle of a municipal park and wrestle him to the ground.

All in good time, I promised myself. I hoped.

By the time we had completed our walk around Stephen's Green I was well and truly besotted. I liked this man, I wanted to be with this man. He seemed to be everything I was looking for: nice, decent, kind, GSOH, solvent – and not bad looking to say the least.

Once outside the park we hovered again. The thought of leaving him now was almost unbearable. But, I considered, even if he suggested something else now, I should decline. It would be totally uncool to be free at a few hours' notice for a Saturday evening.

However, he clearly realised that it would be rather insulting to assume I'd be free on such short notice. Either that or he had had enough of my company. Perhaps he had plans for that evening. Whatever the reason, he turned to me and placed a hand lightly on each shoulder. My body thrilled to his warm touch.

He said, "Sally, that was wonderful! I really enjoyed it. Thanks so much for meeting me. I wonder," he continued anxiously, "would you like to meet again sometime?"

"I'd love to!" I said, and if my shining face gave away how keen I was, I didn't care. He was showing himself equally keen on me, after all. And I didn't want to get into playing games. There was too much game-playing in my opinion.

"Great!" he said, his anxious face relaxing as he smiled back at me. "What about, say, Wednesday evening?"

"Wednesday's not good," I told him ruefully. I was due to baby-sit for Gaby on Wednesday. "What about Thursday?"

It was his turn to look chagrined. "Can't do Thursday. Aren't we fascinating people with full, busy lives! I hardly dare ask . . . what about Friday?"

"Friday's good," I told him, relieved.

"Would you like to go out for dinner?"

"I would," I told him warmly. "That would be great."

"Will we swap phone numbers in that case? I'll make a reservation somewhere, and ring you with the details. How about that?"

That sounded good to me, very good. He programmed my number into his mobile phone, and I programmed *his* number into *my* phone, and that was it. We were contactable.

"Grand so, I'll ring you soon," he told me, putting his phone away. "Sally," he paused a little, "I really, really, enjoyed this afternoon. It was great to meet you, and I can't wait till Friday."

"I enjoyed it too," I told him. "Till Friday, then."

He bent then and kissed me on the cheek, his hands still on my shoulders. His breath was warm against my face and his mouth was soft on my skin. Involuntarily I took a sharp intake of breath, of desire. He laughed a little to himself then, at the effect he had had on me. He wore a half-smile of delight and anticipation and satisfaction.

"Till Friday," he said and his voice was a bit croaky. He moved his hand away from my cheek, reluctantly it felt like, and then with a wink he turned and walked away. I turned also and gently floated my way towards the LUAS stop.

Chapter 5

I was *dying* to talk to somebody about it. As soon as I got home I rang Gaby. "Can I come around?" I asked her.

"What makes you think that we will be available at such short notice on a Saturday evening?" she asked me mock-frostily.

"Because you have two young children and your life as any sort of party animal is therefore over!" I answered cheekily.

"True," she said disconsolately. "But think of it this way, since Haley and Jack are now six and three respectively, in fifteen more years, or even less, I'll be free, free, freeeee! Whereas you have your eighteen years of purdah still to go – it's all ahead of you."

"I should be so lucky," I told her.

Mind you, maybe I was being a bit premature, but the possibility of having a family seemed a little more likely now than it had been a week previously. Which brought me straight back to the purpose of my call.

"So can I come around?" I asked her again. "I've loads to tell you."

"Ah, you didn't say that. If you've loads to tell me, *of course*, you can come around. We stay-at-homes are *desperate* for news. Especially since Peter's abroad on business right now, and I'm on my own. So, yes, pick up a bottle of wine. Actually, pick up two bottles of wine, pack a toothbrush and stay the night."

Accordingly, I ended up in Gaby's house within the hour.

While Gaby prepared our dinner I played with Haley and Jack: laughing and wrestling and giggling and hugging together until, upon Gaby's gentle suggestion, we went upstairs to organise their bath. It was a treasured tradition that if I was at their house at bedtime, it would be I who gave the children their bath and put them to bed.

It was a win-win-win situation. It gave Gaby and Peter a rare break, the children loved it because of my novelty value and because I allowed them longer in the bath than their rushed parents usually managed to do – and it was a win for me as I cherished the time with that gorgeous laughing little girl and that robust solemn little boy who were both so precious to me and whom I loved so much.

As I wrapped them afterwards in soft warm towels I marvelled – as I always did when I had the gift of this experience – at the seemingly contradictory strength and delicacy of their small bodies. So small, so fragile, but yet so healthy and solid. And so faultless, with the scars and wrinkles of life yet to mark their perfection.

I read them a story or two, tucked them in, and kissed them goodnight.

After I came downstairs again, Gaby and I ordered Chinese takeaway, opened a bottle of wine and sat down for our chat.

"So, tell me," she commanded, and willingly I did so.

"I met this man today," I told her, "through the dating agency I told you about. And Gaby, he's *gorgeous!* I really like him! And he seems to like me! He asked me out again, for next Friday!"

"That's great!" she said smiling broadly. "I haven't seen you so energised about somebody since . . . well, since forever, really. What's he like? What does he do for a living? Where's he from?"

So I provided for Gaby all the details which I had learned about Chris. Every single detail. Probably more than she ever wanted or needed to know. But, credit where it's due, she listened attentively and showed every appearance of being engrossed. She was even leaning forward in her chair, the better to hear me.

"He sounds fabulous!" she said, sitting back in her chair when I, having run out of minutiae to share with her, finally ground to a breathless halt. "He sounds like every woman's dream. He really does. I'm quite jealous myself!"

"And you with Peter!" I protested. "What on earth have you got to be jealous about?"

"Nothing, nothing at all," she said hurriedly. And totally unconvincingly.

This disconcerted me completely. If all wasn't well

in Gaby and Peter's marriage then there was absolutely no certainty in this whole universe. There was nothing to which I could cling as making some sort of sense in a crazy world. It was like finding out that the whole map of the world was an elaborate fiction designed to fool us and that Australia didn't really exist. Although, if that were the case, where did all those soap operas originate?

She sighed deeply. "I know it sounds mad, but sometimes I envy single women like you."

"*You* envy single women like *me*?" I repeated, not sure if I had heard her correctly. It was like somebody saying they envied people with halitosis.

"In a way. Don't get me wrong. I'm delighted to be married and I love Peter. I really do." She looked at me to see if I had got this. I nodded, and she continued, "But, Sally, it's like this: once you're married, that's *it*. No more grand passion, no more wild romance, no more choices or options or maybes or that excited *does-he, doesn't-he* fluttering of the heart. No more delicious uncertainty or excitement." She sighed and continued, "I envy you single women all that. For you it's still all potential, all possibilities. For me . . . it's all a known quantity. A great, wonderful, fabulous, known quantity for sure. But sometimes I feel a sense of bereavement for the single woman I was, the woman whom men desired before I got the *Keep Off* sign of a wedding ring. I grieve for that woman who'll never exist again. Oh, listen to me," she said, a little embarrassed, "waxing lyrical about a condition I was delighted to leave behind. But still . . ."

I listened, aghast. I had thought that Gaby had the

perfect life; it certainly was the life to which I aspired. And now to hear that sometimes she found it cloying . . .

"And as well . . . I love Peter," she said. "I *do*. But you've seen how he adores me. And sometimes, just sometimes, a tiny little bit, that adoration can be a little suffocating, a little overpowering. It's like being wrapped in a warm downy duvet: cosy and comfortable. But sometimes it's like the duvet is covering my head and I can't breathe properly. Sometimes I can't help feeling a little bit of envy for the independence you have, the choices, the freedom."

"That's *ridiculous*," I said crossly. "You are so, so lucky. You should appreciate what you have. This freedom and independence you envy is pure loneliness. To continue your own metaphor, it's the equivalent of a bed with only a thin sheet to cover you – no warmth or comfort anywhere. And how can you be so unfair to poor Peter? God, if I could get a man even half as nice as he is, half as cherishing, I wouldn't complain about him, I can tell you."

"You're right," said Gaby, chastened. "I suppose it's just the human condition. Far away hills are green and all that. For God's sakes, though," she stressed urgently, "don't ever let on to *anybody*, especially not Peter, that I feel like this. I've never told anyone, and I suppose I shouldn't even have told you. But isn't that what friends are for?"

"Yes," I said uncertainly. I wasn't at all sure if I had wanted to know that Gaby and Peter weren't this totally blissful unit I had supposed, or that marriage itself wasn't the totally idyllic experience I had imagined it to be.

They were my role models, the standard to which I aspired. How dare they prove themselves any less than perfect?

But that was the point, I supposed. They weren't perfect, and it wasn't fair of me to expect them to be. Life and love would never be flawless, and once I grew up I would realise this. And maybe Gaby's revelation had progressed that growing-up just a little.

"Don't worry," she urged. "We're really happy together, honestly we are. Everything's okay. It really is."

"Good," I said, relieved as my universe settled back into its accustomed groove with only a little residual rocking as it regained its equilibrium. "Mind you," I said, grinning at her, "I'd love the chance to discover whether adoration really is suffocating, all the same."

"Well, if this man is all you say, then you should be getting that chance really soon!"

"You may well be right," I said, delighted to be back talking about Chris. "We shall see!"

I certainly wasn't going to get the chance to experience adoration unless he phoned as he had promised, to finalise the details of our date the following Friday. I did have *his* number, but if he didn't ring me, I couldn't possibly ring him.

I shook my head wearily, wondering how many hours and days of my lifetime I had wasted wondering if some man would ring me. I was so worn out with this. Would there *ever* be an end to it? The dating game, which had seemed so much fun when I began it in my teens, had long lost its novelty.

In my darker moments all I could imagine was this continuing on for the next few years, with me getting older and older and the pool of available men growing smaller and smaller, until even hoping for a phone call seemed like a long distant memory which belonged to a golden past.

Oh, they were the days, I'd be reminiscing, *when at least there was a chance, no matter how small, that somebody was going to ring me.*

I was going to end up a sad and lonely spinster, I told myself. Well, I was already a sad and lonely spinster – I'd soon be an *old* sad and lonely spinster.

Stop it, I told myself briskly. That way lies total depression. Go and do something more empowering. *Don't* sit around waiting for him. Have you no self-respect? Get a life.

* * *

But in the event I didn't have to wait too long. Chris defied all expectations created by the rest of his gender and actually phoned. In fact, he phoned on Monday evening. I was so excited when his name appeared in my mobile phone screen that I forgot to be cool, and I answered with an exuberant "Hi Chris! How are you?"

"Do you know," he said, his voice warm and chocolaty, deliciously intimate this close to my ear, "I still haven't got used to people knowing who's ringing. It still surprises me. I'm thinking, is she psychic, is she a witch? Although, Sally, the way you've taken over my thoughts since Saturday, I'd have to suspect that you really are a witch."

"Oh," I said, thrilled silly at his words, at which all poise seemed to have deserted me. "Well, I'm definitely not a witch, I can assure you of that. I failed the exams."

He laughed. "So," he said then, carefully casual, "you still on for Friday?"

"Sure," I said, "if you are."

"I am, of course! I'm glad you're still on for it, because I've already made a booking. *Fauna* at eight o'clock. That suit you?"

"Oh yes," I breathed. Not only was I going out with the most gorgeous man this side of Hollywood, but he was bringing me to *Fauna*! Only *the* hottest place to eat, for this week at least. It seemed to me that the media photographers must practically live in the place, so frequently was it featured in celebrity magazines and newspaper glossy supplements.

"Grand, I'll meet you inside at eight. Okay?"

"Sure thing."

"So . . . how have you been in the meantime?"

"I've been great," I told him, and soon we were chatting away like old friends. When we finally said goodnight and hung up, I glanced at my watch, and was amazed to note that over an hour had passed. It didn't look as if we'd ever have awkward silences, anyway.

Chapter 6

Once Friday finally arrived, I dressed with great care for the date, delighted with the chance to dress up and wow him. Obviously I hadn't been able to do that before – it's difficult to make too much of an impact on a Saturday afternoon coffee date.

I wore a sleeveless black shift dress which I had bought in a second-hand shop in Paris. It was special because of the thousands of tiny jet beads with which it was covered, beads which swung and glistened as I moved. I didn't know if the dress actually dated from the thirties, but it certainly wouldn't have looked out of place being worn to dance the Charleston. With that I wore sheer black stockings and high-heeled black shoes. No jewellery apart from a pair of tiny jet studs in my ears – the dress itself was enough of a statement.

I took ages over my make-up though, brushing dramatic dark neutrals onto my eyelids, lining my eyes in black kohl and highlighting my lips with a dark red lipstick. With my blonde hair freshly washed and blow-dried to a sophisticated sleekness, I was ready. And though I say so myself, not looking too bad at all. Scrubbed up well, as usual.

I often wondered if I could make a living as a professional before-and-after model, because I looked so ordinary before going through the extensive grooming, and so . . . well, not great, but improved afterwards.

On my way to *Fauna* I reflected on the difference a week makes – last Saturday I had been nervous about meeting Chris, but now, six days later, I was experiencing only excitement and anticipation. I pushed open the door into the restaurant, and he was rising from a chair in the foyer area to greet me even as I was walking through the door.

"Hi," he said, his face lit up, "I'm delighted to see you," and he bent and kissed my cheek, and I was suffused with the enticing healthy scent of him.

He pulled away to look at me, holding me literally at his arms' length so he could view me, and his approval was rich in his eyes.

"My, my," he said appreciatively. "I thought you looked nice last Saturday – and you did! – but look at you now! You look absolutely beautiful, Sally. I'm so delighted and honoured to be with you."

It was pretty obvious that he had also made an effort – he was wearing a dark grey suit, sharply tailored and expensive-looking. Definitely a suit for upmarket socialising rather than the office. His shirt was thick cotton, pure white, and was opened one or two buttons with no tie. His short black hair was clearly freshly washed and combed into place. He looked totally edible.

So for some moments we just looked at each other in pleasure and delight until a polite 'ahem' distracted us and we broke eye-contact to see the maitre d' standing beside us. He had a carefully (but not carefully enough) hidden expression of benign amusement on his face, and it occurred to me that restaurant staff must be witness to many a burgeoning romance and the oblivion to the outside world that comes with it.

Of course, I reflected dryly, they must also be spectator to the other end of the spectrum: the thick bitter silences and the hissed arguments. But I put that thought aside. I didn't want to think of sour endings when there were sweet beginnings happening. To me!

So we sat at a table and ordered food which we were bound not even to notice eating, and chatted and laughed in the manner of lovers-to-be everywhere, and I could scarcely breathe for the sense of excitement and joy and anticipation and *what-ifs* coursing through me. I was so aware of his every breath, his every gesture, everything about him. Sometimes I wasn't even too aware of what he was saying, suffused as I was with the joy of being there experiencing him saying it, and the music of his melodious voice.

At one stage he asked me something.

"Hm?" I asked, not having heard him due to having been engaged in admiring the way the blue of his eyes contrasted so well with the black of his long lashes and strong eyebrows.

He laughed a little, kindly, and repeated what he

had said, "I was asking you about your family. I remember in your e-mails you said you had four siblings. That's a big family these days! I don't envy your mother at all! Where do you come in the family?"

"The eldest," I said automatically and a bit shortly. I hate talking about my family. But then something about his interested expression and the compassion in his eyes, something about all that made me decide to tell him.

"I was born when my mother and father were both eighteen, the summer they did their Leaving Certs," I told him, taking a therapeutic sip of my wine. "Not married, needless to say. Not living together, not earning a living, nothing. They were only children themselves."

"That must have been tough for them," he said sympathetically.

"It probably was," I agreed. "At least GanGan – my grandmother – was able to help. I lived with her while my mother went away to college. She used to stay with us during holidays, seemingly, although I don't remember it. When she got her degree she got a job near us and lived with us. However," I took a deep breath and continued, "GanGan died very soon after that."

His expression screwed up in a grimace of sympathy. "Was it expected," he asked, "or sudden?"

"Very sudden. It was a huge shock to everybody – she wasn't even sixty yet, and was in great health by all accounts But she had a brain haemorrhage. I was about four. That was the earliest memory I told you about in the e-mail, remember?"

He nodded and I continued, "It worked out quite well, if you can say such a thing, as I was able to start school that September. I went to a child-minder's after school and Mum minded me when she was at home."

"I see," he encouraged.

"But she was busy and stressed, trying to get ahead in her career. I remember it being a scary, bewildering time. I had been used to living with GanGan, and she adored me. Spoiled me, probably. But I certainly felt so loved and . . . right, somehow. And Mum was impatient sometimes, and abrupt, and not very cuddly."

"It must have been awful for you," he sympathised.

"It was. But, you know, when I look back on it now I could cry for her sake too. There she was, still only twenty-two with a dependent child, responsible for paying all the bills, looking after everything by herself."

"That sounds hard for her."

"It was. At least she had GanGan's house, which she inherited outright as she was an only child. But everything else was down to her. It must have been a very lonely, scary time for her too. And she was truly doing her best. She could have had an abortion, she could have put me up for adoption, but she didn't do either, and I have to honour her for that."

"I'm glad she didn't," he said, and I smiled briefly at him.

"I understand a lot more now, as I've said. But at the time all I was aware of was this cold chill after the warmth of GanGan's love and lap. I was aware of bewilderment at the way everything you ever knew could just be taken away from you, just like that," and I snapped my fingers to illustrate just how quickly it could all go.

"And your father?" Chris prompted gently.

"He and Mum didn't stay together even until I was born by all accounts. He went to college too, and he came and visited me whenever he could, and sent what money he could, and presents for Christmas and my birthday. Stuff like that. When he got a proper job he did support me properly, financially." Chris nodded to show he was still listening, as I continued, "And then when I was about eight Mum got married. To a nice decent man. My stepfather. But I always called him by his given name, Barry." I took a deep sip of my wine, and sighed, and continued, "And a year later I had a new baby sister, and at the same time I heard the news that my dad had got married too. A year after *that* my mother and Barry had another baby girl, and my father and his wife had twin sons. So each had two children with their spouse, and then there was me."

Chris was listening intently, his blue eyes full of sympathy.

"And you know," I said with spirit, sorry I had ever started this but impelled to finish, "it has been *awful*. I never felt as if I belonged. I lived with Mam and Barry, and he's been very good to me, don't get me wrong. You hear awful stories about stepfathers and their stepdaughters – but he never ever laid as much as an inappropriate finger on me. He was a good stepfather. He always ruffled my hair and asked about my day at school, and gave me lifts to hockey practice and friends' houses without a word of complaint. But it was quite clear that his heart was completely and utterly and totally devoted to Mum and his own two girls, and all he had left for me was mild affection. I sometimes used to think he even preferred the family dog to me!" I laughed, but it was the laugh of near-hysteria rather than amusement.

"That's awful," murmured Chris.

"But to be fair," I continued, "why *should* he feel anything for me? I'm not anything to him. I was just some baggage Mum brought along with her, and he loved her enough to take me on as well. I'm sure it wasn't easy – I was hurt and bewildered and that showed itself as belligerence and sulks. But he did try and as I say, I've no complaints. He's been very good to me."

"Sounds like a decent bloke," said Chris. "But what about your mother? Did things get easier between you two after she married?"

Dimly I was aware that I was pouring my heart out to this stranger, telling him more, probably, than he ever really wanted to know. But all credit, he was showing every appearance of fascination.

"No," I said, answering his question, "things with my mother weren't great afterwards. I didn't want her to marry. I didn't want yet more changes."

"Well, that's understandable."

I smiled my appreciation of his understanding and continued, "I didn't want to share her. I was already sharing her with her job and her social life – there was little enough left for me as it was. But she did marry and I had to share her with Barry. And then with Laura and Eva."

"Your sisters?"

"That's right. She gave up work as soon as Laura

65

was born, and while I know she had no choice while I was small, with nobody to bring in an income, it still rankled with me."

"It must have hurt," he said softly.

"Oh, it *did!*" I could hear the pain etched in my voice, and I was sure he could too. "She was devoted to those two babies. It's not that she didn't love me, I'm sure she did. And it wasn't that she was cruel to me. But . . . it's just that herself and Barry and Laura and Eva made this perfect little family and I was superfluous to requirements."

Chris nodded. "And are you still in touch with your father?"

"Well, it's the same story there. He had his wife and his two sons and there was never really room for me. I used to be sent over there for some weekends and for a week or two during the summer holidays. But it was even worse there, because I genuinely wasn't part of the family. At least Mam and Barry's house was my home. But I always felt like a guest with Dad and his wife."

"I can see that might have been difficult."

"Mmm. Well, I was a reasonably welcome guest. Don't get me wrong. But one with whom they didn't have anything in common, whom they didn't really know how to handle, and whom they were always glad to see the back of after she left."

I suddenly realised the extent to which I had been parading all my baggage and issues, in the middle of what was supposed to be a fun date.

"Sorry," I told him, "I'm going on a bit."

"Not to worry – I asked you after all. It does seem, though, that you had a hard time."

I shrugged again. "I suppose I didn't really. It was just unfortunate. There were no baddies at all, after all. Mum and Dad just made a mistake – not that I like to think of myself as a mistake – " I laughed humourlessly, "and did their utmost to make the best of it."

"You're not a mistake at all," Chris said gallantly. "How could you be?"

"Thank you," I told him, smiling at him in gratitude. "And you know, maybe I should just get over it. My mother and father have both been very good to me, their respective spouses have both been very good to me, my half-sisters and half-brothers are nice, genuine people. It's not their fault that I never really belonged to either family, not properly."

I smiled at him. Time to change the subject.

"What about your family?" I asked him. "You said you have only one sister, didn't you? And what about your parents?"

"Just the one sister," he confirmed, "and I'm the product of what appears to be that rare thing, a truly happy family. We didn't have much money growing up, but we always had enough. My parents were very much in love, they both adored my sister and me, she and I got on pretty well considering, and we're good friends now. There isn't really much else to say," he shrugged and grinned. "Happy stories are so boring."

"You said your parents *were* very much in love," I prompted.

"They're both dead," he said sadly. "Isn't it always

67

the way? The good ones go young. My mother died ten years ago, aged only forty-five, of breast cancer, and my father died two years after that. They said it was heart failure that got him, but Sheila – that's my sister – and I always believed that it was actually heartbreak. He just couldn't live without her."

There was silence for a moment as we digested that, and then I said, "At least you still have Sheila."

"I do," he said, "but unfortunately she's living in Australia now. She went over there for a year after university. But she met this man, and she's settled there now. And you won't believe this, his name's actually Bruce!"

"And her name's Sheila!" I gasped. "Oh, I don't believe you! Are you serious?"

He was laughing. "Never more so. It *is* hilarious, isn't it? But it causes all sorts of trouble for them. When they applied for their mortgage they didn't hear back for ages, so they rang to check it out. And the frosty voice the other end told them," and Chris put on a strangled Australian accent, "that the application had been binned as soon as it was received, and that they, the bank staff, were busy people and didn't appreciate one bit having their time wasted like that!"

I was laughing so loud now that other diners were looking at me but I didn't care. It was just so nice to be laughing after having revisited my bleak childhood, which was a stupid thing to have done anyway.

That laughter lifted my mood completely and set the tone for the rest of the evening, and we chatted and laughed our way through the rest of the meal.

I was in a state of heightened awareness, registering every breath he took, every move of his arm, every millimetre of his expressive mobile face. God but he was gorgeous and I desired him so much.

Would we be together tonight? It was way too early, really. Especially if I wanted him to take me seriously, which I did.

But as I watched his mouth as he spoke, I could barely hear his words for imagining that mouth on my own mouth, on the arc of my shoulder, on my belly and beyond. As his large strong hands wielded his knife and fork I stared, fascinated, imagining those hands touching me in every secret crevice and curve.

It was a real strain keeping up any semblance of normal conversation.

After the meal he said to me, "Would you like to go for a drink now? Or . . . say no if you don't want to, but my friend Mike's having a party and he's invited us."

"Us?" I questioned.

"Well, sure. Hasn't he been deafened hearing all about you for the whole week, so of course he invited you. His exact words were, 'Come to my party on Friday and bring Sally if you dare risk it because, with the write-up you've given her, I'll be giving you a run for your money'."

"Oh, right," I said, delighted with the implied compliment and *thrilled* at the realisation that he had been talking about me to his friend. He must be reasonably keen on me if he was already mentioning me in despatches.

"Now, it's okay if we don't go," he said, "if you

don't want to. It's just that it's his birthday party and I should never really have arranged a date for tonight, but when none of the other days suited you I didn't want to rule tonight out as well."

"But you'd like to go?" I said.

"I don't really want to – I'd much rather spend the time with you. But . . . it *is* his birthday, and we *are* very good friends. He might be hurt if I didn't turn up."

"Of course, we'll go, then! It could be fun."

"Great!" he said, his face relaxing. "That way I get to spend time with you without letting Mike down."

And even though I didn't really want to go to this party it was ample consolation to learn that Chris was so thoughtful and considerate.

Accordingly, once we left the restaurant Chris took his mobile out of his pocket and switched it on. "I'll just ring him and see where they are," he told me, "find out if they've left the pub yet."

Wherever they were, it seemed there was bags of *craic* going on. I could hear the background noise from where I stood, and Chris was having to listen with a finger stuck into his opposite ear and shout, "Where? *Where*? I can't hear you?" Eventually, however, he managed to decipher the information, and he yelled, "Grand, see you there in a while!" and hung up. "They're at his place," he informed me. "It's not far so we might as well walk. Is that okay?"

"Sure," I said, even though the thought of walking even a short distance on my high heels didn't really appeal. Also the night had grown chilly enough and all I had was my wrap – glamorous but not exactly known for its thermal qualities.

"Come on then," he said, taking me at my word the way men always do, and we turned and walked off.

I gave an involuntary shiver and he asked solicitously, "Are you cold?" and he whipped off his jacket and placed it around my shoulders. Warmth immediately coursed through me as the rich material – still warm from his body – settled around me. As his too-big-for-me jacket swamped me, embraced me and surrounded me, I relished the intimacy of warming myself on his body heat.

And then the icing on the cake: he put his arm across my shoulders as we made our way.

The stars were shining in the clear sky as much as the city lights could show, and there was a nearly full moon beaming down on us.

And as we walked hip-to-hip, chatting animatedly, it was as near to heaven as I could remember achieving. I could almost – not quite, but almost – ignore the agony of my feet as they trod the city pavement in shoes which were never designed for actually walking in. Soon, despite my awareness of Chris, I still gazed longingly at each taxi which passed. Each time I thought, I'll ask him if we can get a taxi, and each time I told myself, no, it's okay, I can walk a little further.

Just about the time that I was *definitely* going to have to insist on a taxi, if not an ambulance, Chris said, "We're here."

Chapter 7

He buzzed the intercom on the door of a purpose-built block of apartments, and without anybody trying to figure out who it was, the door buzzed in return to let us in.

"Which floor does he live on?" I asked, thinking that there was no way, no way whatsoever, that I would be able to climb those stairs. Not without taking off my shoes, at least, and I didn't want to do that. It would have been like Cinderella's dress returning to rags while she was still with the Prince. Couldn't be done, not until we were together a *lot* longer than this. Not until well after the first sexual encounter, and just before the first wear of grey saggy knickers out of the emergency *way-behind-in-the-washing* stash.

But to my relief he answered, "The ground floor." He pushed open an internal door the far side of the stairs and said, "Actually, right here."

He needn't have bothered saying that – as soon as

the internal door opened I could hear the party noise pour out through the apartment's own opened door. People were spilling outside into the corridor, drinking and laughing. I hoped Mike had neighbours who were: a) very accommodating, b) at the party or c) away.

One of the corridor-inhabitants peeled himself away from the crowd when he saw us.

"Chris, my man," he shouted, and came up to us, "how the devil are you?" and he gave Chris a mighty slap on the back.

To Chris's credit he stayed vertical, managed a sickly smile and said back, "Hi, Paul, how are *you*? Look, I'd like to introduce you to Sally," and he turned to indicate me.

Paul focussed (I use the term loosely) glazed eyes at me. "Hiya, Sally!"

"Where's Mike?" Chris asked. "Inside?"

Without waiting for an answer he steered me through the door of the apartment and into a heaving mass of people, redolent with thick sweet-smelling smoke, loud music and louder conversation.

Now, don't get me wrong, I'm up for a party with the best of them. I personally have made my own contribution many a time to a heaving mass of party-ness and loud noise. It's just that usually I have been in on these parties from the beginning, and have had a chance to evolve into party-mode with everybody else. It was a shock to the system to arrive, mostly sober after a restrained grown-up couple of glasses of wine, at such a Bacchanalian scene.

It didn't help that both Chris and I were both way overdressed compared to everybody else's statement torn jeans. My beautiful dress was going to be ruined, I realised, with all the smoke. And, I realised after a frantic look around, there was nowhere whatsoever to sit down and rest my agonised feet.

I looked up at Chris and he looked down at me and grimaced.

"Sorry, Sally," he told me. "I didn't expect it to be like this, I really didn't. We won't stay long, I promise. Let me just find Mike and let him know we're here. We'll just do the showing-our-faces thing and then leave. Hang on till I get us a drink."

He disappeared into the crowd and I was left standing there in the crowd, lost and disoriented. Not belonging. A feeling I'm prone to, given my background.

Nobody likes being out of their comfort zone, I know that. But as all these strangers swirled around me, laughing and joking and teasing each other, I experienced again exactly the same sensations I had felt all my life in my two para-families. As if I was standing on the outside, accepted but not belonging.

Added to all that, my feet were now hurting so much that I totally empathised with the Little Mermaid, for whom every step was agony. Actually, come to think of it, didn't she have to give up her beautiful voice in return for her legs? I, too, had lost my voice right then. It could never compete against all the noise, and I had nothing to say anyway, and nobody to whom to say it.

It was a bizarre, almost surreal, experience, standing there with a half-smile pasted on my face, which was meant to demonstrate that I was totally relaxed and confident here; don't you worry about me.

The air was fragranced with the sweet smell of cannabis and on the sofa two women were kissing exuberantly.

A young man – medium height and build, long hair, thin moustache – approached me and inwardly I cringed. This was already bad enough – I didn't need the experience of fighting off the attentions of some drunk, half-stoned youth who was chemically induced to the belief that he was God's gift.

But he surprised me, "Hi, I'm Mike," he said pretty coherently, proffering his hand.

"Happy birthday," I told him as I shook his hand.

"Thanks! I'm thirty today, a big milestone and worth celebrating. So . . ." he looked at me speculatively and I recognised that the small talk was over and we were moving onto a new stage of proceedings, "you're Sally."

"I am indeed," I agreed.

"Well, do you know what?" he said and I realised from his maudlin tones and glazed expression that he was drunker and/or more stoned than he had first appeared. "You're a very lucky lady. A very, *very* lucky lady."

"I am?" I enquired calmly.

"You are. You are indeed." He was even waving an illustrative forefinger in my face, "And do you know why you're a lucky lady?"

"Why's that?" I asked mildly, even though really I wanted to say sarcastically: *No, but I've a feeling you're going to tell me.*

"Because you're going out with Chris Malley. Any woman who's going out with Chris Malley is a very,

very lucky woman. He's such a nice guy, he's my best mate, me and him are like that!" and he held up two fingers together.

"*That* close, huh?" I laughed.

"Absolutely! I hope you appreciate how lucky you are," he continued once he was satisfied that I knew just how much *like that* he and Chris were.

"Oh, I do," I assured him.

"And I hope you treat him right. He deserves to be treated right. He's been unlucky with women – he's ended up with some right bitches who take advantage of how nice he is, and it's just not fair."

"Really?" I leaned forward a little, the better to hear him.

"Yes! Take his last girlfriend, Angela Hanly, what a bitch she was!" he said as I listened avidly. "Treated him like shit, she did. I was so happy when they broke up; she was making him so miserable. But even now she won't leave him alone. Ever since they broke up she's been stalking him practically – it's driving him mad."

"*Stalking* him?"

He swayed slightly as he tried to focus on me. "That's right. Stalking him. It's *awful* for him. She made his life hell before they split up and she's making his life hell now. She's psychotic, she is, totally crazy." He swirled his finger around his ear to illustrate how crazy she was.

God, yes, she'd be boiling rabbits yet.

"Well, I can assure you of my stability!" I said to him.

"Glad to hear it! It can often be like that, though. You get a run like that. I went through a stage where every girlfriend I hooked up with was a shopaholic. What are the odds, eh?"

"What indeed?" I echoed politely.

"Are you chatting up my new girlfriend, like you threatened?" asked Chris, coming back with the promised drinks.

"Just keeping her company, mate," Mike held up his hands in surrender, which wasn't his best idea given the can of beer in his hand. Some of it sloshed out over his shoulder down onto his back. But he didn't seem to notice so I said nothing.

"Here you go." Chris gave me my drink – a can of beer. I dislike beer intensely, and never drink it. But it was probably all that was available. I smiled my thanks and said nothing. I opened the can and took a polite sip (there were, it goes without saying, no glasses), and found that the beer was warm. Even worse.

As Chris and Mike chatted about computer technology (at least, that's what I thought it was – I understood about one word in three) I stood there, my feet in agony, pretending to take occasional sips of the beer, carefully smiling. The over-crowded room was hot and uncomfortably close, and the air was thick with cigarette smoke, acrid and pungent.

Just then something caught Mike's eye.

"Christ on a bike," he breathed, "speak of the devil. Chris, it's Angela. How the fuck did *she* know you'd be here?"

Chris and I both turned towards where he was

looking. We had a clear line of vision as the crowd had moved away from her, leaving a pathway almost between her and us. There was an air of nervous anticipation in everybody's demeanour. It certainly wasn't to their credit, but this anticipation was sharply reminiscent of schoolboys' excitement as they eagerly form a circle around a fist-fight by two of their peers. The music stopped abruptly and the room was almost silent.

Chris muttered a curse under his breath as Angela began walking towards us, shouting incomprehensible abuse as she did so.

I quailed as she grew nearer. She appeared to be literally mad. Her long red hair was unkempt and tangled, and as she shouted at him her face was twisted in a feral snarl. I was surprised spittle wasn't flying out of her mouth.

Chris shrugged in resignation and walked towards her, so the two of them looked like gunfighters in a Western film.

"Angela, Angela," he was saying gently, holding his hands out. "Angela, everything's okay."

"Everything is *not* okay!" she spat. "Everything is far, far from okay!"

"Shush now," he soothed. "Shush now."

"Don't you try to shush *me*!"

He raised his hands in a gesture of defeat. "I'm only trying to help," he told her gently.

"*Help!*" she screamed. "*Help?* Don't make me laugh!"

It didn't look as if anybody was in immediate danger of making Angela laugh.

The party guests were watching the exchange avidly,

turning from one participant to the other as they spoke, like spectators at a tennis match.

Suddenly Angela burst into tears. "I loved you," she sobbed. "I loved you so much! Where did it all go wrong?"

Mike, still standing beside me muttered, "When you went mad, you stupid woman. That's when it went wrong!"

But Chris was saying compassionately, "I don't know, Angela. It's hard, I know it's hard. Look, there's no point having this conversation here. Let me bring you outside, get you a taxi. We'll talk tomorrow, I promise. Okay?"

Her tears came to a hiccuping stop. "Do you promise?"

"I promise."

"Okay – okay then," she acquiesced, and allowed Chris to lead her away, the crowd parting before them, out of the apartment and, presumably, out onto the street to call a taxi.

Somebody gave a shaky giggle and said, "Remind me not to invite her to *my* next party!" and everybody laughed and then, as I still stood shocked, not sure what to do, there was a buzz of conversation as people began to share their enjoyment of the drama.

Thankfully Chris came back a few minutes later.

"She's on her way home," he said to me. "Look, I'm so, so sorry. I wouldn't have inflicted that on you for *anything*. Needless to say I never dreamt she'd be here . . . when I mentioned her to you I didn't go into details. It didn't seem to be fair to talk about her behind her back.

But that – well, what you've seen is why we broke up."

"She seems totally crazy," I said, still shaking

"She is, really," he sighed. "It's such a shame, she could be so lovely, but whatever went wrong . . . I knew she had a troubled background but I had thought she could get over it. I was wrong. I know that now. Anyway, I'm sorry, truly sorry you had to see that." He gave a nervous laugh, "You probably won't want to see me again after this, and I wouldn't blame you."

"Of course I want to see you again," I quickly assured him. "It's not your fault that she landed on you like this. I thought you dealt with it very well. Very kindly and gently. But, I wonder, can we go now? Or at least, I'd like to go. It's been a long evening."

"We'll both go," he said quickly. "I'll text Mike tomorrow to make our apologies. Come on."

I didn't need a second invitation.

To my delight an available taxi passed within a few moments of our reaching the street, and we flagged it down. As we got in and I was at last able to rest my poor agonised feet, I wondered was there any pleasure as intense as the cessation of pain. Sex doesn't even come close.

"Where to?" asked the taxi-driver.

"Dundrum," I told him, and gave the address.

"And then Ballsbridge," said Chris firmly.

I breathed a sigh of relief at his sensitivity. It was really too early to be considering anything more intimate anyway and, besides, the encounter with Angela had spoiled the mood totally.

Flickering yellow-light and darkness alternated as we travelled through the city streets. Chris took my hand, and leaned a little towards me.

"I'm really, really sorry about tonight," he said in his chocolate voice, his breath warm and comforting in my ear, a certain shallowness of his breathing indicating the tension he was still experiencing.

"It was awful, truly awful," I told him.

"It was," he agreed.

"Will you phone her tomorrow, as you promised?"

He sighed deeply. "I'll have to. I'm a man of my word, I'm afraid. Don't know how much good I'll do her," he sighed again, "but it's all I can do, to try to help her."

"You're really kind," I told him. "Any other man would have totally washed his hands of her."

"Oh well . . . " he said modestly. And then he leant towards me and said in a whisper: "But will you see me again?" and in the flickering darkness his head beside mine and his voice reverberating gently against my cheek was intimate, powerful, sexual.

Maybe that spoiled mood could be restored.

His voice held a tone of uncertainty, of vulnerability which appealed to the nurturing instinct in me. And the combination of deep masculine sexual voice and nervous, somehow uncertain, tone was a potent mix and my heart turned over with . . . with what?

Not love, I told myself, surely not love so soon? But something strong and powerful and compelling. Something that definitely felt like love.

"I do want to see you again," I told him truthfully,

and a part of me rejoiced to hear his sharp out-breath of relief as I said it.

"You doing anything on Sunday?" he asked me then.

"Sunday?" I said nonchalantly, and paused as if I were mentally checking through a crowded schedule. Inside I was chortling in delight: here it was, Friday night – Saturday morning actually – and he was proposing meeting on Sunday! Only two days between dates, not a cool, casual, week or so apart.

"No, I don't think I'm doing anything," I said, and my voice was a little breathless.

He moved a fraction of an inch closer to me then, so that when he spoke his lips were moving on my ear, on my cheek, and I couldn't help it, I squirmed with desire as he spoke to me, and I had to concentrate to hear what he was saying, "Why don't you come over to my place around twelve? Though I say so myself, I'm not a bad chef, so I'll cook you a nice dinner, and then we can do something for the afternoon. Take the DART to the seaside, maybe, or go into town and be cultural in the National Gallery. What do you reckon?"

"Sounds . . . ahhh . . . sounds wonderful," I managed to say at last.

At my barely restrained writhings and obvious lack of concentration, he gave a deep, delicious chuckle. A chuckle, it seemed to me, of male virility and honest pleasure at being able to give such pleasure to his partner. A chuckle of anticipation and expectation, of masculine power and revelling in it and enjoying it. A chuckle which was sexily deep in his throat and seemed to hold all sorts of promises within it.

I began to revise my notion that the evening had ended too traumatically for intimacy.

But just then the taxi-driver said laconically, "Here we are, the address in Dundrum."

"Right, right," I said, sitting up straight, struggling to regain my equilibrium, "thanks very much. How much – ?"

"Don't be silly," said Chris immediately before the taxi-driver could respond, "I'll get it."

"Thanks," I told him, "but really . . ."

"Won't hear of it," he said firmly. "Honestly, it's my pleasure. Hang on," he said to the driver, "I'll just see my guest to her door and I'll be back."

The driver grumbled a little but accepted this – he still hadn't been paid after all – as Chris and I got out of the car and walked to the front door of my apartment-block.

"I'll say goodnight here," he told me. "Don't want to upset the driver any more than I have to! I'll e-mail you my address and directions, okay? And I'll see you on Sunday."

"You will indeed," I told him. "Thanks for a lovely evening."

"We-ell . . ." he grimaced.

"No, it was lovely," I insisted, "despite that – unpleasant incident. I loved being with you."

He beamed at this. "And I with you. So, goodnight then," and he bent and kissed me on the lips, lingering just a little.

Despite myself, before I even knew I was doing it, I had breathed in sharply.

"You're delicious," he said and his voice was gravely. He chucked my chin then and said, "I'd better – " and gestured towards the cranky driver. And with that he winked at me and turned and ran lightly down the steps to the path, and into the waiting vehicle. I watched but he didn't turn around as they sped off into the night.

Chapter 8

I floated around the house all that next day, Saturday. Not even the stink of smoke off my beautiful dress could diminish my rapture. Nor the memory of Angela.

I replayed every moment we had been together, picturing again and again Chris's perfect face, hearing again his church-bells voice saying nice things about *me*.

I so wanted to go around to Gaby's and tell her all the news – I had the strongest urge to talk about the previous evening, talk about Chris. Probably non-stop.

But I restrained myself. Peter had been due back the previous day, and I didn't want to play gooseberry. I mean, I quite often play gooseberry, and they assure me they don't mind. When you've been married as long as they have, they tell me, laughing, there's no romance left to be interrupted by a third party. However, I usually try to play gooseberry when they haven't just been parted for a week.

It was a strain not to ring her, but I managed it and I was very proud of myself.

And maybe virtue is its own reward, but sometimes something a little more tangible can happen as well, because Gaby rang me!

"Hi, Sally," she said, "I was wondering, are you doing anything tonight?"

"Not tonight, no," I told her, wondering what she was going to suggest.

"Well then, would you like to come over and spend some quality time with your honorary niece and nephew? Say from around eight o'clock till midnight or even later?"

"You mean the 'B' word, don't you?" I asked her, laughing.

"That's right!" she laughed right back at me. "Baby-sitting. Any chance, Sal? Peter wants to whisk me off for a romantic dinner and needless to say I'd quite like to be so whisked!"

"Sure, of course I will," I told her, and battled briefly with my conscience but it gave in, wimp that it is, with scarcely a fight. "But Gaby, any chance I could come over a little early, say around seven? And then I could talk to you while you're getting ready. I was out with Chris last night and I've loads to tell you."

"Of course you can, my sweet," she told me. "Come over whenever you like. I'm dying to hear your news. And if you want to bring your overnight stuff you can go to sleep in the guest bed whenever you like – you won't have to wait up for us to come home. We might be all hours."

She giggled a little in excitement and anticipation,

and I wondered if the children had been bribed at all with a new video to keep them busy for half an hour or so while Gaby and Peter had already had some mummy-and-daddy time together.

Just before I left for Gaby's house I checked my e-mail and as promised Chris had sent me directions to his house. I printed them out, folded the sheet carefully and put it in my bag. I then packed overnight stuff and suitable clothes for the next day.

I got to Gaby's around seven as agreed, and once I had peeled Haley and Jack off me with loud promises of undivided attention later, and whispered promises of extended bedtimes, I had Gaby's undivided attention all to myself.

Undivided, that is, except for herself and her mirror. Credit where it's due, she did listen very attentively, even as she was holding different tops against herself as she considered with pursed lips which one she should wear that evening.

So as Gaby put on her make-up I spoke to her reflection in the mirror and told her about our meal, and our laughter, and details of our conversation – everything but the incident with Angela. That had left a sour taste in my mouth and I didn't want to review or revisit the scene of Chris caught in the crossfire of whatever was going on in that poor girl's mind.

At last, I finished breathlessly with, "And, oh, Gaby, he's perfect!"

She paused in her making-up then, and turned to face me directly as though it was no longer enough to speak only to my reflection, and her face was lit up by a huge smile. "Oh Sally, that's *great* news! I'm so happy for you!"

"Isn't it wonderful!" I enthused. "I know that this pure excitement doesn't really last," I said, trying to be sensible, "but still, it's great when it happens. And I'm so going to enjoy it."

"Do," she said sincerely, "do. Cherish it while you have it," she said a little sadly, and I guessed she was still thinking of the lack of excitement in a secure happy marriage.

* * *

That evening as I was snuggled up on the sofa with a child either side of me, reading them their fifth bedtime story, I wondered where Chris was and what he was doing.

Was *he* sitting in baby-sitting a friend's children? Hardly. He was probably out at some trendy venue with trendy people having trendy drinks and trendy conversations.

I wondered what he would think of my own Saturday evening occupation. It wasn't very cool, after all, was it?

I wondered if, as he lifted his glass of champagne at the book launch or film première or whatever glittering function he was at, he was thinking at all of me.

* * *

I was still in bed next morning when my mobile rang. It was Chris!

"Hi, Sally," he said in his deep voice, and I writhed

against the bed a little in pleasure at having his voice right in my ear in so intimate a setting as my bed. "Hope I haven't phoned too early."

"No, no, not at all," I told him, squinting at my watch. "Why, it's eight o'clock already, practically midday."

He laughed. "I've been up since six, myself," he told me.

"Well done," I told him, gleefully thinking to myself that he couldn't have been out on the tiles the night before, then.

"Are you still on for this afternoon, then?" he asked anxiously.

"I surely am," I told him. "I'm looking forward to it."

"Me too," he said. "It looks like being a nice day – do you fancy going on the DART to Howth after lunch?"

"Sounds great!"

Just then my bedroom door opened and there was a squeal of excitement as Haley confirmed to herself that I was still there. She ran across the room, pulled back the covers and dived into bed beside me. I grunted as a sharp young elbow landed heavily on my stomach.

"What's going on?" came Chris's amused voice in my ear.

Mentally I cursed the timing. No chance now of being mysteriously inscrutable about my activities the previous evening. No chance of giving the impression – without lying in the slightest, of course – that I had been doing something interesting and cool.

"That was my friend Gaby's daughter squealing with excitement to find me here in bed, and my grunt as she caught me with her elbow. I stayed over last night in Gaby's house."

"Ah, right. So you're still in bed then?"

"Of course! Where else would I be at eight o'clock on a Sunday morning?" I laughed.

He ignored that last and repeated softly, "You're still in bed. Well, you know, I think I'm with your friend's daughter – I'd also be squealing with excitement if I found you in bed. And I'd have you grunting too, but not in pain."

"Really?" I whispered, my own voice low as he whispered these seductions to me. I coughed then as Haley caught my attention with her ever-louder demands that I tell her a story.

"Chris," I said laughing, "I'd better go."

"So I hear," he said good-naturedly. "We can resume this conversation later. See you then."

"See you," I told him and, hanging up, I turned my attention to a delighted Haley.

Gaby and I met up at the breakfast table. She was looking tired but there was a glow about her despite the weariness.

"Did you have a good time?" I asked her.

"Oh yes," she said, and there was a half-smile about her, something secret, some remembered experience which she wasn't about to share – although it wouldn't have taken Sherlock Holmes to figure it out.

"We went to Lanigan's," she told me, relaying the shareable part of the evening, "and the food was great. We had a fabulous Merlot with the meal and – " and she went on to describe the evening, sounding more like a restaurant critic than a lover.

But I looked at her face and realised that what she wasn't saying was more important. She was describing in detail the publicly acceptable parts of the evening as a metaphor for what she couldn't say: the laughter, the meaningful glances, the hands clasped, the shared memories, and later the love-making, the low murmurs and the sharp intakes of breath and the coming together and recommitting to their love and their relationship.

And I was very, very glad for her.

After a leisurely chat-filled breakfast with Gaby and the children (and Peter when he eventually surfaced, rubbing his eyes and with his hair sticking up), it was time to leave. I was glad to go. I had been counting the minutes until it was time to leave to see Chris.

I would have been leaving early, even if I had no plans. I didn't want to outstay my welcome. You see, no matter how close I am to Gaby and her family, no matter that I know they love me and, in Haley's case, adore me, no matter how welcome they make me feel . . . I am still an outsider. I'm still a welcome stranger rather than a proper member of the family.

I'm still only a guest. A welcome temporary addition to their family, but not a necessary and permanent component.

Being with Gaby and her family was always bitter-sweet for me, bringing up as it does those childhood feelings of the Victorian orphan pressing her face against the window of the warm lighted family inside.

Anyway, I didn't have to think about that today. I had my afternoon with Chris to look forward to!

Chapter 9

Clutching my directions I headed off and found my way to Chris's house without any difficulty. He lived, it transpired, in a 1930's-looking redbrick semi-detached house on a leafy road a few minutes from the DART train station. I studied the house when I reached it – it was in immaculate condition, which is always a good sign. Sometimes bachelor accommodation can be a celebration of function over form, to put it mildly.

The door and window-frames were painted in a rich glossy bottle-green which contrasted well with the red brick, as did the overflowing window-boxes. Terracotta pots filled with summer flowers enlivened the red-tiled porch and made it all look very inviting.

I pushed open the wrought-iron gate and walked up the short tiled driveway to the porch. I rang the bell and the door opened immediately – Chris must have been waiting for me. Which was good, showed how keen he was, but it also meant that he possibly would have witnessed my perusal of his house.

He had.

"Hi, Sally, come in. You're very welcome," he told me, and as he ushered me in he kissed my cheek. "I saw you checking the place out. What do you think?"

I blushed a little and said, "It's lovely. I was just admiring it."

"It is nice, isn't it? I know I shouldn't say that, but I'm really proud of it. I've put a lot of work into it. Come on in and I'll show you around."

The house probably had a tendency to be dark, I noted, built as it was at a time when people weren't as aware of the need for natural light as we are now. But Chris – or whoever had decorated – had done his best to compensate for this and had decorated in a minimalist style and neutral colours.

Real wooden floorboards throughout were stained in a rich oak colour, and all the walls were a creamy buttery yellow. Heavy cream curtains hung at each window. Accents of colour were dotted around – red cushions and a rug in the sitting-room, a dominating orange abstract canvas in the office (which was in the former dining-room), and green accessories in the kitchen.

The kitchen door opened onto a small garden, most of which was laid out in a charming Mediterranean-style patio complete with barbecue, plenty of seats and colourful pots everywhere.

"Would you like to see upstairs?" he asked me, and I followed him up the wooden staircase to the traditional layout above. The bathroom faced the stairs with what looked like the original suite in it – substantial and white, with a claw-footed bath.

The two smaller bedrooms were simply decorated and had that slightly dead atmosphere of rooms which had not been occupied in a very long time.

The master bedroom at the front of the house was large enough not to be overwhelmed by the free-standing oak wardrobe which stood in the alcove one side of the original-looking fireplace, nor by the large oak bed. I looked at the bed and couldn't help wondering what action that bed had seen . . . and more to the point, what action it was going to see in the short-term future.

On a dresser in the other alcove sat a modern hi-fi system, and CDs lay carelessly on the dresser and I realised that that was the first sign I had seen of any mess, or indeed, of any personal aspects to the house at all. I had seen a big hi-fi in the sitting-room, along with the wide-screen TV, but any music, or any sign that the hi-fi had ever been used, were well hidden.

Now that I thought about it further, the whole house seemed totally impersonal. Like a show-house almost: perfectly designed, perfectly kept, perfectly personality-free. Or . . . the thought came unbidden, I don't know where it came from or why, but it came . . . or . . . like a stage set.

"It's lovely," I told him truthfully while we were still standing in that final room, the master bedroom. Equally truthfully I told him, "And it's so well kept. Are you a neatness freak or something?" I asked, laughing.

"Well, it's true I like things neat and tidy. I can't stand clutter."

"I see," I said. Was there no end to this man's perfections? A tidy man! However, I wondered at the total lack of anything personal around – there wasn't, now that I thought about it, a single photograph displayed in the house, for example. No matter how anti-clutter a person is, they would surely display a photograph or two.

Mentally I shook myself. It didn't matter; some people just weren't into photographs after all. After all, look at my own place – very few photographs there, either.

There was the one of me and Gaby in the Isle of Man when we were eighteen that hung in the little hallway. And the photo of me holding Haley at her christening which graced the top of the television. And the one of myself and my mother and father at my graduation which hung on the sitting-room wall.

Actually, that one had been worth hanging up for scarcity-value alone. To have a picture of my mother and my father together, without any members of their real families, was unheard of, before or since. I suppose we wouldn't get another such photo until my own wedding, if that ever happened.

Which thought brought me back to where I was, and why I was there.

"It's a lovely house," I said again. "It's a credit to you. Well done. How long are you living here?"

And he took my cue and began to lead the way downstairs to the kitchen, chatting to me about his purchase of the house six years previously and the work he had done to it since he had it, and its history as far as it was known to him. Safe conversation to be getting on with.

He sat me at the kitchen table with a glass of crisp white wine while he chopped and sautéed and grilled and roasted and chatted away to me. I had a sudden image of us as we would appear to outsiders – it made a lovely tableau.

There was I, dressed in jeans, and a cream knitted cotton top, my blonde hair in a pony-tail and my make-up very subtle and girl-next-door. I had a chunky bead necklace around my neck, and matching earrings, and I wore pristine white running shoes with thick white socks. Wholesome, I think you'd call the image I was trying to purvey and which I think I had achieved. Think Meg Ryan.

And there I was sitting at this table, watching and listening intently to the man there with me, a man who by any reckoning was super handsome, who was looking adorable and sexy and kissable, but somehow also cute and vulnerable as he engaged in the task of cooking. He too was wearing jeans but his were topped with a spotless white T-shirt whose short sleeves showed off his strong muscular arms with their dusting of black hair.

Around us the kitchen looked as if it were straight out of a home-style magazine and between us – me, him and the kitchen – I thought we created, as I've said, a lovely tableau.

I could nearly picture the Celebrity Magazine captions: *'Sally Cronin and Chris Malley in their beautiful Ballsbridge home. 'I've never been happier,' declares Chris as he deftly cooks dinner for the celebrity couple. 'Sally's definitely the woman for me.'*

And maybe the next picture would be a close-up of

me as I daintily sipped my wine in that fine kitchen. The caption might read: *'I knew it was meant to be,' says well-known beauty, Sally.*

Just then I remembered the Curse of the Celebrity Magazines and quickly banished *that* particular image from my mind. At least I had remembered the famous curse *before* we had had the crew around, not after.

"That's right," I mused aloud as I thought of it. "You had cooking down as one of your hobbies on your profile, didn't you? I had forgotten that."

He laughed. "You probably thought that it was a lie anyway, something to impress the women. But it's all true, and, of course, it *does* impress the women!"

It was lightly said and lightly delivered and I laughed when he said it. No matter that a fine sharp pain went through my chest at the thought of all the women he had had occasion to impress. Which was a pretty stupid thing to get upset about. Did I really think he had lived in a box before he met me?

And would I really want a man who had at the advanced age of thirty-four never had a relationship before . . . that would be a bit strange, a bit spooky.

Of course he had ex-girlfriends, just as I had ex-boyfriends. As long as they weren't all like the psychotic Angela, we'd be fine.

"*Et voilà*," said Chris with a tongue-in-cheek flourish as he served the meal just then. It was wide ribbons of home-made pasta (bought by him, he explained, not made by him), served with lots of vegetables finely chopped – tiny pieces of sun-dried tomatoes, sliced olives, diced sautéed aubergines and courgettes, all cooked in a rich fresh tomato, red wine and basil sauce, enriched with fresh cream. It was served with a glass of earthy red wine and the whole thing was a feast indeed.

"Cheers," he said, raising his glass to me, and I raised mine, and the beautiful sound of quality crystal resonating rang across the room, and the light caught the facets of the glasses and they sparkled like diamonds as we toasted.

"To us," he said, "and all that we may be to each other."

"To us," I echoed, delighted and thrilled that he would be making such a profound (albeit, when you actually studied the statement, ultimately uncommitted) toast so early.

"You know," he said, taking a sip from the heavy glass, "this is just perfect, Sally. This moment. Being here with you. It's as if – now, you won't laugh, will you?"

"No, no, I won't laugh," I promised him, leaning forward a little, the better to hear what he was going to say.

"Okay," he said, and cleared his throat before continuing, and as he spoke he studied his wine glass intently, turning its stem in his hands so that the dark red liquid trembled gently. "The thing is," he said after a moment, "it seems so totally and absolutely right that you're here. Not just nice, I mean. Or enjoyable, although of course it's those things too. But it's more than that." He glanced up at me to see how I was reacting.

I smiled at him and tried to make my smile as encouraging as possible. *Don't let him stop now,* I was thinking frantically, *I've got to hear what he's going to say.*

My smile must have been reassuring enough as he continued then. "It's as if, I don't really know how to explain it, but it's as if there was a Sally-shaped hole in my life before. And only you can fill it, obviously, since it's a gap made by your absence. This probably sounds really silly," he said, looking extremely vulnerable and nervous about how I would greet this declaration.

"It doesn't sound at all silly," I rushed to reassure him. "It sounds wonderful! You have no idea how much that means to me, to hear that."

I was almost delirious with joy at what I was hearing. A Sally-shaped hole which only I could fill? That I wasn't just welcome, but necessary? Could it be true? Could it be true that I was finding what I had been lacking all my life – a place where I belonged? A man who needed me, rather than just amicably tolerating me?

There was a strange sensation in my chest and I realised after some reflection what it was: it was an absence of pain. A pain I'd been carrying around so long – ever since GanGan had died in fact – that I had stopped even noticing it.

It was the pain of there being nowhere I truly belonged and nobody who profoundly needed me. The pain of being merely tolerated rather than being an essential to somebody's life, to somebody's happiness.

That pain had been with me almost all my life. And now it was gone. As Chris told me about the Sally-shaped hole which only I could fill, the reason for the pain evaporated, and the pain with it.

I felt light-headed suddenly, giddy. With the pain's absence came a lightness, and an ease and an elation which I had never before experienced, and I began to laugh for the joy of it, and Chris smiled at me, enjoying my laughter.

Maybe that's all any of us wants, to know that we matter, that at least one person is better off and richer because of our presence, happier for our existence. And on that sunny Sunday afternoon, in that cream and green kitchen, Chris gave me that gift. Or what seemed to me then to be that gift.

"Thanks for saying that," I told him.

He smiled his acceptance of my thanks, but shook his head at the same time, "No need to thank me, it's all true." He gestured at my meal, changing the subject, "Eat up before it goes cold."

As I ate the meal, and sipped at the robust wine, and chatted and laughed with this handsome man I thought to myself that this was the nearest to happiness I had ever, ever been.

No, I corrected myself, this wasn't near to happiness – this *was* happiness. And more, or maybe entwined, it was belonging. I felt so right there, so accepted, as if there were indeed a Sally-shaped hole which only I could fill. *This* was the feeling of belonging I had always been searching for.

And although Chris had not promised anything tangible – it was too early for that – it seemed clear to me that there was an unspoken promise in the long looks he was giving me, in the laughter and chat we shared, in the knowing that we would have a future together. Not a defined future, not yet, but a future nonetheless.

Chapter 10

It was perfect. At least, it would have been perfect if the phone hadn't rung just as we were finishing our meal. Its shrill tones echoed from the hallway, summoning, peremptory. *Don't answer it*, I thought. *Don't break the moment.*

But: "Sorry, Sally, I'd better get that." He patted his lips with his napkin and then went out to the hallway.

Through the open doorway I heard him pick up the phone and say cheerfully, "Hello, Chris Malley."

Then: "Oh, it's you." There was silence for long moments as he listened and then he said, "Now that's enough, Angela. I said, that's enough," his voice was rising, "I don't have to listen to this shit, and I won't! I've done everything I can. I can't help you any more – no, Angela, no. I won't." A pause. "Don't say that," he hissed. "It's not true. You are mad. You know you are. Nothing you say has any basis in reality. Oh," he said in impatience, "I'm stupid to be even engaging in this conversation. Don't ring here again, do you hear me?" and he hung up the phone.

He stood in the hallway for a few moments and then I heard him give a big sigh before he returned to the kitchen.

"Sorry about that," he said, and smiled at me with a visible effort.

He seemed almost to be vibrating, like a high-voltage electrical wire, with the tension of the conversation.

"Would you like another glass of wine?" he asked, and upon my nod he refilled my glass and with that we spoke no more about the phone call and deliberately tried to recapture the previous good humour we had been sharing.

After lunch we cleared up together and it seemed as if I had always been there in that sunny warm kitchen with this handsome fascinating man.

After we had finished he said, "So, what do you think? Will we DART out to Howth?"

At that stage I would have happily agreed if he had suggested we give up everything and go and be Buddhist monks in Nepal, orange clothes and shaven head notwithstanding. So a trip to Howth was a mere nothing to agree to.

We strolled out of the house and towards the DART station. Before long we were heading north along the coastline to the gorgeous town of Howth.

We walked along the seafront and then onto the pier. As we did so Chris took my hand and I thought my heart would literally burst out through my chest wall with the excitement and joy and happiness I was experiencing.

Even God was on my side, creating the perfect atmosphere for two lovers to come together. The sky was a clear cloudless blue and the day was warm and clement. The tranquil sea reflected this bright blue, and twinkled like diamonds where the sun caught it.

Many other people were out strolling together on this beautiful Sunday afternoon: teenage couples with eyes for nobody but themselves; youngish couples like us, chatting and laughing; traditional families with mummies and daddies and one or two children running laughing ahead, and maybe a baby in a pushchair or sling.

I tried not to look enviously at those, or at least, not obviously so.

There were elderly couples walking together slowly and cautiously, and on their lined faces I seemed to be able to read the text of a lifetime of love and commitment and laughter and joy and problems surmounted and bad times overcome.

And if there were single fathers there trying to amuse over-excited children, I didn't see them. And if some of the elderly couples were walking in bleak silence and thin compressed lips, I didn't see those either.

I was walking in a haze of happiness and nothing which contradicted that could possibly get access to my consciousness.

How can I describe what that magical afternoon was like? I can't even really remember what we spoke about. It wasn't anything earth-shaking, I know that. It was conversation for the sake of conversation. Conversation in which the medium *was* the message, in which dialogue was important for its own sake.

I cherished the sensation of his hand holding and surrounding mine, and the lightness of touch as our upper arms brushed occasionally. I cherished the sound of his voice, his very presence.

We had a glass of wine in a pub after our walk, and even as we talked more and chatted and shared childhood anecdotes and political opinions, even as that was happening and we just looked like any couple enjoying a drink, even then I was thinking: *I'm in love with this man. It's happened already. We're soul mates.*

And even though part of me cringed at the corniness of that thought, the bigger part of me realised that it was true. Or at least, this is exactly what it felt like. It truly seemed to me that Chris and I were like soul-twins separated at birth and now that we had found each other again that awful empty place inside was filled, and everything – my whole life – made sense for the first time ever. We laughed together at the same things, we had remarkably similar, but not spookily identical, opinions on stuff, we seemed to be completing each other's thoughts even.

And it was both more than all that and less definable than all that . . . it was just a knowing, a believing, a heart thing. I grow frustrated trying to describe it – perhaps it's like trying to describe the sensation of the wind on your face to somebody who has been indoors all their lives: unmistakable once it's experienced but impossible to describe with the meagre tool of mere words.

After our drink we slowly made our way back to the DART station. I could feel my feet dragging in sadness that this wonderful day was nearing its end. I didn't want it to end, ever. I didn't want the inevitable separation from Chris to come about. I didn't want to have to wait the number of days – no matter how few – until it was time for our next date.

"I've had a great day," he told me as we sat waiting for the train, and he reached over and took my hand, "and I don't want it to end. I'm wondering, what are you doing this evening? Would you like to spend the evening with me?"

"I would," I told him, and again we looked deep into each other's eyes and smiled.

When we got back we cooked and ate a light meal before taking our coffee into the sitting-room. But it wasn't long before he put his mug on the coffee-table, leaned over and gently took my own cup out of my hand and placed it carefully on the table beside his. And then he leaned over me and kissed me.

It was our first kiss, our first proper kiss. He laid one hand gently on the back of my neck but apart from that, and his mouth on mine, he didn't touch me at all. But his lips caressed mine and his strong tongue slipped through my softened lips and gently probed my mouth.

As we kissed he groaned deep in his throat and moved a little closer to me. Without conscious thought I lifted my hand and placed it around his head, clasping the back of his neck, revelling in the sensation of his skin and strong muscular neck under my hand, and I pulled him even nearer to me.

I didn't have to pull very hard as he took the invitation, the command, and moved towards me. I leaned back under his onslaught until I was half-lying on the sofa and he was half-lying on top of me, and I experienced for the first time in ages that delicious unique pleasure of a man's weight on top of me.

But after some time he lifted his head from me. I felt bereft, abandoned, but he wasn't going far, just far enough to whisper in my ear, "This isn't very comfortable. Will you come upstairs with me?"

And I whispered back, "I will."

He stood and took my hand and gently pulled me to my feet, and then led me out of the sitting-room into the hall, and up the stairs towards his bedroom. And all the time I was dimly aware that this was very, very early in a relationship to be sleeping together, but it just felt so right – the whole relationship felt so right – that it was okay.

We drifted, floated, up the stairs, or so it seemed, and before there was a chance for the mood to break or self-consciousness to arise I was lying on my back upon his bed and he was lying half-on, half-beside me, and he was kissing me again, strong and sweet, enticing and demanding all at the same time. I could feel myself responding with my nipples hard and straining and aching for his touch, and other parts of me softening but equally straining and aching for his attention. And I could feel him responding to me, that sublime experience of a man desiring me and making it clear with another presence, a presence which wasn't there before, insistent against me.

Chris moved his hand and caressed my breast and I gasped and arched my back the better to meet him. "Do you like that?" he whispered, and although I couldn't see his face I could hear a smile in his voice.

And then cohesive thought faded and it all blurred into one powerful sensation of touch, of skin upon skin, and mouth against mouth, and mouth and tongue searching and finding, and groans and pleas and low chuckles, and anxious request about contraception, and confirmation regarding same, and then a sliding and a filling and a completion and a rushing and a satiation.

And then it was a lying together, curled tight, feeling incredibly complete and floaty.

I said sleepily, "I feel so comfortable here, it seems a huge effort to get up to get."

"Don't go then. Stay here tonight with me."

"I have no overnight stuff with me."

"I've a spare toothbrush, and I can lend you a T-shirt, assuming you have to sleep in anything at all. And maybe you could go home in the morning before going to work. Or wear today's clothes – it won't matter for once, surely."

"True," I said, "and it would be lovely to stay. The thought of having to get up out of this warm cosy you-filled bed and drive home now is awful. But I've make-up on me and need to wash that off, and I've no make-up for the morning."

"Tough," he said. "I'm not going to let you go anyway," and he tightened his grip on me to illustrate how he would be holding onto me, and I felt emotionally as well as physically warm, and wanted and needed and cherished and desired and special, and it was a very, very satisfying feeling.

Eventually we got up and brushed our teeth and used the bathroom, and I washed off my make-up as best I could with a face-cloth and ignored the tightness I experienced since I had no moisturiser with me, and then we snuggled back under the covers together.

"Good night," he whispered, "see you in the morning."

"Good night," I told him, and fell asleep moments later.

And that was my first night with Chris Malley.

Chapter 11

When I awoke the next morning it took me a moment to recognise where I was. Oh yes, I remembered, waking fully now, I was in Chris's house. In Chris's bed, to be precise. I realised that the bed was empty, and even as I registered that I registered also the sound of the shower.

How would it be, I wondered, when he came back into the room? Would we be natural together? Or embarrassed?

I noticed a soft white towelling dressing-gown at the end of the bed, placed there, it seemed, for me.

Grateful for this thoughtfulness – we might have been writhing in each other's arms a few hours previously, but I still wouldn't feel confident walking around naked in front of him – I slipped out of bed and put it on.

I was tying the belt when the sound of running water stopped. I sat on the edge of the bed, nervous enough. Should I go and meet him? Or just wait for him? I could hardly go downstairs and just start making coffee, surely?

But even as I was wondering this he came back into the room, and it very quickly became apparent that I had nothing to worry about. His face broke into a wide smile when he saw me, he came over to me and kissed me hard on the mouth.

"Good morning, beautiful," he said cheerfully. "Would you like a shower now? I'll go down and get breakfast organised."

Once I was washed and dressed I joined him in the kitchen. The smell of coffee was enticing, and Chris in all his vibrancy and enthusiasm was just as enticing. As we were drinking our coffee, cradling our mugs standing up, he asked me, "Sally, will you come back here after work?"

I didn't need to think about it. "I'd love to!"

"Great," he said. "Any time after seven, okay? Actually, hang on," and he lifted his key-ring and removed a key which he handed to me. "Let yourself in if you get here first. Make yourself at home."

"Thanks!" I told him, carefully taking the key. How much he trusted me, so soon!

"I'll see you later this evening then," he said. "In fact, I can't wait to see you then."

We kissed goodbye on the path outside his house and got into our respective cars. He pulled off with a cheerful bip on the horn, and I waved back.

I sank back into the car seat and gave a sigh. A sigh of satisfaction, and delight. What a *wonderful* evening! And he wanted to see me again tonight!

There was no way, I realised, that I could go into work. All I wanted to do was to think about Chris, talk about Chris, imagine Chris, remember last night with Chris. I'd be a liability to them, I justified to myself. I'd be so unable to concentrate I'd do more harm than good.

And so, very bad I know, but I took my mobile out of my bag and rang in to work. And I told Kathleen, who answered the phone, that I was too sick to come in that day. She was concerned and unsuspicious, told me to wrap up warm and she'd see me when I got better.

I assured her that I would, thanked her, and hung up. And I only felt a tiny little bit guilty and remorseful.

I drove home, changed my clothes and grabbed some breakfast – I was ravenous at this stage. And then I rang Gaby.

"Hi Gaby," I trilled into my mobile, "it's me! I was wondering if you're around this morning."

"I am," she told me. "What time were you thinking of?"

"I could be there in half an hour. That okay?"

"More than okay," she told me. "I'll put the kettle on. But, hang on, shouldn't you be in work?"

"I'll explain when I see you," I told her, and half an hour later when I was sitting in her generous kitchen I did so, giving her all the details (well, maybe not literally *all* the details!) of what had happened since I had last seen her on Sunday morning. Only twenty-four hours previously, I realised, but what a difference it had made to me.

"He makes me feel so special when I'm with him,

like . . . oh, I don't know, a princess in a fairy-tale maybe," I told her, trying to explain how it was between us, "the sort of stuff we dreamed of as girls. He makes me feel complete for the first time ever in my life. I love him and I . . . I think he loves me too. He hasn't said it yet, neither have I, but I'm sure he does. And Gaby, don't laugh, but I think he's my soul mate."

"I'm not laughing," she told me sombrely, and she wasn't either. "I'm delighted for you, Sal, I really am. But you know, this is very soon to feel so strongly."

"Oh!" I said, thwarted and frustrated. "Don't try to spoil it for me, please don't. I've been so lonely for so long, I really have, for my whole life really," I told her, near to tears, "and now this magical thing has happened to me and I want you to be happy for me."

She looked at me, her face troubled, and then she seemed to reach some decision. Her face brightened in a brilliant smile, and I refused to look at any effort that that might be costing her. She said, "I *am* happy for you, Sally, I really truly am. If this Chris is as right for you as you're saying, then how could I not be?" She came over to me and hugged me, "You deserve somebody special and I'm so glad you've found him. Tell me, when are we going to meet him?"

"Soon," I promised, recklessly, given that I had no idea how Chris would feel about being wheeled out to be viewed by the pals.

"I look forward to it," Gaby said, a smile still fixed in place.

* * *

112

I was actually quite down as I made my way home from Gaby's house. Why, oh why, couldn't she be happy for me? Yes, I granted, she was right about it all being very quick.

But sometimes these things are, I argued as if she were there to hear me and be convinced by what I was saying. *Just because you and Peter took the slow and steady route to love – friends first, affection turning to romance turning to commitment – that doesn't mean it's right for everybody,* I insisted to her image in my head. *That doesn't mean,* I told her absent self crossly, *that everybody has to do it your way. All those stories about love at first sight, they came from somewhere, surely. You just have no romance left in your soul,* I insisted, *to understand what's going on here.*

When I got home I hovered, uncertain. I was inexplicably jittery, nervy, unable to relax. What on earth was I going to do to fill the day? I wasn't used to this much leisure at a time when nobody was around to play with. I couldn't get to Chris's house before seven . . . at least, I could, I had the key, I reminded myself, feeling again that glow of acceptance and belonging and trustworthiness which giving me the key indicated. I *could* go there earlier, but there was no point when he wasn't there . . . I would have even fewer resources with which to amuse myself there than I did here.

I'd go to the gym, I decided, a good workout would pass the time, and would possibly get rid of some of this nervous energy. So I quickly changed into my gym clothes, packed an overnight bag to take to Chris's and drove the short distance to *Svelte*.

As I made my way there I pondered why I should

feel so jittery. I eventually came to the conclusion that there was a combination of stuff going on. There was excitement and delight at this new romance. There was nervousness in case it didn't work out and I ended up hurt. There was the fear that what I was feeling was all one-sided. All of this was compounded by a nagging feeling that even if he *did* feel the same way, that somehow it was all too good to be true, a feeling that such wonderful things couldn't really happen to *me*.

I pulled into the gym car park and turned off the ignition. But instead of getting out of the car I sat there and forced myself to face the question: could it be too good to be true?

It could, I acknowledged, and there was some relief in facing the worst.

But it didn't *have* to be too good to be true. People *did* fall in love very quickly, after all. Lasting relationships *could* begin this explosively.

And why wouldn't Chris feel the same way as I did? He certainly seemed to.

My doubts were just down to my own lack of self-esteem, I acknowledged. I was really asking myself: how could he possibly be in love with *me*?

But why wouldn't he? Did I think I was truly the only unlovable person on earth?

And if Gaby's doubts echoed my own deeply buried ones and forced me to examine them, then that was probably a good thing. I didn't want to lose my head entirely over this. Take it handy, I told myself. Take it handy until you know exactly what Chris is thinking and feeling.

Thus relieved at having identified my feelings and having dealt with them, I got out of the car and went into the gym. I did a thorough workout which left me feeling weak and wobbly-kneed, but – after a long and hot shower – also left me feeling refreshed and somehow cleansed of all my worries and issues.

I went into the snack-bar and ordered a juice. When it came I went and sat down at my favourite table overlooking the pool, and sipped away, enjoying the feeling in my tired muscles, the soothing sight of swimmers ploughing up and down their lengths. Enjoying, too, the enduring buzz from the previous night's encounter, and the anticipation of the evening to come.

After some time my reverie was interrupted. David had appeared at my side, with a glass of fruit-garnished mineral water for himself, and another juice for me.

"Room for one more?" he asked easily.

"Of course!" I said, gesturing the chair on the other side of the small chrome table. "Always room for you!"

As he sat, relaxed, lounging back in the chair, his long legs stretched out, I appreciated – as ever since realising he was gay, in an aesthetic way only – his physical good looks. From his pleasantly handsome face topped with brown needing-a-cut hair, to his soft brown eyes behind his trademark glasses, to his lean but perfectly toned physique, he was a fine thing.

Not as fine as Chris, of course. Chris was better-built, and his colouring was more dramatic, and his face was far more handsome in a classically chiselled way.

Even as I thought of Chris again, my face broke into a big grin.

"You seem in good form today," David said, smiling to see me so happy.

"Oh, I am! Wait till I tell you – I've met the most fabulous man! I'm so happy!"

"That's *great* news!" he told me, smiling broadly, clearly delighted. "I'm thrilled for you. Who? Where? How long? Come on! Tell your Uncle David all!"

I needed no second invitation, and I spoke of Chris, of how handsome he was, and intelligent, and thoughtful, and wonderful, and special, and . . . and . . . and . . .

Give David his due, he listened with every appearance of a man dying to know every detail. Only towards the end did his attention wander. I noticed that he was looking towards the bar.

I followed his gaze. He was looking at a man who stood there, and I have to admit that the man was well worth looking at. He had a body even Arnold Schwarzenegger would have envied, all muscular curves and hard planes. He had obviously just been working out as he was still sweat-stained, and he wore a short towel around his neck with which he wiped his forehead even as we looked.

I glanced over at David and saw that he wasn't merely looking at this man. He was staring intently at him, and there was a speculative expression on his face. Rating his chances, perhaps.

David must have noticed me looking at him because he came back to me with a little start. "Sorry, Sally," he apologised, swinging in his chair so that he was facing me again. "I was a bit sidetracked there for a moment."

I bet you were, I found myself thinking bitchily

before I caught onto myself. Why shouldn't he eye up the talent. I asked myself. Don't you do it yourself? At least, I used to.

Those days were no doubt behind me now. At least, I hoped so, and all the signs were good.

I could feel excitement bubbling in my stomach again. Oh God, but it would be wonderful not to have to worry any more about getting dates, about meeting somebody. It would be wonderful to be settled, to be chosen. It would be a dream come true. I would be able to relax and enjoy life.

Not that I didn't enjoy life now, I corrected myself quickly, but I would enjoy life much more.

"So you're in love then?" he asked me, turning his attention to me again.

"Well, maybe not yet in love," I said, laughing with joy, "but who knows what the future will bring?"

"Who knows indeed? We should all be so lucky! Anyway, I'd better be going," he said then, draining the last of his drink, "must get *some* work done!"

"See you soon," I told him.

Chapter 12

I finished up my own drink soon afterwards, and
wandered out into the bright sunshine. I looked at my
watch: it was only three o'clock. Time for a spot of retail
therapy.

So I went to the local shopping centre and spent a
couple of very happy hours browsing and purchasing.

Naturally I bought some new sexy underwear. It's
one of the immutable laws of the universe, that: *new
relationship = new underwear*.

And I bought some new tops, and a feminine flowery
skirt which flowed around my calves as I moved. And
fun strappy sandals to go with it. And some perfume, a
light and flowery scent. And a dark and musky one while
I was at it, for evenings and sultry night-times.

Around six o'clock I stopped for a cup of coffee and a
sandwich, and then I made my way over to Chris's
house. As I drove I was aware of a huge mass of
excitement deep in my belly.

I replayed the previous night's love-making and my groin tightened in response. I pictured him – his handsome angular face, his sleek black hair with his piercing blue eyes, the intent expression on his face as he looked at me. I could easily visualise his sturdy broad shoulders, his smooth firm body, his strong hands gripping me, and my own hands gripped the steering wheel more tightly in response.

I couldn't wait to see him.

I reached his house just before seven o'clock. As a courtesy, I rang the doorbell and waited a couple of minutes. There was no answer, however, so I used the key and let myself into the house. It felt very strange to be in somebody's house without them, somebody who was – no matter how much we had shared physically and emotionally – still essentially a stranger.

Where was Chris? He said he'd be here at seven. Oh well, he was probably delayed. He'd be here soon.

I hovered inside the door, uncertain as to what to do next. After a moment I put my overnight bag down on the hallway floor and made my way into the sitting-room. What could I do that wouldn't be invasive? I sat on the sofa and put on the television, but I couldn't concentrate and after a while I switched it off again.

I looked at my watch – it was twenty past seven. And Chris still wasn't here. *Make yourself at home*, he had said, but that was easier said than done.

The silence in the house was loud, a tangible presence. It was almost oppressive. I switched on the television again and watched it mindlessly. Until, about ten minutes later I heard his key in the door. I leapt to my feet and made my way to meet him in the hallway.

On my way there I heard him call out in a faux-American accent, "Hi honey, I'm home!" and I smiled to myself in amusement and anticipation.

We met in the doorway between the hall and sitting-room, and my heart leapt again at the realisation of just how handsome he was . . . it wasn't that I had forgotten as such, more that I couldn't hold this image perfectly in my memory.

"Hi!" he said looking intently at me. "My, but you are so good to come home to!" And even though he was being deliberately corny, I could hear his truth behind the words. He bent and kissed my cheek, caressing the back of my neck with his hand. "Seriously, all joking aside, it was lovely to open the door and realise that you were here, so much nicer than coming back to an empty house."

I hugged him hard, delighted to see him, relishing the solidness of his well-toned body against me.

He cooked dinner for us, a simple cheese, onion and mushroom omelette, accompanied by a fresh green salad with a home-made dressing. All of which was washed down by a perfect white wine.

"I could get used to this," I told him lightly by way of compliment.

But he took it seriously. He looked at me intently, and said seriously, "I hope you do."

"Oh," I said, not sure how to react, aware that I was blushing. "Good," I said after a moment.

He smiled at me, a smile of rich satisfaction, and despite my confusion I was delighted that I could be the cause of so much contentment.

After dinner we moved to the sitting-room. We sat close together on the sofa, legs entwined and hands clasped. We chatted together, getting to know each other better, and I could feel myself relaxing. I was right to be here, I knew that now. I did belong.

And when, towards the end of the evening, he held out his hand to me and said, "Shall we?" I was able in confidence to give my hand to him and follow him as he led me to his bedroom. And in the darkness we came together again and we fitted so well and I felt so belonging and right and wonderful.

As we lay afterwards, with me resting my head on his chest and my leg thrown over him, and he playing gently with my hair, I began to hope that this might be it. You know, *IT*.

And then it got better because as we lay there in this post-coital repletion his voice came through the darkness, dark and rich.

And he said, "Sally, I hope you don't think this is too soon to be saying this. I've tried to be patient and say nothing, but I just can't help myself. And what I want to say is . . . well, Sally, I love you."

"Do you?" I whispered into the darkness. "Do you really?"

"I do," he confirmed. "I know it's way too early to be saying it," he said again, "but –"

"No, no," I hastened to stop him denying it or excusing it, "because, Chris, I love you too."

"That's great!" he said, relief in his voice, and he tightened his arm around me and pulled me even closer against him.

"I was so nervous saying it," he said with a little self-conscious laugh. "I've never said that to anybody before. But to know that you feel the same way – that's just incredible. I'm so lucky," and he bent his head and kissed the top of my head, and I lifted my face to him, and moved up nearer him, and we kissed passionately, and I truly thought that my heart would burst with all this happiness it couldn't contain.

I had been so lonely for so long, and out on the periphery of life and relationships for so long, and now at last I had come home. Now at last I belonged, and was wanted.

* * *

When I woke up the next morning it took a little moment to recall where I was, and why I had this sense of excitement and joy within me. And then I remembered and I smiled to myself in contentment. I grew aware of Chris fast asleep beside me, breathing deeply. *I'm not surprised he's still asleep*, I told myself smugly as I recalled our love-making the previous evening. Both occasions.

I leaned over and snuggled up to Chris and began nuzzling his neck. He stirred and woke.

"Hi," I said, "good morning. How are you? Did you sleep well?"

"I did," he said grinning at me. He yawned then and stretched. "What time is it?"

"Early," I told him, "there's loads of time," and I began kissing him.

* * *

Much later we were sitting at the breakfast table together.

"We should go out to dinner tonight," he told me, "to celebrate the fact that we love each other."

"Good idea!" I told him. "Where, and when?"

We made the arrangements and left for work together, for all the world like a couple which had been together forever. As we walked to the DART station, he asked me, "And will you come back here tonight?"

"Sure I will," I told him happily.

When I arrived at work Kathleen was both surprised and delighted to see me. "Don't you look well!" she told me. "I didn't think you'd be back at work so soon, I really didn't. Not the way you sounded yesterday. But you look fabulous today. That day's rest did you all the good in the world."

"Thanks Kathleen," I told her, feeling very guilty. "I do feel great today, thanks."

* * *

That evening at dinner I suggested to Chris that I would like him to meet Gaby and Peter.

"She's been my best friend since forever," I explained to him, "and Peter and I are great friends ever since they got together, and it would be fabulous if you could meet them. Now that you're so important in my life . . . and they've always been important to me, it would be good if you could meet."

"I'd love to," he told me. "When would you suggest?"

"Could you let me know when suits you," I asked him, "and then I can give them a selection of dates. It's not as easy for them to get out as it is for you and me, because they have to get a baby-sitter."

"Understood," he told me. He took his Palm Pilot out of his jacket pocket and, referring to it, began giving me a selection of dates.

I wasn't quite so cool, scribbling the selection of dates down on a mere piece of paper.

That night as he moved within my body he whispered to me, "I love you. You complete me. I needed you all my life and I never realised it. Don't ever leave me."

And as I arched my back the better to have him fill me I whispered back, "I won't, I swear I won't, not ever."

As we moved together in our love-making, my heart sang, He loves me! He loves me! And once we were lying together in post-coital glow, I told him, "I love you too." And he held me tight, burying his head in my neck, and I felt so, so joyful.

* * *

The next morning I said to him, "I'll probably go home this evening after work."

"If you like," he said. "I'd much rather you were here, but I understand that you might need some space."

"It's not that," I told him, which it wasn't. I just didn't want to assume that he would want me around yet again. It's very awkward this, wanting to spend every minute with somebody but not wanting to assume that he felt the same way.

"Tell you what," he suggested, "you'll have to come

back here anyway to collect your car, if we get the DART together. Why don't you eat with me, and you can head home then?"

"Good idea," I said, because in truth Chris was fast becoming like oxygen to me, and I needed my daily dose. I was greedy to spend every second with him that I could.

Chapter 13

Later in work I rang Gaby and arranged to go over to her house during my lunch break. I'd take a taxi and hang the expense.

We hadn't spoken in a couple of days, so there was lots of news to share when we met: the minutiae of day-to-day lives shared by good friends.

"So," she said, once I had caught up on her doings, "how are you? How's it going with Chris?"

"Great!" I told her, "In fact, that's why I wanted to call around. I was wondering if you and Peter would like to come out with us some evening soon, for a meal maybe." Even saying that, saying '*us*', gave me a thrill. It was so wonderful to be able to casually toss it into the conversation. "I'd like you both to meet him, to get to know him."

"We'd love to!" she said warmly. "When were you thinking of?"

"I have a few dates here, and we thought we'd let

you pick from those, depending on when you could get a baby-sitter."

'*We*' again! I was saying '*we*' like I was born to it, as if I had been saying it all my life! I could get used to this.

"Right you are," she told me when she had written them down. "I'll ring Emma as soon as she's back from school, and I'll get back to you then. It'll probably be Friday, though. That's her usual baby-sitting day. So . . ." she paused for a second and then continued, "so it's going well with you and Chris then?"

"Oh Gaby!" I said, heartfelt, and she laughed in delight. "Gaby, I love him. And he loves me! It's official, we've both said it to each other!"

"That's great," she said, but I sensed some reservation.

"What?" I asked.

"It's just that . . ." she said, her face troubled, "is it not very early for you to be in love?

"It *is* quick," I admitted, "but it's real."

I leant forward towards her, the better to share with her. "Love at first sight isn't just a myth. I know that now! We love each other. And it feels so right, Gaby! I feel so good about this."

"That's wonderful!" she said. "If you're sure . . .?"

"I am," I told her. "I am. I really am."

"Well, then . . ." She stood and came towards me, and wrapped her arms around me, leaning her head on mine as I sat there. "I'm so happy for you, Sally," she said into my hair. "You really deserve somebody special."

"He is special," I told her. "You'll see that when we all meet."

"I'm looking forward to it. I'll text you when I've spoken to Emma. We'll aim for next Friday, though, okay?"

* * *

That afternoon Gaby texted me to say that it *was* Friday that suited Emma and hence suited herself and Peter. I wrote it into my diary and sent a quick e-mail to Chris confirming the date.

However, no matter how pleased I was that the logistics were working out, there was something going on within me. I paused to consider and realised that there was a tension in my stomach. Some well-spent moments of introspection revealed why I might be nervous. There was a lot riding on this meeting. I so badly wanted them to get on well together.

I so wanted them to get on because it's so awkward when your boyfriend (*Boyfriend! I was saying 'boyfriend'!*) doesn't get on with your friends, and they all have to put up with each other for your sake. It's so much nicer if they do genuinely like each other, makes things much easier.

But also, I wanted them to get on because – and now we were reaching the crux of it all – if Gaby and Peter got on well with Chris then it would change the dynamics of my relationship with them. It would make it all a lot more balanced. I could be, with Chris by my side, an equal partner in the friendship, rather than what I was now – the recipient of their kindness in allowing me to be a hanger-on to their family.

For example, each year they invited me to spend

Christmas with them, and most years I ended up doing so.

I did have other options, of course I did. I could go to my mother's and Barry's house. But the very fact that each November Mum rang me to assure me that I would be very welcome, simply (it seemed to me) emphasised my outsider status. Did she ever ring my sisters to let them know they were welcome? Or was that already simply known by both Mum and themselves? I was pretty sure I knew the answer to that, but one year I asked her.

I said, "Mum, I'm curious. Do you do this for Laura and Eva?"

"Do what?"

"Invite them for Christmas."

There was silence for a moment and eventually she said, "Well, no, I don't. Why would I? They know they're welcome. But I'm not *inviting* you either, Sally. I'm simply *reminding* you that . . . that . . . you'll be welcome," she finished weakly.

So that was one option I had, to bury my pride and go there for Christmas, a place where I had to be reminded that I was welcome.

Another option was to go to my dad's. At least, I supposed it was an option I had. Dad had never specifically invited me for Christmas, but he had many times told me I was welcome "any time, any time at all, Sal. Just ring and let us know you're coming," and I assumed that that included Christmas. But such a vague invitation is no invitation at all, and having to ring and invite myself never really appealed to me.

When I was younger I had often gone away with

other single friends, and that had been fun. But as the years had passed, and everybody except me had paired off, that was no longer an option.

Another alternative was to remain at home on my own, or go away with other single people – strangers – to an organised Christmas celebration. Neither of which ever appealed to me.

And so remained the alternative of spending Christmas with Gaby and Peter, and that was the choice I usually made. Not always – pride and a desire not to impose too much on them prevented me from going every year. On the years I didn't go to Gaby and Peter's I either went to my mother's house, or did take one of those solitary holidays, cursing the single supplements and the enforced jollity.

I had always enjoyed Christmases with Gaby and Peter hugely, don't get me wrong. But there had always been a feeling within me, nagging away at me like a small stone in a shoe, a stone which isn't quite uncomfortable enough to remove but which is nagging by its presence. That feeling was this little image in my mind, an image of Gaby saying to Peter, "Do you mind if we invite Sally again this year? I know Christmas is for family but she's practically family, and she has nowhere else to go." And I could picture Peter saying easily, "Sure thing, you know she's always welcome."

And that image of charity offered and accepted always rankled with me.

But if Chris and I were to make it as a couple, then it would all be different. He and I would spend Christmas and other such occasions in our own house, and I could meet Gaby and Peter as equals rather than just as the recipient of their goodwill.

Because, I might as well admit, I had an image of the two couples, me and Chris, and Gaby and Peter, getting on so well that we were important in each other's lives even unto old age. I visualised us, for example, going away on holiday together. Not just us, but our respective children as well . . . because in this particular reverie Chris and I weren't just a committed long-term couple, we were parents too.

I know, I know, counting my chickens before the eggs were even laid, never mind hatched.

* * *

That evening after work I went, as planned, back to Chris's place and we cooked a meal together. And somehow I didn't end up going home that night either.

I did, however, by a huge effort go back home the next day, Thursday. Chris looked gratifyingly sorry to see me go, but I was sure the break would do us good. Make him appreciate me even more. The meeting with Gaby and Peter was arranged for the day after that, so we weren't going to be apart for long.

I breathed a sigh of relief, however, as I got into my flat on Thursday evening after work. It was the first time I had been alone since . . . since the previous Saturday afternoon, I realised. The previous week had been the most sublime experience of my life, and I was thrilled and delighted with the way things were going between us. But I was tired – sleep had not featured overmuch. And I needed some space. I enjoyed the solitude for an hour or so, but after that it chafed. I was getting used to having company, it appeared. Just as well. But I was bored and disorientated at home.

I'd go to the gym, I decided. I hadn't been all week, not with everything else that was going on, and I needed to keep fit and trim. No way was I going to stop looking after myself just because I'd got myself a man.

And not going to the gym meant that I hadn't seen David for a whole week, and now that I had a little time to myself to actually think, rather than being swept away in the emotion of my new relationship, I realised that I missed seeing him.

So off to the gym I headed and did my workout. I went into the snack-bar after my shower, and took my juice to my regular table. David didn't show up. Oh well, I shrugged, it would have been nice to meet him and catch up on all the news. But no matter, I'd see him the next time.

By the time I got home it was nearly time for bed. Some long overdue laundry, some dusting of unused furniture and similar chores filled in the evening very nicely. I hardly had time to miss Chris.

But still, lying in my otherwise-empty bed that night, I ached for him. How quickly I had become accustomed to his presence, to having his body and handsome face near mine. How quickly I had become accustomed to that aching sensation of loneliness being eased. Just as well I was seeing him the next day.

* * *

The next day passed slowly as I waited for the evening

to come. Isn't it always the way, the more you're looking forward to something, the more slowly the time drags towards it? But eventually it was time to finish up work and head out for those precious hours and days of freedom called the weekend.

"Any plans?" Marc asked me as we took the lift together.

"Oh, I'm going out to dinner with a few friends tonight," I said nonchalantly.

"Hope you have fun."

"So do I," I said fervently. "My boyfriend's meeting my friends for the first time, and I just hope they get on well."

"Ouch," winced Marc, "that's a tricky one all right. Good luck with it!"

I went straight home, showered and then, with my towel still wrapped around me, I hovered in front of my wardrobe.

What was I going to wear? I wanted to look stunningly gorgeous, that went without saying. But I also wanted to look as if I wasn't trying too hard. Naturally fabulous, that was the aim.

In the end I selected a simple linen dress in a soft salmon pink. It was sleeveless, knee-length and had an elegant boat-shaped neckline. The dress's shape, and hence my own, came from cleverly sewn darts. A pair of gold strappy sandals, and my hair up in a casual knot added to the effect. Earrings, a fine gold chain, and subtle make-up completed the effect. I scrutinised myself in the mirror after I was ready. Yes, I was happy with that.

Chapter 14

I packed an overnight bag and, as arranged, drove over to Chris's, experiencing that rollercoaster exhilarating sensation of combined nerves and excitement, deep in the pit of my belly.

I'm going to see him again, the thudding of my heart seemed to say. *I'm going to see him again.*

He opened the front door as I reached it, and my heart leapt at the realisation that he must have been waiting for me, looking out for me. I drank in the sight of him – tall and broad-built, his dark hair brushed sleekly back from his face, his generous mouth wide in a welcoming smile, and thought again how lucky I was that such a fantastic man should be interested in me! I went into his arms and we hugged tight. He held me at arm's length then, the better to examine me.

"You look great!" he told me. "Really special. Such a pity we have to go out . . . no chance we could cancel?"

Laughing, flattered, desired, I shook my head. "No way. But there's always later."

"That'll keep me going," he said, and there was a promise in his eyes, "as long as we're not out too late."

"We won't be," I assured him. "Gaby and Peter have a baby-sitter, after all. They'll have to be home at a reasonable time."

"Oh, that's right," he grimaced, "the curse of being parents. Come on and we'll go now. I'll just grab my jacket."

As we walked toward the DART station I pondered his reaction. Everybody knows that being a parent limits you, that you're not nearly as free as you were before. But that's just the nature of it, the nature of life. It's nothing to grimace at, surely.

I wanted to know his opinion of children, I really did. Clearly if we were going to stay together, which seemed likely now that we loved each other, we'd need to decide about children.

And I really, really wanted a baby. I ached to hold a baby of my own, not a borrowed-for-a-minute baby who had to be handed back. I wanted to be the one to whom a hurting toddler automatically turned. No matter how much Haley loved me, if she fell or got upset, only Gaby would do, and I was never more forcibly reminded of my guest status, my expendability, than at such moments. I wanted to be the one who was necessary, the one who carried the magical power to kiss better.

And so I needed to know what Chris thought about having a family. But yet I hesitated to mention it. It's such a cliché after all – the woman trying to talk about babies. And I didn't want to scare him off. I did need to know before I committed myself any more to this relationship, but not at the cost of frightening him away.

These circular thoughts were floundering around in my head as we waited at the station, and continued as we got onto the DART and headed towards the city centre. And Chris must have noticed because he said to me, "You're very quiet."

"Hmm. I was thinking."

"About me?"

"Oh," I laughed, "you're very vain! I could have been thinking about tax returns or *anything*!"

"Were you thinking about tax returns?"

"Well, no," I admitted, "I wasn't. And yes, I was thinking about you, you'll be glad to hear."

He certainly looked glad to hear it. *Gratified*, that would be the word I'm thinking of.

I decided to bite the bullet and ask him. What had I to lose after all? Nothing. Except having a relationship with him, I reminded myself. But still, I needed to know.

"I was just wondering," I told him, "how you felt about the idea of children. You grimaced when I reminded you about Gaby's children."

"No, I wasn't grimacing about children," he corrected me. "I was grimacing about the limitations of having a baby-sitter. When I have children I'm going to have a live-in nanny," he said, expansively, "so I can stay out as late as I want."

"A nanny!" I echoed, "You mean, to go along with the butler? And the parlourmaid?"

"Exactly!" he agreed, laughing.

And we didn't talk any more about children then, but I certainly didn't feel the need to do so . . . he had said "*When* I have children . . ." and that was enough for me, to know that he was agreeable in principle, to know that he saw himself as having children in the future.

And it seemed to me, as the DART pulled into our station and we got out, that all the pieces of the jigsaw entitled 'My Perfect Life' were coming together. All I needed was for this evening to go well.

* * *

Gaby and Peter were already at the restaurant when we got there. Introductions were made all around, and there was certainly goodwill and bonhomie to spare. Everybody, it seemed, was determined to get on with everybody else.

We sat at a table and drinks were served, menus were perused and meals chosen and ordered.

"So, Chris," said Peter then, "where do you live?"

And so began the small talk. It was fine. It fulfilled its purpose which was for these strangers to get to feel comfortable with each other. Different public transport systems were compared and contrasted. Opinions were sought and exchanged about the current political scandal. The current reality TV show was sneered at amid tentative admissions about having viewed it.

When the food came it brought with it more opportunities for conversational fodder.

After some time of this, and a couple of glasses of wine, we began to relax into each other's company, and it began to get easier. Soon we began trading travel anecdotes and roaring with laughter together. I tried to steer the conversation away from this topic because I knew what would come up. But it was impossible to do this without making a big deal of it, and thus arousing curiosity.

And sure enough, I was right. What I thought would come up, came up.

"Oh, oh, oh," gasped Gaby, "but wait till you hear what happened when Sally and I went on holiday to Greece together."

"No!" I told her, in a last attempt to prevent the inevitable, "no, don't tell that story."

But: "Oh, do," said Chris interestedly, and even Peter chimed in with his own request to hear. So much for all these years during which I had managed to keep it from him.

So there was nothing to do but to smile as gracefully as I could as Gaby told her story.

"We went to Crete the summer we were both twenty. It was our first major holiday abroad so we were determined to enjoy it. And Sally decided she was going to get an all-over tan. I mean, *all over!*" she emphasised in case they hadn't got it.

They had, Gaby. They had.

"And so we found this secluded beach and Sally stripped off."

"And did you strip off too?" Peter asked her with a gleam in his eye.

"No, I didn't. Not quite. But Sally did, and we sunbathed all day. And that evening Sally discovered that she had got burned all along her back. And that included her bum! She had to sleep on her front, but the worst was during the daytime because she literally couldn't sit down. I mean, *literally*!"

Chris and Peter were both trying to look suitably sympathetic. But little snickers of laughter were forcing their way out of their mouths, which soon turned into full-scale guffaws of laughter.

Gaby was laughing too as she continued, "When we were in bars she had to stand, but that wasn't too bad, lots of people stand in bars. But she had to stand in restaurants as well. I tell you, she looked so incredibly stupid just standing there by the table. It was hilarious."

"Hilarious," I echoed bleakly, my face as red as my bottom was back then. Great, this was really going to impress Chris. Thanks, Gaby.

He was smiling at me though, along with his laughter. "You care a lot about how you look, don't you, Sally?" He leaned forward and whispered in my ear, "I'd like to see you with an all-over tan. We might try it some day – the sensible way of course."

Thankfully the rest of the conversation passed less humiliatingly, and we joked and laughed and I began to relax. It was okay. They liked each other!

* * *

In the taxi on the way home Chris said, "They're nice, your friends."

"I'm glad you like them," I told him accurately, "and I think they liked you too. I could tell."

"Do you see a lot of them?"

"Quite a lot. They're my closest friends, really."

139

He gave a cheerful laugh. "I just hope that they won't take up too much of your time. I need to know there'll be time for me!"

"Oh, there will, Chris," I promised him fervently. "There will."

And when we got home (and see, already I was thinking of his house as *home*) it all got even better as he began kissing me powerfully.

"I've waited all evening to do this," he said gutturally, "I've waited long enough," and he showed me the strength of his desire for me right there in the hallway. His desire inflamed mine and I responded wildly to him. We didn't even make it into the sitting-room.

Afterwards we crawled up to bed and slept curled together.

When I awoke the next morning we made love again, and eventually surfaced towards noon. We had brunch in his bright kitchen and then I regretfully said, "I'd better go."

"Oh?" he said, disappointed. "Do you have to?"

Well, I didn't really. I just didn't want to assume I could stay.

"I could stay if you liked," I told him, and his face lit up.

So we spent a wonderful weekend together – I stayed all day Sunday too.

We laughed and played, and went to a craft fair, and took walks and cooked together, and gave each other an aromatherapy back rub with some oils I bought at the craft fair, and took hot sensuous showers together and made love all over the house.

During the weekend I managed to text Gaby from the privacy of the bathroom. I just sent one word, *"Well?"* and she texted back, *"He's gorgeous! And really nice. Talk soon."*

So, Chris even had Gaby's seal of approval. Perfect.

On Sunday afternoon I told him, "I'll head home after dinner."

"Don't," he implored.

"I have to," I told him. And it was true. I did have to. I couldn't really explain it further . . . it was because we weren't *officially* living together, and I couldn't assume that we were *unofficially* living together. Going home was my way of asserting my independence, of subliminally telling him that I did have a life of my own. Also I was running out of clean clothes.

So I forced myself to go home on Sunday evening, and in one way I was sorry I did. My tiny flat seemed huge and empty and silent. But in another way it was good to be back in my own space.

Staying with Chris was wearying in one way, in that I was neither guest nor occupant but something strangely in between. I could comfortably make myself a cup of tea, but I didn't have any drawers or wardrobe space allocated to me so I was living out of my weekend suitcase. I didn't put any clothes washes on, that was a resident-type thing to do, not a short-term guest activity. I didn't answer the phone if it rang but yet I could go upstairs as I chose.

And it was tiring not knowing the etiquette of this undefined role. Several times I was aware of Chris's expression tightening a little as he kindly didn't comment on some *faux pas* I was inadvertently committing regarding the routine of his house. It was good to have a break from all that, from wondering if I was doing the right thing.

And I didn't even see him on Monday evening either. When I was leaving I had told him, "I'd love to see you on Tuesday if you're free."

"Oh?" he said lightly. "What're you doing on Monday? Seeing your other lovers?"

"Nothing so exciting. I'll go to the gym – I have to do that regularly or my body just starts dissolving! And I'll go and see Gaby."

"I'm very jealous," he told me, "of anything that takes you away from me."

"Don't be silly," I told him, "going to the gym and seeing Gaby doesn't take me away from you. It just means spending a little time apart. As I told you, I'll see you Tuesday."

"Sure thing," he said easily.

So after work on Monday I went straight to the gym. As ever I dreaded going in and it took willpower to make myself go through with it. And as usual, once I was under the shower having my post-workout wash, I was feeling on top of the world and so glad I had come.

I didn't stop for a juice when I finished – Gaby was expecting me. But as I left I passed David talking to somebody in the lobby. He waved at me and I saluted back as I rushed past.

It was bedlam when I got to Gaby's house – Peter was trying to get the children to bed and they were up to high-doh, and it didn't help matters when they saw me.

Gaby grinned helplessly at me as I fought my way from under them.

"Sorry," she said, "they were at a birthday party today and they're hyper from all the sugar. And their darling Sally arriving – well! That's finished them off entirely!"

I agreed to help them get to bed, there were hard negotiations done on the amount of stories which constituted proper bed-putting, and eventually they were in bed, curled up like little angels.

Exhausted I went downstairs to discover that Gaby had opened a bottle of wine in honour of my visit. Or possibly in honour of the achievement of getting the two whirling dervishes to a stationary mode.

Peter popped an affectionate kiss on my cheek, accepted a glass of wine, and muttered something about checking something out on the Internet, and disappeared giving us two women space to be together.

I wasted no time. "So, what did you think?" I asked her, snuggling more deeply into the deep ruby-red sofa.

She knew immediately what I was asking her opinion about. Or rather, who.

"He's *lovely!* Really, really nice. He's got a lovely way about him and a really pleasant manner about him. Peter really likes him – he really appreciated that advice Chris gave him about his computer. And isn't he *handsome!*"

"He is, isn't he?" I said proudly. Honestly, you'd swear it was all my own work. "I'm glad you like him, though."

"What's not to like? And, you know, he was so nice when I was talking about Haley and Jack. I try not to go on and on about them, but he was so interested. Or at least, he made me feel he was fascinated. And he was asking me about how long Peter and I had been married, how we met and stuff like that. He was so kind, or interested, or both."

This was *great!* Gaby and Peter liked Chris, and he liked them. Maybe my fantasies hadn't been too far out after all.

Chapter 15

On Tuesday Chris came over to my place after work and we went for a drink at the local pub. It didn't take me long to realise that he had something on his mind, and my heart skipped a beat. Was he going to tell me we were finished?

"I missed you," he told me. "I really missed you Sunday evening and last night. It's amazing how quickly you've become part of my life. I told you that you filled a Sally-shaped hole which I didn't even realise was there. But now I know it's there and it feels awful when you're not around."

As I listened I could feel my heart-rate decrease. This wasn't bad news. Whatever he had to say, it seemed it didn't have anything to do with us finishing. Quite the contrary it appeared.

But having said that, Chris was shifting uncomfortably in his seat. Whatever he had to say, it wasn't coming easily.

Eventually, however, he came to the point, talking down into his hands, showing an avid interest in the beer mat he was busy shredding, "The thing is, Sally, I know that it's very, very early days in our relationship. Probably way too early to say this, but I'm going to anyway."

I sat tense, waiting to hear what he would say.

He looked up at me then. "Would you like to move in with me? I know it's early days," he said again, speaking quickly, nervously, "but I miss you so much when you're not there. Would you?" he asked, waiting anxiously for my verdict.

But he didn't have to wait long. "Oh Chris, I'd love to!" I told him, reaching over the short distance between us and resting my hand on his leg. "That would be so great!"

This just kept getting better and better! Living together! Oh, wait till Gaby heard this! My loneliness would be over, my despised single status would be gone! I would be one half of a couple. I would be with Chris every day . . . it was just so perfect.

"Brilliant!" he said, his whole face relaxing in relief. "So, when can you move in?"

I shrugged. "The weekend?"

"So long?"

"It's only five days until Saturday," I told him, secretly delighted with his impatience.

"True," he conceded. He laid a hand over mine where it still rested on his leg. "It's going to be an adventure," he promised. "Wait until you see."

He stayed with me that night, and I ended up

staying with him each of the nights until the weekend, so I might as well have moved in immediately.

* * *

On Friday evening as we ate dinner together I said to him, "You know, we should discuss exactly how living together is going to work. Things like sharing bills, my paying my way, things like that."

"Right. Good point. We really should sort that out. About the mortgage, don't worry about it," he told me. "I'm paying it anyway, it's not going to cost me any more because you're here. Same goes for the heating costs. For food and phone bills and stuff like that, maybe we could split it down the middle. How does that sound?"

"Sounds good," I told him.

"It's going to be fine," he said winking at me. "There might be teething troubles, we'll both have to get used to living together, but we'll work it all out. We love each other after all."

"Yes, we do, don't we?" I said, grinning hugely at him.

And in that declaration of love it seemed churlish, or perhaps unwise, to ask my other question about living together. Such as: what exactly does living together mean for us? Does it mean shacked up together temporarily until we get bored? Or is it a halfway house to marriage, like a modern version of being engaged? What exactly was he offering when he wanted me to move in with him?

I wanted to know. I really wanted to know. But I

couldn't ask. What if he said it was just a casual thing? What would I do then? I could hardly move in with him under those circumstances. But yet I didn't want to risk finding out that that was the case and have my dreams shattered.

I would just go with the flow, I decided. Take each day as it came. Not need to have every 'i' dotted and every 't' crossed. And after all, he *had* said he loved me.

Stupid I know. If we were close enough to be moving in together, we should have been close enough to discuss such hugely important issues. But I was just too excited about finally getting my dream – a steady relationship, to have been chosen, to belong – to question too much. Chris was offering me all this, and I couldn't afford to look too closely to see if there was any small print.

Accordingly, the next morning I drove back to the flat in Dundrum. When I entered it I walked around as if I had never seen it before. It seemed now, suddenly, like a stranger's place. But yet I was a little sad as I walked around. I had been very happy here.

I had phoned the landlord and given him the required month's notice. We had always got on well to the limited extent that our paths had crossed, and he agreed to refund me the difference if he got new tenants within the month.

"Give me your new address," he requested, "so I can send the deposit cheque on," and as I gave it to him I fully experienced the thrill of saying it for the first time.

I packed all my belongings in suitcases and then when they were full, in plastic bags. A bit less-than-cool, I considered, looking at them. But it would have to do. There was a *lot* of stuff. It was going to be a challenge to get it all into the car.

But get it into the car I did, even though I could have done with the help of those people they hire for the crowded Tokyo underground trains, whose job it is to push people in even more tightly.

I drove around to Chris's house and parked in front of it. The door opened as I pulled up and Chris came down the driveway towards me, a huge grin on his face. He helped me in with some of my stuff and we carried it upstairs.

"Look here," he said, showing me proudly, "here's wardrobe space I've cleared, and look, two empty drawers. I hope that's enough room. There's furniture in the other rooms if you need more."

"I think I will," I told him, touched by his naivety about how much clothes-storage space the average woman needs. I ended up getting a full wardrobe and chest of drawers in the box-room allocated to me. My own dressing-room!

Eventually we had unloaded the car and put everything away, and we looked at each other, and I don't know about him but there was a sudden sense of *what now?* It was different, so different, living together. Even though it was what I had wanted, now that I had it I didn't know what to do with it. What would we say? Or do?

But Chris had no such difficulties. He whisked me off to bed for the afternoon where we thoroughly celebrated our new status, and then he brought me out for a meal that evening.

* * *

I rang Gaby on Sunday morning. Although we had texted trivialities we hadn't spoken since Monday evening.

Each time I had considered telling her I was going to move in with Chris, something had stopped me. And so the week had passed until I was actually ensconced, *in situ* so to speak, before telling her. Which had the effect of making sure I wouldn't be talked out of it. Which does beg the question as to whether I was as certain of this as I wanted to think, if I feared being so easily talked out of it.

But no, I reassured myself, it wasn't that. It was just that Gaby had been a sceptic about this relationship since the beginning. About the speed of it more than its existence, and moving in with somebody after knowing them for two weeks did count as fairly quick in anybody's terms. But as well, I was in love, I was excited about the launch of My Perfect Life, and I didn't want to study too closely any doubts which Gaby might be expressing.

"Hi," I told her when she came on the phone, "I have some news for you. Some *good* news," I emphasised, giving her her cue. "I've just moved in with Chris. We're living together!"

There was a pause on the far end of the line and then her voice came brightly, "Well, that's great news, it really is! It's brilliant that you've found somebody so special. I'm very happy for you."

"Thanks," I told her. "I'm pretty delighted myself. Have you got a pen and I'll give you my new address and phone number?"

Once she had the details, and had offered her congratulations again, I rang off.

Who else should I tell? My mother, naturally.

I wouldn't tell her about the new boyfriend, and certainly not about living with him. She'd only insist on meeting him, on having a 'nice dinner party' for him. And I really, truly, couldn't cope with that.

She would no doubt patronise him when she first heard his well-spoken-but-not-posh accent. And then she would possibly begin to fawn over him once she realised that he was a reasonably well-off businessman. Either way it would be nauseating and I would put neither Chris nor myself through it.

So I simply texted her my change of address and land-line phone number, and the same for my father. In due course I got acknowledgment texts in return.

My sisters texted occasionally but as we had never been close they didn't need to know about my move either – we could just continue to keep in touch by text. My half-brothers, same story. I saw even less of them than I did of any of the other members of my divided family, which meant virtually never.

I ran through the list of my friends, and quickly texted those who might have occasion to ring me at home, giving them my new number. Before long I had received a rash of texts in return, congratulating me on the move and promising to ring soon. The curse of a busy society, always genuinely intending to phone, to keep in touch, but without the time to keep that promise.

I set up my laptop in the dining-room office and Chris did some fancy stuff with wires and cables and organised a connection to the Internet for me, which meant I had access to e-mail. So I e-mailed Majella in New Zealand and Jan in London and advised them of my new status.

I would advise the HR department in work tomorrow of my change of details and write letters to my bank and insurance companies and so on, and that would be it. The formalities taken care of.

Chris called me just then, telling me that dinner was ready. I joined him at the kitchen table and we tucked in.

As we were eating he said to me, "Now that you're living here you'll have to take your turn cooking – you're not a guest any more, you know!"

"Fair point," I told him, taking a sip of my wine. "As you've been doing all the cooking, and fabulously so, since we met, I just hope you won't be expecting the same standard as you provide! I'll do my best, but you're a hard act to follow."

"I'm sure you'll be great," he reassured me, but he looked pleased, as well he might, at my compliment regarding his own cooking skills.

The weekend passed in blissful love-making, and laughter, and meals cooked and eaten, and walks taken, and pub-drinks consumed.

* * *

All too soon it was Monday and back to the real world of work. As we left the house together I realised that this was *it*! We were genuinely living together and routinely going to work together was the proof of it.

That evening I checked my e-mails to see if anything had come from Majella or Jan. Jan had sent her congratulations and best wishes, and Majella hadn't answered yet, probably due to the time difference.

But hang on, what was this? An e-mail from smalley@kangaroo.au. Who was that? I opened it and began to read:

Dear Sally,

I hope you don't mind, but Chris gave me your e-mail address. He's been singing your praises these last few weeks! I have to say, you sound wonderful! Sorry, let me introduce myself – I'm his sister Sheila. I'm living in Oz now. I don't know if he mentioned me at all? He e-mailed me the news that you've just moved in together, and I'm writing to offer you my congratulations. You're a very lucky woman. Chris is a great guy, and you probably don't get too many women saying that about their brothers!

Mind you, I wouldn't have said that when we were growing up – we fought like the proverbial cat and dog in our childhood – I suppose all brothers and sisters do. Anyway, my congratulations again to you both, I hope you'll both be very happy together.

Virtual kisses,

Sheila.

How nice! I thought. And how envious I was of Chris having a sister to whom he could be so close.

I quickly typed back: *Dear Sheila, thank you so much for your e-mail. How kind of you to send your congratulations. Yes, Chris and I are very happy together! I'm settling into his house well, as if I always lived here! And yes, I do know how lucky I am to have met him. I really do. How do you like*

Australia – is it as fabulous as we all think here, barbies on the beach and so on? All best, Sally.

Once I had sent the e-mail I started making dinner. It was simple enough, a spaghetti bolognese. But I was using fresh basil in it, and a dash of red wine, and I was very pleased with how it turned out. I found it to be delicious. Not so Chris however. He ate a mouthful or two and then put his fork down with an attempt at hiding his grimace.

"Do you not like it?" I asked anxiously.

"Well, no," he said reluctantly. "It just tastes a bit . . . a bit funny. I don't know how to describe it better."

"I'm sorry," I told him, full of remorse. The first meal I had cooked us, and I had ruined it. "Can I get you anything else?"

"I'll just make myself some toast," he told me, and got to his feet. "You carry on."

I ate a few more mouthfuls and I have to say, I genuinely couldn't see anything wrong with it. But nonetheless the pleasure was gone out of it for me and I put my fork down almost immediately.

Chris ate some toast and honey, but I couldn't eat anything else. I didn't know if I was overreacting but I had so wanted to make this a success and I was so disappointed at how it had turned out.

* * *

On Tuesday morning he knocked on the bathroom door while I was putting on my make-up.

"Mind if I come in," he called, which I thought was really decent of him seeing as the door was ajar so it was clear I wasn't engaged in anything too private. I called back that no, of course I didn't, and he entered and began combing his hair.

We stood side by side, and I could see him watching me in the mirror as I completed my make-up. I smiled a little to myself – *this* is what it was all about, *this* is what I had wanted: the easy intimacy, the relaxed feeling of making up while he did his hair. He saw my smile in the mirror and smiled back at my reflection.

"You look so well with make-up on," he said appreciatively.

"Why, thanks!" I told him.

But as I continued brushing my hair, doubts began to nibble. He said that I looked well with make-up on . . . did that mean that he thought I *didn't* look well unless I was wearing make-up?

Chris was still smiling, and humming a little to himself as he finished combing his hair, and I realised that there was no way he could have meant that. He was only passing a nice compliment for heaven's sake! No need to analyse it to death. The fact that this was my own deep-down secret – that I knew I was plain until I reinvented myself each morning – was making me paranoid.

That evening I got my expected e-mail from Majella who professed herself delighted with my news. And I also received a reply from Sheila.

Hi Sally! I was delighted to get your e-mail so quickly. Glad you're settling in well. What's the weather like over in Dublin? It's summer so it must be oh, at least, ten degrees! Only joking, hope you're getting lovely weather. It's winter

here in Sydney, and yet it's about seventeen Celsius. Heaven!
Must dash, will write soon. Hugs, Sheila

I sent her an e-mail telling her what the day was like, telling her that I envied her getting seventeen degrees even in winter, and hoping that she was keeping well. I was delighted with this correspondence – it was a real bonus of my relationship with Chris that I was getting to know his sister. Would we ever meet, I wondered? A holiday to Australia would be nice, I mused . . .

Chapter 16

When I look back now on our life together, it amazes me how quickly I settled into Chris's house. It was as if I had always been there. Our days soon fell into a pattern. As Chris had clients all over the place, sometimes he was working in the city centre and on those days he and I would get the DART into work together. Other days he would have to drive to his clients' premises and on still other days he would work from home.

Sheila and I e-mailed reasonably often. We began to get to know each other, we shared thoughts and ideas and perceptions. It was the first time ever I had had a pen-friend, and her being Chris's sister made it all the better. She shared with me little anecdotes about him, swearing me to secrecy, saying he would *die* if he knew she was sharing these. And I, avid for every detail of my lover's life, agreed with alacrity.

They were the anecdote equivalent of baby pictures

– sweet, poignant, harmless but yet a little cringe-making for the subject.

For example, she told me to check out the tiny scar he had on his shoulder-blade. *That happened the time he climbed a tree to rescue my kitten*, she wrote, *and fell out of the tree and caught his shoulder on a twig on the way down. He was lucky to get off so lightly; he could have killed himself. I wouldn't mind but the kitten found its own way down!*

Or: *He saved up all his pocket money for weeks and bought me the single by the boy-band all the girls were on about. I never had the heart to tell him that by the time he had enough money to buy it, they were no longer in fashion! I still have that single, although needless to say I never listen to it!*

As Sheila and I e-mailed I began to feel very close to her, and it was great to be able to tell her of my feelings about Chris with somebody who shared them, albeit in a sisterly way. After swearing her to secrecy in the name of the sisterhood (*after all, don't want to let him know* all *my secrets*, I typed) I felt comfortable sharing how much he meant to me.

I was aware that I was probably going on a bit, but I justified it on the grounds that she was his sister and loved him too. Certainly she never complained about reading page after page about how wonderful he was and how much I adored him. When I apologised for possibly boring her, she wrote: *We're still very close as I told you, but obviously he doesn't share that kind of stuff with me, being a man! It makes me feel even closer to him to hear all this, so keep writing it!* I needed no further invitation.

It helped me too, to get a better sense of Chris, to

learn about his childhood. I envied him so much his close relationship with Sheila, his loving and lovable parents.

* * *

On the home front, too, things were great. We were enjoying hugely living together, being together, being a couple. Sure, we had a few moments of adjustment, doesn't every couple? It's a big change, living together.

One issue which was particularly significant was the tidiness-quotient. Chris was a bit of a neatness freak. And I, frankly, am a lot more relaxed about mess. I don't like living in a slum, don't get me wrong. But it doesn't upset me if a newspaper is left on the coffee table overnight, for example.

However, it was important to Chris, so I tried really hard to be as tidy as he was. It helped that he had a cleaning lady come in three times a week, the wonderful Mrs Butler. But even so it was a bit of a strain on me making sure I never left any mess behind me, no matter how little and how temporary.

It was a minor price to pay, however, for the happiness Chris and I were experiencing.

Our happiness was also marred a little – at least, mine was – by the all-too-frequent phone calls from Angela. Whenever Chris was there he took the call and spoke to her in soothing tones, trying to calm her down, until his patience ran out.

I only answered her call once, and hung up as soon as I realised who it was. I copied her number from the Caller ID onto the back of an envelope which I then placed face-up in the drawer of the hall table. And every other time the phone rang, I pulled the drawer open and checked the number before answering it and if it was Angela I just didn't pick up. Of course I soon came to recognise that number very well.

It was uncomfortable, though, listening to the phone ringing unanswered. She didn't give up easily, I'll say that for her. On and on and on the phone went, while I waited in the empty house for it to stop.

But when Chris was home he would take her calls, and speak to her in soothing tones, trying to calm her down, until his patience ran out.

Actually, I'm wrong. I said this marred our happiness a little. That was me trying to be philosophical. The reality was that I pretty much felt under siege. I tensed whenever the phone rang, not knowing if it was going to be a genuine caller, or Angela with another diatribe.

One evening after he had had to deal with her on the phone I asked him, "Is there nothing you can do about it?"

He grimaced and shrugged. "What *can* I do? Go to the police? Tell them that she's stalking me by phone? I don't think there's anything they can do. And even if they could . . . I'm worried about her mental stability. I don't want to push her over the edge."

"Why don't you just stop answering her calls then? She might get bored and stop ringing."

"I wish I could. But, same reason – her stability – I can't. She's threatening suicide, and I can't risk that. I'm trying to handle it all very carefully, to speak to her enough to calm her down, not enough to encourage her.

It's a delicate balancing act." He grimaced and shook his head.

"It sounds it!" I thought, not for the first time, what a kind and decent man he was, and how lucky I was to have him.

He lifted his palms and his shoulders in that quintessential gesture of defeat. "I feel so guilty about her, even now. I know it's not my fault that she's so unbalanced. But her – whatever we call it – madness or whatever, has got worse since we split up. I do try to calm her when she's on the phone, and that's all I can do. That's all I can do," he repeated bleakly. "I'm terrified that she'll kill herself, and I couldn't cope with that on my conscience."

Well, Chris might be a candidate for canonisation but I certainly wasn't, and I hoped, I fervently hoped, that I wouldn't have to speak to her again. And it transpired that I had my wish because, for whatever reason, abruptly, about two weeks later, she stopped phoning entirely.

Her silence seemed to disconcert Chris. He would check the caller ID as soon as he came home, he would enquire of me if I had taken a call from her. It seemed she was occupying his thoughts – and hence my own – more in her silence than in her diatribes.

"You seem almost worried that she's not phoning any more," I said to him.

"Well, yes," he said uneasily. "I suppose it makes me feel tense because I'm wondering what she's up to. I hope she's okay . . ."

"She probably is," I reassured him. "Everyone

moves on eventually after an affair, however disastrous."

"I suppose. But, also . . . it's like the calm before the storm. Just as well I don't have a rabbit," he joked, "or I'd be checking for its safety each day."

But it proved not to be the calm before the storm, rather the calm before the continuing calm, and after a while we forgot about her and just carried on with our lives together.

* * *

Gaby came to see me one Saturday afternoon. Without the children. Much though I loved them I knew that they were, in common with all children, patented mess-creating devices, and I shuddered to think of what they would do to this pristine house. So Peter had the pleasure of their company while Gaby came to see my new residence.

She pronounced herself well impressed, both with the house itself, and with the glow of happiness on my face.

"I was wrong," she acknowledged. "I was just concerned for you, worried that it was all happening too quickly, that you weren't giving each other time to know each other. But you both look so happy together. You make a lovely couple."

And Gaby's approval was all I needed to make my happiness complete.

* * *

Contentment dulls the mind, though, I began to think. At least, I hoped that's what it was, not incipient

Alzheimer's. Because I started having what Americans call 'Senior Moments'. Moments in which you forget things you should know. Moments when your mind just doesn't operate the way it should.

The first Moment happened the next time I cooked dinner. Chris was drifting in and out of the kitchen, chatting, laying the table for me, catching up on the news of the day. And I must have been distracted by his conversation. Or maybe I was concentrating too much on his handsome body and on planning a seduction scene later, and not concentrating enough on cooking. Because dinner was literally inedible. This wasn't just Chris's opinion either. I had seriously oversalted it. If we had a dog, even the dog wouldn't have eaten it.

"I'm so sorry," I told him, distraught. "I don't know what I was thinking of. I mustn't have been concentrating properly. But God knows how it happened. There must be half a cup of salt in here."

"It doesn't matter," he told me kindly as he began putting bread in the toaster. "It could happen to anybody. Sure, it could happen to a bishop."

And as we laughed at that archaic phrase I mentally shrugged and let go my upset. It was a mistake, people make mistakes all the time, it was just one of those things.

But it happened again, except this time it was half a tin of curry powder in the saucepan. And there was no mistaking it. I had opened up a new tin and put in, or so I thought, the recommended tablespoon of powder. But we nearly burned the mouths off ourselves when we tried to eat it, and when we went to investigate, the evidence was there: a half-empty tin of curry powder.

I just stood looking at this half-empty tin shaking my head in disbelief. "I can't believe it," I kept saying. "How could I have done this?"

And Chris was so good. He calmed me, putting an arm around me, pulling me against him for a reassuring cuddle. "It's okay," he told me in soothing tones. "You were just distracted, that's all. Maybe concentration isn't your strong point, but so what? We can't all be good at everything."

Later when I had calmed down and we were relaxing in the sitting-room, me curled up against his strong body, he said, "Tell you what – maybe I'll take over the cooking, hm? You can do your share in other ways. I hate ironing for example, and while I know it wouldn't be exactly your occupation of choice, you don't hate it as much as I do. What about it?"

"Sure," I agreed tearfully, glad to give up on this hated job of cooking which was proving to be such a disaster.

So, at least we were eating well after that.

But I was still having these Senior Moments.

Such as the time Chris didn't arrive home from work until one o'clock in the morning. As the evening passed I was all but climbing the walls with combined worry and anger – one of them was applicable but until I spoke to him (if indeed he ever got home safely) I didn't know which. His mobile was switched off, and he wasn't responding to texts. When he eventually safely arrived home I realised that I didn't have to worry, and therefore anger was the appropriate emotion.

"Where were you till now?" I challenged him

furiously. "I was *frantic* with worry. I thought you were dead or worse."

He looked at me, totally shocked at this assault. "I was out with Mike. But you knew that. I told you I was going out with him tonight after work. I told you last week when it was arranged, and I reminded you this morning."

"You never said a word about it," I told him.

"I did," he said, looking more and more concerned about me. "Honestly, Sally, I did. When we said goodbye at the DART station this morning, I said, 'See you later. I don't know what time I'll be home so don't wait up.' Do you not remember?"

"You never said that," I persisted.

He shook his head in worry and disquiet, "But I did, Sal. You obviously just don't remember."

As he was so certain I began to doubt my own memory. I searched my mind but I couldn't actually remember our parting that morning. Didn't that mean that it had been so routine there was nothing to remember? Or did it mean that he was right, that he had reminded me about the meeting with Mike and I hadn't remembered.

Or maybe I just hadn't heard. Yes! I grabbed that thought with relief.

"I mustn't have heard you," I told him. "It's as simple as that."

And I refused to acknowledge that I must have not heard him twice – that morning *and* the previous week when he first mentioned it.

He pursed up his mouth at that. "If you say so," he

said dubiously, "but I had just kissed you goodbye. I said it right into your ear. But, yes, clearly you just didn't hear me." And that was worse, that he was obviously just humouring me.

These Moments, although worrying, were reasonably infrequent. I just forgot having the occasional conversation, mostly. Or I would set the video to record a documentary on Channel 4, as I thought, and discover that I had taped an hour of Sky News. Or I forgot to post letters, that sort of thing.

Apart from my concern about this, though, we were having a great time together. We didn't see much of our other friends; we were content just to be together, the two of us. We went out with Gaby and Peter on a couple of occasions, and with Mike and his girlfriend *du jour* on another, but apart from that we were wrapped around each other, both emotionally and physically.

It seemed to me that we were more in love with each day that passed, and I thought to myself: *Nothing can go wrong now!*

Chapter 17

Summer changed into a blustery autumn, and mid-September found us celebrating our two-month anniversary of living together. We celebrated in the bedroom with champagne and love-making.

As he was post-coitally peeling off the ubiquitous condom he said, "You know what, Sal? Maybe we should knock these on the head."

"What do you mean?" I asked, sated and indolent, but intrigued nonetheless.

He disposed of the condom and turned to me, gathered me into his arms, "We could start trying for a baby," he said into my ear. "I'd love a baby with you and, after all, you're not getting any younger."

"No, I'm not getting any younger, thanks for reminding me," I said dryly, "but are you serious? Having a baby? We're not even . . ." I hesitated and then courageously went for it, taking a deep breath first, ". . . we're not even married yet."

"Married?" he repeated, aghast. "Sally, what century are you living in? Marriage is so irrelevant. I don't believe in God, you know I don't, so we wouldn't get married in church anyway. And as for a State marriage, what's the point when you can get divorced? It's no more of a commitment than making a commitment to each other privately."

I said, "I see," and tried to keep the bleakness out of my voice as I saw my fantasies of a traditional white wedding drift away. Fantasies I hadn't even realised I was entertaining until any hopes of them were ruined.

But yet, he was right. If you didn't believe in religion there was no point getting married in church. Indeed, that would be downright hypocritical. And what the State meant by marriage was, as he had said, nothing more than a temporary arrangement anyway.

"I love you, Sally," he continued, "I want us to stay together forever, but I wouldn't stay with you just because I had signed a piece of paper, not if we were irrevocably unhappy. And I won't leave you on a whim just because we didn't sign a bit of paper. Do you see what I mean?"

Was I really hearing what I thought I was hearing? Had he really said he wanted to stay with me forever? My heart leapt in excitement and joy at that prospect. Because, up until now, we had never actually said what living together would mean. And I still hadn't felt right about asking him.

"So you're saying that we're totally committed anyway?" I asked him, making sure I had heard correctly. With my Senior Moments I could never be certain.

"Well, of course," he said in amazement. "What else is this about? Of course, we are! At least," doubt came into his voice, "that's what *I* thought. That's certainly how it is for me." He cleared his throat nervously. "Is it not the same for you?"

"Of course, it is!" I assured him, and turned in his arms to hug him tightly. As we held each other close I realised that, compared to the fact that he was proposing a lifetime together, the loss of my fantasy white wedding was nothing.

And, of course, this whole conversation had begun by him mentioning a baby!

"You mentioned trying for a baby?" I reminded him.

"I did indeed. And I don't think we need to be married to have a baby. What's the point? There's no stigma for the child any more, so why bother? And I'd love a baby with you. So, what do you think?"

I thought about conceiving a baby. Imagined telling him one day, proudly, that he was going to be a father. Visualised my pregnancy, the bump getting bigger and bigger and the big day getting nearer and nearer. Conjured up an image of me holding a tiny newborn infant to my breast (you'll note my fantasy jumped quickly and effortlessly over the birth itself), my head bowed Madonna-like over the baby as he or she nursed peacefully.

I pictured Chris and me playing in the park with a two- or three-year-old, pushing him or her on the swings. I could hear the sound of abandoned laughter, the sun was shining and everything was perfect.

"Yes, please," I whispered, 'I'd love that."

"Grand," he said with satisfaction. "I can't wait!"

* * *

When I woke up the next morning, for a moment or two I couldn't remember why I felt so happy, so excited. And then I remembered: we were going to have a baby! Well, to be exact about it, we were going to try to conceive a baby. I couldn't exactly go and tell the world about this baby yet given that it's surely more sensible to wait until the baby's actually conceived before you announce its impending arrival.

But it was tough. I so wanted to share this exciting news with somebody. Anybody. But I couldn't, I just had to contain myself. I quickly calculated: as luck would have it I was, or should be, right in the fertile part of my cycle right now. So now that we had stopped using protection, well, I could conceive at any time!

One thing I wanted to sort out first, however. In work that day I rang my doctor and made an appointment for that evening. I then quickly e-mailed Chris to let him know that I'd be late home. Not wanting to worry him, I didn't mention where I was going – I could tell him later, if there was anything to tell.

* * *

Dr Carolan was his usual kindly, if harried, self. "What can I do for you, my dear?" he asked.

I explained: "I'm hoping to conceive soon, and I'd like a check-up to make sure I'm healthy enough. I'm especially concerned because I've been doing strange things recently."

"Have you?" he asked. "Like what?"

I explained about the Senior Moments and whispered to him my barely expressed worries that I was beginning to lose the use of my faculties.

He laughed, "On the basis of messing up a few meals and forgetting a few conversations? I don't think so, my dear. That happens to us all. I wouldn't worry about it, I really wouldn't. Maybe take some Evening Primrose Oil if you're concerned. Now, let's check your blood pressure."

As I rolled up my sleeve I debated stressing my worry about these Senior Moments. But no. Dr Carolan wasn't concerned, and he was the expert after all.

He took my blood pressure, listened to my heart rate, weighed me and pronounced me to be in the peak of health. He also took some blood samples which he would send away for testing – we should have the results in a few weeks, he told me. Having said that, he was only doing this to reassure me, he wasn't expecting any surprises from them, so I was to go ahead and conceive as soon as I wanted.

Greatly reassured, I went home.

To be met by Chris in a rage. I had never before even seen him angry and it was a huge shock. He didn't even wait until I was inside the house – he opened the door to me and his expression was grim: all tight lips and narrowed eyes.

"Where have you been?" he demanded loudly of me, his fury evident in his carefully enunciated words. "I've been worried sick about you."

"I told you in my e-mail that I'd be a bit late home."

Despite myself I immediately felt defensive and fear was a knot in my stomach.

"What e-mail?" he asked sharply.

"The e-mail I sent you," I whispered to him, as a greater fear began to grow icily in my bowels. I *did* send that e-mail, I know I did. But it was as if I was trying to reassure myself.

He was shaking his head, and his rage was dissipating, to be replaced by a worry and concern which had me equally worried and concerned. "I got no e-mail," he said more softly.

"But I sent it," I said, and there was a note of pleading in my voice. "I know I did."

"I never got it," he told me. "Look, come here," and he brought me into the office. "Look, here's my inbox, and I downloaded my most recent mails not half an hour ago. There's nothing from you at all."

Frantically I read the list for that day. Sure enough, there was no e-mail from me.

"I sent it around eleven o'clock," I told him, my voice high-pitched and squeaky. "It must have got lost in cyberspace. I'm sorry you were worried."

"It's okay," he said, calming down now that he knew it wasn't a case of me just not bothering to let him know. "Although," he continued, "maybe you could ring in future if you're going to be late, to make sure I know."

"I will," I promised, grateful that his anger seemed to have gone and anxious never again to incur it.

"Where were you anyway?"

"I was at the doctor."

"The doctor?" he repeated, concern sharp in his voice. "Is everything okay?"

"Just for a check-up."

"Did you mention your mental confusion?" he asked anxiously.

"I did," I said, and noted the grave concern in his expression, "but he said that it was nothing to worry about."

"Oh, that's great!" said Chris, releasing a big sigh of relief. "That's very good news!"

"Actually, the reason I went for the check-up was, you know, for conceiving a baby," I told him shyly. It was one thing to whisper conversations about babies in dark post-coital intimacy, it was another to discuss it in broad daylight. Would he have changed his mind?

But he hadn't. And he approved of what I had done.

"Good idea, it's you carrying the baby after all, growing my baby. You need to know you're in good nick first. And speaking of conceiving babies, come on upstairs and let's get going on it!"

And we made love and the passion and love were heightened now by the prospect of our love-making being powerful enough to conceive a baby, a whole new human being. And in that love-making I was able to forget those nagging doubts about that e-mail. At least temporarily.

* * *

My first thought upon wakening next morning was: *Am I pregnant?* Was there, even now, a little zygote, too small even to be called an embryo, busy dividing its cells over and over? I placed a hand on my stomach and wondered. I didn't feel any differently, but then I wouldn't, not so soon. How strange that there could be a whole new life being created literally inside me – I mean, how bizarre when you think about it! – and I wouldn't know.

My second thought, less welcome, was *That e-mail. Did I send it? Or did I just think I did?*

As soon as I got into work later that morning I rushed to my computer and called up the Sent Items section of my e-mail account. There was nothing there. At least, there were lots of e-mails there – my regular business correspondence. But there was no e-mail to Chris. And staring disbelievingly at the screen didn't change that fact.

I sat and shook. I was sure I had sent it. I had been *certain*.

Kathleen noticed me. "Are you okay?" she asked me.

"I'm fine," I told her, gritting my teeth to try to stop the shaking.

"You're clearly not," she told me.

"It's just," I said shivering despite the warmth of the office, "that – " and then I stopped. I could hardly tell her the truth: that I was cracking up. I finished, " – it's just that I think I'm coming down with the flu."

She appraised me kindly, and I wanted nothing more than to fling myself into her arms and tell her the truth – that I was losing my mind – and have her comfort me and make it all okay. But how could she? All wasn't okay, it clearly wasn't.

"I think you should go home," she told me.

"I think you're right," I told her, and I did, stopping at the health food shop on the way to buy some Evening Primrose Oil, which I clutched to myself like a talisman all the way home on the DART. Surely it would make the difference, and stop these Senior Moments, and I could get my life back on track and all would be well.

* * *

The Evening Primrose Oil proved useless. My Senior Moments continued unabated. To tell the truth, they began to happen more often.

They didn't happen incessantly, or even frequently. But I never knew the day nor the hour. It was like constantly waiting for the other shoe to fall. I lived my whole life stressed by the possibility of another such Moment.

I became almost obsessive about checking and double-checking arrangements. Like the time I texted Gaby about arrangements to meet, and then phoned her ten minutes later to check she had got the text.

"Of course I got it," she said impatiently. "Amn't I after texting you back confirming the time?"

True, true, but I still felt better after confirming it verbally to her. Not that that proved anything, of course. It was always possible that I could have *thought* I'd phoned her to confirm, without actually having done so.

I didn't speak of this again to anybody. If I was cracking up I didn't want to announce it before it happened. I didn't want to admit to people how little of a grasp I had on reality. Nobody could have known that I was a very, *very*, frightened woman. And totally isolated in my fear.

Even the results of the blood tests coming back totally normal didn't reassure me. They were only checking for stuff like diabetes and rubella. They weren't checking – how could they, and why would they think to even if they could? – for incipient madness.

These Senior Moments were beyond terrifying. And I hugged them to me like a guilty secret, petrified lest anybody find out. Even Chris didn't know the half of them. I hid from him every example I could.

But there were many of these Moments which I could not conceal. Like the time I burned his best shirt.

I went into the kitchen to discover the iron face down on the shirt.

"Oh my God," I breathed, *horrified*, and ran over to it. I lifted off the iron – but too late, there was now a perfect iron-shaped burn mark on the shirt.

"What is it?" asked Chris, coming into the kitchen. "What's that funny smell?"

In answer I held up the shirt, trying to put my guilt and apology and shame into my expression.

"I'm sorry," I whispered, tears threatening. "I thought this shirt was over there, hanging up with the others. I could have *sworn* I did that. And I *did* leave the iron on the ironing-board. But standing up, and unplugged. Just until it cooled. That's why I was coming into the kitchen now, to put it away." But my voice didn't sound certain even to my own ears.

"You couldn't have done that," he said in the most

reasonable tones, but I could tell he was struggling to keep his patience. "Otherwise the shirt would be hanging up safely with the others, not in your hands with that burn mark."

"I was *sure*," I said again.

In answer he looked pointedly at the burned shirt in my hand.

"Look," he said wearily, "just bin the shirt, and we'll forget it. What's done is done. There's no point worrying about it."

He turned and left the kitchen and I was left replaying my previous actions in my mind. *Had* I unplugged the iron? I thought I could remember doing it, but when I thought about it, I could also 'remember' leaving the iron face-down on the shirt. Which was memory, and which imagination?

It was beyond terrifying.

The constant stress meant that I was finding it extremely difficult to eat. The spectre of whatever was happening to my mind was robbing my appetite. The ever-present terror of what would happen next kept me in a state of constant nausea, and my stomach turned further at the thought of having to cope with food as well. It meant that I was only managing to keep down the bare minimum of food.

Be careful what you wish for, I told myself bitterly. All these years when I wished I could be effortlessly slim. Now I was, but at what price?

Added to all this, I had my first disappointment in the form of my period. And then, a month later at the end of October, my second one.

Six months is average to conceive, I reassured myself, and anything up to a year is normal. Particularly for a woman of thirty-three. For I was thirty-three now, I had had my birthday during this time. It wasn't a very happy birthday, dealing as I was with the bitter disappointment of not conceiving, and the frantic worry about my mental state.

Actually, part of me was glad that I had not conceived. I wasn't fit to be a mother. To tell the truth I knew that I was being completely irresponsible even trying to conceive. But I clung to the possibility of a baby like somebody clinging to a life-raft, thinking that somehow having a baby would help me. At least until I absent-mindedly left it in a shop one day and went home without it.

Chapter 18

I often noticed Chris looking worriedly at me when he thought I wouldn't notice. Even though he didn't know the half of what was going on, the half he did know was bad enough.

One evening after work he said, "Maybe you're too stressed. Perhaps your job is too much for you."

"I don't think so. In all honesty it's not that taxing. And I enjoy it, and get on well with my colleagues."

"Still. Something has you really stressed. And you need to be relaxed to conceive, after all. So, I've been thinking about this, and I have had an idea."

"What's that?" I asked him.

"Do you remember telling me, back when we first met, that it was your dream to be a novelist?"

"I do. Well, I said if I won the Lotto and didn't have to work it's what I'd do."

"Come upstairs with me," he said proudly.

He led the way upstairs and stood outside the door

of the boxroom, the room in which my clothes were kept.

"*Voilà*," he said with a flourish, and opened the door.

He had been busy since that morning – although the wardrobe and chest of drawers with my clothes were still there, the bed had been removed (to the second bedroom, I later learned), and the walls had been painted over with a light moss green. The fresh chemical smell of new paint hung in the air.

My computer sat on a new mahogany-look desk, and a matching filing cabinet and bookcase had been placed in the room. On the bookcase shelves were five or six books with titles such as *Writing a Best-selling Novel,* and *Plotting Vs Characterisation.* And on top of the desk sat my laptop computer and a new printer.

I looked at it all, not sure what to say.

"It's for you," he said anxiously at my silence. "It's for you to write your novel."

"But how can I do that and work as well?" I asked him, even though I knew fine well that absolutely everybody who wrote a first novel did it as well as the day job. But it seemed as if he had decided something for me that I mightn't have decided for myself.

"This is the genius of it," he told me proudly. "I'm suggesting that you give up your job. I'm earning more than enough to keep us both. If you're at home you won't be as stressed, you can take your time over the novel. And then when the baby comes you can combine both! You were saying you didn't want to go out to work when you had the baby."

This was true. I *had* been saying that. I wanted to

give my baby what my mother hadn't given me but had given Laura and Eva. Maybe we all have children in the hopes of making up to them for the flaws in our own upbringing.

"It seems to me you'll never have this chance again," said Chris persuasively. "You know yourself that you'll be so busy when the baby comes. If you do it this way you'll have at least nine months, maybe more the way things are going, to write your novel and see if you can make a success of it."

I was tempted. The picture he was drawing was very compelling. No more early morning rush, no more strap-hanging on the DART, no more dealing with sometimes-awkward customers. Instead I would be sauntering upstairs with my coffee, ready to write all day.

It sounding idyllic. Except for one thing.

"What about money?" I asked him. "I've never been dependent on anybody for money. Wouldn't that change the balance of our relationship?"

"I've thought of that. I'll take over all the household bills and everything. I'll put you on my credit card so you can use that to buy groceries or whatever else you need. And I'll give you money each week for cash purchases. What do you think of that? It means you would never have to ask me for a penny, so you would be keeping your independence."

It sounded good. It sounded very good.

"Are you sure?" I asked him.

For answer he gestured towards the set-up office. "I've already put the money and effort into arranging this – surely that tells you how sure I am." He laughed. "It was so funny, nonchalantly seeing you off this morning, and then rushing around putting everything into place! I had the painters parked around the corner ready to dive into action as soon as you had left. It was like something out of a TV makeover programme!"

"Thank you," I said, touched that he loved me enough to go to this trouble for me. I went to him and hugged him tight. "Thank you, I'd be delighted to do this. Thanks for making it possible."

"It'll be great," he said, "and even on the days I'm working from home, I'll be downstairs, so we won't disturb each other. Maybe we can meet up for lunch in the kitchen, though – a romantic assignation!"

* * *

It was hard breaking the news to my colleagues that I was leaving. They were gratifyingly sorry to see me go – although, I have to be honest and say that there was some well-hidden relief too. I had been making too many stupid mistakes recently.

No matter. That was put aside. There were extravagantly complimentary speeches, and promises to keep in touch which deep down we probably all knew we wouldn't keep for long, and a wild leaving-do after my month's notice was up. Just as well I had my period again – I couldn't be drinking like that if there was any chance I was pregnant.

* * *

It was strange not going out to work the following

Monday morning. Mind you, it was no hardship not to go out into what turned out to be a wild and stormy late-November morning. But I was disciplined nonetheless. I got up at eight o'clock on the dot and was sitting in front of the keyboard, fully washed and dressed, by nine o'clock.

Except, I was thirsty. I had to go downstairs and get a drink of water. I brought it back upstairs and started again. And then my body informed me that it was time to visit the bathroom. And just as I was going to definitely start, I heard the morning post drop through the letter-box, so I had to go and investigate that.

Eventually, at about ten o'clock, I managed to sit down and type in earnest for a couple of hours, after which I thought I deserved a break.

I logged onto the Internet, checked my e-mails – nothing exciting – and then browsed for writers' websites.

I came across an excellent writers' forum, and I avidly read the recent posts. There was a thread headlined: *What Writers Do Instead Of Writing*, and it was hilarious. The main thrust of it was that since writing is so challenging and so tough and so scary our brains and our bodies conspire to make us do *anything* except write. Hence the constant thirst, and the constant feeling of need to use the bathroom. Playing computer card games, I learned, could eat up *hours* of the writer's day.

Spending hours on writers' forums was another one, actually, come to think of it. I forced myself to return to the keyboard.

Slowly, a story began to come together. It was about a young woman who was born when her parents were only eighteen (don't they say all first novels are semi-autobiographical?) but who was given up for adoption. It explored a life spent feeling like an outsider (see a pattern here?) until she met the love interest.

There was something which would stop them getting together – I didn't know what yet, had to think about that. Also she goes to find her biological parents (maybe she meets the love interest through that search?), and it turns out there's some big secret in her background. Again, I didn't know yet what it would be.

But on reading the books on writing with which Chris had so thoughtfully provided me, I learned that there are two schools of thought about writing: one was that you should know every single thing that's going to happen in your story before you begin it, the other was that it should all be a big surprise even to yourself.

I would belong to the second school of thought, I decided. By default.

By the end of the day I was delighted with how much I had written, and – I tentatively hoped – how reasonably good it was.

* * *

The next morning, however, I got a huge fright when I opened the file and re-read the last page or two of the previous day's work. It was rubbish. I don't mean that it wasn't of a very high quality. I literally mean that it was pure drivel.

I had written the scene where my heroine Maria

decides to trace her birth mother. I thought I had written it lucidly, logically, chronologically. But when I looked at it I discovered that the two last paragraphs were what I can only call stream-of-consciousness stuff. And I'm no James Joyce. Stuff like: *"Winter waxy warmer. Feathers stood bleak against a pewter rainbow. Fun fun fun. Maria walked like a rhinoceros on speed."*

The worst thing wasn't that this was incomprehensible gibberish. The worst thing was that it was incomprehensible gibberish which I couldn't even recall writing.

Petrified, I erased it. Nobody need know that my Senior Moments were infiltrating even my writing. I'd just rewrite the missing paragraphs.

So that is what I did. And that is what I did each and every time I discovered that somehow I had written such nonsense. There was no pattern or logic to when this happened. I could go up to a full week without writing drivel, and then it might happen three times in a row.

And on those days when I discovered that I had been writing gibberish, it would put me out of sorts for the rest of the day, and I would struggle to write even one page of text.

Still, I reminded myself, I was so lucky to have this opportunity. Think how many people would envy me this chance to follow my dream.

However, it was lonely. I could go from one end of the week to the other without leaving the house except to go to the gym three evenings a week, or occasionally to see Gaby. I missed my colleagues, missed the relaxed camaraderie, the Friday lunches out, the occasional drinks after work.

E-mail was great, though. I was in regular touch with Jan in London, and Majella in New Zealand, and of course, Sheila in Australia. But I mentioned my doubts and my fears to none of them.

* * *

My mother rang in the first week of December.

"I just wanted to let you know that you're welcome to come for Christmas," she told me kindly.

"That's okay, Mum," I told her back, "but I'm sorted for Christmas. Thanks anyway. I might come over Stephen's Day if you're available."

"Oh no, what a pity! We're going to your Auntie Margaret's on Stephen's Day."

That's what I'd been banking on. I didn't want her to see the mess I was making of myself.

"Oh well, we're sure to catch up some time over the period," I said vaguely, and we left it at that. We both knew it was unlikely we would meet up, and we were both pretty okay about it. It was just that, for some reason, we both felt we had to go through the motions.

* * *

A couple of days after that Chris said to me, "I was thinking, Sal. I know you like to go to the gym regularly, and I think that's great. But now that you're not working, maybe you could go during the day instead of the evenings. It would be much more efficient, really, and it would mean you're here in the evenings with me. I miss you when you're not here."

"I see," I said, considering it. I wondered if I should mention that I *was* actually working during the day. If we were to take this novel-writing seriously, then it *was* work. But it seemed churlish to say that when all he wanted was more of my company. Wasn't that something to be appreciated, rather than challenged?

But no, it was important.

"The only thing is, Chris, I'm supposed to be working full-time on this novel. I'll never get it written if I keep taking too much time off."

"I see your point," he said, "but you know, Sally, we're supposed to be living together to spend time together. What's the point if you're regularly out three times a week? It seems a bit unfair on me if I'm supporting you so you can swan around doing whatever you want – *your* novel, *your* time at the gym, while I, who am paying for it all, never get to see you."

"Good point," I acknowledged. "Okay, I'll go to the gym during the day."

I was beginning to see that the problem with Chris . . . or rather, the problem with me . . . was that Chris was extremely logical. I suppose anybody in IT, dealing with computers all day, *would* be logical. And it meant that I could never come off best in any discussion, coming from a place of emotion and intuition as I did. Arguments – discussions, I mean, discussions – were something to be avoided, I was quickly learning, because I could never win them.

Chapter 19

And so I began to go to the gym during the day, three times a week now, down from my original five. I rarely went for a coffee afterwards, however. Chris had suggested that it was better if I didn't. "It would take too long," he said. "You won't get a novel written that way."

True. He was too nice to point out that since he was subsidising me doing this, it was only fair that I get the head down and do it so that I wouldn't be a burden on him indefinitely. But I realised this nonetheless.

So now I just did my workout and came straight home. This went on for a couple of weeks until one day David intercepted me in the lobby as I was leaving.

"Sally," he said, stopping me in my headlong rush with a gentle hand on my arm, "Sally, how are you?"

"Great!" I said. "Couldn't be better. And you?"

Even as I was asking I was edging towards the door. But David didn't take the hint, didn't release my arm.

And short of blatant rudeness I couldn't just tug it away.

"I haven't seen you in ages," he said, "except in passing in the gym. Do you not go for a drink any more?"

"I don't really have the time," I said apologetically. "Not as a rule."

And then I felt sorry for him, and aware how unfair I was being. Also I had missed seeing him, had missed our light and cheerful chats.

So I said, "But I have some time at the moment. Would you like to go for a drink?"

"Sure," he said easily.

We went upstairs to the snack bar and ordered a coffee each, and then sat together.

There was an awkward silence for a moment or two.

"How come you're coming here during the day, these days?" he asked me then.

"I've left my job," I told him. "I'm a full-time writer now, so I can work my own hours."

He gave a whistle of appreciation, "Well done, you! How is it going?"

I told him about the joys and tribulations of being a writer, and how it was going very slowly. How I had started off flying but had hit the solid wall of writer's block about forty pages in, and it was very tough. I didn't mention the irregular but frequent lapses into writing gibberish, needless to say. And I didn't admit that 'tough' meant 'at a practical standstill'.

He listened interestedly and asked pertinent questions.

At the end he said, "Well done for following your dream! And I'm *sure* you'll get over the writer's block.

Keep the faith. But tell me," he paused and took a sip of his drink, "tell me, I still don't understand. How does that mean you come here in the days rather the evenings? Surely *full-time* means exactly that."

"I know. But my boyfriend," (I still got a huge thrill out of saying that), "wants me there in the evenings with him, which is very romantic. And he's the one subsidising this career change, so it's the least I can do."

"Understood. I see his point. If I was your boyfriend I'd be the same, trying to get you to spend time with me instead of the reprobates you find around here," and he gestured humorously around the room, not excluding himself.

"You're very charming," I told him, gratefully accepting the compliment, "but I don't think there're any reprobates around here!"

"You'd be surprised," he said mock-darkly, and we laughed.

I seized the moment to explain: "That's why I can't go for drinks as a rule. I *do* have to get this novel finished."

"I totally understand," he said. "It's a pity, and I miss you. But still, you'll be coming to the Christmas party, won't you? It's on next Wednesday."

I couldn't believe it but I had forgotten about the Christmas party. I had practically forgotten about Christmas, being so engrossed in my work and my life with Chris.

But the party . . . it was tempting . . . Each year *Svelte* had a party for all its staff and members on the 23rd of December, the day they closed. I had gone every year and it was always great fun, with the staff putting on a mini-panto – a skit on David's gentle earnestness and Darius in his Don Juan mode.

It was great to see everybody – staff and fellow members – dressed up instead of in our usual leisure wear (and just why, I ask, when I'm on the subject, is that stuff called *leisure wear* when leisure is the last thing you manage in it?).

Wine and canapés were brought in by outside caterers, and there was lots of laughter and flirting (partners were never invited) and just plain old-fashioned fun.

It was *very* tempting.

"You *are* coming, aren't you?" said David, almost horrified as he read in my expression that this wasn't a done deal.

"I don't know," I said slowly. "My boyfriend mightn't like it. But, look, I'll see," I said. "I'll run it by him and see what he says."

David wrinkled up his eyebrows in an extremely dubious and sceptical way, but declined to comment further. "Well, we might see you there, then. And if not, have a happy Christmas anyway."

"I will. You too. Thanks for the coffee."

* * *

When I got home Chris was there before me. "Were you at the gym?" he asked, indicating my gym-bag on my shoulder. "You were gone a good while."

"I had a coffee there afterwards."

"It's well for some," he said lightly, "being able to take all day to gallivant off wherever they want. How's the novel going, by the way?"

"It's going fine," I said, taking his point. I decided that I wouldn't stop ever again for a drink with David. It wasn't fair on Chris, when he was working so hard to keep us and give me this chance.

I also judged it politic not to mention the party.

* * *

I got my period again that evening. This was now the fourth month that I hadn't conceived. I knew rationally, of course, that it doesn't automatically happen like clockwork, just because you want it to. But still, it was upsetting.

I went downstairs and broke the news to Chris. He was very sympathetic.

"Poor you," he said, rubbing my back. "God, I just hope you don't have a problem."

That stung.

"Four months doesn't mean a problem," I told him, "and anyway, if there *is* a problem, it could be at your end as much as at mine!"

He surprised me then. "I've already had tests," he told me.

"You have? Why? Were you trying for a baby before?"

"No," he laughed, "hardly. But I got mumps about eight years ago, very embarrassing all around I can tell you! And afterwards I had to get my sperm checked to see if I was still fertile. And I was. Olympic swimmers, they told me," he said with a little justifiable swagger (if somebody can be said to swagger sitting down).

"Oh," I said morosely, "then if there's a problem, it *is* my problem."

"There won't be a problem." he asserted confidently. "Although," he looked a bit concerned then, "it would be an awful shame never to have children. I hope that you aren't infertile, I really do."

"So do I," I said, heartfelt.

And maybe my upset got between me and my concentration. Or maybe my hormones were acting up. Or more likely it was another Senior Moment. Who knows?

All I know is that later that evening there was this almighty roar from the kitchen.

"Ah for *fuck's* sake!" Chris yelled. "Sally, look what you've done now!"

I ran, heart thudding and stomach sick with nerves, into the kitchen.

Chris was standing in front of the washing machine, and there was a huge puddle of water on the floor. He was facing towards me and holding out an object for my scrutiny. I checked it out and it turned out to be a mobile phone. My mobile phone. Soaking wet.

"You put it through the wash," he said through gritted teeth, clearly hanging onto his patience by the proverbial thread. "It's ruined now. Not to mention the mess on the floor. I heard this awful clanking and I had to open the machine mid-wash."

I stood with my hand over my mouth, staring aghast at it, shaking my head in denial and disbelief. "It was in my handbag. I was *sure* it was in my bag. But I must have left it in my jeans pocket. Oh, Chris, I'm so sorry."

He sighed deeply. "I've been very patient with you,

Sally. I've said nothing as you've forgotten arrangements. I've said nothing as you've burned toast and ruined dinners. I've said nothing when you forgot to post my car insurance renewal and I was driving around uninsured for three days until I checked it out."

"I didn't know I was supposed to post your insurance," I protested again, but feebly.

"Ah Sally," he said impatiently, "the letter was sitting in your handbag, and probably would still be there if I hadn't realised that I hadn't got the certificate back from the insurance company. I have been very patient," he said again, "but it's getting beyond a joke."

"What's wrong with me?" I wailed. "I don't know why I'm getting like this."

"I don't know either. Do you think you should go back to the doctor about it? The only thing," he sighed, "is that if you get involved with doctors you've no idea where it'll end. They could diagnose anything. You could end up carted off by those funny white men in their funny white coats. You surely don't want that."

I shook my head helplessly. That was a deep terror for me, going to the doctor, making it official. I could end up in a loony bin yet.

"No," he said more softly, "I don't want that either. I love you, forgetfulness and all. We'll just have to beat this ourselves. I'll look after you. I'll make sure you're okay. Will you trust me?"

Still weeping, I nodded my head, and when he held out his arms I went into them, and he held me as I sobbed.

More than Friends

Is there anything more awful than the prospect that you're losing your mind? I couldn't then, and can't yet, think of anything more terrifying. In one respect, you *are* your mind. If you lose that, what's left? Just a dark and horrific chasm.

Chapter 20

The next week passed quietly and uneventfully until it was Christmas Day. Chris was taking all of Christmas week as holiday, and I was delighted to announce that I would do the same. Delighted, because I needed the respite from the stress of pretending to write, forcing myself to try to write, sitting staring blankly at the screen.

We went over to Gaby and Peter's early on Christmas morning to exchange presents. After that we returned home to our own Christmas dinner cooked by Chris.

It was a dull and sombre enough occasion.

What are Haley and Jack doing now? I wondered as I pulled a cracker with Chris, feeling most strongly like I was only going through the motions. The day seemed so quiet with just the two of us. Christmas is for children. Maybe, though, by this time next year we would have our own baby.

I got him a CD for Christmas – it was difficult to know how much to spend on somebody's present when they were going to end up paying for it. But I was optimistic that he'd like it – it was by a band he had been mentioning recently, saying how much he liked them.

But his face told a different story. "Oh," he said when he saw it, "thanks . . . thanks, Sally." He was clearly trying to hide his disappointment, but I sussed it nonetheless.

"I thought you liked them," I said nervously. "You said you did."

"No, Sally," he said patiently, "I was saying that I *didn't* like them, that I thought they were over-hyped and useless."

"Oh. Oh, I'm so *sorry*, Chris. I was *sure* you had said you liked them."

"It doesn't matter," he said gently. "I can change it when the shops open again."

My own present was a beautiful gold chain. "I was going to get you a new mobile phone," said Chris, "to replace the one you washed. But I decided it would be a waste of money getting you a phone just yet. We'll get you one when you've got over these . . . lapses in concentration, shall we call them? When you prove you're able to mind one, we'll get you one."

As I fastened the new necklace around my neck I wondered if Chris realised how condescending he was coming across. He was speaking to me as if I was a six-year-old child. But . . . still . . . he *did* have a point. I wasn't proving myself as being able to look after stuff, was I?

On New Year's Eve we went out for a meal with Mike and his current girlfriend. But the food was mediocre, the service was resentful, and the nightclub we went to afterwards was crowded enough to contravene the Geneva Convention.

This time next year, I thought hopefully as I stood in a dark, airless and sweaty cavern, drinking warm white wine, unable to hear a word of conversation, *I'll have a two or three-month-old baby, and hence the perfect excuse not to do this.*

* * *

The New Year began quietly. My New Year's resolution was to concentrate better. I could do it if I really tried, I resolved.

But it was easier said than done, and by the second week in January I had already had two Senior Moments: I put a wash on at 90°C when I was sure I had put it on a delicates 40°C wash, and ruined several of Chris's jumpers. And I somehow deleted the last ten pages of my novel. It was no great loss, to be honest, but I was still horrified at having done that without remembering.

Gaby rang at the end of that first week of the New Year.

"Hi, how are you doing?" she asked me. "Listen, I was wondering if you'd like to come over for dinner tomorrow. I know it's short notice, but Peter's after getting a promotion at work, so we're celebrating!"

It was the last thing I wanted to do, to meet people and have to pretend to be normal. But it was important to them, I couldn't let them down.

"I'd love to!" I told her. "Let me just check with Chris."

I turned to Chris and swiftly ran it by him.

"Sure," he said, "Why not?"

I relayed this to Gaby, and we agreed a time.

"See you then!"

"Look forward to it."

When I hung up I said to Chris, "She wants us there at eight o'clock. Will you be sure to remember that, in case . . . in case I forget. I'll go and write it in my diary as well. Straight away, before I forget. And I'll write it on the kitchen blackboard."

I was taking no chances.

* * *

Accordingly we turned up to Gaby and Peter's house the following evening. The promotion was obviously a big thing because we were eating in the formal dining-room. Two other couples were there – a colleague of Peter's and her husband, and a neighbouring couple they're friends with, who I met reasonably regularly at Gaby's parties.

I was very apprehensive about this meeting. What if I messed up? It was horrific not even being in control of my own actions. There was no telling what I might do. I could do *anything*, I believed. So far I had mostly – I hoped – managed to keep my craziness hidden from Gaby, apart from minor eccentricities such as phoning her to confirm that she had received texts.

So I was tense and nervous, and I know I didn't come across too well. I so wanted to act normally that I was trying too hard. I was jittery and highly-strung, talking way too much about nothing in particular. I saw

Peter and Gaby exchange a worried glance with each other, and that made me worse.

I'm mortified to admit it but I knocked over not one, but *two* glasses of wine.

"Oh!" I gasped, holding my hand over my mouth in horror. "I am so, *so* sorry."

"It's fine. Sally, it really is," said Gaby, mopping up the spill with a handful of napkins. But she didn't *sound* like it was fine. The gritted teeth were a bit of a clue. Once she had mopped up as much as she could she said brightly, "I'll get dessert now. Sally, would you give me a hand bringing it in?"

"Sure, sure," I said, reluctantly. Not that I minded helping her *per se*. But I had a suspicion that this request for help was only a pretext to have a serious talk with me, which I would rather avoid. And I wasn't wrong.

As soon as we got into the kitchen she turned to me, concern etched on her face. "Sally, what's wrong?"

"Nothing," I told her. How could I even begin to explain? It was gone beyond words now.

"There's *something* going on," she insisted. "You've been acting all evening as if you're on speed or something. And you're moving so jerkily you're like a marionette. And you've lost too much weight. What's going on?" she asked again, her hands on her hips and a determined expression on her face.

"Nothing . . ." I said squeakily. I coughed to clear my throat and started again in a more convincing voice, "Nothing's going on, Gaby. Honest," I added when she looked sceptical.

But her sceptical expression didn't noticeably clear.

She looked at me, and I forced myself to look her in the eyes with my most sincere expression.

Eventually she sighed in defeat and shook her head a little. "Here," she said, and handed me some plates, "would you bring those in for me?"

"Sure!" I said, relieved that the questioning was over.

For the rest of the meal I sat like a statue, hardly daring to move lest I knocked something over, or dropped something. I was silent too, to prevent myself from talking too much, and by tacit consent everybody gave me space and didn't speak to me.

I now felt like the spectre at the feast as the conversation swept around and over me. I couldn't help but be aware of the stress and tension in the air as everybody tried to pretend that everything was normal when it patently wasn't.

I was so glad when, as soon as coffee was served, Chris said, "That was wonderful, Gaby, thanks so much. But, you know, we should head now."

"Sure, sure," she said, womanfully trying to keep the relief from showing in her voice.

As for me, I was so relieved I was like a dog who has seen its lead being picked up – already at the front door, tail quivering so hard its whole back half was vibrating.

"Goodbye," I said. "Congratulations again, Peter, and thanks Gaby."

And off we headed and pretended not to hear the collective sigh of relief as the door closed behind us.

There was silence for the first few minutes of our drive home, and then Chris said, "Well, that was truly awful. What on *earth* were you thinking of? I was so embarrassed, and they weren't even my friends. You were talking non-stop, and you were talking such *drivel*! And so clumsy. Bad enough knocking over one glass of wine, but two . . ." he shook his head in despair.

"Sorry," I said numbly.

"Well you might be," he said, and sighed.

We drove in silence the rest of the way.

Chapter 21

About a week after the ill-fated dinner party I went to the gym. I might as well; I was getting no writing done. No matter how many hours I sat in front of the screen, no words would come to me. My characters sat there, inert, like puppets with their strings cut.

Even as I was on my way to *Svelte* I was thinking that I really shouldn't be driving at all. Suppose I had one of my Moments and killed somebody during it? I was being highly irresponsible and unethical to even get behind the wheel of a car. But I was going anyway. I had to cling to some sort of normality, or I was finished. And I wouldn't have an accident; I was determined upon it. I gripped the steering wheel hard and forced myself to concentrate really, really hard.

Once I got there I did my routine. But really I was only going through the motions. I just didn't have the strength for a proper workout. I suppose it wasn't surprising, given how little I was eating these days.

As I left I saw David looking down at me from the balcony of the juice bar, waving to catch my eye, but I pretended I didn't see him.

As I drove home, concentrating hugely again (and the effort of such deliberate concentration was exhausting all by itself), I thought to myself how glad I was to be getting back to Chris, to somebody who knew what was going on and who loved me anyway.

Maybe I should resign my membership of *Svelte*, I thought as I drove. I certainly couldn't keep going there if I wasn't fit to drive. And if I didn't have the energy to work out, then what was the point?

When I pulled up outside the house I saw to my surprise that Gaby's car was parked there. What was she doing here? I certainly hadn't been expecting her. Or, oh God, had I? Had I arranged to meet her and then forgotten all about it? It was all too possible.

I went into the house and opened the door to the sitting-room. Gaby and Chris rose abruptly when they saw me, turning towards me with a strange expression on their faces. An expression of . . . what? They were sitting apart from each other – Chris on the sofa and Gaby on the armchair beside the fireplace, but still . . . I definitely got the sense that I had interrupted something. What was going on? Or was this my own craziness making me see things which weren't there?

"Hi, Sally," said Gaby, and I now identified her expression as guilt. That was it. Guilt. Her eyes were wide and she had a shocked caught-in-the-act expression on her face. Caught in what act?

For his part Chris was looking distinctly uncomfortable.

"What's going on?" I asked, looking from one to the other of them.

"I . . . I just popped in to see you, to see how you're getting on," said Gaby hastily. And most unconvincingly.

"But something's going on," I said. "It's clear that I've interrupted something. What is it?"

In answer Gaby looked desperately at Chris. *Help me out here*, her glance said.

Chris wouldn't meet her eyes. He simply said, "I think you'd better go now, Gaby. I'll explain everything to Sally."

Relief flooded Gaby's face. She grabbed her bag and stood, and was out the sitting-room door before you could see her move.

"I'll ring you, Sal," she said from the doorway. "I'll ring you tomorrow once Chris has spoken to you."

And she opened the front door and fled the house as though the gods of the underworld were after her.

"What's going on here?" I asked Chris then. "What's going on between you?"

"Nothing," he said.

"Oh come on! I'm not stupid. There was *something* going on. It was obvious."

"Okay," he said, opening his palms out in a gesture of surrender. "I'll tell you."

"No!" I said, changing my mind. I didn't want to hear it.

My legs suddenly swayed. They had no strength

with which to support me. I fell into the nearest chair and closed my eyes to shut out the world.

But the knowledge wouldn't go away.

There was something going on between Chris and Gaby. My partner and my best friend. I would have laughed at the pathetic cliché-ness of it all, but I somehow seemed to have no amusement to spare.

And where did it all leave me? I would have to move out. Rent somewhere – but how, with no job?

Okay, I'd have to get a job first. But where would I live while I was job-hunting? I had an urge to laugh hysterically at the realisation that up until ten minutes ago, Gaby's would have been the first place I sought refuge.

I'd have to impose on my mother's hospitality. Oh God. Could it get any worse?

I hadn't just lost my lover, and my friend, although that was bad enough. I had lost my whole way of life. It was too much. I wanted to just curl up and go asleep and make it all go away.

Chris interrupted my reverie. "Are you ready to listen to me?" he asked.

"Listen to your excuses and justifications?" I asked wearily, my eyes still closed. "No, thanks."

"It wouldn't be justification, because I've nothing to justify. If you are going to find me guilty and sentence me without even giving me a chance to tell you what happened, then that's your choice. I can't stop you. I'm not going to try to tell you the truth over your blocked ears or shouted accusations. You'll either give me a chance to prove my innocence as best I can, or you won't. You'll either value this relationship enough to give it every chance, or you won't. Make up your mind and let me know. I'll be in the kitchen."

I heard him move away and into the hallway and a few moments later I heard the kitchen radio with some overly cheerful DJ spouting inane nonsense for the delectation of his listeners.

A moment later I heard the sitting-room door open.

Chris said, "I'm going to tell you anyway. It's not fair otherwise. The truth is that she made a pass at me."

"She made a pass at you?" I echoed, incredulous, my eyes still closed. "Come on, Chris, don't be *ridiculous*. This is my best friend we're talking about. She's happily married. She wouldn't do that."

Although, what had I seen if not something like that?

"That's the truth," he said. "I swear it to you. I know how it looks. I know that she's been your friend for years, and I'm only a newcomer in your life. I know you'll probably believe the worst of me and the best of her. I know I'm in danger of losing you now, and it would be so unfair, it really would. I love you and I would never be unfaithful to you. Please – I beg you – come and find me in the kitchen when you're ready to talk."

The door closed again with a gentle click.

I thought about what he had said. It was true that I hadn't given him a chance to defend himself. But come on! They had both been demonstrably guilty, it was in their expressions . . . actually, as I thought about it, that culpability had only been in Gaby's expression. Chris had merely looked uncomfortable.

But come on! Really! Gaby making a pass at him . . . how ridiculous a story!

But yet . . . but yet . . . Chris wasn't stupid . . . why would he make up such an absurd story? Maybe its veracity lay in the very fact of how ridiculous it was.

Or maybe it was a double bluff.

Oh God. My head hurt trying to think about it. How could I, a woman who couldn't even remember to unplug the iron, be expected to figure all this out?

Take it slowly. Take it logically.

Okay.

The first point was: despite it being totally unbelievable, Gaby had done *something*. Whether it was a mutual thing, or whether she had made an unprovoked pass at Chris as he claimed, she certainly felt – and looked – guilty of something.

So it was possible – unlikely, but possible – that Chris's claim was correct.

But that's ludicrous, I told myself again. Gaby making a pass at Chris was as unlikely as the earth spinning backwards. Quite apart from Gaby's loyalty to me, of which I was certain, she loved Peter. They were the quintessential happily married couple.

But yet, she had done *something* that she felt guilty about.

And she and Peter weren't as happy as I liked to insist to myself. Hadn't Gaby expressed dissatisfaction with being married?

But Gaby wouldn't do that to me.

Around and around went these thoughts, until I empathised with a rat in a wheel, spinning to exhaustion but getting nowhere.

Okay, I decided at last, exhausted into capitulation,

having no other ideas whatsoever – let's hear what Chris has to say.

I pulled myself unenthusiastically to my feet and made my way to the kitchen. Chris was reading the evening paper and was drinking a cup of coffee. The pungent smell made my stomach clench. He put down the newspaper as I came in.

"Go on then," I said cynically, leaning against the door jamb. "Let's hear what story you come up with."

He looked at me for a moment, appraisingly.

"Okay," he said then. "I'd rather you listened with an open mind, but I can see that's asking for too much. It's good that you're listening at all." He sighed and trailed off.

Then he took a deep breath and said, "Gaby arrived over here after you had left. She didn't realise you were going to the gym during the day now, and she thought you'd be here. And she didn't realise I would be here. So, to be fair to her, I have to say I don't think it was premeditated."

Oh, that makes all the difference – that makes it okay then.

"I invited her in for coffee, needless to say. I didn't think anything of it. I wish now that I had been more circumspect. But you don't think. You just don't think." He shook his head sadly. "Anyway, we were having our coffee when out of the blue she began talking about how she was bored in her marriage, how she would love it if something exciting would happen to her, that she was ready to experience something mad, something outrageous."

I stared at him as he spoke, just listening, numb to all feeling.

He continued, "I didn't know what to say to that, Sally. I was panicking, to be honest, but trying to stay calm. And maybe she took my silence for encouragement," he said anguish in his voice. "I don't know. Anyway," he took a deep, shuddering breath, "she told me then that she had fancied me since we had met. That she would love to have a fling with me. Just a fling, she said, nothing to rock either of our relationships."

"Gaby wouldn't do that to me," I said flatly, with the certainty of years of loyal friendship behind me, "and she wouldn't do that to Peter."

"You saw yourself her reaction when you came home," he said. "She *did* try to do that to you, to Peter. She told me that her marriage to Peter is suffocating her, that he adores her too much, that sometimes she can't breathe. She said that she longs for the excitement of a new relationship, that she doesn't want to die without having experienced that excitement just one more time."

I looked at him in shock. For the first time a trickle of doubt began to filter through. Gaby had said as much to me. True, she hadn't suggested that an affair was the antidote to that suffocation, to that boredom.

But the point was this: there was no way Chris could have known that Gaby felt suffocated, not without her telling him. I had never told him.

And so – my poor tired brain reasoned – if Chris knew Gaby's secret about feeling suffocated and bored, it lent much more credibility to the rest of what he was telling me.

Chris was watching me intently as I digested this information, and he visibly relaxed a little when it became clear that I had accepted it.

"She wanted a fling," he went on to explain, "just to experience the wild side for once. That's my words, not hers, but that's the gist of it. She does love Peter, she told me. She doesn't want to leave him. But she just wanted to do something wild, something for herself. And I happened to be it," he finished dryly. "I happened to be what she decided was her key to some excitement."

"And why me?" I asked dully. "Why did she have to pick on *my* partner?"

The pain of betrayal was knives impaling me with each breath I took.

He shook his head. "She said that she found me attractive," he said uncomfortably, "and that her opportunities to meet potential lovers were limited – not so many available men in the playgroup. And as for you . . . she did say that she felt dreadful about doing this to you –"

"Decent of her," I muttered sarcastically.

" – but that what you wouldn't know wouldn't hurt you. She said that neither you nor Peter need ever find out."

"But I have found out."

"Only because Gaby was looking so guilty," he pointed out. "She's obviously not experienced at this kind of deceit, to be fair to her."

I looked him in the eyes then for the first time, and he gazed back at me and there was a maelstrom of emotions in his eyes. I could see hurt, and fear, and trepidation, and tension and a high level of alertness, and concentration and love and hope.

"Do you believe me?" he asked, his voice cracking slightly. "I have nothing without you, Sally. I love you and I need you, and to lose you like this . . ." he shook his head in despair.

That was the crux of it – did I believe him?

Well, of course, I did. He was my boyfriend, my lover, my life-partner. Of course, I believed what he told me.

Except when he told me that Gaby had betrayed me. She wouldn't do that, I told myself.

But now I sounded as if I was convincing myself. How else had Chris known about her boredom, her suffocation?

It was an impossible situation. I trusted Chris totally, and I trusted Gaby totally – but I couldn't believe them both. Either Chris was telling the truth and Gaby had betrayed me. Or Chris was lying.

And there was another point. Why on earth would Chris lie? What could possibly be gained for him by such a thing? Nothing, that was the answer.

But yet, Gaby wouldn't betray me. Or would she?

"I'll ring Gaby," I decided aloud. "I'll listen to what she has to say."

"So you don't believe me?" he said sadly. "You don't trust me enough. What does that say about our relationship? Even if Gaby confirms what I've said – and there's no reason to suppose that she will – why should she tell the truth? But even if she does, I think you might be inflicting a fatal blow to our relationship by refusing to believe me or trust me."

I hovered, uncertain. He was right. The truth was that I didn't know whether to believe him or not. I wanted to, God knows I wanted to. If he was telling the truth then my life could continue as it had been, with me being part of a couple in a settled relationship. All would be well.

Apart, of course, from minor details such as my mental aberrations and my infertility and the absence of Gaby.

If he was lying then everything was gone and I was left with no job, no future, no boyfriend, no baby and no possibility of a baby, no home, and little or no sanity.

I really wanted to believe him. There was a lot of incentive to believe him.

But I needed to know for sure. I couldn't stay with him if he had been a party to any infidelity. Or if he had lied to me. No matter what upheaval it cost in my life. And I suppose that needing proof was an admission that I didn't trust him to that extent.

So be it. I needed to know.

"I have to ring Gaby," I told him.

"I see," he said sadly. "You don't trust me enough. Well, ring her if you want. There's no guarantee, though, that she'll admit it. I've no idea what she'll say. But you go ahead and ring her. I can't stop you."

"I'm sorry, Chris. I really am. But I need to speak to her."

I went out into the hallway where the phone sat, and Chris trailed after me looking anxious.

With shaking hands I dialled Gaby's number and listened to the phone ringing, my heart pounding harshly in my chest. Chris stood behind me, waiting to hear what she would say. He was right, really. More than likely she would deny it. And where would that leave me? I would be no better off. I would still have to make a decision as to who to believe.

After a couple of rings she answered: "Hello?"

"Gaby, it's me."

"Hi," she said warily.

"I've spoken to Chris, and he's told me everything."

"Sally, I am so, so sorry. I feel terrible about it, I really do."

My heart plummeted. "So he's telling me the truth! Gaby. Why did you do it?"

"I never meant it to happen. I just dropped in to say hello to you, like I told you. I was worried about you after the dinner party."

"Big of you," I sneered, hurt making me vicious. "Dressing all this up in concern for me!"

"No, Sally –"

"Gaby, I have never, ever, felt so betrayed in all my life. I'll never forgive you."

"I didn't mean it as a betrayal, honestly."

"Oh come on, what else would you call it?"

"Okay, okay," she conceded sadly. "But I never meant you to find out. I wouldn't hurt you for the world, Sally. You must know that."

I exploded then. "You think that makes it okay?" I shouted into the phone. "It was all okay as long as I didn't find out? God, you are *despicable*, and I'm glad I found out now rather than later," and I slammed the phone down, shaking.

I turned to Chris behind me and went into his arms. Dimly through my tears I could see his expression of relief and satisfaction at how it had turned out.

"She actually thought it would be okay as long as I didn't find out!" I howled. "The *cheek* of her! And Chris," I wept into his shoulder, "I'm sorry, I'm so sorry I doubted you. Please forgive me."

"It's okay," he soothed, patting my back. "It's okay."

"How could she do it?" I wept then. "We've known each other for years. We were best friends. We told each other everything. At least I have you." I kept sobbing. "At least I have you."

Chapter 22

Over the next two weeks Gaby incessantly texted me and e-mailed me. *"I'm so sorry,"* she wrote over and over. *"I never meant to hurt you. Please contact me. I love you."*

I ignored her messages for a time but in the end e-mailed her tersely, *"I'll never forgive you. We are no longer friends. I don't think we ever were. I don't want to hear from you again."*

And she took me at my word, and did not contact me again.

Her absence left a big huge hole in my life. Not only had I lost my friendship with her, but I was already missing Haley and Jack, and Peter.

And despite my acid hatred when I thought of her, I missed Gaby herself. I missed her warm abundant manner, her hugs and deep laughter, her brisk and no-nonsense advice. Even as I loathed the person I now knew her to be, I missed, missed desperately the Gaby

I had thought I knew. I missed the person I had believed her to be.

But at least I found out what she was like. That was good, I told myself.

* * *

However, the downside was that Chris was unable to come to terms with my not trusting him.

"After all," he said once, "if I were as distrustful as you, I could question what you actually do at the gym. Are you even really going to the gym?"

"Of course I am!" I protested.

"But how do I know? You could have an afternoon lover for all I know. We're obviously not in the business of trusting each other, are we, Sally? At least, *you* don't trust me. And now you see what it's like to be on the receiving end of being mistrusted. It's not very nice, is it?"

"No," I said miserably, "no, it's not." I stood and went over to him, put my arms right around him. "I'm sorry I doubted you," I told him for what seemed like the hundredth time.

But poor Chris, he obviously wasn't as confident as he appeared, needing this reassurance over and over. "And I promise you, I'm not unfaithful to you," I assured him, "I *have* not been unfaithful to you, and I *will* not be unfaithful to you."

He clung to me. "Good," he said. "I need to know both that you trust me, and that you will be faithful to me. I need to know that."

"I do," I promised him, "and I will be faithful forever."

And I began kissing him and we made love there in the sitting-room. And as we did so I wondered would this, would this at last be the moment I conceived our longed-for baby.

Because it still hadn't happened. We had been trying for five months now, and each month had brought its red flowing disappointment. I was getting quite down about it actually, try though I did to keep my spirits up. And each month when I realised that yet again I hadn't conceived, I knew it was my fault, my body which was letting us down. To use an archaic phrase, but one which seemed appropriate: I was barren.

Probably just as well I hadn't conceived yet, having said that. Not while I was still having these Moments.

I determined to get myself healthy so that I could get over those episodes, so that I could give my body the best possible chance of conceiving. I gave up alcohol, tea and coffee. And one day I went to the nearest health food shop and stocked up on herbal teas, a multivitamin, more Evening Primrose Oil (even though it hadn't worked for me), iron tablets and whatever else I saw that I thought might help me.

I also stocked up on fruit and vegetables although I wasn't at all sure how much of them I would be able to force myself to eat. My appetite was still minimal

Chris laughed when he saw my purchases. "And you think that'll make the difference?" he said. "You think a few vitamins and minerals will sort out whatever's wrong with you. Well, I wish you luck."

"I have to try *something*," I told him. "We can't keep going on as we have been."

"True," he said in heartfelt tones, "that is so true."

My heart quailed when he said that. There was an implied threat there.

What if I didn't get well? What then? Would he break up with me? I remembered that he had promised he wouldn't leave me on a whim because we weren't married. But he had also said no marriage certificate would keep us together if we were irrevocably unhappy.

And God knows we weren't being that happy right now. My Moments came between us, kept us both tense. My infertility was a further source of unhappiness. And now we had the chasm caused by my having mistrusted him.

But this relationship had to work. It just *had* to. I had been lonely enough before we got together, how could I possibly go back to that? How could I possibly relinquish my dreams of a partner and baby and settled lifestyle?

Maybe this healthy eating would help. I certainly had no other ideas.

It was difficult though. I stoically took my supplements each morning, forcing myself past the gagging reflex. However, I was so stressed at this stage that it was difficult to eat much of anything. I forced one or two florets of broccoli past my lips, or half a boiled egg, and could manage no more.

I had tenaciously continued to go to the gym three times a week. I had to keep fit in order to conceive a baby, and surely whatever was going wrong with me mentally would be helped by being healthy and fit. But because I wasn't eating I wasn't strong, and I didn't have enough energy to do good workouts. I was really only going through the motions. But I persisted with a kind of dogged determination, in the absence of any other solutions.

Until one day David intercepted me as I was striding purposefully – if shakily – across the lobby, my hair still wet from having been washed.

"Sally, Sally," he called, catching up with me and laying a hand on my arm, "how are you? I haven't seen you in ages! How's everything going? Tell you what, have you time for a drink now?"

"No, no time, David, sorry," I said, edging towards the door. I was this side of being rude, but only just. "I'm very busy these days, have to get this novel finished you know, finding it hard to justify the time out of that work each day."

"Too busy for one drink with an old friend?" he asked, smiling, but I could see the vulnerability in his expression.

"Yes. Yes. Much too busy. Sorry," I said as I saw the hurt in his brown eyes behind his glasses. "Must dash."

I felt so guilty as I drove home. But I couldn't risk upsetting Chris. I couldn't risk putting our relationship under any more strain than it was already. He already had enough of a face on him whenever I got back from the gym. And I didn't want to upset him. I really didn't.

So I stopped going to the gym. It seemed the easier option.

I had to admit to myself – sometimes I really wearied of anticipating Chris's moods and trying not to upset him. But then I would give myself a big shake and a reality check. Real life isn't like a fairy tale. Real life is about two people working together to create a relationship. Real life is about compromise and adjustment. Happy Ever After without effort only happens in fairy tales and schmaltzy films.

Mind you, I could have coped with real life better if I had been feeling well. The supplements weren't helping. My Senior Moments continued unabated. And I never, ever knew when the next episode would occur. In a peculiar way, it was nearly a relief when the next Moment was revealed, because then the worst had happened. Waiting for one to happen was *awful*, particularly as time passed since the last one, and the tension built with each passing day as the next one became more and more imminent.

I began to get a bit obsessive, I have to admit. One time I lost my car keys and we searched absolutely everywhere for them until Chris found them in the bin (he thought to look there because a scrunched-up envelope was in my bag when it should have been in the bin). After that I got myself a little hook just inside the door and I hung my keys there as soon as I came in.

But I might be doing something else – washing up, perhaps, or putting on a load of laundry – and it would suddenly occur to me, *Did I really hang my keys up, or did I just think I did?* and I would have to drop everything to go and check. And ninety-nine times out of a hundred the keys would be safely on the hook. But the hundredth time they wouldn't be, and then it was anybody's guess where they were.

Even if I had found them there, some time later I might think, *Did I really check that they were there, or did I just imagine it? Or maybe when I remember checking, I'm actually remembering yesterday's check, not today's,* and I would have to go and check again.

Chris tried to remind me of things that I might otherwise forget. He encouraged me to keep going with the supplements (apologising for having sneered before), told me that I would surely get better with all this healthy living I was doing, that it just was taking time to kick in, without having to go to the doctor and get sucked into the medical system.

"They'll do brain scans and all sorts of awful stuff," he said to me, "and they'll label you mentally ill, and you'll never, ever be free of that label. They might even section you against your will – they can do that, you know, if they think it's in your best interests."

"No!" I gasped, horrified.

"It's true," he said anxiously. "They go to court and the court makes you a ward of the State. It means they can put you in a mental hospital against your will. You don't want that, surely. We'll sort you out ourselves without going through any of that."

And because I was terrified of admitting my problems to any outsider, and absolutely petrified of the picture he was painting, I agreed with him. But it put an extra burden onto me, the burden of keeping this guilty secret, and the dread of being found out.

I began to find reasons not to go out lest I betray myself to the check-out woman in the supermarket, or my fellow-passengers on the LUAS. I was probably capable of any action at any time, no matter how bizarre, and I had to stay at home lest I do something mad like taking off all my clothes in the street or something.

So, more and more I didn't go out of the house at all. There was nowhere I needed to go, nobody I needed to see. Outside seemed so big and wild and intimidating to me now. I was much safer inside in the house.

With all that was going on in my head, it's not surprising, perhaps, that my writing still wasn't progressing. I would spent hours staring at the screen, mentally flailing myself for my lack of ideas, struggling for the next piece of dialogue, the next action.

But they rarely did come, and on the rare occasions when I did manage to write anything, it was immediately apparent on reading it back that it was dreadful. Beyond wooden. Dull and formulaic and awful, and worth only deleting.

"How did your writing go today?" Chris would ask each evening . At first I would answer, as brightly as I could, "Well, thanks."

But as February turned into March he once responded sharply, "Really?" and I broke down into tears and admitted that, no, it wasn't going at all well. It hadn't progressed in months, to be honest. I was never going to make a writer. I was a failure.

And what's more, I had got my period *again*.

"It's okay. It's okay," he said, cuddling me. "Just keep trying, both with the book and for the baby. Perseverance, that's the key."

And so I spent more weeks staring blankly at a screen, mentally straining after a story which was out of reach.

And we spent more time in soulless sex, sex just for the aim of conceiving, with the joy and laughter and desire totally absent now.

Chris was also so patient, so good to me. But then, as time passed, his patience began to slip.

"Sally, you forgot to flush the toilet after yourself. That's disgusting," he said one morning, returning from the bathroom to the bedroom, and his face was twisted with repulsion. "I had to do it for you, and I never signed up for that, Sally. I truly didn't."

"Sorry," I said, my heart breaking. I tried and tried to think but I honestly couldn't remember flushing the toilet. It's something you do so automatically it doesn't stick in the memory. But I obviously hadn't done it automatically. And I blushed with embarrassment at the thoughts of what he must have found as he lifted the lid.

Another time he came to me and said right into my face, "Sally, this is *beyond* stupid. I come home to find the phone off the hook. No wonder I couldn't get through all day. And what if a client had been trying to get through to me? Business is slow enough, you stupid woman, without you doing that!"

"Sorry," I whispered, which is all I seemed to be saying to him these days, "some telemarketer rang this morning and I suddenly remembered I had left toast under the grill and I ran off to check it and I must have forgotten to come back to the phone."

"For God's sake," he shouted at me, "I don't know how much more of this I can take! You are such a burden to me, Sally. I didn't realise when we started this that I was going to have to act as nanny, safety officer and psychologist rolled into one." He ran his hand through his hair. "I don't know how much more of it I can take," he said again.

It was as if he had kicked me in the stomach. I could physically feel the impact hit me. Adrenaline flooded my system as I considered what he was saying. He couldn't leave me. He couldn't. What would I do then? How would I cope?

I couldn't get another job, not like this. And the option of going to stay with my mother was just not doable. To crawl back to her, a pathetic mentally ill failure? No way. I'd rather live on the street. Although the way things were going, it was entirely possible that that preference would be put to the test sooner or later.

"Please don't leave me," I begged. "Please don't. I need you. I love you."

But he turned such a look of repulsion and abhorrence at me that my soul withered a little.

"I don't want to leave you," he told me wearily, but any relief was short-lived as he went on, "but you're going to have to start pulling your weight, Sally. I can't support your novel-writing any more. I was trying to keep it from you, trying not to worry you, but the truth of it is that my business isn't going at all well. I've been worried about money for months now. You're going to have to start helping."

"Anything," I promised, weeping now.

"You can hardly get a job," he said looking derisively at me again. "Nobody'd hire you like this. You can barely manage to get yourself dressed in the morning."

It was hard to listen to all this, but it was true.

Chris continued, "But what about this: I've had to let Mrs Butler go. I can't afford a cleaner right now. Maybe you could take over the responsibility of keeping the house seeing as you're doing nothing else. Writing a novel, hah!" he laughed derisively. "That's a good one. Instead of sitting pretending to write, maybe you could make yourself useful."

"Yes, yes, of course I will," I said, delighted to be able to legitimately abandon the travesty which this novel had become. Delighted too, to prove myself, to make some contribution to this household.

He was right. I had been coasting all this time while he had been responsible for everything. No wonder he was being short-tempered, the poor man. Not only did he have me and my vagaries (to put it kindly) to worry about, but he had business and money worries as well.

He continued, "And I'm going to have to ask you to watch what you spend. I won't be able to give you that weekly money any more. And run all credit-card expenditures past me first, okay?"

"Sure," I said. "No problem." That didn't bother me. I was going nowhere, what did I need money for?

And so I took responsibility for the housekeeping, all except the cooking.

* * *

It was awful. It was a nightmare. I spent all of each day trying to keep up with the housework, and it just wasn't happening. I kept losing concentration and finding that I had been gazing into space for ages. And I kept getting things wrong – housework had so many opportunities for one of my Moments that it wasn't funny.

I left irons on again, I paired socks completely wrong – I mean, a grey and white striped one folded in with a red and black one, not even ones that were similar. I washed coloured items with Chris's white work shirts so they ended up bizarre colours – he was spending a fortune on shirts, replacing the ones I had ruined. Just at a time when he couldn't afford to.

Oh, I could go on and on, but I would rather not.

I was getting more and more stressed about it, feeling that my sanity was eroding more and more with each day.

I had this constant tension pain in my chest, trying to think continually of the millions of things I had to remember, trying to do the jobs I was supposed to do, waiting for the proof of my latest Moment to present itself. Waiting for the smell of burning, the roar of annoyance from Chris, the sound of falling and crashing which indicated where I hadn't put something fragile back properly.

And I still wasn't conceiving. What with my illness, and the stress Chris was under, we were making love less and less. But still we made sure to make love in the middle of the month, even though it was a joyless sorry experience each time.

But even so, it never worked. I remained barren. It was probably as well, to be honest. I was in no fit state to look after a baby. As Chris said, I couldn't even look after myself. But I clung pathetically to the idea of a baby. If I could conceive at least I'd have managed *something* right.

Chapter 23

"Got your period again?" Chris said one day at the end of March, obviously having spotted the sanitary protection on the bathroom shelf. "So you didn't manage to get pregnant this month either? God, Sally, but you're useless. Can't write a novel, can't keep house, can't even manage to get pregnant. Probably just as well, though," he sneered. "Fine mother you'd make, crazy as you are. Probably fuck any child up for life, if you had one. Just as well you're infertile."

That hurt, that really hurt. But it was true. A small part of me whispered, he shouldn't be talking to you so harshly. But the rest of me was so weary, so scared that he would leave me, so beaten down, that I just accepted it. And, true, it wasn't terribly kind perhaps. But it was understandable. I, and my problems, had driven him beyond endurance. As he had told me, he hadn't signed up for this.

As I quailed under the onslaught, I promised

myself: *I'll get better*. I'll get better and start behaving more rationally. And then he'll have no reason to be so abrupt and cutting. It'll get back to where it was before, when he adored me and thought the world of me and we were so happy together. That love and joy couldn't be lost forever; they were just temporarily put aside because of these problems. I'll fix it, I swore. I'll make it all better. All I had to do was to get better.

I realised that Chris had still been speaking –

"– and you know what, I have *totally* gone off you. When we met I thought you were attractive, but you're not. You just use make-up and clothes well, but it's not really you, is it? It's all a con, because basically you're totally plain."

This was going straight to my deepest secret, and it hurt. It hurt so much.

But still, fear and misery kept me silent. *I'll make it better*, I was swearing. *It'll all be okay.*

He continued, "And now you're not even making any effort any more, so you're pure ugly. You've lost so much weight, you're only skin and bone. It's like fucking a skeleton. You're about as responsive as a skeleton as well."

That was true too. Sex seemed such a chore now, all my former joy in it totally eroded.

"And the only reason I fuck you now is to try to get us a baby, but that's not working, and I'm pretty sure a baby's not right for us now. To put it bluntly, Sally," – like he hadn't been blunt already? – "you disgust me now, you really do. I'm certainly not going to have sex with you again." His face twisted with revulsion at that thought, and my heart twisted with pain at such patent rejection.

I reeled under the onslaught of his words, but I couldn't deny the truth of what he was saying. It *was* true that I wasn't that attractive – hadn't I always known that myself? And I *had* let myself go. It was ages since I had had a haircut, and my hair was straggly and shapeless. My roots were visibly showing too. I hadn't had a manicure or a facial in about the same length of time, and my hands and face told that story clearly.

My skin, despite the supplements I was still tenaciously taking, was looking distinctly grey. Partly because I still wasn't eating very much of anything (hence the scrawniness of which he complained), partly because I had abandoned my previous skin-care routine in favour of a quick wipe with a face cloth, and partly because I rarely got outside nowadays.

I wasn't even wearing any of my nice clothes any more – what was the point? For the past two months or so I had been exclusively wearing draw-string leggings and sweatshirts.

So I could see his point, and I couldn't blame him for going off me, but still . . . it was devastating to know that he found me totally repulsive.

And there was no way I was going to be able to conceive a baby now, after all.

* * *

Our days fell into a pattern. Chris went out each day, submitting proposals to prospective clients, he told me.

While he was gone I attempted to clean the house.

There were only two of us, we didn't make much mess, it should have been easy. Except that it wasn't. My brain was such a fog that I kept forgetting what I was supposed to be doing. I'd suddenly come to with a start, and find myself in a room with no idea what I had gone in there for, and no idea how long I had been staring into the middle distance.

The simplest jobs were enormous chores as I had to force myself to concentrate so hard, to make sure I did them right, and check over and over if I had finished the job, closed everything which needed closing, put away everything I had used, switched off everything which needed switching off.

As the day progressed I would get more and more stressed as three o'clock came around. That was the earliest time I could expect Chris to come home. Or, he might be out until ten o'clock. I never knew, and I didn't dare ask in case – as was likely – it would turn out that he had already told me and I had forgotten. So with every minute after three o'clock my tension rose higher and higher.

Eventually I'd hear his key in the door, and with my heart pounding and my hands kneading each other I'd go to meet him, with a smile on my face which I knew to be ingratiating and timid but which I couldn't change.

"Good day?" I'd ask nervously.

He might grunt at me, or he might shake his head silently, or he might laugh derisively. He would say with a sigh, "Let's see what you've messed up today, shall we? Let's see what chaos I have to face now that I'm home, will we?"

He would walk through the house and comment on jobs unfinished or not properly done. I would anxiously follow him, apologising where it proved I had been deficient; sometimes, despite my better knowledge, offering an excuse or a reason.

"That's because we ran out of polish," I might say. "I was going to put it on the list and do it as soon as we got some more."

But such attempts always backfired as he turned his wrath on me, accusing me of using up the polish too quickly, of being profligate, easy knowing it wasn't I who had to earn a living, who had the worry of it all. I quickly learned it was more sensible to just keep quiet and meekly apologise when he discovered things undone.

Chris would then cook a meal over which we would sit in near silence. He always ate with relish, but I could barely manage a few mouthfuls, even though I knew he would get on at me about my tiny appetite.

"Food not good enough for madame, is it?" he would sneer. "Not what you're accustomed to? Of course, you'll hardly have built up an appetite with the little exercise you've done today. I've seen faster sloths, I really have. You are useless. You really are."

Later we would watch television in more silence. He almost always picked the programmes we were to watch. Once or twice he would ask me for my choice, but I learned quickly not to offer an opinion.

"You want to watch a documentary about the Ice Age?" he'd laugh bitterly. "God knows you move with the speed of an Ice Age yourself. Looking for a few hints, are you?"

So now whenever he asked me for my suggestions I would say, "I don't mind. Whatever you like," and no matter that he always sneered, "God, have you no opinions of your own? Would require thinking, I suppose, and that's too much to ask, isn't it?" It was still easier than having him dissect whatever choice I ventured to make.

Looking back, part of me still finds it impossible to believe that I allowed myself to sink so low, to accept such verbal and emotional cruelty. But most of me understands it perfectly.

Because I was losing my grip on reality I could trust none of my own perceptions. So Chris, no matter how he was behaving, was the one certainty in an otherwise uncertain existence. I needed him as one true thing to which I could cling. Otherwise I could lose myself entirely in a maelstrom of illusion and doubt. I needed him totally. And he was already wavering about staying in this relationship. I couldn't afford to do anything which might sway his decision towards leaving me.

With Chris, no matter how unhappy I was, there was security. Without him there was chaos and uncertainty.

And my confidence was zero. Less than zero if that were possible. I couldn't begin to imagine a situation in which I could function normally, among normal people. The Sally who used to do this seemed like another woman entirely, and I often thought of her in awed amazement and admiration.

Did I love him still? I don't know. I don't think so, but the dynamic was such that such questions seemed irrelevant.

Perhaps there are those who would call me pathetic that I was putting up with this, tell me to get a grip on myself, cop onto myself, pull myself together and so on. I certainly used to have no sympathy for women who let themselves be bullied, so other women's scorn and impatience is probably all I deserve.

I kept clinging to the fact that he had never, ever hit me. Abusive men hit their women. He wasn't hitting me, therefore he wasn't being abusive. And he was really nice to me until I started losing my mind – it wasn't his fault he got sharp when he had so much to put up with. Or so I argued.

Whatever it was, it certainly wasn't doing either of us any good. I was frequently miserable. Well, actually, perpetually miserable. And Chris surely wasn't happy, or if he was he had a strange way of showing it.

* * *

My mother phoned towards the end of March to tell me that Laura had just got her Master's degree and to invite me to the graduation party. I thanked her, and asked her to pass my congratulations onto Laura, but said that I would be unavailable that day.

She said, "I haven't told you yet what day it's happening."

"True. But I will be unavailable no matter which day it is."

"That is so selfish," my mother said, "so typical of you. This is Laura's big day, and you can't even be generous enough to be there for her. She was at *your* graduation."

"She was told to be there. She was thirteen; she had no choice."

My mother said frostily, "I will be sure to tell her that you congratulated her. Perhaps you would be good enough to let me know when you are ready to participate in this family. I look forward to hearing from you – although I don't hold out much hope. Goodbye."

I had a nasty tinny taste in my mouth after she rung off. The taste of guilt. It *was* a bit unfair to Laura who, after all, had never been mean to me. If anything she had hero-worshipped me as the all-knowing all-wise older sister.

Ha! If she could see me now, with huge black marks like bruises under my eyes, skin so translucent that it was blue, no job, no prospects, no proper home, a dysfunctional relationship. Yeah, she'd really know how wise I was then.

And that was the very reason I couldn't go. I couldn't go back to that family as they celebrated the success of the favoured daughter while I, literally the ugly stepsister, turned up and admitted what a mess I was. I had so little of anything left, I had to cling to my pride. Even at the risk of hurting Laura.

Chapter 24

Who's to say how it would have ended? Would we have gone on like this in perpetuity? Surely not, something would have had to give, and I hate to think what that would have been. I was on a downward spiral and although I didn't know what was on the end of that spiral I surely knew I wasn't going to like it.

Unless there was a catalyst, something that could stop the spiral and even reverse it.

That catalyst was closer than I realised.

About a week later the doorbell rang. It startled me out of whatever reverie I had been experiencing as I stood in the sitting-room with the vacuum cleaner roaring unused in my hands. Surprised, I wondered who could possibly be there. We had very few callers now.

I went to answer the door and my jaw literally dropped. My caller was David! I dimly registered his essential warmth, and the tall lean height of him, his visible health and wonderful wholesomeness.

"Hi . . . hi," I said to him nervously, clinging to the door for security.

He didn't seem able to respond with the social niceties, staring at me with horror as he was. "My God, Sally, what have you done to yourself?" he demanded. "What's going on?" When I didn't answer he persisted, "What is it? Are you on drugs? You look like it."

"No, no, I'm not," I said, still dazed to see him there. A hundred questions floated through my mind and I grabbed one at random: "How did you know where I was?"

"I've been very worried about you," he said, "and when you suddenly stopped coming to *Svelte* I tried ringing you. Your mobile number was on your application form. But it was unobtainable."

It *would* be, I thought half-hysterically, once it had been through the 40°C cycle.

David continued, "So I went to the address you put down – to find new tenants living there. But they were able to give me the contact details of the landlord, who gave me this address. And I'm bloody glad he did. I'd never have found you otherwise."

"Why are you even looking for me? Is it because my membership has now lapsed and you're that desperate for business you're hounding old members?" I asked cruelly.

Inside I quailed at such rudeness to David of all people, who had never treated me with anything less than courtesy. But I was on the spot and defensive, and like all threatened creatures I was using any possible method of protecting myself.

David's mouth tightened but he ignored that, saying

only through gritted teeth, "I told you. I'm really, really worried about you. I've been watching you over the past few months, getting thinner and thinner, and more and more jittery. No time any more to talk to anybody, coming in, doing an excuse of a workout and then leaving without talking to anybody."

I bowed my head, chastened.

"No time to talk even to somebody like me, who thought," he said with heavy irony, "that they were your friend. And then you disappear entirely. Christ, Sally," he brushed his hand through his hair in frustration, "I didn't know what to think. I didn't know if you were dead or alive. And now I see," he said looking critically at me, "that you're something in between. "Come here," he said abruptly, and he firmly but gently took hold of my arm and shoved up one of my sleeves. He examined my inner arm intently, turning it sideways after a moment.

I tried to seize my arm back but his grip was implacable. "What on *earth* are you doing?" I demanded. "How dare you!"

"Looking for needle tracks," he said brusquely. "But I can't see any – what about your other arm?"

And even as I protested, "I told you – I'm *not* on drugs. I don't have needle tracks anywhere," he had exposed my other arm and was studying it. Eventually he conceded defeat.

"Well, you're not injecting, unless you started injecting in places other addicts usually end up in, and I don't propose to examine there. So either you're taking drugs in some other way – "

"I'm *not* taking drugs," I protested uselessly.

"Or there's something else seriously wrong."

That silenced me. Something else *was* seriously wrong but I certainly wasn't going to admit to insanity.

"What is it? What's going on with you?"

"Nothing," I said quickly, "nothing at all."

He gave a short unamused laugh. "Nothing? Don't insult my intelligence, Sally. Over the past few months you've changed from a beautiful, vibrant, outgoing wonderful woman into what I can only describe as – sorry, but it's true – a total wreck."

Oh God, did *everybody* think I looked awful?

But David wasn't finished. "You're severely underweight, no doubt suffering from malnutrition, you're shaking – look at you, you're doing it now – and the way you opened the door, you're moving like an old woman. What's going on?"

"Nothing," I said again. How could I possibly begin to explain what I didn't understand myself? How could I admit to this man who I admired so much and whose good opinion I craved, that I was half-psychotic? I couldn't.

And so I just repeated stubbornly, "Nothing's wrong, David, honestly."

He stared at me then, his frustration clear in his flight-or-fight stance, the hooded eyes of his expression, his closed fists.

"Have it your own way," he said then, reluctantly. "I can't force you to tell me. But Sally, know this. No matter what's going on, I still consider you to be my friend. So if you can ever admit to needing help – just ring me and I'll be there."

"I don't have your number," I said without thinking. I wasn't going to ring him, so what did it matter whether or not I had his number?

"No problem," he said, "here you go," and he reached into his pocket and took out a wallet, from which he took a business card and handed it to me.

I took it automatically. "Thanks," I said. I curled my hand around the card.

But he wouldn't be so keen to help me if he knew my guilty secret, if he knew I was mad. I would rather, I decided, have him annoyed and bewildered, than see the disillusionment grow in his eyes as he realised the levels to which I had descended.

David gave a deep sigh. "Look," he said, "you need help, Sally. You really do. I've never seen anybody go downhill as far and as fast as you've done. You need help and I'm offering my help to you."

Tears prickled the inside of my eyes at his kindness and generosity, at the compassion and concern in his voice.

"No matter what you need," he said, "someone to listen, money, a place to stay – I'll give it to you. But I can't force it on you. It breaks my heart, but you need to take the first step back to yourself. I can't do it for you. I would if I could, but I can't. So –" he shrugged in despair and turned to go. "Keep the card," he said over his shoulder. "Ring me any time."

And he turned and walked out of my life.

I stared after him and thought about what he had said. What had he called me? Beautiful, vibrant, outgoing. Wonderful. Was I ever really that woman?

I uncurled my hand and smoothed out the crumpled business card. *David Corrigan*, it stated, *Managing Director, Svelte Fitness Centre*. It had the business phone number on it, and a mobile number. His mobile number. I had only to lift the phone that was sitting right beside me here in the hall, dial that number, and in thirty seconds or less I could be talking to him, and maybe two or three minutes after that he could be back here with me.

That way lies madness, I told myself. Even more madness. I looked again at the card in my hand, and then folded it carefully and placed it into my jeans pocket. I wouldn't use it, I knew, but somehow it was good to know it was there.

I went back into the house, into my life, and closed the door behind me.

* * *

But all hell broke loose when Chris got home. As soon as I heard the door slam I knew he was, to put it mildly, not in good form. I hastened to the hallway to try to appease him, whatever it was that was upsetting him.

"Hi," I ventured even more nervously than usual.

"How dare you!" he spat at me. "How *dare* you!"

"How dare I what?" I asked him, shocked at this onslaught. "What are you talking about?"

"How dare you entertain your lover here today! After all your talk, 'I'll never be unfaithful to you, Chris'," he mimicked cruelly, "and then you have him here in the house!"

David! He was talking about David. But how did he know David was here?

241

Then he said, "He gave you something. A bit of paper. What was it? Where is it?"

"Nothing," I said, "he gave me nothing." That business card suddenly seemed the most valuable item in the world.

"Don't lie to me," said Chris. "Just don't. I *know* he gave you something. I saw it."

"How could you have seen anything?" I asked.

"Come here," he said, and grabbed my wrist. He pulled me out onto the little porch and pointed up. And then I saw it: a tiny camera, with a red light blinking, hugely conspicuous now that I knew it was there.

"You forget I work in security," said Chris when he saw I had seen it. "You don't think I'd actually trust you, do you?"

"You've been *spying* on me!" I said, stunned enough for courage. "How dare you?"

"Oh I dare," he said, "I dare what I like. And what are you going to do about it, eh?"

His face was twisted with venom and I suddenly wondered how I had ever thought him handsome. That open-faced, charming character with whom I had fallen in love seemed like a different person entirely. And I had the sudden sensation that this was the real him, that it was the other who was the fiction, all the better to entice me into his world, into his grasp.

I became aware of a cold knot of fear in my throat, a nausea of terror in my stomach.

"I dare what I like," he said again when he wasn't getting any reaction from me, "and what are you going to do about it?"

"Nothing," I whispered, "nothing," my ephemeral courage fading under his venom.

"No," he said, satisfied, "you're not going to do anything about it, are you? Now," he asked again, menace in his careful tone, "give me whatever paper he gave you."

"I threw it in the bin," I told him. "I didn't want it. I told you, I have nothing to do with David. If you were watching you'll have seen that he had to press it on me. And you'll have seen that he never came into the house."

"True," he said begrudgingly. "Okay, let's go and get the card out of the bin and burn it so you don't have any temptation to retrieve it. Come on," and he led the way into the kitchen, and opened the bin.

Of course, the business card was nowhere to be found in the bin, and my trepidation grew as he searched more and more extensively without finding it, his anger and his frustration growing with each passing minute. As his anger grew, so did my own tension. Oh God, maybe I should have admitted to still having it, should have given it up. It wasn't worth this, surely.

"It's not there," he said finally, having searched the contents of the bin thoroughly. He went and washed the detritus off his hands, grimacing with distaste at it all.

"So," he said softly, turning to me, "if it's not in the bin, where is it?"

"I don't know," I said, putting on my best confused expression. It was a pretty good confused expression. After all I had had plenty of practice over the past few months. "I was *sure* I had put it in there," I said. "God, Chris, it's another of my Moments."

He looked at me sharply then. "You're sure you binned it?"

"I *thought* I did," I said. "But it's not there, clearly. Where could it be?" and I looked around the room as if for inspiration.

Chris took a deep God-give-me-patience breath. "On the film it shows you putting it into your jeans pocket. Let's check there."

I tried to keep my face expressionless as I said, "Okay," and began putting my hands into my pockets. My sluggish mind was struggling to think. Would I pretend not to find it? But there would be no harm – I decided – in letting him have it. I wasn't going to ring David anyway, and if I ever needed to, I could find *Svelte*'s phone number easily. All I would be lacking was David's mobile number.

"Oh, here it is," I said, giggling nervously. I shook my head in confusion. "I could have *sworn* I put it in the bin."

Chris didn't say anything, just took the card off me, turned on the gas hob and made to hold the card over it. He paused for an instant and then seemed to think better of it. "No," he said, "maybe I'll hang onto this," and he put the business card into his own pocket.

Not good. I was sure David wouldn't want him having that information. But there was nothing I could do about it.

Chapter 25

The evening passed as ever they did: soundlessly watching endless television together.

That night I couldn't sleep. I listened to Chris's deep breathing and tried to think, although concentrating on any thought for long was difficult for me these days.

Chris had been awful when he had come home. I had been literally scared for my life in that moment. Aren't most women murder victims killed by their partners? I know he had a lot to contend with, what with my illness and his money worries. But still, did that excuse him intimidating and bullying me the way he was doing?

I had always shaken my head in disbelief at women who stayed with abusive men. Have they no self-esteem, I used to ask myself. Could they not see what was happening?

Now those smug opinions were coming back to haunt me. It wasn't as easy as that. Yes, easy to say: just leave him. But not easy to do. After all, where could I go?

I couldn't go to Gaby's obviously, no matter that that would otherwise have been my first choice. I couldn't go to my mother's house. Well, I could. Who was it who said: home is the place where, when you go there, they have to let you in? By that definition I supposed my mother's house was still home. If I turned up and threw myself upon her mercy she would take me in.

But I couldn't go back as such a failure. It would have been one thing to make a grand triumphant return, with a three-book novel contract and six-figure advance, for example. But to turn up at her doorstep thin and shaking, with no job and dubious mental health, fleeing from an unsuitable man . . . it just was not to be countenanced.

Same thing applied to going to my father's house: a triumphant return perhaps, but not creeping back wounded and disillusioned.

I would rather sleep in the streets. I really would.

I even would rather stay with Chris. So what if he was a bit short-tempered sometimes? None of us was perfect.

Ah, now I was rationalising his behaviour. As probably thousands of abused women did all the time. Not that I was abused. Of course I wasn't. He was insulting and contemptuous. He was intimidating and oppressive. But he didn't hit me or physically hurt me in any way.

It really all came down to this: I *had* to rationalise his behaviour and excuse it. I had to do this in order to make it bearable. And I had to make it bearable, because I had to stay with him. I had no other options.

I had already ruled out going to either of my parents.

I couldn't go to Women's Aid. They were chronically under-funded, they needed all their resources for women who really needed their help. Women who were being hit and beaten up. Not for women like me who were too spoilt to be able to take the rough with the smooth, who caved in as soon as somebody got a bit cross with them once in a while.

And then my thoughts turned to David. He had said he would help me. Anything I needed, he said. But he said that without knowing how mentally unstable I was. He certainly wasn't signing up for that.

And besides . . . I had invested so much in this relationship with Chris. I had been panicking before I met him, how much worse would it be now that I was nine months older? And I didn't even want to contemplate the shame of explaining to everybody that I was now single again after having grandly announced that I was shacked up and settled . . . and chosen.

Also, in a bizarre way I felt safe with Chris. I knew what to expect. His house was a kind of sanctuary for me. The outside world seemed so big and quick and loud and scary, compared to the relative tranquillity of this little house.

Within this house I had only to worry about my Moments, and about not annoying Chris. But that was it. I didn't have to worry about anything else: not holding down a job, nor making decisions, nor juggling a busy lifestyle. My life had imperceptibly shrunk over the past months until it was a small thing in its scope.

If I could make Chris happy, then all would be well. I just had to stop annoying him.

I would change, I decided as I lay there listening to Chris's breathing. It would all be fine. I would make sure not to upset him, and then he would be always nice to me, and we would be happy again. And I'd start taking care of my appearance so he would find me attractive again, and we could start making love, and then I would conceive and we would have a beautiful baby.

I decided: tomorrow I would plan a perfect homecoming for him. I'd make everything all right.

My Perfect Life could get back on track. It would. I was determined upon it.

Chapter 26

The next day I prepared well for Chris's arrival home. I knew it was a cliché, the little woman dressing up for her man's return, but I still did it. I was going to sort out whatever had made our relationship such an arid ugly thing these days. I intended to make everything okay between us.

I took a long bath, scented with a fabulously expensive bath oil left over from my old life. I shaved my hairy legs, and I rubbed in matching oils so that my skin was soft and perfumed. I put on make-up for the first time in ages. For tonight I was going to ditch the ubiquitous leggings (really, was it any wonder that Chris had gone off me?), and wear something really nice.

Accordingly I chose a pair of plum velvet wide-leg trousers and a red sequinned waistcoat. I put them on – and viewed my reflection in acute disappointment.

The clothes hung off me. The waistcoat had been

dashing and risqué when I had had breasts. Now it just looked stupid and pathetic as it sagged off my narrow shoulders, exposing too much of nothing of a bosom.

As for the trousers – instead of sitting on my waist and snugly cupping a curvaceous bottom, they hung off my hips, and the back of them sagged sadly.

Okay, not them so. What about that white linen skirt?

Nope, it was too big too.

It turned out that *everything* in my wardrobe was too big. It was scary how much too big everything was. Given that I had been wearing draw-string waistband leggings for the past two or three months, I hadn't realised exactly how much weight I had lost. I mean, I knew I was losing weight, but this was beyond a joke.

In the end it came down to a choice between a wrap-around holiday skirt, whose reds and yellows and greens and oranges and purples looked warm and vibrant with the clear southern light and brown legs of holidays – but which now looked merely loud, gaudy and tasteless in this cold blue northern light, against my blue-white legs – or the ubiquitous leggings.

I couldn't bear the thought of trying to have a romantic evening in my leggings, so the skirt it was going to have to be. I chose a plain blue T-shirt in the hope of toning it all down a bit.

I considered going to the hairdresser's, but I couldn't face the enormous challenge of going out. Besides, I rationalised, we were supposed to be saving money. But I did wash my hair *and* use conditioner, *and* blow-dry it sleek and as glossy as I could. It didn't look too bad when I had finished. It didn't look great, granted. But it didn't look too bad.

I can't say I was pleased with how I looked when I finished. I wasn't, not in the slightest. Picture the scene: gaunt body draped in gaudy clothes, drawn face topped by a haystack of two-tone blonde and brown striped hair, anxious expression in too-large eyes.

But I was pleased with the effort I had made, an effort which had been lacking for months now. And I hoped that Chris would be too, would appreciate it.

I laid the table prettily, got out the candles – so far so clichéd, but a cliché, after all, is just a poor man's tradition.

And now, food. I wasn't stupid enough to attempt to cook the food. I'd get a take-away from Fantastic Foods, which was an open secret for culinarily challenged hostesses. They delivered oven-ready food. The sort of food hostesses liked to pass off as their own, which their guests kindly pretended to believe.

I looked them up in the phone book and rang them. I got them to talk me through their newest menu and made my choice. They would be able to deliver within the hour, they promised as they took the credit-card details.

This was great, I told myself, even managing a little hop of joy and exuberance. We would have a pleasant, relaxed meal. We would chat and joke as we used to. All would be well.

As I polished wineglasses and chose from the small collection of wine, I was so happy that I was humming to myself. So I wasn't best pleased to be interrupted by the phone.

"Hello, Ms Cronin?" said a male voice. A highly embarrassed male voice. "It's Damien here from Fantastic Foods. You were on to us about half an hour ago, placing an order . . ."

"That's right."

"Well, the thing is, Ms. Cronin, I'm afraid the credit card has been declined. I just wanted to check in case I had written the number down wrong or something." He was way too kind and way too professional to suggest any other possibility.

"Oh dear," I said, grasping at that, "okay, let's check the number you have."

But that possibility was ruled out very quickly – he did, indeed, have the right number.

"Can I leave the order for now and ring you back in a few minutes?" I asked him, totally bewildered as to what had happened.

"Sure thing," he said easily, sounding relieved now that the awkward conversation was nearing its end.

I hung up and thought about it. The card number I had given him was the card on the joint account I had with Chris. It shouldn't have been declined. God, we were probably even deeper in financial trouble than I had realised.

What would I do? I wondered, staring at the phone as if it could give me answers. I was vaguely aware that I was biting my lip. I still had my own credit card, I could use that. Apart from the minor detail that I had no income with which to pay the bill when it came in.

Or should I ring Chris and find out what the story was? Maybe it was just a mistake, and could be sorted out. No, I wouldn't do that. Not only would it spoil the surprise, but it would more than likely annoy him if I rang him.

But I couldn't have no dinner when he came home, I told myself in frustration – that would be defeating the purpose of the whole thing.

Okay, I decided, I'd take a risk and use my own credit card. The cost of the meal wasn't *that* much, I'd sort it out somehow when the bill came in. So I lifted the phone again and spoke to the lovely Damien, and re-ordered the meal. I held on while they put the card through, just in case, and it was fine. Great, sorted.

The meal was duly delivered on time, along with printed instructions for its cooking. Even I could do that, I thought, and I'd put the timer on the oven clock, *and* the alarm on my mobile phone to make sure I wouldn't forget in yet another Senior Moment.

And so it was that Chris walked through the door of the house that evening to be met by something unusual: the delicious, fragrant scent of cooking food.

"Hi!" I said to him, going up to him and kissing him on the cheek. "Welcome home."

He looked down at me with suspicion in his eyes. "What's all this about? Your outfit? That smell?"

"I just decided to make it a nice homecoming for you. Don't worry, I haven't cooked the meal myself," I laughed coquettishly (and, I hoped, reassuringly). "I got a catering company to deliver it. Come on into the kitchen. I have the wine breathing. Would you like a glass?"

He followed me into the kitchen. "A catering

company? For God's sake, Sally, why did you do that?"

"I wanted a nice meal for us," I said stubbornly, "and I couldn't risk cooking it myself."

"But the cost – "

"It has worked out even cheaper than going out to a good restaurant, but instead we're in the comfort of our own home," I purred seductively as I poured him a glass of wine and handed it to him.

He didn't thank me, but took a sip of it, which I considered a good sign. As I donned oven gloves and checked the contents of the oven, still all Stepford Wife-ish, I was aware of his appraising glance on me. Maybe, I thought hopefully, the proper grooming had worked. Perhaps he had realised that I was still an attractive woman.

"Tell me, Sally," he said conversationally, "what on earth are you thinking of, wearing that *hideous* outfit?"

"It's not the nicest, is it?" I said calmly, determined to keep the conversation upbeat, "but it was the only thing I had that fitted me, apart from leggings. It's just that I've lost so much weight. And at least it's cheerful."

"Cheerful is one word," he conceded, "cheerful enough to give somebody a migraine."

"You're so witty," I smiled brightly at him, "and I hope you're hungry because the dinner is ready. Sit down. Sit down," I gestured.

He sat as I served him a generous portion of lasagne, a rich red tomato sauce oozing enticingly out from between the layers of pasta. With that I served a fresh green salad with Fantastic Food's special honey-and-mustard salad dressing, and creamy garlicky potatoes.

"Tell me," he said, tucking in, "how did you pay for this?"

"With my credit card," I told him through my own mouthful of food, "but that reminds me, Chris. Something very odd happened when I tried to pay with our joint credit card – they said the card was invalid."

"Well, of course it is," he said calmly, taking a sip of wine.

"What do you mean?"

He sighed deeply and put his glass down, "Sally, this is getting very, very tiresome, you forgetting half of what I tell you. Since you weren't going out any more, and since our finances are so tight, I didn't see the point in paying the government stamp duty on a card which wasn't being used. So when my card was up for renewal I didn't renew yours. I did tell you this," he said with heavy patience.

I was shaking my head. "I don't remember you telling me that."

"I'm sure you don't," he said ironically. "I'm quite sure you don't. I'm surprised you can remember your own name, to be frank. Your memory these days is about as good as your dress sense and your looks."

I stared at him as if he had hit me.

"Why are you being so mean to me?" I asked him then. "Why? The reason I organised all this," and I gestured around at the meal and my own appearance, my voice catching with tears, "is that I wanted us to have a nice time together, to make it a little bit like it used to be." I could feel a stray tear trickling down my left cheek and I brushed it away.

"I know things haven't been great between us, and I wanted to try to sort it out. But you're just rejecting everything I've done, all the effort I've made. Why are you being so mean?" I asked again.

He sighed wearily. "Okay, here we go with the martyr bit," he said resignedly. "Sally, have you any idea – *any* idea – what it's been like for me these past months? You don't, do you? It's all *me, me, me* with you, isn't it? There's no pleasing you."

I bowed my head, so that I couldn't see the scorn and disgust in his eyes, and quailed under this tirade.

"I should have sussed this a lot sooner, but I was blinded by love," he said. "And instead of having a healthy woman being an equal partner to me, I have this total wreck dragging out of me. Don't start with the waterworks," he snapped as my tears started in earnest. "You women are all the same. The minute somebody dares tell you any home truths it's all tears. Well, tears won't work with *me*."

He took a deep dragging breath and continued. "I gave you *everything*, Sally. I even gave you the chance to write your novel. Have you *any* idea how many people would have died for a chance to be a full-time writer? And you have just wasted it. I have been supporting you these past months and what have you written? Sally, look at me. What have you written?" he insisted when I didn't answer as I stared at him in numb misery. I still couldn't answer.

"How far have you got?" he asked sarcastically. "Halfway? A quarter? A tenth? Maybe even a hundredth? Surely you've done one per cent, Sally. A novel's what, four hundred pages long? One per cent is four pages, surely you've written that much?"

He paused to let me answer.

"I didn't think so," he said when I didn't – couldn't – answer him.

"So, you're living off me without producing *anything*. And you can't even keep your head together to remember simple things like messages and conversations. And I have to put up with all that confusion. I have been so patient with you. Haven't I?" he demanded.

I nodded miserably. It wouldn't take a genius to figure out that acquiescence was the correct response.

"So I have somebody who's living off me, who's creating chaos in my house and my life, who's let herself go so much that she's physically repulsive to me now, who is practically a hermit and to be quite frank, Sally, adds nothing to my life but grief.

"And that *somebody*," he said, the pitch of his voice rising in disbelief, "has the gall, the *temerity* to think that ordering a fancy meal which *I'll* have to pay for, and putting on a hideous outfit, will make all that okay." He shook his head incredulously.

"And now that we're on the subject, Sally, I'm not sure how long we can go on with this. I've been very patient, I think you'd have to agree with that . . ."

I nodded as he clearly required, but I could feel the hard knot of fear in my stomach as he continued, "There really is nothing for me in this relationship any more. I have thought about ending it, Sally. I really have. But I couldn't do that to you. So we'll keep going as long as we can, as long as I can, I mean. And maybe you'll get better, and we can resume a normal life. That's all I'm hoping for now, to be honest. And I don't know how long my patience can last."

I stared at him in horror, my stomach churning. He was putting me on probation. Or rather, I had been on probation for some time and he was now telling me so. With a muttered apology I put my hand over my mouth and ran upstairs to the bathroom where I retched and retched the mouthful or two I had managed to eat.

Once my stomach had calmed down a little I rinsed my mouth and then sat on the edge of the bath with my head in my hands, experiencing complete and utter and total despair. I was actually beyond tears at this stage.

What on earth was I to do now? I had reached that proverbial place between the devil and the deep blue sea. I couldn't go and I couldn't stay.

I couldn't go because, as I already had realised, there was nowhere to go. And how could I stay when we were so unhappy together, when I was miserable and he was miserable?

How could I stay when I knew he was always watching me and checking me and judging me, and how could I live with this fear that at any moment I might be kicked out?

But where would I go? Which brought me straight back to the realisation that I couldn't go.

I hate to think of it now, I hate to admit it, but as I sat there, there seemed to be only one option available to me, only one solution which would solve my dilemma. An ultimate solution, from which there was no coming back. And as I sat there on the edge of that bath, the taste of fear still in my mouth, I realised that I could make that choice.

But some vestige of courage came to me. A tiny, fragile atom of courage, that was all. But it was enough to whisper: *You can get over this. You can prevail. Don't give up*.

No, I decided, I wouldn't give up. I had no idea what I would do, but I would do *something*. There must be some way out of all of this. And I certainly wouldn't find it if I was dead.

I was exhausted now. I would go to bed and let the oblivion of sleep overtake me. I'd be fresher in the morning. I could think of some solutions then.

I lay in bed, willing the blessed unconsciousness of sleep to come so I could forget this awful day, this awful life. It truly couldn't get any worse than this.

And just then something stirred in the back of my mind. Some memory. What was it? Whatever it was, the more I tried to catch it the more it skitted away. Eventually, even as I was trying to remember, sleep claimed me.

Chapter 27

I slept fitfully, tossing and turning all night, dreaming wild dreams with horrible creatures chasing me, so that I woke up as tired as when I had gone to bed.

And when I woke I lay there for a moment and wondered why I felt so awful. And then I remembered why, and I felt worse. I lay there for ages, with nothing to get up for. Chris had clearly gone already, either that or he hadn't slept in with me at all.

And then it came to me – the memory which had been out of grasp the previous evening. Angela. Chris's ex-girlfriend Angela. I could contact her. She had spent time with Chris. She might be able to help me.

Any relief I might have felt drained away. *That* was my solution? To get in touch with Angela? Yeah right, that was really, really going to help.

I thought of the huge mess I had made of my life and how irretrievable it all seemed.

So ring Angela, my internal voice suggested. *What have you got to lose?*

She's mad, I countered.

So are you, it countered back. *You'll have lots in common.*

Ha, ha.

But I was truly at the infamous rock bottom, and I had nowhere to go but up.

Either that or stay at rock bottom for ever, for however long *forever* proved to be down there in the mud and the darkness.

Or I could take my tiny flicker of courage, and cup my hand around it to shelter it and maintain it, and coax it into growing into a strong brave flame, and reclaim my life.

Right now I had no idea how I would do that, or even what my life would look like once it was reclaimed – but I couldn't continue as I was. I *wouldn't* continue as I was.

I certainly couldn't see the big picture, I didn't have a grand plan or anything. But I realised, I decided, that if I was proactive in any way, that was better than nothing. That was a tiny step with my tiny embryonic flame of courage. And right now, the only thing I could think of was to ring Angela.

Another memory came to me. Mike at that party, telling me that Chris had had a run of crazy girlfriends. And my smug assurance, I cringed to remember, that I wouldn't number among them. Ha bloody ha.

A run of crazy girlfriends . . . including Angela.

Why? Could he really be that unlucky?

And Angela had seemed angry with him. Furious. As though she somehow blamed him for it all.

I needed to know her side of the story.

I would ring Angela, I decided. Being that proactive would be good for me, even if the call itself produced nothing tangible.

And . . . I truly could think of nothing else to do.

Of course, that was easier said than done. I didn't know anything about her, not even her surname. And I could hardly ask Chris.

But . . . hang on . . . something was stirring in my memory. Hadn't Mike mentioned her surname at that party? I remembered the scene, I remembered him telling me about Angela being Chris's ex, and he had used her surname when he mentioned her. But, even though I clearly remembered the scene, there was nothing but a blank at the bit where her surname was. There was no reason for me to have remembered it, I acknowledged glumly.

I tried to sneak up on the memory, hoping that by getting a good run at it I'd recall the name. Slowly a sense of her name began to come to me. It was two syllables, I felt certain of that. And it was an Irish name. Gradually, like a flower carefully unfurling, my mind partially gave up more information. It started with a 'H'. Hand? No, that was only one syllable. But it was nearly right. Handy? That wasn't a name at all, but it was on the right track. *Hanly!* That was it! Her surname was Hanly.

Energised by this remembrance (and by the fact that my brain was at least working to some extent!) I jumped out of bed, or at least, did what passed for jumping these days. I quickly got dressed without even bothering about a shower (not exactly a rare occurrence by then, I'm ashamed to admit), and went downstairs. I took the phone book out of the drawer in the hall table and looked through it. D . . . G . . . H . . . Hab . . . Hand . . . Hanly. I scanned down the 'A' section of the Hanly list . . . but there was no Angela listed.

Despondently I closed the phone book and replaced it, listlessly closing the drawer.

What would I do now? Was this a sign that I should give up?

And, anyway, what help could an emotional wreck like her be to me anyway? What was she going to do – wave a wand and stop me losing my mind? I didn't think so. I might as well give up on this idea.

Except . . . what else would I do? As I had debated endlessly with myself, every other option was a cul-de-sac. Speaking to Angela was the only option which held even the possibility of a solution. And an answer to the question – *why* did Chris have 'a run of crazy girlfriends'? I could suddenly hear Mike's voice saying: "What are the odds, eh?"

I *would* find her phone number, I decided. I would succeed, and even if she couldn't help me, the achievement – no matter how insignificant – of carrying out a task to its completion would be good for me.

I stood in the hallway, irresolute, not knowing what to do next. If only she would ring here as she had done before! And then something flickered deep in the recesses of my mind. What was it? What memory was hovering just out of sight? I probed and dug at the memory, but it remained elusive. Frustrated, I decided to stop thinking about it for now. Maybe the memory would come back to me if I stopped nagging at it.

I would have a shower, I decided. If I was refusing to let myself sink totally, then I was going to start taking better care of myself. Having a shower was a small gesture, and far from a solution to my situation. But it was something proactive which I *could* do.

So I went back upstairs and, having stripped off my clothes, stepped into the shower. And as the water rained down on me, warm and benign, my mind drifted, thinking of nothing much at all. And in that relaxed state, it came to me.

I had written Angela's phone number down, taking it from the Caller ID.

But . . . where had I written it down? And did I still have it?

As I soaped and rinsed my skeletally thin body, and then dried myself, I thought about it. Unsuccessfully.

As I dressed myself in fresh clothes (more leggings and sweatshirts, but at least they were clean), I tried a different tack. Being relaxed in the shower had worked before, so I endeavoured to disengage my mind, to achieve that tranquil state into which memories could drop.

And it must have worked because I remembered: I had written her number down on an old envelope.

Okay, so far so good.

But what had I done with the envelope afterwards? Did I keep it? Or did I bin it?

I simply could not remember. And no matter how determined I relaxed my mind and disengaged my thoughts, I still could not remember. I probably *had* binned it, I acknowledged to myself, even though I couldn't remember doing so. But, truly, there was no reason to have kept it.

However, since I couldn't remember binning it (not that me being unable to remember signified anything), there was a tiny possibility that I hadn't. But if not, where was it?

I thought back. I was using the number to check the Caller ID. So it was logical that the number would have been handy for the phone. On the hall table, or in its drawer. If I had left it on the hall table, then it was long gone – it would have been tidied away ages ago.

But if I left it in the drawer, it might possibly be still there.

It was certainly worth looking.

I went downstairs to the hall table, and opened the drawer. Typically for Chris, it was well-organised. But there, at the back, was an envelope. I took it out and looked at it. And there it was! A mobile phone number which I recognised, now that I saw it, as being Angela's.

I stared at it. *Well, what am I waiting for?* I asked myself. Taking a deep breath I dialled the number.

A few rings later she answered brusquely, "Angela Hanly." Hard to judge in just those two words, but she certainly *sounded* normal enough.

"Hello, Angela," I said nervously, "you don't know me, but my name is Sally Cronin."

"Who?" she asked, not crossly but briskly.

"Chris Malley's new girlfriend," I explained. I rushed in with my explanation, hurrying lest she hang up on me, "I know this sounds mad, ringing you. But I didn't know who else to contact, what else to do . . ."

"It's okay," she said, and her voice slowed right down and softened and she seemed to be indicating that she had all the time in the world for me. "I understand. Let me guess – you're at the end of your tether, you're about to crack up and you think you're losing your mind?"

"Yes! Yes . . . how do you know?" I asked her, confused. "Are you psychic?"

She gave a short unamused laugh. "No. I'm not psychic. I guessed this for a completely different reason. I think we'd better meet. I'll explain then."

"Can we meet now?" I ventured. I needed it all to happen immediately. I didn't think I could wait for hours never mind days.

"Now? I don't know if I can . . ."

"Please," I said, and waited for her verdict. I had no other pleas to make, couldn't even begin to describe the courage getting this far had taken me, nor the desperation I was feeling.

And maybe she heard all that in my voice because she said sympathetically, "Okay, hang on a second and I'll see if I can get away."

I held on, clutching the phone to my ear and I could hear voices in the background: Angela's voice brisk and efficient, and a lower voice, a male voice, rumbling in response.

After some moments Angela came back onto the line. "Okay," she said. "I can meet you now. Where?"

Gratitude and relief flooded me as I told her, "What about Murtagh's pub? It's just around the corner from –"

"I know where it is. I can be there in about half an hour, forty minutes," she said. "That okay?"

"Sure," I said, "thanks, Angela."

"See you then," she said, and hung up.

* * *

About twenty minutes later I put on a coat and left the house. I hadn't been outside in ages. Everything seemed so strange. The wind felt so strong against my face, the passing cars so noisy, and the sound of other people's voices and footsteps so intrusive. It was all so oppressive and intimidating, threatening to overwhelm me.

I looked longingly at my car. Maybe I could drive to the pub? *Don't be ridiculous*, I chastised myself. *It's only a ten-minute walk. You can't possibly drive that distance.*

Part of me – a large and scared part of me – wanted to rush back into the house, back to safety, but the small courageous part insisted that I keep going. One step after one step. Until after about ten minutes I reached our local pub, Murtagh's.

I went into the pub and ordered a mineral water, as a licence to sit in the pub more than any innate desire for it. I paid with my lone five-euro note, and there wasn't much change. I wouldn't even be able to afford to buy Angela a drink, and I cringed at the thought.

I took my drink and sat down in a little alcove. There was a fire burning cheerfully and the dark wood, ornate wrought iron, and tumultuous stained glass all worked together surprisingly well, creating a warm and inviting atmosphere.

I looked at the meagre change in my hand, and realised how pitiable this was, and how far I had fallen. I studied the pathetic pile of coins and there and then something gave. It finally dawned on me – really, really, dawned on me – that this wasn't right. Things were going to have to change. Regardless of whether Angela could help me or not, I was going to have to make some changes.

While I waited for her, and sipped my drink carefully, I began breathing more deeply. There was something about the air in this pub which was easier to breathe than the air in the house.

I began feeling a sensation which I couldn't identify. What was it? It was . . . I realised . . . an unaccustomed sense of freedom. A sense of not being observed. Of not having to watch my every word. A sense of space, both literal and metaphorical. The freedom wasn't total; there was fear there too. Fear at what Angela would say. Fear about my future which seemed as formless and as intimidating as ever. But I could still breathe more easily.

About twenty minutes later the door opened and a tall, elegantly slim woman came into the pub. Was it Angela? Not as I had last seen her, certainly. This woman was sharply business-suited, and although she did have long red hair, it was decorously plaited rather than wildly chaotic. She had a calm expression rather than the snarling mouth and feverish eyes I remembered so clearly.

The woman glanced around the room, caught sight of me and nodded a greeting. It *was* Angela.

She indicated my drink and mouthed, "Same again?" and without waiting for an answer headed off for the bar, while I sat, humiliated beyond belief. She was here at my request after all – the least I could do was to buy her a drink. But that was beyond me.

She came back a few minutes later with another mineral water for me and what looked like a double brandy for herself.

"I'm going to need this," she said, gesturing towards her glass, "for this conversation," and I experienced an icy wash of fear at her words. What was she going to tell me?

Chapter 28

She took a deep nervous breath, and for the first time I saw a crack in her poise.

"Right," she began, "tell me why you contacted me."

Believe it or not, it was only then that the inappropriateness of it all hit me. Chris had broken it off with her, upsetting her enough to drive her demented, and here I was about to cry on *her* shoulder about my own relationship with him.

"I'm sorry I had to contact you," I said. "I didn't know what else to do."

"It's okay. I think you did the right thing. I'm exactly the right person for you to talk to. That is, if your problem is what I think it is."

"My problem . . ." I echoed as the enormity of it hit me again.

"You'd better tell me what it is."

"Okay," I said, and came to an abrupt halt. I didn't have a clue what to say next.

"Start at the beginning," she suggested.

"Okay," I said, and took a sip of my water and a deep breath. "I met Chris through a dating website, *MoreThanFriends,*" I began.

And then I told her, in a huge rush, how it had been. All about how Chris and I had met, and fallen in love so quickly, and moved in together in such excitement and joy. But how it had all started to go wrong then. How I had started having these Senior Moments and feared I was losing my mind, how I couldn't do anything right and Chris was understandably fed up with me.

Almost without taking a breath I continued, telling of Gaby's betrayal, of how Chris had given me the chance to write a novel and I couldn't do it, and now I had no job and no prospect of one, and how I couldn't even conceive a baby – which even sixteen-year-old heroin addicts managed to do – but that was all academic as Chris didn't want to come near me as I was so ugly, and how his business was doing so badly that we had no money and I was such a drag to him because I couldn't earn and I couldn't even sign on for unemployment benefit as I had voluntarily made myself unemployed, and with all the stress I could hardly eat and had lost too much weight, and couldn't even go out of the house now, that it had been a huge challenge even managing to come here to meet her.

When I finished I just sat there, totally drained.

"I'm going to get another brandy," she said, and I saw that she had finished her first one while I had been speaking. "Would you like one? For medicinal purposes."

I nodded gratefully. I don't normally like brandy,

but right now its heavy aromatic warmth seemed exactly what I needed.

"I'm sorry I can't buy my round," I said. "I don't have any money."

"It's okay," she said compassionately. "I understand. I'll be back in a minute."

The pub was quiet this early in the day and she was back with our drinks in no time. I cradled the substantial roundness of my glass gratefully.

"Okay," she told me, "I have some good news and some bad news, and in a way they're the same thing. Sally, almost nothing of what you have told me is true."

How *dare* she! Hugely irate, I began to say, "Now, Angela – "

But she held up her hand to forestall me. "I'm not saying you're lying, Sally, honestly. I *know* you're not. But you *are* mistaken about a lot of things. Some of that is good," she insisted. "For example, you're wrong when you say that you're losing your mind."

"What do you mean? Were you not listening?" I demanded. "Have I not told you that I keep doing totally odd and sometimes even dangerous things? Are you suggesting that they are the works of a well-balanced person?"

She was shaking her head as I was speaking. "I'm not saying that. On the contrary, they certainly are *not* the works of a balanced person," she said dryly. "But the unbalanced person who did them wasn't you. It was Chris."

"What?" I stared at her in disbelief, beginning to

regret having contacted her. Maybe she wasn't as well-adjusted as she appeared.

"All those episodes that you called your Senior Moments – they were orchestrated by Chris," she said patiently.

I was shaking my head now. "This doesn't make sense."

"Okay, for argument's sake just answer this: *could* he have done them? Was he there when the stew was over-salted, the curry was ruined, the shirt was burned?"

"Well, yes, but . . ."

"I'm telling you, it was *him* doing these things to make you think you were losing it. And those conversations you had forgotten – I'm certain that you never had them; he just said you did. And that he put letters in your bag, and then insisted he had asked you to post them."

I stared at her in horror. "Why on earth would Chris want to do such a thing? That doesn't make any sense at all." But, even as I spoke, I was engaged by the tantalising possibility that what she said was true, that I *wasn't* crazy. That would be *so* wonderful!

And then I realised one flaw in her theory.

"But that can't be right. There was one time I was sure I had sent an e-mail from work, but when I checked, I couldn't have done, because it wasn't in my Sent Box. And Chris wasn't ever in my office."

"Sally," she said, exasperated, "Chris is an IT security consultant. He's an expert on hacking into other people's computer systems. It would be simple for him to get into your e-mail account and simply delete it."

"Are you serious? Could he really do that?"

"No problem to him," she said confidently.

"And my novel!" I gasped. Angela raised an enquiring eye at me, and I went on to explain. "I used to find gibberish in the text of my novel. Which I didn't remember writing. That could have been him! And if so, I didn't remember writing it because I *didn't*!"

"Absolutely," said Angela approvingly, like a teacher with a not-too-bright child who has finally grasped some concept.

"But hang on, there were things that I definitely did," I told her, deflating at the thought. "One day I forgot that a saucepan was on, and it boiled dry and burned so badly I had to throw it out. And he was out at the time, so he definitely couldn't have done that. And by the time I left work I was making way too many mistakes there."

"Yes," she agreed, "but we all do things like that sometimes and it doesn't mean we're crazy. It was just his good luck that it happened to you and you took it as further proof that you were losing it. Or maybe you were more prone to forgetting things at that stage because you were so stressed."

"True," I mused.

"Also, you've said that you haven't been eating, and I must say," she said acerbically, "you certainly look as if you could do with a good feeding. And malnutrition makes you stupid. So maybe some of those Moments *were* down to you. But that makes you stressed and hungry, not crazy."

"But even though Chris could have done those things, that doesn't mean he *did*," I said sadly.

"Listen to this," she said triumphantly. "He not only did the same things to me, but he *told* me he had been playing these tricks on me. He admitted it!"

"Oh come on, Angela, why would he do that? If he was doing it, it would make no sense for him to own up to it!"

"He told me later, when it was all over between us, because he wanted to impress me with his cleverness. And an awful lot of this whole situation is about Chris wanting to impress people with how clever he is, so it *does* make sense for him to admit it."

The delicious possibility was percolating through me. *Maybe I'm not crazy.* And at that thought it felt as if a weight literally lifted from my shoulders, a dragging weight I hadn't realised I was carrying. I wasn't crazy!

Or maybe, of course, we both were.

"I would go further," she said. "With all you have been through, it's a sign of your mental stability that you are bearing up as well as you have been."

"You know," I said, thinking now, "if this is true . . . you know, Chris never wanted me to go to the doctor with this problem. I went once, and when I told him, he looked extremely anxious until he learned the doctor had dismissed it as nothing. I thought it was concern for me that had him anxious," I laughed bitterly, "but, from what you're saying, it was the worry that I would be found totally sane, and he would be found out."

"Sounds about right," she agreed.

"And ever after that," I remembered, "he discouraged me from seeking medical help. He painted an awful picture of brain scans and being committed against my will. I was terrified of that."

"Of course, you were," said Angela, softly. "Anybody would be."

"Am I really not going crazy?" I whispered, still hardly able to believe it.

"No." She smiled kindly at me. "No, Sally, you're not."

I could feel tears pricking the inside of my eyes. Tears of joy, of sheer total and utter relief from the ever-present and oppressive worry. I wasn't losing my mind. I was still sane!

At least, according to Angela I was still sane.

"So, what else was going on with you?" she said, thinking back to my monologue. "Oh yes, your friend's betrayal. I would bet large sums of money that that never happened, that he just managed to convince you it did. All in order to isolate you and make you more vulnerable."

"Oh, that did happen," I assured her. "He knew something about her marriage she would never have told him otherwise, and she admitted to me that it had happened."

"Well, maybe it did happen," she acquiesced, "but it's also possible that he figured out that secret about her marriage – he's very, very, good at reading people – and used that to convince you. It might be worth having a talk with her."

"Hmm," I said sceptically.

Angela looked at me and clearly decided not to pursue that one any further. She continued, "As for the chance of writing a novel, it sounds as if you were a bit coerced into accepting that."

"I was very happy in my job," I said reflectively. "He kind of insisted I tell him what I would do if I won the Lotto, and that's what I came up with. And then he arranged the opportunity for me, and it seemed churlish to turn it down. And to be fair, I *was* excited at the prospect."

"Right. Well, arranging to have you at home writing a novel had two benefits for him – by giving up your job you were becoming isolated. And it was much easier for him to mess up your success at that than it was to mess up your job. And you never suspected anything."

"No, no, I didn't."

She took a deep breath and a sip of her drink, and said dryly, "Let me guess – you're not too close to your family either?"

I stared at her, "How did you know? You *must* be psychic!"

She gave an unamused laugh. "No, I've just realised how Chris operates. And picking vulnerable women who are easy to isolate is his style – I was one of those myself – so it's not a criticism, honestly."

He had chosen me from the start. The thought chilled me.

"Now about you being infertile," she said going back to my list. "Of course you're not."

"How do you know?" I asked sceptically.

"Well, to be fair, I don't know that for sure," she said, "how could I? But I do know that not conceiving with

Chris is no indication that you're infertile. He has had a vasectomy." She gave a little laugh, a sardonic laugh, at my dropped jaw. "Oh yes. Many years ago. He told me that information pretty early in our relationship – or what I thought was a relationship," she added ironically. "It meant that I had to pay the highest price to have a relationship with him: that of relinquishing any chance of children. Which I did. Which appealed to his vanity no end."

"That's *cruel!*"

She shrugged wearily. "Of course it was cruel. But he obviously thought of a new, maybe even crueller, twist for you . . . make you think it was your fault, and use it to assault you even more. Clever," she said begrudgingly, "very clever."

I was shaking my head in contradictory disbelief and all-too-possible belief. She saw me and smiled sardonically.

"My dear, I swear to you that you will some day do as I have done, and that's to thank God from every atom of your body that you never ended up carrying that man's child."

"But he told me he had been tested, and proven fertile," I said, not really able to keep up with this rapid revision of what I had thought was reality.

"Sally, part of what is going on with Chris is that he's a pathological liar. I started off by saying that almost nothing you told me is true. Reason being, *nothing* Chris says is the truth. Nothing. He tells lies to manipulate people, but he also lies for the fun of it, and he lies for the sheer heck of it."

278

"So . . . I'm probably fertile after all?" I asked her, hardly able to believe it.

"As good a chance as anybody else."

"This is . . . it's wonderful! You're giving me back everything! My sanity, my future babies, *everything*."

"I'm only giving you back what's rightfully yours," she told me, "what Chris has stolen from you. But look at how he manipulated you. It was all very clever," she said begrudgingly. "I have to give him that, although I'm loath to give him anything other than the deep end of the ocean and an anchor." There was bitter venom in her voice as she spoke.

My pleasure at what I was regaining was short-lived. "But why would he do all these things to me? Why? He said he loved me. Why would he want to hurt me?" I asked her in total bewilderment.

She shook her head sadly and said, "Not only does Chris not love you now, but Chris never loved you. Chris never even liked you. Your whole relationship is a lie."

I looked at her, feeling the stirrings of panic acidic in my lower stomach. "That's not true," I protested. "You don't know me. You don't know us or our relationship. You can't say that."

She looked at me shrewdly. "I'll ask your own question back to you, then. Why would he do these awful things to somebody he loves? He wouldn't. There *is* an explanation, though, which I shall tell you now. But first, another brandy?"

The first brandy had gone straight to my head, unaccustomed to drink as I now was, and on an empty stomach. I shook my head. "I'd love a water, though."

279

She went to the bar and when she returned I realised how drawn her face looked.

I said, "You're looking tired."

She gave me a weary grin. "Talking about Chris exhausts me."

"Thanks for doing it."

"No problem. Right," she said brusquely, all business, "it's like this. Chris did exactly the same thing with me as he did with you: he built me up, then systematically tore me down, and eventually, when he was tired of playing with me, broke it off with me." I listened avidly as she continued, "I was devastated for a while, deranged almost – well, you know that – you saw me at that party and you were in the house when I was making those phone calls. I'm not proud of it, but it's the truth. I mean, relationships break up all the time. It wasn't that. It was the whole thing about the – well, I can only call it the deconstruction of my personality. It seemed to me that he had done it deliberately. But that didn't make sense. I was asking the questions you've just asked – why would somebody do that?"

"And did you get answers?"

"No. Well, not from him. I did some research and found the answers myself. And what I came up with was this: I think – or rather, I'm pretty certain – that Chris is suffering from Narcissistic Personality Disorder, or NPD."

She looked at me to see how I was taking this, and I could only look back at her and shake my head in confusion.

"I never heard of it," I told her.

"No, neither had I. Neither have most people. Well, I'll try to explain this as best as I can, but don't forget, I'm only a layperson. I shouldn't even have offered this diagnosis, really. But having said that, I've been to a therapist since, to help me recover from this experience, and she has put me pretty much back together, thank God, and as best as she can judge from what I tell her, she agrees with me." She took a sip of her drink and then a deep breath. "Okay, here goes. Have you ever heard of Multiple Personality Disorder?"

"I think so," I said cautiously, "but I'm not sure exactly what it is."

"It's where a child experiences such awful abuse that he or she creates different personalities to go through the abuse, so the core, real, personality can safely retreat from experiencing it. Well, as far as I can gather, NPD is similar – it's also often caused by severe childhood abuse – but instead the core personality just retreats, disappears, and leaves *nothing* behind."

"Nothing?" I echoed, not really understanding.

"Nothing," she confirmed. "So you have somebody without a personality of their own. I can't even imagine what it must be like, to have no personality at all. To be literally Nobody."

"But he certainly seems to have his own personality," I said, confused.

"It can seem like that," she agreed. "NPDs like Chris construct what's called a False Self to portray to the world in place of their absent True Self. But truly, there is nothing there."

"It sounds terrifying," I ventured.

"Exactly!" She was doing her proud teacher thing again. "And it *is* terrifying to them. And because they can't ever know if they really exist, there's only one way they get proof of their existence and keep the terror at bay. And that's if somebody is paying them attention. Because obviously people don't pay attention to non-existent people. Okay?" she asked, to see if I was following her.

"Okay," I said tentatively. "It sounds mad, though."

"It does," she agreed. "It *is* mad. But it's a real disorder, recognised by professionals. I'm not making this up. Wish I was," she muttered.

"What happens then?" I asked her. "Why is this need for attention such a problem?"

"It's a problem because this proof that they exist only lasts *as long as* somebody's paying them attention. As soon as the attention is removed, so is the proof, and they're back to being Nobody. So they need this attention *constantly*. It's like a drug to them. Or more, it's like fresh air is to us. As basic and as essential as that. And everything they do, *everything*, is aimed at getting it."

"I see," I said for want of anything better to say. I didn't really, but hopefully it would start making sense at some stage.

"And that's where *you* come in," she said triumphantly, "and where *I* came in. We are the providers of the constant attention he needs."

"What do you mean?"

"An NPD creates his False Self to be your ideal, so that you will like and want to be with him, and therefore provide the attention he needs. He clinically studies people, gathering information about their desires and weaknesses. That's why he seemed so perfect when we first got to know him. He made it his business to seem perfect. To provide what we wanted."

"But Angela," I protested, "we all like attention. And we all put our best image forward in a new relationship."

"True. But although we all like attention, we can live without it. We don't *need* it. And we put forward the best aspects of our real genuine personality. We don't design a totally false personality based on our cynical study of what the other person wants."

"I wanted to belong," I said wonderingly. "I never felt I belonged in my family of origin. But Chris made me feel as if I belonged. In fact," I said, remembering now, "he even said that there was a Sally-shaped hole in his life that only I could fill."

"That's exactly what I mean," she said compassionately. "That's the sort of thing they do. Discover your weakness and then exploit it."

"You sound like an expert," I said, fascinated at what she was saying, but with a feeling of revulsion as if I was attending the autopsy of a slug.

"Do I? Well, I have spent hours and *hours* of my life learning this stuff. And I have resented every minute of that learning because it meant I was still defining my life by him, still playing his game. But I needed to understand in order to be free."

"But hang on," I protested, putting a halt to her gallop. "You're saying that he keeps us paying attention to him by being our ideal person, our perfect lover. But he *wasn't*, Angela, at least not for long."

"No –"

"It's true," I conceded, "that at the beginning he was like that. But he soon changed, and he has been cruel, insulting, intimidating, and downright *horrible* to me. And if you're right, he's even been going to a great deal of trouble to make me believe I was crazy."

Angela nodded. "I know it sounds contradictory. But it is a classic pattern of narcissists. It's called the Idealisation-Devaluation Process. They build you up until you think you're the most incredible person out – and of course, we all love feeling like that. But then they bring you down, and you have so far to fall it's not funny."

"Why on earth would they do that? It doesn't make sense."

"It does actually make sense, in a bizarre twisted NPD way. There's a couple of reasons. One is that the idealisation is so wonderful, and the devaluation so devastating, that some women spend their whole life trying to get back to the idealisation part. They think that if they just try harder, or love him more, or be more what he wants, that they'll get back to that magical place. And what the narcissist gets is what he wants – increased attention. Don't get me wrong," she said hastily as I opened my mouth with a gasp, "all relationships begin with a kind of idealisation and then move into a more reasonable rational place. But that's very different to the narcissist's method of deliberate idealisation and devaluation."

"No, no. That wasn't what I was going to say. I was going to say that's *exactly* what happened to me! I kept promising myself I'd make it all better, and that then he'd be nicer to me."

She shrugged, gesturing with her open palms, as if to say, *There you go.*

"But hang on," I continued, "you said they want attention. And I certainly wasn't adoring him after he changed. I was too tense, and scared, and worried about upsetting him."

"Hmm. Well, they do prefer positive attention like adoration, it's true. One of their unpleasant traits is that they think they're superior to everybody else, that they're God's gift to the rest of humanity, simply because they exist, and hence such positive regard is merely their birthright."

"He is a bit like that," I admitted, thinking back to how he had walked down Grafton Street on our first date, as if he owned it, and the crowds had parted to let him through.

"So, they would prefer positive attention like adoration. But, Sally, for them, *any* attention is good attention. Even bad attention proves to them that they exist, which is, always and forever, the object of the exercise. And when you were tense and scared and worried about upsetting him – what were you thinking about?"

"Well, him, of course."

"Exactly! It was bad attention, but it was still attention. In fact, there *are* good reasons – good reasons in the twisted logic of NPDs, at least – for them to actively choose the bad attention. Hang on until I get us another drink, and I'll explain it to you."

She stood and went to the bar, and while she was being served I tried to make sense of it. There were good reasons why he was being horrible to me? Why he was trying to make me think I was insane? I certainly could think of no good reasons, and I was dying to hear Angela's explanation.

"I got a soft drink for myself this time," Angela said when she came back. "No matter that talking about this could drive me to drink, I must keep a clear head. Anyway, I was going to tell you why NPDs start being horrible, wasn't that it? Even though they prefer the positive attention."

"That's right. I've been trying to figure it out and I just can't think of any reason why they might do that."

"You can't figure it out because you're a normal person thinking like normal people think. NPDs have their reasons though."

She began to enumerate on her fingers: "The first reason is that pretending to be the ideal lover is emotionally exhausting. It wears them out to do it for long. Second, acting as your ideal partner and making you feel wonderful has served its purpose of enticing you into their clutches, so why keep doing it? Do you keep washing a plate once it's clean?"

"No," I conceded, "I don't."

Angela nodded and continued, "And thirdly, they despise you, and so they treat you as the pathetic person they think you are."

"Why on earth would they despise me . . . us?"

"Oh, lots of reasons," she said cynically. "One is the very fact that you're in love with them. Because they see love, like all emotions, as weakness. *They* don't have any feelings. Only inferior people, the common herd, have feelings. So the stronger the love you feel, by definition the weaker a person you are and hence the worthier of being despised."

"This is *horrific*!" I said, shaking my head in disbelief.

"You don't know the half of it," she said sadly. "Another reason to stop treating you nicely is because they have a big conflict going on. Although they need your attention, they *hate* intimacy – both physical and emotional. But they had to pretend to want intimacy to entice you into the relationship."

"You mean he never wanted to be close to me, just pretended he did?"

"Exactly. And he soon had a problem. He had to stop this intimacy, but at the same time keep you around as an attention-provider. The perfect solution is this abrupt change in their treatment of you. They know there's a very good chance you'll stay, no matter the abuse, because you'll be trying to get back to the idealisation stage, trying to fix whatever's broken. But while that's going on, they don't have to be at all intimate with you."

"That's probably why the sex stopped," I realised.

"Oh, certainly. He soon found an excuse to stop sleeping with me too. No loss," she said bitterly. "Anyway, there's still a few more reasons to mistreat you. Do you want to hear them?"

"Go on," I said resignedly. Awful as it was, I needed to hear it.

"Okay. One thing is that they're angry. They're not angry because they're so different from everybody else – that's not a problem to them; they *like* being different from the rest of us – it's part of what's special about them."

"Why are they angry then?"

"Because the world won't acknowledge how unique and special and superior they are. And you're a handy target for taking that anger out on."

"Bloody hell," I said, shaking my head in despair.

"And here's another reason: They realise, at some level at least, that they need you for this constant attention, and they *hate* being needy, because that's a weakness. So they hate you because they need you, in the same way as smokers often hate cigarettes even as they long for them."

"This is incredible," I said on a sigh. "It's like a distorted fairground Hall of Mirrors."

"And there's more!" she declaimed sarcastically. "Another reason to mistreat you is that they hate, they absolutely *detest*, the idea of you being happy."

"Why would they possibly hate us being happy?" This was just getting more and more twisted.

"Because, if you're fundamentally happy you might get joy from anywhere, anywhere at all. I mean," she said ironically, "you might experience joy at a sunny day with fluffy clouds, or smile affectionately at overhearing a child's laughter, anything at all. And they cannot *stand* it that you are experiencing something, even as little as that, that doesn't come from them. They have to be the centre of your universe, and they can't do that through happiness because happy people get joy from everywhere." She gave a big sigh and continued, "But they can do it through misery, because the misery they inflict on you puts such filters in place that you don't even see the blue sky, or hear the laughing child."

It was so painfully true.

"*That's* why Chris tried to isolate you, convinced you to give up your job, and split you from your friend. The smaller your world is, the bigger a place he takes, proportionally, in it. The more important he becomes to you. The more he consumes your thoughts. The more attention you give him. So," she finished at last, "does *that* answer why he changed from being nice to you to mistreating you?"

"It all sounds so complicated. My head hurts even trying to follow all this."

"If it's hard for you to follow it, think what it's like to *be* it. An NPD's head must be a truly desolate, terrifying, nightmare place. I could nearly feel sorry for them. Until I think of the misery they cause. Having been Chris's victim," she said slowly and seriously, "has been almost beyond words. I have thought long and hard about how to describe the experience. And in the end I have come up with this: being an NPD victim is rape of the soul." Her face was drawn and haggard as she spoke.

"But," I wailed then, near tears, "I thought he loved me. I thought it was love at first sight because it all happened so quickly!"

"Speed isn't an indication of love," she said sadly, "not where Chris is concerned. He needed attention, and quickly. He just didn't have the time, nor the interest quite frankly, to woo you slowly."

"That's dreadful," I said. "And now, with what you're telling me, I have to rethink my whole future, but as well . . ." I paused to swallow back tears, "I'm having to rethink the past. Nothing is as I thought."

"I know," she agreed sadly. "And you need to hear the rest of it. I think Chris broke it off with me because it was time to move on to the next stage of his game. They also get easily bored, you see, so they change the game. I reacted as he expected, with total devastation. I begged him to come back to me – so he got even more attention."

"He liked you begging?"

"Of course! He got the attention *and* the proof of his wonderfulness. Then I went through a stage of being *furious* with him. Through furious and out the far side, actually. I had to vent my rage upon him. I was practically stalking him, ringing him all the time."

"I knew that," I murmured.

"And he *loved* it. All those phone calls . . . they were all wonderful attention to him."

"You know," I said slowly, "now that you say it, I remember a kind of heightened tension in him after those incidents. I put it down to stress, but it could have been enjoyment. It was as if he was energised by it all. And – " it was coming back to me now – "when you finally stopped phoning, he seemed disconcerted . . . in retrospect, almost *disappointed* . . . though at the time I thought he was just concerned . . . You know," I went on, realisation dawning, "that explains why he continued to take your calls. He said it was about letting you down gently. But he was feeding off your fury, isn't that right?"

"Exactly!"

"So how did you get over your anger enough to stop ringing? I could do with a few hints here," I gave a hollow laugh. "I can feel my own anger rising rapidly."

She laughed in acknowledgment and took another sip of her drink. "Get over my anger? I don't think I have. I may never get over having been so comprehensively used. But I signed up for an excellent forum on the Net for victims of NPDs. And one piece of advice kept coming up, over and over. And it was the hardest thing to do, but I recognised that they were right. It was this: let it go. Let it go."

"What do you mean?"

"What NPDs want from you is attention, remember. So, to win, stop paying them attention. Stop responding to them, or trying to contact them, or *anything*. It's so hard, because you feel you won't get closure unless they admit what they've done to you. But the only way to win is to stop playing."

"I don't understand."

"Can't you see," she said urgently, laying a hand on my arm. "It's a game you can never *ever* win. You will *never* get through to them, because there's nothing to get through to. And, by the very fact of playing the game, you're losing because you're providing them with attention. So the only way to even partially win is to quite simply stop playing." She laughed bitterly. "They *hate* when you do this. Chris certainly did. Once I stopped ringing him, he was lacking that source of attention. Even though he was getting it from you at that stage, they can never have too much. And so he started sniffing around me again. Ringing me, texting me, e-mailing me. Begging me to come back to him."

"What!" I shrieked, loud enough that people at

other tables looked around at me. "He was doing that! When he was with me?"

"Sally, Sally, Sally," Angela said wearily, "what bit of 'To him you only matter as a source of attention' did you not understand? He doesn't love you, he didn't ever love you, he doesn't even like you or acknowledge your humanity. Nothing personal," she added dryly.

"Right." It was all hurting so much. I could feel the pain sharp in my solar plexus.

"His begging me to come back is meaningless, Sally. He only wanted me back to prove he could, anyway. He only wanted me back so he could devalue me again."

"So I presume you told him to take a running jump?"

"Not immediately. You see, he came to me wearing his False Self personality. Like a shape-shifter in a medieval forest in the old fairytales. Wearing the personality I had fallen in love with. The one I had thought lost forever. And now here he was, come back to me, and begging me to return to him."

"And did you?" Not that it should matter. I now knew that Chris and I had had no relationship for him to betray.

She sighed and shook her head. "I wanted so much to do it. Even though I knew – from reading other people's experiences on the forum – that this was standard behaviour – even so, I was tempted. He was so convincing, so persuasive."

"And?" I breathed.

"And I somehow found my strength and I turned him down. He didn't believe me, of course. He had such confidence in his powers. He pursued me, but I ignored him. I used ignoring as a proactive tool."

"Ignoring as a proactive tool?"

"Yes. I simply deleted his texts and e-mails. I binned his letters unread – I wouldn't even return them, because even that would have been communicating in some way. I was pretty sure he was following my on-line communications, so I stopped reading the NPD forums, although that was tough – they were a source of support and comfort for me. But if he knew I was reading up on NPD he'd know I was still thinking of him."

"Does he know he has NPD, then?" I asked, and then a thought hit me. "But, Angela, if he has NPD then he's ill, not bad. And he can be cured, surely. He could go to a psychologist and get sorted. What? Why not?" I finished, because Angela was shaking her head.

"I think he *does* know he has NPD. I've certainly told him I think he does. And he was *fascinated*. We spoke about it at length one evening. Until finally it occurred to me what was going on – he and I were involved in an hours-long in-depth discussion about *him*. Narcissistic heaven!"

"But *could* he get treatment?" I persisted.

She shook her head. "Forget it. NPDs think they're superior to everybody else – why on earth would they want to be cured of that? They despise the common herd who are prey to messy emotions – they don't want to become one of them."

"Oh." I realised that my throat was very dry. I took a sip of my water.

Angela continued, "Having said all that, NPDs *have* gone for therapy – but it's always a farce. They actually love therapy because it's talking about them! But they don't want to make any changes, and so they don't. According to my therapist, psychologists consider NPD to be incurable."

"So there's no hope, then?"

"Not for Chris. Nor for your relationship. But there's hope for you, Sally, if you'll take it."

"I'll take it!" I promised her. "I'll be out of there so fast . . ."

"One thing you might remember. You might blame yourself for having fallen for this, for letting him treat you so badly. And others might blame you for putting up with it. 'You should have had more self-respect than to put up with this. Why didn't you get out sooner,' they might well think. Or say."

"I see what you mean. Now that you're pointing it all out it seems so *obvious* that it was an awful situation. Why *did* I put up with it? I was even rationalising his behaviour, saying that he was under stress and so on. And I remember deciding that he wasn't abusive, because he never hit me."

"Well, emotional abuse is just as real as physical abuse, you know. But he was clever. He eroded your self-esteem so gradually and skilfully you weren't aware of it And, too, you thought you were cracking up."

"That's true," I said thoughtfully.

"Also," she said, taking a sip of her drink, "NPDs have the gift of being able to make the abnormal seem normal. And seemingly all victims – of any trauma – are prone to doing that too, as a survival mechanism. So it's not surprising that we start accepting what's going on as being totally normal. It's natural human behaviour, Sally, not weakness. Also, there's another advantage for them in isolating us. Whether they know this or not, it creates Stockholm Syndrome."

"What's that?" My head was spinning with all this information.

Angela was happy to tell me. "It's a process whereby hostages actually bond with the hostage-takers, but it applies to abuser and abused too."

"Why on earth would they do that? That's ridiculous!" I told her indignantly.

"It's *not* ridiculous. Being in a hostage situation is stressful for hostage and hostage-taker alike, and going through something deeply emotional with somebody bonds us to them. And everything's so uncertain when you're a hostage, and the hostage-taker provides your only chance of certainty, and your food and other needs. Exactly," she said with emphasis, "as Chris provided *your* certainty, and food and so on."

"I see," I said slowly, "that's exactly right. That's what I was doing with Chris, clinging to him as my only security. The more miserable I became, the more I clung to him."

"Now you know why," she said kindly. "Forgive yourself for it."

"I will," I promised her, although I suspected it mightn't be as easy as that. "But what made him be like that?" I asked wonderingly. "You said it was very bad abuse, but he told me he had an idyllic childhood."

She snorted her derision at that. "Pathological liar," she reminded me. "By definition, if he has NPD he didn't have an idyllic childhood. Though there is a twist: NPD is the result either of severe abuse or, some psychologists think, such an amount of indulgence and devotion that it amounts to abuse."

"How can indulgence and devotion amount to abuse? I wouldn't have minded a bit more of that myself," I said dryly.

"Normal indulgence and devotion are great. Essential even. But sometimes parents love, not the child themselves, but their image of the child. They don't care about the child himself, but what that child represents for them, and how well the child reflects on them and their success as parents. And so the child grows up not existing as a person. That's where such NPDs have the twin aspects of thinking they're superior, because they've been over-adored all their lives, and at the same time having no personality of their own." She sighed. "So, I suppose that an NPD *could* think that the over-indulgent childhood was idyllic. But Chris belongs to the other category. I'm a researcher by profession, Sally, and I did some digging. Resenting it all the time, but I needed to know."

"And what did you find out?"

"I spoke to old neighbours, and they spoke of alcoholic parents, a filthy house, an extremely thin and underdressed child – you know, going out in the depths of winter in just a shirt, that sort of thing."

"Why didn't they do anything?" I asked, horrified.

She shrugged. "Sally, it was thirty years ago. The

culture was very different. People just said to each other how awful it was and let it go."

"True," I acknowledged. It was heartbreaking, but weren't there similar stories all too often in the paper?

But even as I was saying this I was thinking, *There's something inconsistent here. Something Angela is missing. Or leaving out.*

"Look," she suddenly said, "it's lunch-time already. Would you like some food?"

I looked around to see that, unnoticed while we spoke, the pub had filled up. I became aware for the first time of the sound of other people's conversations, the clink of glasses and crockery, and above all the smell of hot comforting food. Suddenly I experienced something I had not felt for a long time: hunger. I was ravenous.

"I'd love to," I said. "I'm starving. Let me get it, to thank you for your help. I'll put it on the credit card."

"How will you pay the credit card?" she asked shrewdly. "No, let me pay."

"Thank you." It made sense, but it was still so, so, humiliating.

We made our way to the food counter. I was dizzy with the excitement of realising that I *wasn't* going mad, and I piled my plate high. "Some more potatoes please," I asked, and even though the chef looked in disbelief from my tiny frame to the already-laden plate, he complied.

We went back to the table and I tucked in, with more panic and savagery than actual enjoyment. But still, the physical sensation of food going into my mouth, into my stomach, was hedonistic in the extreme, and I was enjoying every moment of it.

"Steady," warned Angela. "You've said you haven't eaten properly for a while. Take it handy enough. You don't want to get sick and spoil it all."

"True," I said through a mouthful of food, and after that I forced myself to slow down, to chew each mouthful, to savour it all.

We didn't speak much as we ate. But as I chewed in near silence it came to me: the flaw in what Angela had been saying about Chris's childhood.

"You're saying that Chris was lying when he claimed an idyllic childhood. But you know, it isn't just Chris saying that. It's his sister too." For I had remembered those e-mails from Sheila, in which she described a most enviable childhood.

"His sister?" queried Angela, one eyebrow raised.

"Yes," I said, "his sister Sheila. The one who lives in Australia."

She shook her head. "Chris doesn't have any sisters, in Australia or anywhere else. He's an only child."

"He *does* have a sister. We e-mail every so often."

"Indeed," she said, looking less than certain of herself for the first time. "Well, that's very interesting. Chris certainly never told me about any sister. And none of his old neighbours mentioned one either. But, to be fair, they didn't specifically say he didn't have a sister either. Maybe he lied to me about being an only child. Who's to know? But, you know, that still doesn't take away from my basic premise. *Something's* seriously wrong with Chris, and my best guess is this NPD caused by an abusive childhood. But maybe there's something else wrong with him. Or maybe he does have a sister and she's equally messed up, equally in denial about their childhood. I don't know. But, I repeat, it doesn't take away from the basic fact that Chris has been emotionally abusing you and messing with your head."

"True," I said, but I was still puzzling over this inconsistency.

After we had both eaten all we wished, and our plates were cleared by a smiling waitress, Angela sat back into the chair, took a sip of her cola, and asked me, "How are you feeling?"

"Delighted to discover I'm not crazy! Or infertile. But terrified now of the future."

"You'll manage," she said confidently. "You're strong. You must be, to have managed as well as you have."

I glowed under her praise, the first kind words I had heard in many months.

"So . . . you said you're going to leave him . . . " she said, her tone casual but her intent expression belying that.

"Absolutely! Can you even doubt it?"

She shrugged. "It's a hard step all the same, especially when you're so demoralised anyway. But, well done for deciding it. Having said that, you need to know this. Remember that NPDs are very simple. They want attention, as we've said. Any kind of attention. And there's one kind of attention they can get from you even in your absence."

"What's that?"

"Fear," she said. "If you're scared of them, you're still thinking of them."

"Are you saying he might be violent towards me?" I gasped, sitting forward in my stress and fear.

"I don't know. It's not likely. They're not usually violent, by all accounts."

"Oh right," I said, relieved, relaxing back into my chair.

However, Angela was shaking her head. "But there have been cases . . . NPD was used as the defence in a murder case in England recently. And there have been certainly a few cases here, of husbands killing wives, where I've been certain the men were NPD."

"Oh God," I breathed, and Angela grimaced sympathetically at me.

"Also, don't forget their inherent arrogance. Because they think they're superior to others, and cleverer than anybody else, they often think they're above the law, or too clever to be caught. By the time they're proven wrong, it's too late for the victim."

I was feeling most anxious again. Actually, *petrified*.

But Angela was continuing, putting the other side of the argument. "But on the other hand, a dead woman can't provide any attention. And because he's so superior he won't want to end up in prison with all the *criminals*. That would be *so* beneath him. Besides the attention they need is probably very limited in jail. So you're probably okay."

"That's good," I said, relaxing a little back into my chair.

"Hopefully so. But when I mentioned fear, I was talking about the fear involved in stalking."

"Stalking?" I echoed. This wasn't much better.

"A lot of narcissists end up stalking their victims. I'm sorry," she said, seeing my strained expression, "but you need to know this. You're trapped in a web and it mightn't be that easy to free yourself.

"Oh God," I whispered.

"It mightn't happen, Sally. It all depends. If he soon gets a new source of Narcissistic Supply, he might just write you off with a shrug and forget you. But if he's a bit short, he might stalk you just so you're always thinking about him, and wondering when he'll next show up, and planning your days around avoiding him."

"That's terrifying," I whispered.

Angela shrugged. Not, it seemed to me, that she didn't care. But she shrugged the way one shrugs about inclement weather or politicians: in a way which simultaneously acknowledges both their adverse impact and the impossibility of doing anything about them. "One thing that's bound to happen is that he'll try to discredit me and all that I have told you. That is, if he finds out somehow that we've met – and I wouldn't put it past him. If he can discredit what I've told you, then you have no reason to leave."

"No, that's true," I agreed.

"And NPDs are very, very good at using what looks like logic to get their way. They spin your head around so much you'd end up agreeing that black was white. So just watch out for that."

"Okay," I said.

"At the end of the day, you've got to trust your

instincts. And while people with NPD are very charming when they want to be, all the information I have read is that people, real people like us, always recognise them at some level. And when we trust our instincts, we recognise them. Trust your instincts," she urged.

"Okay," I said again.

"Now," she said, leaning forward in her chair and speaking very intently to me, "I have done, I think you'll agree, far more than my fair share. I had to rearrange meetings at short notice. I've given you," she glanced at her watch, "all this time, and I've taken this full day off work – I certainly won't be fit to go back to work now. But, more important than any of that, for the sake of my own recovery, this meeting has to be closure on Chris Malley for me."

"I understand. And I'm so grateful, Angela. More than I can ever say."

"In that case, pay it forward. See if you can help his next victim, as I have helped you."

"I'll try," I promised.

"Good. I'll be off now. Goodbye." She stood and began to gather her belongings.

"Goodbye. Thanks again." The words seemed so weak compared to the gift she had given me. The gift of returning to me my sanity, my fertility, my self-esteem and the key to my freedom.

She nodded at me, said, "Oh, yes, and don't forget – believe *nothing* that comes out of his mouth."

Then she turned and walked across the room, out the door and out of my life.

* *· *

I sat there and thought about what she had said. I struggled to assimilate it all.

The last nine months of my life had been a total lie.

Everything I had believed to be reality was now totally inversed.

Chris and I were not lovers and partners, we were consumer and consumed.

My head swirled with the volume and enormity of these thoughts spinning around inside it, trying to make sense of them all, trying to come to terms with the new reality I was now dealing with.

I knew that there was an avalanche of pain and hurt waiting to engulf me when I had the luxury of time and space to be so engulfed, but for now they had to wait.

I knew that as soon as I let myself really realise – really get it – that not only was I nothing to Chris, but I had *never, ever,* been anything to him – not a love, not a girlfriend, not even a fellow-human, just so much material to feed his need for Narcissistic Supply – that then it would be like being whirled through a tornado. But that too would have to wait.

And yet I experienced the most incredible, enormous sense of relief, so much so that I wanted to burst out laughing, right there in the pub, with the joy and release of it all. I *wasn't* crazy, I wasn't! I was tricked into believing so, and then saw the portents of madness everywhere. I was manipulated into this deep dark hole where I could see only Chris.

That was it, I realised as I pursued my train of thought. He wanted me to see only him. Angela had mentioned that he had surrounded me with a filter of misery. But it was more than that. He had enclosed me in a filter of him-ness, where everything had to pass through him before it became part of my reality. And, of course, he was distorting everything.

Now the question was, how was I to regain my sense of true reality? Regain my life? Regain my Self?

I sat there in the nearly-empty pub, nursing the dregs of my glass of water, and pondered this question.

I had to leave him. There was no question about that. I had to go.

It was scary to think of going, of starting again with nothing. But when a small voice whispered to me that I *could* stay, that it would be easier not to rock the boat, I dismissed it immediately. It was a boat which was on the rocks surrounded by shark-infested seas, taking in water and already sinking and breaking up slowly, if that's not stretching a metaphor too far.

But where would I go? All my original arguments still applied: I couldn't go back to my mother as a failure. I couldn't go to Gaby's – no matter what Angela had said, I had heard what I had heard, and that was Gaby admitting Chris's accusation.

I could go to David's! My original reason for not going to him was that I couldn't inflict my craziness on him. But if I wasn't crazy – and yet again I experienced the sweet and delicious elation of knowing that – then I *could* go to him. No matter that I didn't know him that well, he had offered, and I had no other options. That's what I would do! Oh, the relief and joy of a decision made! I had to hope he still wanted me, of course. That the offer was still available.

Oh! The hand which had been lifting the glass to my lips froze halfway as the thought struck me. If I wasn't crazy then I could get a job! I *could* support myself! Oh, this was just getting better and better!

I couldn't get a job immediately, I acknowledged. I was too worn down with stress and exhaustion and, to be blunt, malnutrition, to be able to hold down a job straightaway. But once I recovered, I would! I wouldn't be a burden on David at all, or at least, not for long.

But what was my immediate plan? I looked at my watch – it was coming up for three o'clock. As usual Chris could be back at any time from now until about ten o'clock. That unpredictability, I was now realising, was probably part of his manipulation: to keep me uncertain and always on edge waiting for the sound of his key in the door.

Anyway, I mentally shrugged, that wasn't going to be my problem for very much longer.

But it meant that I wasn't going to be able to pack my stuff today and just leave. Not without risking him arriving home and intercepting me.

I didn't want him to know I was leaving. There was the faint chance that he might hurt me. But even if that wasn't the case, I knew I was too weak emotionally to face whatever tirade or arguments he could come up with as I trundled to and fro from the car with my belongings. Masters of twisted logic, Angela had said. I didn't want to face that.

I would do nothing tonight, I decided. I would pretend it was just another night. And tomorrow morning I would ring David as soon as Chris left for work – I'd get the

TRACY CULLETON

number of the gym from the phone book since Chris had taken his mobile number from me. And assuming he was still agreeable to putting me up, I would pack and leave then, long before Chris got home.

That idea pleased me. After all, I had stayed with him all this time. What difference could one more night make?

306

Chapter 29

Accordingly I finished off the last drops of my mineral water and made my way back to Chris's house.

I was blazing with courage and determination and ambition and freedom, and it felt great! After so long thinking so badly of myself, it was great to be able to consider that maybe possibly – in fact, quite likely – I was competent and capable.

I debated with myself. Maybe I *should* leave today. Just get my passport and other essential documentation, abandon all my other possessions, and go. Because otherwise how would I get through the evening? How good an actress was I really?

On the other hand, I could just be quiet when he came home. He wouldn't particularly notice anything – I had mostly been quiet lately after all. The evening would pass, and in the morning I could contact David, pack and move out before he got back from work.

But, I argued, Angela had said there was a small

possibility he might be violent. And I probably couldn't fool him that everything was as it had been. Not only was I not a good actress, but I would be under such strain. It just wouldn't work.

I *would* leave today, I decided. I would go back to the house, get my documentation and just walk out. Drive over to *Svelte* and throw myself on David's mercy. And if he couldn't help me . . . well, I'd just have to go to my mother's after all. Desperate times call for desperate measures and all that.

But when I opened the front door I realised that all my discussion had been totally academic. To judge from the aromatic smell of sautéing onions and garlic, Chris was home already. I couldn't make a discreet exit now. Okay, back to Plan A. I'd do the best job I could of pretending everything was normal, and leave in the morning.

"Hi," said Chris cheerfully, coming into the hall to meet me.

His expression was open and honest, his demeanour relaxed and happy. No sign anywhere of the perpetual scowl of the recent past, nor the menacing oppressive body language, nor any of the trio of conversational gambits: berate, grunt, or ignore.

"I'm just preparing dinner," he told me. "Would you like to have a glass of wine with me while it's cooking?"

"Sure," I said, uncertainly, and followed him into the kitchen.

"Sit down. Sit down," he said as he poured a glass of red wine with a flourish and passed it into my hand.

"Cheers," he said, raising his own glass to me before

placing it down on the worktop. He then turned the contents of the saucepan into a casserole dish and put it in the oven.

He picked up his glass and joined me at the table.

"Tell me," he said conversationally, "did you have a good time with Angela today?"

I became very, very still. Like a deer does when faced with a hunter, hoping against hope that she will escape unnoticed.

"What?" I asked, stalling. "Wh – what do you mean?" I was searching for the right mixture of confusion and interest in my tone.

He smiled at me benevolently, his smile relaxed and his blue gaze gentle. "I mean exactly what I said," he said kindly. "Did you have a good time with Angela today?"

"How . . ." I swallowed urgently although my mouth was suddenly very dry, "how did you know I was with Angela?"

"Aha," he said, and tapped the side of his nose conspiratorially. He even winked. "I know a *lot* of things, Sally. You should realise that by now."

"I know you do. You're very clever," I said, remembering that his desire was for admiration.

"I am, amn't I?" He preened a little while I still stared at him, totally unsure what I should do, or how this was going to end up.

He seemed to come to a decision then. It seemed that the desire to keep me guessing had been warring with the desire to impress me, and the latter won.

"The thing is, I *didn't* know you met Angela today. I only guessed."

"Guessed?" I repeated for want of anything better to say.

"Yes, indeed. I pressed redial to make an outgoing call, not realising that you had used the phone since I had, and when I got through to her mobile message-minder I guessed you had phoned her – well, it wasn't me! And then when you were out for hours it seemed like a fair bet to guess that you had met her. And your reaction when I said it proved it. That was it," he said, trying for a modest tone, "no mystery at all."

"You were still very clever to think it all through like that," I said, as warmly as I could manage. Thinking: yeah, I really bet you 'just happened' to press redial. You've probably been somehow following all my phone calls.

"Thank you," he acknowledged the compliment. "But Sally, you still haven't answered my question."

"What question was that?"

He shook his head sadly. "Oh, that memory!" he said playfully. "Your brain is still letting you down! The question was: did you have a nice time with Angela?"

"Yes, thanks. I had a lovely time," I said politely.

"Only one thing you have in common," he pointed out.

"That's right," I said, playing to him, "you."

"Yes, me," he said proudly. "I presume my name cropped up in conversation."

"Once or twice," I acknowledged.

"And did she spin you some tale about this supposed disorder she's decided I have?" he asked, his tone a little bit more serious now. But still kind, still benign.

There was no threat emanating from him whatsoever. And that was nearly scarier.

I looked at him, not sure what would be the best way to respond.

It appeared, however, that the question was rhetorical as he answered it himself.

"I'd say she did. She loves sprouting that theory. I mean," he shook his head in disbelief and a little pity too, "how pathetic can you get? A man breaks up with her, and she's so egotistical she has to go trawling until she finds this half-baked theory as to why he did it." He smiled at me, shaking his head in disbelief and inviting me to join in with the joke. "The fact that she's a cantankerous ugly old bat who he couldn't stand to be near for another minute wasn't enough of a reason, oh no. She had to find some explanation which made it all his fault."

He gave a short laugh, and I smiled at him, tremulously, uncertainly.

He continued, "And it had to be illness to boot. No ordinary reason would explain why anybody would break up with Angela Hanly. A man would have to be suffering from a whole personality disorder – *that* would be the only possible reason that she could imagine for somebody to finish with her. The arrogance of it!" He shook his head again. "She's mad. I told you she's mad – you saw it yourself at that party, didn't you?"

"Well . . ." I said neutrally.

"So tell me," he said conversationally, "you didn't happen to buy into that bullshit, did you? By any chance?" He looked intently at me, waiting for an answer.

What on earth was I going to say? I searched for inspiration within a brain which was suddenly blank.

"A lot of what she said made sense," my mouth said, even as my brain was rushing in saying, *No, don't antagonise him*.

"Like what?" Chris enquired lightly.

Anybody coming into the room would have sworn we were engaged in the most frivolous of light banter, two affectionate lovers sitting around a kitchen table, enjoying a post-workday glass of wine and catching up on all the news.

"Like, my so-called Senior Moments *could* all be attributed to you trying to convince me I was going crazy. Like, you were very nice when we met, but have been unremittingly nasty to me for ages. Like, you have systematically isolated me."

I waited for the yelling to start, for him to flail me with derision and sneers.

But he remained kindly. He even shook his head in admiration of sorts. "She did a great job on you, didn't she? Managed to take facts and twist them to fit her bizarre theories. The reality is that you *have* been having these Senior Moments, and I don't know why they started when you moved in here, but it's nothing to do with me. Did she actually suggest," he asked incredulously, "that I – I – was deliberately faking incidents to make you think you were going crazy?"

I shrugged my shoulders in what I hoped was a noncommittal way.

He gave a hollow derisive laugh. "God, she's some piece of work," he said shaking his head at the thoughts of it. "She really is. And don't tell me, Sally, just don't tell me you believed her. That would be the ultimate insanity on your behalf. It really would. Well, did you?" he insisted when I didn't answer.

"It did seem too much of a coincidence," I ventured.

"It probably *isn't* a coincidence," he agreed. "You getting these amnesiac episodes probably *was* related to moving in here. But maybe it was due to the stress of getting used to living with somebody. The pressure of adjustment. But she had the cheek, the sheer *cheek* to suggest that I was doing it deliberately! Why would I even do that? What would be in it for me?"

It did sound silly when he put it like that. "Well," I ventured, "because of this – this Narcissistic Personality Disorder – "

"Ah yes," he interrupted, "this personality disorder I'm supposed to have. Come on, Sally, how plausible is this? I have this bizarre mental illness which nobody has ever heard of, and it makes me be nasty to people for the fun of it, and makes me deliberately convince you that you're mad for no good reason." He sighed and raised his eyes to heaven in frustration. "Christ, how gullible are you anyway?" he asked me rhetorically. "Or is this more likely: that guy was right when he said that hell hath no fury like a woman scorned, and he wasn't even allowing for *her* craziness." He paused, glaring at me. "And what other 'evidence'," he made inverted commas in the air around the word, "does she come up with for this disorder? The fact that I was nice to you to start with and then have been nasty to you, you say?"

"Well, yes . . ." I said, trailing weakly off.

"Sally, we have discussed this before – *I* think that I have been remarkably patient given all I have had to put up with. And yes, I concede, that I have been sharp sometimes, but come on, I've had to put up with a lot. I try to be patient, but sometimes it gets to me. I'm sorry for that, but that makes me human, Sally, not psychotic or whatever else she said I was. And what was the last thing you said? That I was isolating you? Well, I'm sorry," he said, holding his open hands out and shrugging, "if telling you the truth about your friend betraying you, and giving you the chance to make your dreams come true, qualify as isolating you, then yes, I'm guilty of that. I'm sorry." He swore under his breath, and then continued with his speech, "Honestly, if I'd realised I was going to get into this much trouble for it all I would have kept quiet about Gaby's disloyalty and let you carry on with your friendship in blissful ignorance. And I would have left you carry on with your routine job and go to your grave with your dreams unreached for. Guilty as charged on that one, I'm afraid."

He stopped then and looked at me, waiting for my verdict, and there was a world of sorrow in his eyes, and hope, and betrayal, and anguish.

"I'm sorry," I said, not even sure what I was apologising for. Or even if I meant any apology or was just going through the motions.

"It's okay," he said. "Come here to me," and as he spoke he stood and I stood too and we moved towards each other, and he held out his arms and I went into his embrace and he hugged me tight. Into my hair he said, "It'll be okay, Sally. It'll all be okay. You'll see. With patience you'll get your head together. We'll be happy. You'll see. I love you, Sally. I hate it when we fight."

"Me too," I said.

He briefly tightened his grip upon me and then said, "Sit down and I'll top up your wine. I've some good news to tell you."

I sat and as he poured some more wine he continued chattily, "I was going to tell you when you came in, but then we got distracted with that other conversation. Wait till you hear! I've got a new contract! A three-year security contract with a big multinational!"

"That's great!" I said, rather unconvincingly I have to admit. But Chris didn't seem to notice.

"We're back on the pig's back, Sal. We really are," he said exuberantly. "We can rehire Mrs Butler to look after the house – you won't be sorry to hand that task over, I'm sure!" he laughed. "You can go back to your novel – if you want," he added hastily, "only if you want. Or you can take some time just for yourself, time to relax and recover. Go to a spa regularly; pamper yourself; get back to being yourself; figure out what you'd like to do after that. What do you think of that?"

"That's great news!" I said again, making more of an effort to sound enthusiastic. "Well done, you! You must have really impressed them."

"Yes, well," he said modestly, "they obviously were taken with my proposal. And though I say so myself, I did present it very well. And I *do* know my stuff – that always helps, of course."

While the meal finished cooking and then when we were eating it, we spoke of his new contract, and his hopes that that would lead to other contracts – where this huge company led, it was reasonable to anticipate that others would follow.

It was all very exciting and seemed to show that we could get our lives back on track.

But somehow I couldn't really get into it. I was studying Chris as he spoke. Was any of this true? Could I trust *anything* he said?

Chapter 30

According to Angela, nothing of what Chris said was true. She had predicted this turnaround, after all. Crazy things *had* started happening around me just when I moved in with him. And he *had* said awful things to me. And I *had* ended up isolated once I got involved with him.

But away from Angela's strong personality, I realised that Chris's side of it was equally plausible.

Just because he *could* have done those crazy-seeming things, didn't mean that he *had*. His presence at most of those episodes could be explained by – for example – me being tense around him, trying to impress him, a little nervous in his presence. And there *had* been amnesiac moments when he wasn't there, no matter how glibly Angela had explained those away.

And he was right about his saying these nasty things. If he was innocent of orchestrating these Senior Moments, then he did have a lot to put up with. It was reasonable that he should be frustrated and annoyed, and understandable, as he had pointed out, that he sometimes was less than kind.

And as for isolating me – well, he had answered that one himself. Far from accusing him, I should be grateful to him for trying to help me with my dream. True, I hadn't really expressed that dream until he pushed me, and he had been a little heavy-handed in arranging it all without consulting me. But since when was enthusiasm a crime?

And how much of an honest broker was Angela anyway? She wasn't exactly an unbiased party. As Chris had pointed out, she *did* have an issue surrounding him breaking it off with her. She *had* been crazy, even by her own admission, and who was to say she wasn't crazy now, doing her best to spoil Chris's next relationship?

"– wouldn't you say so?" said Chris.

"What? Sorry, Chris, I was miles away."

"And Angela would probably say that's my fault too," he said jocularly, "along with global warming and world hunger. God knows what else she's accused me of."

"She just said that she thought you were ill, that you had this disorder because of your troubled childhood."

"*What* troubled childhood?" he roared, and then calmed himself with a visible effort. "Sorry, sorry. Sorry for shouting. God, this is so twisted. She's saying all sorts about me and for all I know when I react to what she said I'm playing into her hands, showing myself to be less than sane or reasonable. But honestly, Sally, she's making all this stuff up. This is the first I heard of any troubled childhood. I already told you that I had a pretty much idyllic childhood, and that's the truth."

"I see," I said.

"I don't know how I can prove any of this to you. Unless . . . hang on a second. Did Sheila make any reference to our childhood in her e-mails to you? Not that that's proof," he said bitterly. "For all I know Angela has an answer to that too. For all I know she'd say that, because of this bloody disorder, I put Sheila up to describing some perfect childhood even though it was awful."

He shook his head, and part of me felt so sorry for him, but another part didn't know what to believe.

"Well?" he insisted. "What has Sheila told you?"

"That you were both very happy, and had a wonderful childhood," I admitted.

"So it *does* sort of prove that I am telling the truth," he said hopefully. "Circumstantially, at least."

"It does indeed," I said, heavily. "It does indeed."

"Come on and we'll get these dishes into the dishwasher," he said, standing and signalling that the meal was over.

"Sure," I said, standing and preparing to make an effort, if Chris was.

But Angela had said that he would react like this.

How much of it was true? I had no way of knowing.

Trust your instincts, Angela had said. But I had no instincts, or if I had, they were well buried. I didn't know who to believe.

I felt like nothing so much as a scrap of ragged cloth which two dogs were fighting over, and the cloth was getting more and more ragged and saliva-stained as the dogs growled and snarled over possession of it. And neither of them even cared about the cloth *per se*. All each cared about was beating the other.

"Actually, Chris, do you mind if I sit down? My head is pounding." It was too, a pain like a vice right across my temples and forehead, squeezing me so that I just simply couldn't think.

"Of course not," he said, his voice warm and solicitous. He came to me and placed a hand on my forehead. "You do feel warm, poor thing. Will I run you a hot bath, and then you can tuck up in bed?"

"That would be lovely," I said smiling wearily at him. "Thank you." A bath would give me some space away from him, away from my thoughts.

We went upstairs and he went into the bathroom and began running the taps. I went into the bedroom and stripped off my clothes, put on my towelling bathrobe, then lay down on my bed and listened to the sound of the bath being filled. Even that noise seemed to pound agonisingly against my head. It seemed to go on and on and on. But eventually the sound stopped and a moment later there was a gentle knock on the door and I heard Chris call me softly.

"Your bath's ready," he told me.

"Thanks, Chris," I told him, and pulled myself wearily to my feet and made my way to the bathroom.

He hovered hesitantly, then said, "Well, I'll leave you to it."

"Thanks," I said again. "I'll come downstairs after the bath."

He clearly recognised this for the dismissal it was and went to leave the room. But before he did so he turned back to me.

"Get out of the bath before you let the plug out," he suggested. "You're so thin you might slide down the plughole!"

It took me by surprise, the sudden hurtful barb. "That's not very nice," I told him.

"Ah Sally, don't tell me you've lost your sense of humour as well as everything else," he said sadly as he left the room.

I looked after him thinking that some 'jokes' just weren't funny, were downright hurtful.

I shucked off the bathrobe, carefully avoiding the reflection of my wasted body, and slipped into the water. Chris had added some of my remaining lavender bath oil, I noted, and its scent filled my nostrils and calmed me. I lay back in the bath with my eyes closed, and gave myself up to the sensation of heat and comfort and embrace.

He never rings her.

The thought popped into my head with such velocity that my eyes popped open at the impact of it and I sat up reflexively. In all this time that I had known him, Chris had never, to the best of my knowledge, phoned, nor received a call from, Sheila. I know that Australia's a long way away, and there are time difference logistics, and nobody's likely to phone frequently.

But not once in nine whole months? Not one phone call between a brother and sister as close as Chris and Sheila? The only remnants of their family? Chris had

had his birthday in October, and there had been no call even then. There was a card all right. But it was already on the mantelpiece when I saw it – I hadn't seen it arrive in the post. Likewise with a Christmas card. That could all mean nothing – I might just not have been around when the postman arrived.

He never rings her, said a small voice insistently.

But that didn't necessarily mean anything. E-mail has taken over so much of our communication these days. They could be texting regularly and I wouldn't know either. Or they could have been phoning when I wasn't around. Mind you, these past few months I was never not around. It niggled at me.

I lay back down in the water and fanned one of my legs slightly to create little waves which then wafted over me, warming my body further.

I thought about it: either Chris was telling the truth, or Angela was. There was no in-between. Chris had a fair point when he pointed out that Angela had motivation to stir things between us, while he had no motivation to do those things of which she had accused him. No motivation, that is, unless I accepted the diagnosis of NPD, which did seem quite far-fetched, really.

But yet Angela had sounded very sincere, and very calm too – she hadn't sounded like she was in such throes of jealousy that she was going to try to wreck our relationship for the sake of it.

I could do a search for NPD on the Web and see if it was a real disorder. Even if it was, of course, that didn't mean that Chris was suffering from it. But if it transpired that there was no such thing, then it proved that Angela had made everything up.

But if Angela had made everything up, I realised with my heart sinking, that meant that Chris didn't have any personality disorder, and therefore no motivation to set me up with iron-burnt shirts and machine-washed mobile phones. And *that* meant that I was back to square one – I was crazy.

Did that mean, I asked myself, that I *wanted* to discover that Chris had this disorder because, if he did, it let me off the hook of being crazy? And if so, what kind of person did that make me? Not a very nice one, I acknowledged ruefully.

And if I did discover, as best as I could, that Chris had this NPD-thingy, then that meant the end of the relationship. Actually, that meant that we had never had a relationship. But it meant the end of any pretence at one.

And *that* meant I had to throw myself on David's charity and crawl my way back to some semblance of a life for myself. No more boyfriend, no more cosy cohabiting, no more smug coupledom. No more feeling settled and somehow *arrived* in my life.

It meant uncertainty and being alone and starting all over again with nothing. With less than I had had before actually, because now I had nowhere to live, no job, no concentration and no confidence.

Why did they never ring each other? That question was nagging away at the back of my mind.

And then I let myself acknowledge a thought I had been resisting with all my might. A question whose enormity threatened to overwhelm me.

It was this: did Sheila even exist?

Angela thought Chris was an only child.

Of course, Angela could be lying. But why would she tell a lie which could so easily be checked? And when I told her that Sheila's account of a happy childhood seemed to contradict her own theory of an abusive one, her reaction hadn't been one of somebody who had been caught out. She had seemed puzzled and confused, rather. She had genuinely seemed as if she was hearing this for the first time.

And it occurred to me as I lay there in the now-cooling water, that the existence or otherwise of Sheila would prove or disprove Chris's integrity. It was that simple.

If she *didn't* exist, then Chris had perpetrated a major lie upon me, and nothing else he said could be relied upon.

So, did she exist?

The only evidence in favour of her existence was that Chris spoke of her, and she wrote e-mails, and perhaps sent cards.

I could discount the fact that Chris spoke about her. Chris's integrity depended on Sheila's existence.

I could discount the birthday and Christmas cards – Chris could easily have written them himself.

And so. The e-mails.

They meant nothing. Nobody, even somebody as untechnical as I, could fail to be aware of people creating false identities over the Internet. Paedophiles did it all the time. And look how easy it had been to get my own e-mail address. Nobody had checked I was who I said I was. And while I had signed up for an Irish e-mail account, the website on which I had signed up was available to anybody anywhere in the world. Similarly I could go to an Australian e-mail address provider and choose an Australian e-mail address, no problem. And if I could do it, so could Chris who was an expert on such matters.

So, my getting e-mails was actually no proof at all that Sheila existed.

And, following that thought to its logical conclusion – every communication I had had with 'her', was, if I was on the right track, really communication with Chris.

"Oh God!" I groaned as I thought of Chris reading what I had written, thinking he would never see it. Declarations of love, statements of adoration. And Chris could have been reading this, and laughing over it, and sucking his needed attention from it.

It was, as Angela had said, truly a rape of the soul.

If I accepted, purely as a working hypothesis, that Angela was correct and Chris was NPD, then that would make sense.

And look at all the things 'Sheila' had said to me. So many of them were about Chris, and about how wonderful he was.

He got to sneakily sing his own praises whilst continuing to appear modest. And he got to hear my private thoughts about him, getting a double dose of this needed attention. It fitted. It fitted all too well. And begrudgingly I had to admit how clever it was. Devious, evil, nasty, sneaky, deceitful, underhand: yes, it was all those things. But it was also very clever.

I stood up, turned on the overhead shower, and quickly washed my hair and rinsed myself down. I defiantly pulled the plug before getting out of the bath – of such tiny victories are revolutions born – and quickly dried myself before slipping back into the bathrobe.

I could ask him, I realised. I could call his bluff. I could ask him for Sheila's phone number and I could ring her.

What time was it in Australia now that it was about eight o'clock here? I had an idea that they were twelve hours different, ahead or behind. I wasn't sure. But it would be morning there, either this morning or tomorrow morning.

It didn't matter for my purposes. I might catch her before she went to work, or I might get an answering machine. If an answering machine said something like, *'G'day, Sheila and Bruce's house, please leave a message,"* then that would be fair proof that she existed.

And if he refused to give me her number, or he gave me a number which was somebody else's – then that would be proof of a different kind.

Either way, I would know for sure.

I dried myself and then slipped on some leggings and a sweatshirt and went downstairs. Chris was watching the news on the telly, but he switched it off as soon as I came into the room.

"Feel better for that?" he asked considerately.

"Yes indeed, thanks for running it for me," I told him. I then took a deep breath, ignored my heart thumping hard against the inside of my chest and said, "Chris, I'd like to ring Sheila."

"What? Ring Sheila? Why?"

"I just would like to. We haven't spoken in all this time."

"True. But why now? At gone eight in the evening? It'll be morning there, she's probably on her way to work already. We can ring at the weekend if you like."

I looked at him sharply as he offered me that option. He seemed quite comfortable about the prospect of ringing at the weekend, just a bit disconcerted – as well he might be, I conceded – at my sudden and urgent need to phone now.

But still, I had to sort this out right away. I couldn't keep living with the uncertainty. And if Chris *was* NPD, then surely there would be some excuse, come the weekend, why I couldn't ring then. He'd just got an e-mail that she was away for her holidays, or in hospital with something long-term. He might even kill her off, like a character in a soap opera. Or the famous but possibly equally fictitious Bruce had got a three-month contract in Indonesia and they were heading over there. To the deepest jungle. Where there were no phones.

"I want to ring now," I repeated stubbornly.

He looked at me and said suddenly, "This is about checking up on me, isn't it? That bitch Angela's shit has got to you. You've been up there thinking God knows what and you've decided to discuss my childhood with Sheila – and no doubt my supposed 'disorder'. Well, I'm sorry, Sally, but I'm not playing that game. Sure I can give you Sheila's number and you can ring it. But our relationship will be over, because if there's that much distrust, there's no relationship left. Either you trust me and we stay together. Or you distrust me and we split up. Well, which is it to be?" he asked, his eyes hooded and anger blazing out from them.

If he was genuine, I couldn't blame him for being angry. I was making awful accusations, after all.

But if he had NPD, then he had to play games with me to stop me finding out the truth. He had to play games of anger and injustice and hurt.

He was being very clever indeed. He was managing not to give me Sheila's number by claiming the high moral ground. He was skilfully putting me on the defensive.

And Angela said that NPDs were very clever. That they could have you believing black was white. But Angela *would* say that, if she wanted me to dismiss anything Chris said.

My head hurt.

"Look," Chris said placatingly, "a lot of the fault for this is mine. I realise that now. I've been under a lot of strain what with my business stresses and your illness, and it made me short with you. And as I've said, that makes me human, not psychotic. But I truly can see that it wasn't helping, and I'm so, so sorry, Sally. I really am. If I hadn't been so cranky you probably wouldn't even have given Angela the time of day, you wouldn't have gone to meet her, and you certainly wouldn't have believed her lies. As it is," he paused and gave a deep sigh, "as it is, while I have to admit to being hurt that you might believe her, I have to acknowledge my own part in this. And I swear, I *swear*, that I have learned from this. I swear that things will be different from now on."

I stared at him. He sounded so incredibly heartfelt.

He continued, imploring me, "I'll be more sensitive towards you. I'll give you no cause to doubt me in any way. I'm not saying I'll be perfect – I can't swear to that. But I swear to you, on my poor mother's grave, that I'll make every effort to treat you as well as you deserve to be treated. Please give me just one more chance, Sally."

He looked at me then, and seemed to be trying to read my face, to see what my verdict would be.

When there was no immediate response he continued, heavily now, "The thing is, I'm in a Catch-22 situation here. When Angela originally accused me of this mental illness I researched it. And so one thing I know is that somebody with this NPD would say exactly what I'm saying to try to fool you into coming back. And no doubt Angela herself warned you that I might try this." He gave a sardonic laugh at my expression. "She did, didn't she?"

"Yes," I admitted.

"So I'm damned if I do and damned if I don't. Which she was probably counting on." He gave a short hollow laugh. "If I said nothing, how could you possibly even begin to think that I might change? But by saying this I might be playing into her hands. But I have to try," he pleaded. "I have to do everything to give this relationship the chance it deserves."

Trust your instincts, Angela had said, and no matter if she was honest or not, it was still good advice.

And I looked at him as he spoke, I looked him straight in the eye, and I read what was written there.

And I knew. I knew the truth.

Chapter 31

"Fair enough," I said, "you're right. I either trust you or I don't. And I do, Chris. I do."

I was aware of his expression relaxing as I spoke, the relief at my words visible on his face.

I continued to reassure him. "I know now that Angela was just trying to come between us, making up any stupid story. I'm sorry I let her get to me, even a little bit. Will you ever be able to forgive me?"

"I will, of course," he said, his handsome face breaking into a huge smile of joy. "Of course I will. I've forgiven you already, you silly moo! Come here to me," and we drew together and embraced fully, and I buried my face against his chest, feeling so relieved that my confusion and doubt were now over.

I drew away at last. "I'm so tired," I told him. "It has been an emotionally draining day. I think I'll go to bed now."

"I understand," he smiled. "I don't blame you. I think

an early night would be perfect for you. We can start our new life tomorrow, properly. I have a client conference tomorrow that I just can't get out of," he said regretfully, "but I'll book somewhere nice for dinner tomorrow night – would you like that?"

"I'd love it," I told him, smiling. I leaned forward and kissed him full on the lips. "Goodnight," I said softly, "see you tomorrow."

"Goodnight, my darling."

Once upstairs I took off my clothes and put on my pyjamas, brushed my teeth and then slipped into bed. It felt so good to rest my body, to close my eyes and relax. It had, as I had told Chris, been a truly draining day. But at least tomorrow would be good. Tomorrow would be the day my new, better, life started.

* * *

When I awoke the next morning the bed was empty. Cautiously I got up, put on my dressing-gown and went downstairs.

"Chris?" I called, "Chris, are you there?" There was no answer but I found a note on the kitchen table.

"Hi Sally," it read, *"I hope you slept well. I sneaked off without waking you because you looked like you needed the sleep. And you looked adorable. I'll be home around six, see you then. XXX C."*

So he wasn't going to be home until six, I noted as I put on the kettle for a much-needed cup of coffee. After my coffee, which was also my breakfast – my appetite had gone again after its temporary return on the previous day – I went upstairs and quickly showered and dressed.

Then I ran back downstairs to the hall table. I took the Dublin area phone book out of its drawer and quickly leafed through it until I found what I was looking for. As I dialled I was aware that my heart was pounding and my senses were alert for any or all sounds.

The phone rang and after a couple of rings it was answered: "Good morning, *Svelte* Gymnasium. Liz speaking. May I help you?"

"Can I speak to David Corrigan please?"

"Who's calling please?"

"This is Sally Cronin," I said, twisting the phone cord anxiously around my hands.

"One moment please."

As I waited I repeated like a mantra, *Please let him be there. Let him be there. Let him be there . . .'*

And he was!

"David Corrigan," he announced in his deep mellifluous voice. "Can I help you?" and I was left wondering why receptionists so often do that: ask who you are but not tell the person they put you through to. But I didn't have much time to ponder this eternal mystery of the universe.

"David, it's me, Sally Cronin," I told him, and I realised that I was whispering.

"Sally! How good to hear from you! Are you okay?" he asked, his tone anxious.

"I've been better, to be honest. David, you said you would help me out any way you could, even up to somewhere to stay –"

"I did," he said seriously, "and I meant it, and that offer's still open. Are you going to take me up on it?"

"Yes, please," I whispered, "and David, would it be okay if I came over now? In an hour or two, I mean. As soon as I'm packed."

"Of course, it would," he said, then hesitated and said, "How has it been?"

"It hasn't been great – well, you knew that. But I've seen sense now and I'm making my escape with your help." I laughed a little at the melodrama of the words, but they were apt. No others would do.

"I'm delighted to do anything I can," he said seriously. "Do you want me to come and get you?"

"No, no," I said hastily, "I'll be fine. He's – well, I mean to say, I have a good window of opportunity now, I'll be fine."

"Okay. If you're sure . . ."

"I'm definite," I said firmly. "I'll see you in an hour or two. By twelve at the latest. Okay?"

"Okay, see you then," he said, and we terminated the call.

I then quickly dialled a random Dublin number, listened to it ring, then hung up again. Let Chris try to figure *that* one out when he monitored my movements by pressing the redial button.

I hurried upstairs and took my passport, birth certificate and other such documents out of the drawer in which they had been stored, and placed them in my handbag. I then fetched my suitcases and put them onto the bed, and I hurriedly began packing my belongings. I would take everything that belonged to me. And that included my self-respect and confidence.

I need never see Chris again, and even that would be

too soon, I told myself grimly. I would just get over this horrible, horrible, episode which so nearly destroyed me, and move on with my life. (I'd have to think about taking up the burden which Angela had given me, that of warning his next girlfriend, but that was another day's work.)

It didn't take me too long to stuff all my clothes and other personal belongings into suitcases, and into black bin-bags fetched from under the sink in the kitchen. All the time I was doing this I was preternaturally aware of every sound, including my own harsh fast breathing.

Once all that was done I lugged each case and bag downstairs to the hallway, and then brought the first one out to my car. My car! It hadn't been used in ages. Would it even start? I took my keys from my pocket and sat into the driver's seat. It felt strange – the position and experience was at once so familiar and yet so strange. I put the key into the ignition and turned it. The engine turned over but didn't catch. My heart sank with fear and tension.

Chris scared me. Actually, he terrified me. I had looked into his eyes the previous evening and what I had seen there was . . . nothing. I had seen the abyss which was at the core of him and from which he spent his life trying to run. I had seen in his eyes the deepest pit of hell, and I had realised that whatever makes us human – call it our soul if you like, or maybe it's something which has no name – Chris was lacking it.

Eventually the car's engine caught and I let my breath out of me with a big whoosh. I ran it for a second or two before switching it off and going back to the house to collect the next case. Once back in the hallway I bent over to pick up a smaller bag.

"Going on holiday?"

As I turned around to face him my heart was already pounding so fast I thought it might burst out of my rib cage. Adrenalin was coursing through me – the flight or fight response. I'd choose flight, if I could. If I had a choice.

He was standing in the open doorway, blocking it – there was no way I would be able to get past him. His face was blank, his expression inscrutable.

I stood straight and faced him. Flight wasn't going to be an option. It was going to have to be fight. Hopefully verbal rather than physical.

"I'm leaving," I told him evenly. "It's over, Chris."

"But why?" he said, now all bewilderment and incomprehension. "Is it because of what Angela said? I thought you didn't believe her. I thought you saw the truth of it."

"I did see the truth of it, Chris. The real truth. Not your truth-lite."

"Truth-lite? What are you on about?" he demanded, and then I could visibly see him decide to become more gentle. "I don't understand," he said softly. "Truth is truth is truth. There are no different truths. And the truth is that I love you, Sally, and I want to be with you, and I want you to stay with me. We have a wonderful future together."

Should I pretend to believe him, unpack my bags, await another chance to leave? It might be the safest. But no. Everything in me recoiled at that. To pretend to him, to smile at him, to spend even another minute with him . . . it wasn't possible. And even if I could do that, it was a reasonable bet that future chances to leave would be sparse indeed.

"I was so excited about us sorting ourselves out," he said plaintively, "that I cancelled my appointment so I could rush home and spend the day with you, starting our new life together. But then I find this," he said sadly, gesturing at my remaining bags. "I don't understand, Sally. I thought we were making a future together."

"We're not," I said bluntly. "I have to go, Chris. And I think you know why."

"Because you believe I have that NPD! Well, I don't!" he cried and I have never heard such a depth of sincerity in anybody's voice, and for one awful moment I wavered. Could I be wrong after all? Could I be throwing away this relationship in error?

But I soon copped onto myself. Even if Chris didn't have NPD, even if I had been mistaken about that truth I had seen in his eyes the previous evening – and I hadn't – even so, he wasn't good to me, or for me, and I had to take my courage and leave.

"I'm going, Chris," I told him again. "There is really nothing else to say."

I bent and took my handbag with my precious documents in it and put it on my shoulder, then hefted a suitcase in each hand.

"Excuse me," I said politely, "do you mind moving? You're blocking the doorway. I'll just bring these out and come back for the rest of them."

If I could just get out with these bags, make him think I was coming back for the others, I would abandon them and just drive off.

"Yes, I do mind moving. You can't just walk out of here like this, Sally – we've been too much to each other."

Even though I knew discussions were likely to be a waste of time I was goaded into replying, "Chris, we have both been miserable in this relationship. It's time to finish it. We'll both be better off."

At least, I will be, I thought, *and that's all I care about.*

"No, Sally, no," he begged. "Look, let's talk about it. Just put your bags down and we'll go and have a chat about it. We'll sit down and have a civilised cup of coffee, talk to each other. Please," he implored, "at the very least give me the chance to win you back. You can't be so hard-hearted as to deny me that, surely? Let me try to convince you of how well I'll look after you. Please."

"Okay," I said, putting the two suitcases down again. "I'll just go out and lock the car, seeing as there are suitcases already in it."

I'd abandon even these bags, I decided. I was feeling very, very scared at this stage. There was no menace in his tone, nor in his expression, nor in his stance. But there was an implacability which stated clearly, *I will not be moved.* And he was between me and freedom.

I could be in danger of my life, here, I realised, and there was such terror in the pit of my stomach and my still further increased heart-rate as I hope never to experience again.

This wasn't theoretical. This wasn't a film with a

guaranteed happy ending. This was me and a very ill person alone in a house together. And women *do* die in what they euphemistically call domestic incidents, and nowhere was it written, I belatedly realised, that I, Sally Cronin, should be exempt from that possibility.

"I'll just go and lock the car," I said again, aiming for a casual tone, "and you can put the kettle on."

"Oh no," he told me, "no. I'm starting as I mean to go on here, and I wouldn't dream of making you go all the way out to the car to lock it. That wouldn't be a very gentlemanly thing to do. Allow me," he said and he held out his hands for the keys.

"I don't mind," I said breathlessly. "I'm quite happy to lock my own car."

"And I'm even happier to do it for you," he insisted, still implacable, and a smile on his face which clearly indicated he was calling my bluff, and he knew he was calling my bluff, and even more special – from his point of view – he knew that *I* knew he was calling my bluff. "Give me the keys, Sally."

Okay, I decided, I'd give him the car keys. But when he was outside the house I'd follow him out. I'd be safer in the street, there were always people passing by. I could flag down a passing car, anything. I didn't care now about any of my possessions, I just wanted my own freedom, my own escape. Why, oh why, hadn't I just left first thing this morning, without even bothering to pack?

Too late now.

"The keys?" he reminded me.

"Sure, the keys, of course. Yes, right," I said, and took

my bag off my shoulder and took out the keys. I handed them to him, being careful not to let our skin make contact – the very touch of his skin was anathema to me now. I couldn't bear to remember that I had welcomed him inside my body, had clung to him, had begged for him.

He took the keys and regarded me for a moment, then he tossed the keys into the air. "Be back in a sec," he said jovially, and turned and went out the door, closing it behind him.

I immediately stepped forward towards the door, intent on following him, but even as I did so I heard a sound. The unmistakable sound of the Chubb key turning in its lock from the outside.

I turned and ran frantically into the kitchen to the back door. But, of course, it too was locked, and its key nowhere to be seen.

I heard the front door open and close again as Chris returned. He came into the kitchen after me.

"There you go," he said cheerfully, "car safely locked."

But he didn't hand me the keys back. And he looked at me standing helplessly beside the back door, and he gave a little half-smile.

"What now?" I asked him.

By God, but if he saw me as a source of attention, he was getting it in spades now. Every atom of my body was directed towards him.

He shrugged. "Now we sit down," he said, indicating the kitchen chairs, "and I try to persuade you to stay. Please, do sit," he invited courteously, and I sat.

He went over to the kettle, filled it, and switched it on. "Coffee?" he enquired.

"Yes, please."

While the kettle boiled he took the coffee and the cafetière and cups and milk and everything needed to make the coffee, and all the time he chatted inanely. How the traffic had been on his drive earlier, how he liked this brand of coffee but preferred another one but the shop had been out of it. And as he spoke I was thinking furiously, planning and strategising. Or rather, trying without success to come up with a plan.

Chapter 32

David was expecting me. At least there was that. Otherwise Chris could kill me and bury me in the back garden and nobody would be any the wiser. Nobody had seen me for ages, nobody would therefore miss me, or search for me. But at least, now, David was expecting me. There was huge security in that.

Would I tell Chris this? Would it help or hinder? As Chris poured boiling water into the cafetière to warm it, I debated that question.

I had better say nothing, I decided. Not until I had to, anyway. I would keep that in reserve.

Chris brought the cafetière, cups and milk over to the table and placed them on the table. He poured us a cup each. I added milk to mine and held the warm mug tight, drawing comfort from it. The aromatic scent of strong coffee filled the room, and my stomach clenched in response. I couldn't bring myself to take a sip, not even for the sake of pretending normality. But I cradled its warmth.

"Now," he said, and there was an air that we were now getting down to business, "what's all this nonsense about leaving me?"

Time slowed as I thought how best to answer.

Would I try to convince him that I had changed my mind and would stay with him? I didn't see how I could. I wasn't that good an actress. And what good would it do me anyway? I'd have to leave at some stage, and it would only be prolonging the inevitable. It would be unendurable to stay with him, waiting always for my chance to escape, knowing that he was watching me.

But what else could I do? Faced with this implacability, what else could I do?

I would have to convince him to let me go.

But how?

How could I possibly make him let me go?

I tried to make my sluggish mind come up with a solution.

I had to make him *want* me to go.

Okay, but how?

He's NPD, I reminded himself. They have a great opinion of themselves, think themselves superior to everyone else. Can I use that?

"It's not nonsense," I told him. "I haven't been good for you. I've been a burden on your finances. I've been a drag on your emotions with the way I was acting so crazy. You deserve better than me. You deserve the best, Chris. You really do. And I'm not the best. I'm far from that. You need to be free so you can meet a woman worthy of you."

Was I overdoing this? *Can* you even overdo it for NPDs?

He looked at me sceptically. Chris was clever, I reminded myself. I shouldn't patronise him. He'd see through that in an instant.

"You think I deserve better than you?" he said.

His voice and expression were neutral. It was impossible to divine what he felt. Was I on the right path at all? I didn't know, but felt I had no choice but to plunge on.

"Well, yes, Chris. I mean, you're so dynamic," I said, totally winging it. I was going to be *fascinated* to hear whatever came out of my mouth next. "The thing is, I've been thinking. You know the way Angela thinks you have this Narcissistic Personality Disorder? And she said people suffering from it have an inflated sense of their own importance, that they think they're superior to everybody else."

Chris nodded.

"Well, what I'm thinking is this: maybe she's wrong. Maybe it's that these people *are* superior to the rest of us. Very, very few people, of course," I added hastily, "a tiny, tiny elite."

Chris was definitely interested in what I was saying; he was sitting forward and was focussed intently upon me.

I continued, "They are superior beings, but the rest of us just don't recognise this. Or maybe – maybe we *do* recognise it and resent it. And try to deny it." I was beginning to see where this was going and began to feel a tiny flicker of excitement. It could possibly work.

Either that or backfire dreadfully. But it might work. And I had no other ideas right now.

"Yes?" said Chris encouragingly, taking a sip of his coffee.

Impossible to judge if he was cynical. Or falling for it. "And because the rest of us, the lesser mortals, don't want to admit that there are these superior beings among us, they try to deny their existence. They invent this illness, this 'Narcissistic Personality Disorder'," I said scornfully, making inverted commas for the words, "to deny these people their uniqueness, their very birthright."

Chris put down his mug and leaned forward, his eyes bright. "Do you think so? Do you think that's possible?"

He was buying it! Or seeming to.

"More than possible," I assured him. "When you think about it, it's the *only* explanation which makes sense. All your life you've known you were special, right? Superior? Better than the reset of the common herd?"

He was nodding at each example and I told myself, take it handy now; you're not out of the woods yet.

"And yet, everybody else denied it. And worse, tried to convince you that you were ill. No wonder you've found that tough," I hazarded, but he continued nodding so it must have been a good guess. "Such greatness will always be a burden, Chris. All geniuses have found that. It just goes with the territory."

He was nodding sadly at this, but still agreeing with me. Now was perhaps the time to remind him why we were having this conversation.

I said, forcing my tone to sound regretful, "And

unfortunately I cannot *possibly* live up to such greatness. The proof of this is that I started going crazy when I tried – having all those Senior Moments."

I watched him carefully but discreetly, and I could see that he was struggling with a number of conflicting wishes.

He would love to tell me I was wrong. And of course, I *was* wrong! There was a serious flaw in my logic. I was saying that my having Senior Moments proved that I was unworthy of him. But he knew that I wasn't actually having any Senior Moments since they were orchestrated by him, so they weren't any such proof at all.

But he couldn't tell me this without admitting that he had lied to me and manipulated me about the Senior Moments and losing me anyway!

Nor, I was sure, would he want to argue against any proof of his superiority.

I waited anxiously. This was my throw of the dice, and I had to wait and see what numbers were going to come up.

When it became clear that he wasn't going to say anything, I continued, "And that's why I have to go. I'm not worthy of you. I'm dragging you down. I need to free you to find somebody more worthy of you."

This was vomit-inducing stuff, all right. But it seemed to be what was called for.

He said, "But as you're saying yourself, there *is* nobody worthy of me," he said, "so you're as good as –"

But I interrupted quickly before he could get too far with *that* train of thought, "No, there's nobody worthy of you, but there must be many women more worthy of you than I am. I repeat," I said firmly, "you should not be burdened with somebody crazy, somebody *so* far beneath you. And that's why I have to go, Chris," I finished, allowing a catch to come into my voice.

He looked sharply at me, and I got the distinct impression that he was onto me. But he couldn't even call my bluff without admitting what he had done to me.

I waited in silence for his reaction. I could do no more. If this didn't work I was out of ideas.

After some moments his face twisted. "You're right," he sneered. "You aren't worthy of me. I don't know why I even wasted as much time as I did with you. I gave you *everything*! I was so good to you, and you're just contemptible."

I bowed my head as he said this, this and much more. I didn't care what he said – if he needed to persuade himself he was better off without me, then that was fine. I could endure this if it were the price of my escape.

Eventually he ran out of invective.

"Go then," he said. "See if I care. I'll find somebody much better than you."

I made myself wait for a few moments, then, "My keys?" I asked, trying to keep my voice as neutral, as quaver-free as possible.

With a muttered curse he pulled them out of his pocket and threw them onto the table.

Moving slowly, careful not to disturb this fragile equilibrium, I reached out and placed my hand over them, drew them towards me.

"Well? Go if you're going!"

I stood and, grabbing my bag from the floor beside me, moved swiftly into the hall. My stomach was churning with nerves. Even now this could blow up in my face.

Chris was following behind me, so close that I could feel his breath on the back of my neck. He was breathing quickly, shallowly.

Was he playing with me like a cat with a mouse, dangling a tantalising taste of freedom in front of me, only to seize it back?

I took hold of my laptop in its case, everything else could be abandoned, and using the reclaimed keys I turned them in the Chubb lock.

Hardly daring to breathe I opened the door a crack. So close now, so close. If Chris was going to stop me, surely this was the time.

And it *was* the time.

He placed a hand on my arm.

I stifled a scream.

He pulled me towards him. He was smiling at me. It was a travesty of a kind and affectionate smile.

"No," he said, "we can't end like this. You can't leave me. People don't leave *me*! They don't go until I tell them to go, and then they're weeping at having to do without me. You'll stay, Sally. That's a much better idea."

I stared at him in pure panic. I could think of absolutely nothing else to do or say.

But then a thought crossed his mind. I could see his expression change as it did.

"No . . ." he said consideringly, "no, you don't have to stay. I have a much better idea. I'm going to let you go. Go on!" He nodded his head towards the door.

Was this another stage of the game? Was he going to stop me again? But I had no choice. I had to play by his rules.

He allowed me to pull open the door without hindrance, and then suddenly, blessedly, I was through it. I walked briskly down the pathway, every nerve on high alert, almost-but-not-quite running. I didn't dare glance over my shoulder, but somehow I was aware that he had followed me no further than the doorway.

I pulled open the gate, and stepped through onto the pathway. I was breathing deeply, taking huge gulps of city air, and to me the polluted air tasted of freedom.

I wasn't totally free, not yet, but there were cars passing frequently, and pedestrians occasionally. Surely he wouldn't be able to seize me and wrestle me back into the house in front of witnesses?

But even now he hadn't followed me. With a shaking hand I put my car key into the lock and clumsily opened the door. I got into the car, locking the door after me.

Safe.

I put the key in the ignition, turned it – it caught first time. Then I reached behind me for my seatbelt, strapped myself in, flicked on the indicator, checked for oncoming traffic in the mirror, and as soon as there was a break in the flow checked over my shoulder to make sure and pulled into the traffic.

And away. Free.

I drove with my heart in my mouth for a mile or so, before I judged that I was far enough away to succumb to my nerves, and pulled into the kerb. I sat and shook for some long minutes, trying to calm myself, to relax, to force myself to breathe deeply. I'm safe now, I kept telling myself, it's all over now. I'm safe now.

But what had he in mind when he let me go? I didn't even want to think about it. Was it like the hare who has been captured by humans, who feels relief when they release her, until she realises that she's being chased by two greyhounds? Was he releasing me, the better to play some other game with me?

No matter, I was free now. I could worry about any plans he might have another time. No matter what happened, I was far better off outside his house than trapped in it.

I moved off again, experiencing the elation of freedom. Driving seemed strange though, out of practice as I was. And the world around me was too big and loud and discordant. But I didn't care. I was free of Chris Malley and all his works. I hoped.

Chapter 33

I drove directly to *Svelte*. When I got there I parked and made my way into reception.

"Hello, Liz," I said to the receptionist. "Is David here? He's expecting me. It's Sally Cronin."

"Hang on, Sally, I'll ring him for you." She dialled a three-digit internal number and held the phone to her ear, and we both waited. But after a little while she replaced the phone, shaking her head in apology, "He's not answering his extension, I'm afraid. Hang on until I page him," and she spoke into a microphone on the desk: "David, ring reception please, David to reception."

Oh God, was he not here?

"He'll be here in a second," she assured me helpfully, "either that or he'll ring up."

And sure enough, a moment later her phone rang, the long single beep of an internal call. "David?" she said into the receiver, then: "Oh hi, Darius. Did he? Okay, thanks for letting me know." She replaced the receiver and looked apologetically at me. "He's not here, I'm afraid. Darius – that's his partner," she told me helpfully, "said he had to go out unexpectedly on urgent personal business. We don't know when he'll be back."

I stared at her, not sure how to respond. All my attention and energy and effort had been focused on getting here, and I had no reserves left. I had thought that David would take me in and sit me down and feed me coffee or something stronger and generally mind me in some small way for some small period of time. I had now totally run out of ideas.

"I'll wait for him," I told her, having no other options. I collapsed onto one of the nearby sofas. She shrugged and went back to her work.

Tears pricked the inside of my eyelids, like little needles. With a huge effort I managed not to cry. I was drained physically, emotionally and psychically. Now that I was here, I was like a burst balloon. I would sit and wait because I had no choice.

I couldn't believe that David hadn't been here to meet me. Urgent personal business, Liz had said. At least there was that, at least he hadn't stood me up on a sudden whim. And really, I told myself, what claim did I have on him anyway? Wasn't he good to let me stay with him, after all? I shouldn't be complaining about him having other calls on his time.

I wasn't complaining, not really. It was just that I was so exhausted.

Liz looked over at me about ten minutes later. "Would you like a tea or coffee, Sally," she asked me, "or a drink of water ?"

"Coffee, please," I asked her, "and a drink of water if that's okay."

Her simple kindness threatened to overwhelm me, so that when she handed me my drinks a few minutes later, my voice was suspiciously croaky as I thanked her.

"Are you okay?" she asked me with concern.

"I'm fine, thanks," I told her. What else could I say?

I drank my water in one or two gulps, and then sipped the coffee, grateful for its warmth. And then I resumed waiting, looking anxiously at the door each time it opened.

I suppose it was about half an hour or forty minutes later that the door opened to show David hurriedly sweeping his way into the lobby. My heart lifted at the sight of him. His brown hair was newly cut it looked like, and he was wearing a brown leather jacket over a black sweat-shirt and pants.

His broad handsome face lit up when he saw me.

"Sally!" he exclaimed, sounding hugely relieved.

He strode towards me as I stood, and he swept me into his arms and held me tight.

I leaned into him, into the warmth and strength of his body and I couldn't help it, I started weeping. All the stress and upset and worry and *everything* which had been repressed for so long just burst out of me, and I sobbed against his chest. He held me and patted my back, and whispered against my ear over and over, "It's okay Sally. It's okay now. Everything's okay now."

Dimly I realised that this wouldn't be doing his business much good. It surely didn't look that professional to have a bedraggled woman weeping in his lobby. But he never tried to hush me, or to move me to a discreet corner.

Eventually I hiccuped my way to a stop. "Sorry," I mumbled, pulling back a little and wiping my face and nose with my hands. Very elegant, not.

"It's okay," he said, "but tell you what, let's get you more comfortable. Come on," and he guided me over to a door marked *Private* behind the reception desk. Through that door, beyond which all luxury stopped, there was a corridor with several doors, signed with such notices as *Office, Kitchen,* and *Supplies,* and a flight of utilitarian stairs.

"Come on upstairs," he told me, and he led the way to the second floor. There was a long landing with four or five different doors on it. He went to the furthest one, opened it with a key, and led me inside.

Inside, it proved to be an extremely well-appointed apartment. The door opened into a sitting-room with a kitchen at the right-hand side behind a breakfast bar, and three doors off it to the left.

"This is my apartment," he said. "I live above the shop! Although I never really tell people – you don't want the punters, sorry, the clients I mean," he grinned cheekily at me, "realising you're too available. Darius has an identical flat next door, and then there's two bedsits for staff. I'll show you around, look . . ." and he led me across the room and opened one of the doors, "this is my guest room. You'll be staying here, okay? And that's my bedroom," he said pointing to the next door and here," he told me, opening the third door, "is the bathroom. Speaking of which, why don't you take a bath now? You look like you could do with one. A deep hot bath. And while you're doing that I'll go down to your car and bring your stuff in, how about that? And then I'll get us some food from the snack bar – it's gone lunch-time, you must be hungry."

I wasn't, but I didn't like to say so, not when he was being so kind.

"That's great," I said weakly but gratefully. I was safe. I was away from Chris. David was being very gentle and considerate of me, making decisions so I wouldn't have to, even taking the pressure of conversation off me.

"Okay, if you give me your keys and remind me which is your car I'll do that. Any requests for food?"

"Whatever you like," I told him. "Surprise me."

"Will do," he said cheerfully.

I gave him the keys and details of my car and he headed off. I went into the bathroom and ran myself a bath. There were some fabulous essential oils available and I helped myself liberally to one of those. As I sank into the warm aromatic embrace of the water I smiled to myself about the cliché – spot the homosexual man, I thought, with essential oils in his bathroom!

As I luxuriated I looked around me. The room was immaculate, which is always a bit of a bonus for a man's bathroom. It was completely tiled – plain white on the walls matching the white suite, and matt black tiles on the floor. The towels were thick and fluffy and so dark a grey as to be almost black. The accessories were in a brushed steel. Apart from the essential oils there wasn't much in the way of fussiness – no fancy soaps, no pot pourri, no ornaments. Luxurious but functional, I decided, lying back in the deeper-than-average bath and closing my eyes. I lay there, just enjoying the comfort of the water. Just being. Not thinking.

After some undetermined time I heard a knock on the door.

"Hi Sally, I'm back," David's melodious voice came through the door, "and I've got some food. There's a bathrobe hanging on the back of the door, put that on if you like."

"Okay, thanks," I called back, "I'll be out in a moment."

Reluctantly I pulled myself from the bath. I dried myself on one of the luxuriously soft towels. I then put the bathrobe on – it swamped me, going around me nearly twice, and trailing off the ground. But it was soft and comfortable. And totally modest if you discounted my being totally naked underneath.

That's silly, I told myself, amused at my daft thought, sure aren't we all naked under our clothes? And David isn't going to care either way.

I joined David back in the sitting-room to discover that he had got Emmenthal, cherry tomato and basil paninis. There was sparkling mineral water in glasses full of ice and sprigs of mint. It was very simple, and very enticing. I even forgot that I wasn't particularly hungry.

I took a tiny nibble of the panini, and to my surprise it tasted nice, so I took another nibble. Before long I had discovered, to my surprise and delight, that I had eaten nearly all of it.

As we ate David said, "I'm working all afternoon,

can't really get out of it but I'll be finished by about seven. We can talk then. That okay?"

"That's fine," I said. "Listen, David, thanks so much for all this."

"Don't mention it," he said, waving my thanks away. "It's my pleasure. Oh, wait till I tell you what happened to Avril," and he launched into the story of how one of their trainers, whom I had known, had won over eighty thousand euros as her share of a Lotto syndicate and was currently on a year-long round-the-world trip. "Postcards arrive regularly from all sorts of exotic places," he told me. "We're all wildly jealous! Oh, and did you hear that Steve got engaged?" and in this manner he chatted about the staff and long-term members of the gym in a light-hearted way which got us through lunch, avoiding both awkward silences and heavy discussion.

After lunch he asked me, "Will you be able to entertain yourself for the afternoon?"

"I will," I told him. "I think I'll just have a lie-down."

"Fine," he said, smiling at me, and I cannot begin to describe the feeling of safety I experienced then. Everything was going to be okay. I was in good hands.

I thought I was in good hands with Chris, I told myself sourly.

But then I reminded myself that Angela had told me to trust my instincts, and how that had proven good advice, how I had truly recognised Chris when I looked into his eyes.

So I looked deep into David's brown eyes and what I saw there was . . . the world. I saw the capacity for love, and I saw laughter, and compassion, and a sense of humour, and empathy, and a conscience. And then I truly knew that I was in good hands here.

"I'll be downstairs in my office if you need me," he said, perhaps not knowing that he had been evaluated and found more than worthy. "Extension 251 – the phone's over there. Okay?"

"Okay," I smiled back at him. "Thanks again."

"No problem," he told me. "I'll see you later."

After he had gone I went into the bedroom. My bedroom for the foreseeable future. In common with the bathroom it was unfussy but opulent. There was a luxurious royal blue carpet on the floor, and a matching plain duvet cover on the black wrought-iron bed, and matching curtains over the window. The wardrobe, bedside lockers and walls were plain white. One picture graced the wall. It was an original watercolour of some sunny and foreign place – the blue roofs and white walls of the building suggested that it might be Greece – and that painting was the perfect touch to prevent the room from being austere, without taking from its simplicity.

I unpacked, which didn't take long. My toiletries, my sad collection of leggings and tops, my pyjamas and my own dressing-gown. Everything else could stay in the suitcase, placed neatly in one corner.

I took off David's bathrobe and put on my pyjamas and then climbed into the bed. I'd have to ask David how long he was expecting me to stay, I thought sleepily. Perhaps he only meant a day or two. I didn't know how he would take it when he found out I needed to stay indefinitely, that I had nowhere else to go, no job or income and no immediate prospect of either.

I experienced a shaft of fear at the prospect of having to sort that out with him, but I quickly let the fear go. It would be okay, I told myself, and whatever happened, I couldn't sort it out with David until later. I wouldn't worry about it now. And on that thought I closed my eyes and sleep claimed me.

I must have slept soundly because the next thing I knew was waking at a sudden brightness. I opened my eyes and realised it was light from the sitting-room flooding into the now-dark bedroom through the doorway at which David was standing. I must have slept for hours.

"Sally," he was whispering, "Sally, are you awake?"

"Yes," I answered sleepily, and he took this as his invitation to come right into the room. He sat on the edge of the bed.

"How are you?" he asked. "It's gone seven. I thought I should waken you or you'll never sleep tonight. And I've dinner nearly made. Pasta do you? How do you feel about getting up? Are you hungry?"

"I'm fine. And yes I am hungry," I said, surprise in my voice given that I had eaten a whole portion of panini earlier.

"Grand so. Get up when you're ready – I'll be outside."

He closed the door behind him and I reached for the bedside lamp and switched it on, then got up and put on my dressing-gown over my pyjamas. I then joined David.

"Sit down there," he told me, indicating the round dark-wood table with four matching chairs which defined the dining area.

As I sat he served dinner. He invited me to shake

freshly grated parmesan on top of my fusili pasta and sauce. He opened a bottle of red wine and poured us both a glass. It was simple and delicious and I could not recall when I enjoyed a meal more.

We ate companionably, and he chatted away about the doings of the afternoon, a problem with the sauna, a good write-up in one of the Sunday papers. He was very definitely controlling the conversation, steering it the way he wanted it to go. But yet I never got the sense that he wanted to dominate the talk for its own sake, but rather to keep the dialogue light for now, until he judged it was the right time for me to talk.

Eventually we had both finished and he brought the plates over to the kitchen area, quickly rinsed them and left them to dry. Chris would have a hissy-fit at that, I found myself thinking, and rejoiced at the freedom to be a less-than-perfect housekeeper.

He topped up our wineglasses and then said, "Let's move over here," and gestured towards his sitting area. There were two white three-seater leather sofas placed opposite sides of an oak coffee table. Their luxury enticed me. I tucked myself into one and accepted my refilled glass.

David chose the other sofa, sitting opposite me, sitting back confidently and comfortably. My, but he looked good, with his brown eyes gazing intently at me, his long, elegantly lean body sprawled on the sofa.

He took a sip of his wine. "Okay," he said, his deep voice serious now, "tell me."

I took a deep breath. "Remember I told you I was in love, and I was moving in with my boyfriend?"

He nodded.

"Well it has been a disaster, a total nightmare." I told him, and over the next hour or so I shared the whole sorry story from exciting and happy beginning to sad and scary ending.

He listened attentively while I spoke, interrupting only to ask for clarification at points.

I ended by telling him of the previous day's meeting with Angela, and how today I had hit upon the idea of using Chris's own disorder against him, tricking him into letting me go.

"That was clever," said David admiringly.

"I had to do something," I told him simply, then added sombrely, "I probably haven't helped matters though, building up his belief in himself like that. God knows how that is going to impact on him, or whoever he takes up with next. But I was just so scared, David. I really was."

"I'm not surprised," he murmured.

"I would have said anything to get away. But at least he thinks he's well rid of me," I said with satisfaction, "at least he feels he has the high ground by my leaving. What's wrong?" I asked then, because David was looking distinctly uncomfortable as I spoke.

"I have a confession to make," he said. "Thing is, I've been concerned about you for months as you know. And I was so worried by your call this morning that when you didn't arrive as soon as I was expecting, I grew alarmed and, well, I went around to the house to find you. To his house, I mean. That's where I was when you arrived here."

"Thank you. There *was* a time," I confessed, "when I wasn't at all sure I'd make it out of there. I remember thinking that at least you would be expecting me and might come looking for me. And I *am* grateful that you did."

"No problem," he said dismissing my thanks. "But the thing is that Chris is furious. He knows now that you have come to me. And he thinks that you've left him for me. He wasn't impressed, putting it mildly. Of course, if I had any inkling he was suffering from a mental disorder, I wouldn't have gone there."

"Oh. I see what you mean," I said slowly. "I hope it's going to be okay," I worried. "I'm scared of Chris. I'm scared of what he might do."

"You're safe here," David reassured me. "He can't reach you here. Just concentrate on getting better – you're all run down, physically and emotionally – and we'll worry about him later. One thing at a time. You need to get your strength up, build yourself up."

"That's another thing," I told him. "I don't know how long you're expecting me to stay, but it might be for a little while." Wrong: it might actually be for a *big* while, but I thought I'd better break it to him gradually. "I don't have any income, and I can't get a job for a while. I know I'm not well enough for that. As you say, I'm all run down and . . . and it's more than that, David. My brain is all over the place. I can't concentrate for long – it's like my brain was fried, or mangled or something. It's terrifying, really."

"I'm not surprised," he told me. "Don't underestimate what you've been through – it was nothing less than psychological torture. Making you think you were going insane, isolating you from everybody, criticising you all the time, half-starving you."

He shook his head in shocked disbelief and disapproval.

"I think," he went on, admiringly, "that the fact that you've survived this, that you were able to make a break for it, that you're as sane as you are, is a huge testament to your strength of character. You will recover," he told me with such confidence that I began to have confidence too. "You *will* get better. You just need rest, and time, and a period with no stress. And no doubt some counselling will help, to assist you getting over this. I know of one very good counsellor – I can get you the number."

"That's great!" I said feeling more and more relieved. But there was still something nagging. "But David, I can't live here indefinitely!" There, now I'd said it.

"Don't see why not," he told me, laughing and winking at me. "I think we'd have fun together. I haven't had a flatmate for years. I'd enjoy it. But," he said, more seriously, "I can see that you mightn't feel comfortable doing it. And that it mightn't be in your best interests – you need to recover by getting back on your own two feet as soon as possible."

"I do," I agreed, although the thoughts of being on my own two feet were very scary.

"However, I was having a think this afternoon. One of the staff bedsits will be available in about five weeks' time. How about you stay with me in this apartment till then, and then move in there?"

"That sounds *great*!"

He grinned his heart-stopping grin at me as he

continued. He had obviously done a lot of thinking that day. "And maybe in three or four weeks, or whenever you feel up to it, you could start working part-time here in *Svelte*. Some cleaning maybe, or some simple admin. I'm not trying to take advantage of you, honest," he reassured me, "but it seems to me that those jobs wouldn't require too much concentration, but would get you back into the swing of working and get some of your confidence back. We'd pay you," he said urgently, "we'd pay you the proper wage. And once you're living in the bedsit we would make our normal deduction for accommodation so you wouldn't feel like we were giving you charity. What to you think of that?"

"I think that sounds excellent!" I told him, and I'm pretty sure my eyes were bright with unshed tears, but they were tears of joy. My vision was blurry through those tears, but I could see him smiling happily at me even so. "You've given me a blueprint for my future, a plan to get my life back. Thank you, thank you, thank you."

"My pleasure," he said. "I'm just so glad you're here, safe and sound, where I can make sure you're okay. I *have* been worried about you," he told me. "That wasn't just talk. I'll be able to sleep better at night now. So far from you putting me out by being here, you're helping me!"

I smiled at him, astonished at the extent of his sensitivity and kindness.

"I've another idea. I think you could go to your doctor, get a sick-cert, and sign on with Social Welfare. You have been paying your taxes all these years, and you *are* genuinely unfit for work – it wouldn't be at all illegal or unethical to sign on for a few weeks until you could start work here. It would give you some money, some independence, another step in getting your life back. What do you think?"

"Good idea! I'll do that very thing."

"And one last thing, and then I'm finished. You probably know that your membership is out of date now. Well, I've reinstated it for another six months. So while you're here you can get fit and healthy again! There'll be no excuses."

"Thank you," I said fervently.

I probably wouldn't be able to manage more than a couple of minutes on the treadmill, or one length of the pool to start with, but it would be good to build myself up, back to fitness. And if I was exercising, and not stressed, my appetite should improve and I should be able to put back on the weight I had lost.

"Why are you doing all this for me?" I asked, suspicion striking at me. Maybe this, too, was one thing which Chris had stolen which I would never recover – an unthinking trust of people.

He correctly interpreted my question and no doubt my expression. "Your experiences have made you very suspicious," he acknowledged. "But I promise you, Sally – this is a gift, freely given, no strings attached. I'm well-balanced, as well-balanced as anybody else anyway," he laughed, "and I swear to you I have no malevolent ulterior motive. Just believe that you deserve helping, and allow me to help you. Okay?"

"Okay," I said. I yawned then, and laughed at my

yawns. "I can't believe I'm tired again, I slept all afternoon after all!"

"I can believe it. You've been to hell and back, you've used up so much energy just coping, so it's not surprising that now that you are safe your body is coming to a grinding halt. Pop into bed. I'll come in and tuck you in."

"Okay," I said, really liking the idea of being tucked in. I hadn't been tucked up in years. Not since GanGan had died.

I used the bathroom, and then back in my bedroom I took off my dressing-gown and got into bed. A few minutes later there was a knock on the door.

"Are you decent?"

"I am. Come in."

David came in and sat on the edge of the bed as before. I could see him looking down at me, towering over me as I lay prone. But somehow it didn't feel at all intimidating or daunting.

Rather, I felt so safe, almost embraced. I was already well wrapped up in the duvet and didn't need much tucking up, but in any case he pulled the duvet up a little bit, all the way to my neck, and tucked it under my chin, and he tucked it in against my sides so that I was well cocooned and cosy. And I could not recall feeling more cared for or better looked after, and I could feel my heart-rate slow and a deep profound calm overtake me.

"Sleep well," he said. "I probably won't be here when you wake up – just help yourself to breakfast stuff. Relax. You're safe now."

And he bent and dropped a kiss on my forehead.

"Thanks," I mumbled, already half asleep. "Goodnight."

I think I heard him whisper goodnight as he stood and left the room, but I was already nearly asleep so I might have imagined it.

Chapter 34

I awoke early the next morning and lay there for some few minutes until I remembered where I was. And then it all came back to me, all the events of the previous day. And a great sense of well-being overcame me as I lay there.

I was free from Chris, free from abuse! I had been strong enough to be proactive and seize my life. I just had to concentrate on getting well, that was the next step. And today I would arrange to see my doctor as David had suggested, and get a sick-cert.

I got up and put on my dressing-gown and went into the sitting-room. Through the window I could see that it was a bright clear day, which reflected my upbeat mood. There was a phone in the sitting-room and I used it to phone my doctor. I got an appointment for later that morning.

Leisurely, I washed and dressed, and then went to get breakfast. On the breakfast bar I saw a note from David scrawled on a closed envelope.

"Morning, Sleeping Beauty! Breakfast stuff in cupboard and fridge, help yourself. Enclosed to pay for doctor and any other expenses. To be taken out of your first wages!"

I opened the envelope and found three fifty-euro notes, and tears prickled my eyes with gratitude at his thoughtfulness. Not only at providing the money, but at stressing that it was an advance on wages, so that I wouldn't have to feel any more beholden than I already did.

Within the envelope I also found a key which I took to be the key of the flat, and I placed that on my key-ring.

I breakfasted on fruit and yoghurt with muesli on top, and the simple meal tasted of joy and freedom.

By the time I had finished clearing up after me it was time to leave. I went downstairs and out to the car. My doctor was only about a mile away, but I decided I would drive anyway. I was appalled at how weak I was. A mile's walk seemed like the North Face of the Eiger to me.

Just as had happened yesterday, I found it strange to be out in the big world, but it wasn't *quite* as strange. Maybe I was reacclimatising. Mind you, it felt as if the car was handling a bit funny – I clearly hadn't quite got back into the habit of driving.

Typically, even though I had an appointment, and even though it was so early, Dr Carolan was running way behind schedule so I had to wait for quite a while. I chafed impatiently at this delay, never thinking that it might be responsible for saving my life.

But eventually I got to see him. I had grown fairly

used to my changed appearance, and so his reaction to me came as a bit of a shock.

"Dear God, Sally, what's going on?"

I quickly explained what had happened, and told him that I needed to go on Disability Benefit just for a little time while I recuperated.

He knows me well, he knows I'm not a scrounger by nature, he knows I'm truthful, and anyway, one look at me corroborated my story.

He quickly filled out the correct forms. "That'll keep you going for two months, Sally – if you need more after that just ring and we'll organise them."

"Thanks, Dr Carolan, I really appreciate it."

"Look after yourself," he said sincerely, but he was already reading the notes of the next patient in the queue. Not lack of caring, just lack of time.

That was enough for one day, I thought. I had accomplished more already than I used to in a full day.

I'd go back, I thought happily, check out where the nearest Social Welfare office was and arrange to go there the next day. And for the afternoon I'd treat myself to a swim, a sauna and a session in the Jacuzzi.

My jubilation vanished abruptly when I got back to my car, however. My front near tyre was flat. So was the back tyre, I noticed with horror. But hang on, the car wasn't listing. I walked to the other side and discovered that both tyres on that side were also flat – every single one of my four tyres was flat! This couldn't be coincidence, surely. Was it Chris who had done it? He knew my car. But he didn't know where I, or my car, would be.

But hang on. He *did* know where I was. He had

David's business card, I remembered, cursing. With *Svelte*'s address on it. Outside which my car had been parked all night. I looked around fearfully. But I saw nothing untoward.

But what was I to do now?

I had very little choice really. I turned and walked the mile back to *Svelte*. Each step challenged me, weak as I was and terrified that Chris was going to approach me at any moment.

Maybe the four punctures were coincidence, I tried to convince myself. Maybe I had driven over a large amount of broken glass. Maybe.

I was nearly in tears by the time I got back to *Svelte*. And I could think of nothing to do but to ask for David's help. I really didn't want to do that. He was already behind in his work for all the time I had cost him yesterday. But my tired mind couldn't even begin think of any other possibility than to run to David and lay the problem in his large capable hands.

I went up to the reception desk. "Hi, Liz, I wonder could you ring and see if David's around?"

"Sure thing, Sally."

She dialled and then spoke into the phone before handing it to me.

"Hi, David, it's Sally. Look, I'm really sorry to bother you, but have you a few minutes?"

"Sure thing," he said, "come on into the office."

I hung up the phone and went through the door behind reception and into the office. David was standing up as I walked through the door, obviously on his way to meet me.

"What's wrong?" he asked anxiously. "Is everything okay?"

"Oh David," I said and burst into tears. Again. This was getting boring.

"Come here," he said, and led me to a chair into which I sank gratefully. I was dimly aware of him pulling up another chair and sitting beside me, taking my hand and holding it while I cried.

After a few minutes I pulled myself together enough to say, "David, Chris has sabotaged my car tyres."

"*What*?" he demanded, shock in his voice. "How? Is your car outside?"

"No, it's outside the doctor's," and I explained what had happened. "I don't know for sure that he's done anything, but unless I drove over a huge lot of glass, and I certainly don't remember that, *somebody* has done something with my tyres. And it would be a bit of a coincidence if it was anybody other than Chris, wouldn't it?"

"Okay, okay, don't worry about it. I'll look after it," he said, but his expression was grim and furious. "Look, just give me details of where the car is, and I'll sort it out. Don't worry about it, Sally. It's going to be okay. Why don't you go and have a swim or something? Just leave me the car keys first."

"Okay," I said, "I'll do that. Thanks, David, I really appreciate it."

I handed him the keys, then went upstairs and got my swimsuit and bathrobe and went back down to the ground-floor swimming pool.

I didn't feel up to any exercise after that walk, so I

went and sat in the sauna for as long as I could manage, and then the reward: the Jacuzzi. I sat there in its pervasive heat and closed my eyes and refused to think of anything.

And so it was there that David found me. "Sally," he said softly, and I opened my eyes to discover him squatting beside me. "Ritchie – the mechanic – found your car. He's got all the tyres repaired and replaced. The car is fine now. Do you want to come with me to collect it?"

"Sure. Just let me get dressed." I got out of the Jacuzzi, fetched my bathrobe from the changing room, and we went upstairs.

Once we were in the flat David said sombrely, "Sally, there's something you should know. Ritchie found out what caused your punctures. Six-inch nails," he said heavily.

"Six-inch nails?" I repeated, not sure if I had heard him correctly.

"Yes. One in each tyre. So it was obviously deliberate. Ritchie told me that it's a fairly well-known way of messing someone around. You wedge a big nail against the tyre, with the point of the nail slightly penetrating the tyre to keep the nail in place. And when the person begins driving, the car rolls over the nail and its weight pushes the nail into the tyre. Usually you do it on both the front and back of the tyre, so it doesn't matter if the car is driven off forwards or backwards. It can be dangerous enough," he said worriedly, "because there's a good likelihood of a crash as the car becomes less responsive to the steering wheel."

"I *thought* it was handling funny," I said.

"You were lucky you had such a short journey, and the car did most of its deflating while it was parked outside the doctor's surgery. No thanks to . . . whoever did this."

"We both know who did it," I told him. "Chris."

"We've no proof," he said. "But . . ."

"Yes. But. We know it was him, David. Angela told me that these NPDs often start stalking their exes. And in fact . . . it's only occurring to me now . . . I did wonder why he did eventually let me go that time at his house. Angela said that they get bored, have to change the game. Maybe this is it."

David cursed under this breath at that. Then he asked, "How did he know you were here, though? That's what worries me."

"Oh yes," I said slowly, "I think I know the answer to that. And I'm so sorry, but do you remember you gave me your business card? Well, he forced me to give it to him, so he knows who you are and where you're based."

"Shit!" he said in heartfelt tones. "That would explain –" he paused abruptly.

"What?"

"Nothing."

"Come on, David. I insist you tell me. Otherwise I'll be worrying and I'll probably imagine much worse than what you're not telling me. And you know that I need to be calm in order to build my strength up."

"Okay, okay," he capitulated. "It's just that I got a couple of rather strange e-mails messages today."

"What did they say?"

But that he would not tell me. "They weren't very nice, that's all. I have them deleted now. Don't worry about it." He sighed. "We should report the tyre issue to the guards."

"We should," I said.

"Look, you get dressed and we'll go out for lunch. I could do with a break. We'll drop into the Garda Station while we're out. And on the way back we'll collect your car. Okay?"

So that's what happened. David went downstairs while I had a quick shower and got dressed. In the ubiquitous leggings and sweats.

I didn't dry my hair, and I didn't put on make-up. It was only David, after all, and he didn't care what I looked like. Oh yes, and strangers, and I didn't care any more what they thought. One huge step for womankind, I decided as I went downstairs to collect David.

As we left the building David said, "I have an idea. Let's look at where you parked last night, and see if there are any nails there. If Ritchie's theory is correct and he put nails both in front of and behind your tyres, there should be four nails just lying there, and it would be some sort of evidence."

"Good idea," I said, "but I parked facing the wall. He would only have had to put nails behind the tyres."

So that was no use to us.

David didn't say anything, but it was clear that he was *furious*. His normally cheerful eyes were hooded and grim, and his hands gripped the steering wheel tightly enough to turn his knuckles white.

Mind you, I wasn't exactly thrilled myself.

We walked into the Garda Station and presented ourselves at the front desk. The garda who dealt with us was very nice, very helpful and very, very young.

When we told him what had happened he said, "There's not much we can do, unfortunately. We just don't have the resources to chase up every incident of petty crime like that."

"Petty crime!" burst out David. "She could have been killed!"

"I know, I know. But really it's just petty vandalism. Look, I'll take a statement and we'll have it written up."

"That's only useful if any harm comes to her later," said David astutely. "So you have more evidence for the assault investigation. Or any other kind of investigation," he said heavily.

The garda didn't deny it. Instead he said, "And would you have any evidence, sir, that she is in any danger?"

"No, Guard," he said, "but we have reason to believe that somebody might be stalking her."

"And what other incidents have led you to this conclusion?" asked the garda. "Given that stalking is a pattern of behaviour."

It was our turn to be silent. The damage to my car was the sole incident. And we could hardly start explaining about NPD. Not without being locked up ourselves anyway.

"Well, anyway," said the garda, taking pity on us by not insisting on an answer, "I have to tell you, sir, madam, that although stalking is now legally a crime, it's almost impossible to prove. We have the problem that the alleged stalker also has his – or her, of course – civil rights, and is quite entitled to walk down any street, or attend any venue, and if you, madam, are also there, who is to say that it is not a coincidence? It's very difficult."

"Great," said David sarcastically. "Well, thanks for your time, Guard."

He turned and walked away, and I followed him, passing an apologetic look over my shoulder.

"Come on and we'll get that lunch I promised you," said David. As we drove off he said begrudgingly, "I can see their point. I don't like it, but I can see it." And then I could see him deliberately rise above his anger and upset at what Chris was doing, and the helplessness of the gardai, and he turned and smiled at me.

"Do you know what this is?" he asked.

"No," I asked, smiling back at him, "what is this?"

"It's the first time you and I have ever been together outside *Svelte*. Ridiculous that all this time we never took our friendship any further, absurd that it had to be something like this which motivated us."

"Good point," I agreed.

"Oh well, at least we're doing it now. And let it be the first of many," he predicted. Or requested, I wasn't sure which.

Either way, I was quite happy to acquiesce. I was enjoying his company hugely. There was just something about his tall, strong presence which made me feel so safe, so . . . right. As if I fitted my skin, and I knew at last who I was. Fanciful, I know, but that's how it was. Also it was no hardship to enjoy his good humour, his relaxed demeanour. And he wasn't too hard on the eyes either.

We went to a local pub for our lunch.

"Tell me," said David in between mouthfuls, "you mentioned something yesterday which puzzled me. You said your friend Gaby made a pass at Chris – shortly after that dinner party at her house, right?"

"That's right," I said, feeling again the pain of her betrayal.

"I don't believe it for a moment!" he declared.

"She admitted it," I said shortly.

"Still don't believe it."

"Come on, David. How much more proof do you need than her admitting it?"

"None," he said, "but it seems too much of a coincidence that just when it suited Chris to have you isolated, your best friend is out of the picture. And it seems like a whole lot of coincidence that your best friend, who has always been loyal to you before – right?"

"Right," I conceded.

"– that she would all of a sudden betray you. *And* betray her husband with whom – and I remember you talking about them – she is very much in love. I think you should talk to her again."

"Look, I take your point. But coincidences do happen, friends do betray and – I have to keep coming back to it – she admitted it when I challenged her."

"I still think you should talk to her again," he repeated. "Humour me, Sally, and do that."

"Okay," I agreed reluctantly. After all he was doing for me, I could hardly refuse the only request he was making of me. "I'll go to see her tomorrow, okay?"

"Okay," he said. "And if she admits it again, then I'll eat my hat."

"You don't wear a hat," I said, smiling broadly.

"No, I don't," he conceded. "Do you think I should? Do you think it would add to my already extremely debonair style?" and with that he lightened the conversation and we laughed our way through the rest of lunch. I couldn't remember when I had last enjoyed just pure simple uncomplicated laughter and I experienced this deep rich centre of contentment, right in my belly. Life was good.

When we got back to *Svelte* Liz intercepted me on my way in.

"Oh, Sally, this came for you," she said, and she reached down behind the desk and produced the most enormous bouquet of flowers I have ever seen. Possibly even the Botanic Gardens couldn't rival these flowers. A riot of reds and pinks and yellows lay within the cellophane wrapper.

"Aren't they fabulous!" she enthused as she handed them over. Puzzled, I took them and lifted out the card. It read: *It would be a long day's walk to find somebody as beautiful as you. This is not flat-tery.*

"Dear God," I breathed, and I could feel the bouquet heavy in my hands and the cellophane seemed slimy and corrupt. I all but flung it onto the nearby sofa, and handed the card to David. He read it and his face tightened and a nerve ticked in his jaw.

"Hand me the phone, please," he instructed Liz.

Puzzled but compliant, she did so, and he quickly dialled the number on the florist's card.

"Hello," he said pleasantly, "you just delivered a bouquet of flowers to Sally Cronin at *Svelte* Leisure Centre . . . yes, we got them okay. No, it's a beautiful bouquet. Don't worry about that. No, we have no complaints, honest!" He held up a hand as he tried to stem the torrent of questions. "Miss, excuse me, hang on . . . I just have some questions about the sender . . . you see, Sally is uncertain who it is . . . right, I see. Did he pay by credit card? No? And can you remember what he looked like? Hmm . . . right . . . okay . . . right, thanks very much."

He hung up and turned to me. "Paid by cash, natch," he said ironically, "and the description could be Chris, but could also be half the male population. She only remembers him as well as she does because it was such a romantic message." He twisted his face as he said that. "As he was in the shop she offered to let him write the card himself, but he declined and asked her to do it, which did puzzle her a little. But of course, that doesn't puzzle us at all, does it?"

"No. No handwriting equals no fingerprints equals no evidence."

"Exactly." He gave a deep sigh. "Liz, would you mind binning those flowers?"

She began to protest but one look at David's expression clearly persuaded her to subside and say nothing except, "Sure thing, David."

Upstairs in the flat, David paced the sitting-room.

"We can't let him away with this," he said vehemently. "That's classic stalking behaviour."

"Do nothing," I stressed. "Do you remember I told

you about the way they work? He's looking for a reaction, so don't give him one."

"Goes against the grain," he mumbled crossly.

"He'll eventually learn that there's nothing to be gained by doing this. Then he'll get bored and move on."

"Hm," he said, acquiescing but not agreeing. "Look, I'd better go and do some work. I'll probably be a bit late finishing this evening."

"You must be way behind in your work now," I said guiltily.

"Not your fault," he said. "Look, catch you later, okay? There's loads of food in the freezer and cupboard. Help yourself when you want dinner."

"Thanks," I said, and with a wink and a wave he was gone.

What now? I didn't feel up to going back to the gym. I wasn't yet ready to contact any of my friends. What would I say? I needed to assimilate and process what had happened to me before I could ever begin to articulate or share it with the world at large.

I had nothing to read, nothing with which to entertain myself. So I switched on the television. It failed to distract me for long, however.

With space to think, the reality of what I had been through hit me. Hard.

First to land with a thump was the true realisation of just how comprehensively Chris had used me. As Angela had said, I was nothing to him – *nothing*. He cared nothing for me as a person. He didn't even really acknowledge that I *was* a person. All I was to him was the gratification of his narcissistic needs. He had just taken me and sucked me dry emotionally to fulfil those needs. Like a spider sucking the juices out of her prey. And that hurt. That hurt a lot.

I sat cross-legged on the sofa and clutched my torso, trying to wrap my arms around myself in comfort. And I literally could feel the sharp pain of it in my stomach. And I bawled.

How dare he? I asked myself as I wept. *How could he do this to me?*

I let myself acknowledge that this is the question asked by all victims. And the answer is: *They didn't see you as a person. They saw you only as product. Yes, it does hurt. But you just have to accept that hurt. That's the reality.*

Also I had to deal with the loss of my relationship. Not the relationship I had – I knew now that that was, as Angela had said, only the relationship between hunter and prey. Nothing to mourn the loss of there. But I was bereaved by the loss of the relationship I *thought* I had had, the fictional relationship which was a lie on his behalf and wishful thinking on mine.

All those visions I had had: of Christmases together, of playing with a child in the park, of growing old together – each and every one had to be laid to rest and mourned. As the afternoon passed, that's exactly what I did – mourned that loss, and laid it to rest.

I had to deal with the total rewriting of the past. Every moment since we met had its filter of delusion stripped away, and was laid naked for me to scrutinise coldly and analytically. It was slow work, and heavy work, and it brought its share of tears and bewilderment and doubts.

And who was left? Now that Chris had sucked everything out of me, who was I? Was there anything left in the husk which remained?

Thrown into the pot too was the fear and uncertainty about my future. I had thought that my life plan was all sorted, and now I was beginning again with nothing.

Add a soupçon of terror about what was looking like a stalking campaign.

Season with pure, white-hot anger, with potent rage at what he had done to me.

During this process, several conclusions came to me. As I wept enough to feel that I was surely dissolving, I thought of a caterpillar in a chrysalis. That caterpillar has to liquefy before it can be reborn as a butterfly. It doesn't *grow* into a butterfly, it dissolves and is reborn as a butterfly. And perhaps that was what was happening to me here.

I had been through the most appalling experience – truly, the rape of my soul – and in some ways I had not survived. Certainly the old me had not survived. The lonely, questing, *love-me-love-me-love-me* woman had been destroyed. But what was to replace her?

It was a basic human need to want to belong. That would never leave me.

But I could make sure that while I *wanted* to belong, I didn't *need* to belong so badly that I would attach myself to just anybody who seemed to provide a niche for me.

Looking back on my time with Chris, a strong image came to my mind of myself as a barnacle attaching itself to the side of a ship. Attaching, clinging, willing to sacrifice any quality of life just so I could cling on. And all the time the ship sailed inexorably towards the rocks.

Never again.

From now on I was going to be *me*. And I was going to have fun figuring out who exactly this *me* was. I had been – I faced the uncomfortable truth squarely – more like Chris than I would like to admit. I, too, had been prepared to *be* whoever I needed to be in order to get what I wanted.

True, the similarity ended there. I didn't deliberately ruin people's lives, after all. But I had been looking to him to define me. *I need to be a settled chosen woman*, I had been saying, *in order to be successful, or acceptable, in order to feel good about myself.*

No more. In future I was going to get my self-esteem from myself. How, I didn't know quite yet. But I would figure it out.

The truths came tumbling towards me. Each one was astringent. Each one was liberating.

I *had* been in love with Chris – or at least with the False Self which he had portrayed. I searched my conscience and I could truly say that. But that love had been fertilised and encouraged to grow by my need to be settled and to belong. That didn't make my love for him any less real, but it made it less pure. But that love was now severed and cauterised by the truth. I was free of it now.

The proof of this was that I didn't miss him at all. Sure, I was still devastated at how I had been treated, at what I had gone through, at being used. But my heart was untouched.

At least . . . here came another relentless truth . . . my heart was untouched by *Chris*.

But my heart was very much touched by David. I was in love with David. The genuine article this time. It wasn't about what I could get from him, or how he made me feel. It was just . . . love. It was knowing that he was a wonderful decent man, and the world was a better place for him being there. It was me smiling each time I thought of him. It was wanting to be in his presence.

I probably had been halfway in love with him already, even before any of this happened, no matter how in denial I had been about it.

But now, having spent this intense time with him, having seen his gentleness, his sense of humour, his strength . . . well, I loved him. It was that simple. And that useless.

Oh well, I'd get over it. Or . . . more likely, I *wouldn't* get over it, but I'd get over wishing things could be different. I'd learn to carry that love like a secret, and just get on with my life.

And, I swore with determination, I was *not* going to go looking for another man. If I met one, great, I wasn't going to retire to a convent either. But I was sufficient to myself now.

I had been looking all this time to belong. Well, I surely was going to belong. To myself. To a select and exclusive club of one person. I would give myself whatever I needed: love, acceptance, a sense of belonging and being wanted and needed.

I realised with a gasp that when I was depending on other people to provide these things for me, I had been giving my power away. I was effectively saying to them, *I can only be happy, and content, and feel good about myself if* you *do certain things.*

What a totally scary precarious way to live.

No, I was going to be happy and content and feel good about myself regardless. And if people chose to give me love, and acceptance, and to seek out my company . . . well, that was a bonus. I would like that, I would enjoy it, but I would no longer *need* it. And if I ever did meet anybody else, I would meet him halfway, as a partnership of equals. I would go to him from love and choice, not from need.

Not surprisingly, at the end of this process I was completely and utterly and totally exhausted. Drained. Shattered. I went to bed early – earlier than David came back – and slept deeply.

Chapter 35

I slept right through the night, and when I awoke curtain-diffused daylight indicated that the day had already well begun. I looked at my watch – heavens! It was gone eleven o'clock. I threw back the covers and got up.

I checked in with myself. How did I feel? Good. Still drained, but clear and refreshed. Ready for the rest of my life.

I was still very fragile after what had happened to me, though. I knew that. I had so nearly lost my personality, my Self. I had to find it again, to build it again. And what better chance would I ever get to decide who exactly I was? Would the real Sally Cronin please step forward?

I went downstairs for a swim. On the way I popped my head around the door of David's office to say good morning.

David waved cheerfully at me from behind the desk. "Good sleep?" he enquired with a grin. "You obviously managed to hack your way through the briars, anyway."

"I wasn't asleep for *quite* a hundred years!" I laughed back at him, leaning on the doorframe, "and I woke myself up rather than waiting for some prince to happen along. Sisters doing it for themselves, don't you know! I've had enough of expecting handsome princes to sort me out. Some of them are frogs anyway."

"Not all of them. Don't lose your faith in human nature," he said, serious now.

"True, but even if it's a real prince, I'm going to meet him awake and whole, not look to him to rescue me. That's not fair on real princes, and gives frogs too many opportunities to hurt you."

"Good point! Well thought out!" he said, giving me an approving nod. "You off to the pool?" he said, indicating the towel bundle under my arm. "Have a good one, and I'll catch you later."

I managed two lengths! True, my legs and arms were literally shaking afterwards, but still . . .

I then went upstairs, showered and dressed and breakfasted, or more accurately, lunched.

I located my nearest Social Welfare office in the phone-book, and went downstairs to drive over there with the sick-certs.

I approached my car with trepidation. Chris was still winning, I realised. I was still thinking of him, still fearing him, so he was winning. But at least my car seemed untouched, and so, relieved in the extreme, I drove off.

The staff in Social Welfare expedited me efficiently and pleasantly, organising for my payments to be lodged to my bank account. It was far from a huge amount of money, but it was a fortune to me, and would be the means of my re-establishing myself.

As soon as the first payment went through I was going to get myself a good haircut, I decided. And no more blonde – I'd get it all dyed my natural brown and stop trying to live up to some sort of standard imposed by God-knows-who.

From now on, what you saw was what you got and you could like it or lump it. Not that I would stop wearing make-up, or stop presenting myself as well as I could. But I would wear make-up because I *wanted* to, not because I had to.

After my visit to the Social Welfare office, I grabbed a bite from a sandwich bar and ate it in the car. And then . . . it was time. I was going to honour my promise to David and call on Gaby.

I drove to her house with my heart thudding uncomfortably. Maybe she won't be in, I thought, even though I knew her schedule – unless it had changed – and knew that she would be back from collecting Jack from playschool and wouldn't yet have gone to collect Haley from school. But I hoped against hope that she wouldn't be there, that she and Jack had gone shopping, maybe, or to a friend's house for lunch.

No matter that that would only be delaying the inevitable. Today I was quite happy for the inevitable to be delayed. As I drove towards her house I could still feel the bitter taste of bile which was the flavour of anger and betrayal. I hated her for what she had done to me.

And how would I broach the subject? I wondered to myself as I drove. Not the sort of question you can just drop casually into conversation, in between enquiries about the children and chat about holidays: "Why did you try to shag my boyfriend?" Didn't fit, somehow.

I pulled up outside her house and saw her car. She was here after all.

Getting out of my own car I braced my shoulders and took several deep breaths as I walked to her door. With a hand I was interested to note was trembling, I pressed the round ceramic doorbell.

A couple of minutes later the door opened and Gaby stood there.

"Hello, Gaby," I said quietly.

"Dear God," she said, her hands flying to her mouth in shock. "Sally! What are you doing here? And what's happened to you? You look – " she shook her head, words failing her.

"It's a long story," I said calmly, no matter that my heart was racing now and my fists were clenched.

My anger and sense of betrayal had expanded now that I was actually in her presence. But that wasn't too bad; I had half-expected that.

What I hadn't expected, and what was unsettling me, were the other emotions I was experiencing: joy at seeing her beautiful round face which was so dear to me, the pain of having missed her company (which pain I had not even really acknowledged before to myself), the overwhelming desire to fling myself at her and wrap my arms around her and hug her tightly and never let her go.

"Come in," she said once she had recovered from her shock. And her own voice was now neutral and restrained, and not terribly welcoming. No matter the truth of what had happened in Chris's house, this was awkward for both of us.

She moved back and I stepped into the house, and my breath caught in my throat as I found myself in that familiar place: scene of so much laughter and even some tears, meals cooked and eaten, of discussion and laughing argument, of glasses of punch at Christmas time, of the rich history of friendship.

In the hallway she hovered, seeming unsure. After a moment she opened the sitting-room door and led me in there. I was acutely aware of the nuances of this decision. Her warm yellow kitchen was the venue for friends and welcome visitors; the sitting-room was, except for parties, reserved for formal guests and business callers.

Once in the sitting-room she turned to me.

"Please sit down," she said in her best hostess voice, indicating one of the chairs. I sat where directed, and she sat on the sofa.

"So?" she asked, still neutrally.

The question just burst out of me: "Did you really make a pass at Chris?"

Her face registered shock and confusion.

I continued, "Did you tell him you wanted an affair with him? A fling, to be exact. That you wanted more excitement in your life and he would do? Did you tell him that?"

"No," she said and her face was red and flushed

390

with some unidentifiable emotion. "No, I never did. Did he say that? Did he say I did?"

"But you admitted it!" I burst out. "So why are you denying it now?"

"I never admitted any such thing," she said loudly, and I began to be able to identify her emotion: it was anger, pure and hot, "because I never *did* any such thing!"

"But you did!" I wailed, beginning to feel again that awful sensation which I had experienced so often with Chris: of my own memories being totally at variance with the facts. "You told me you did! And you must have. Otherwise how could he have known your secret?" I cried out. "About feeling overwhelmed and suffocated by Peter's love, and of regret about never again having the excitement of new love?"

She looked even more shocked, if that were possible. "*I* never told him that – never ever."

"But you must have! Because he knew."

"I never told him," she insisted grimly.

"Well, how on earth could he have known, then?" My voice was rising.

"*I* don't know! Maybe it was a lucky guess."

That put a bit of a halt to my gallop. "He *is* very good at reading people," I admitted.

"But if you knew that, why did you take it as proof that I had done what you've said?" she asked.

"I didn't know it *then*," I protested. "I only learned it afterwards. And anyway, I *didn't* take it as proof. I rang you about it. And you *admitted* it."

"I never admitted any such thing," she insisted.

"You *did*," I said, near tears now, "when I said that Chris had told me everything, you said you were so sorry about what had happened. What was that if not admitting it?"

"But Sally – "

"You said you never meant for it to happen, so you were admitting that something had happened! And you said you had never meant it as a betrayal, and that you never meant for me to find out. And now you're denying it!"

She was looking very pale.

"I remember that conversation. But none of it was about making a pass at him!" She looked aghast at the prospect. "It was about . . . about something else entirely."

"What?" I demanded immediately.

She stood and began to pace around the room, her agitation clear in her movements, in her kneading hands.

"I was worried about you, Sally. That last time you came for dinner you were frantically talking, but making no sense. And you were looking agitated and jittery, so uncoordinated that you knocked over two glasses. And you had started losing a lot of weight – although not nearly as much as you've lost now," she said, shaking her head at the state of me. I was worried about you," she said again.

"Funny way of showing it," I muttered.

She glanced at me but carried on. "So when Chris rang and said that *he* was worried about you and wanted a chat, I jumped at the chance. When I got there he was saying how mentally unstable you were, but that you were terrified of the idea of going to a doctor."

I let a gasp out of me at his audacity.

Gaby continued, "He was asking my opinion about – about options. Like . . . getting you committed."

"He *what?*"

"I swear, he was. As you can imagine I wasn't a bit happy about talking about that. I felt guilty for even getting into a position where I was plotting – it felt like to me – behind your back. But yet, you *were* ill, there *was* something wrong with you. And Chris started telling me that you were hallucinating, that you thought he was trying to poison you, and that you were threatening to jump off a bridge if he didn't leave you alone. He was telling me that he was seriously worried for your safety, and even for his own."

"That's all untrue. I was bad, yes, but not that bad!"

"That's what he said. And I was *horrified*. I had been concerned about you anyway but this was way worse than anything I suspected. So I . . . well, I discussed options with him . . . But I felt awful about it. And yes, guilty. As if I was betraying you. That's the point at which you came home. If I looked guilty, it's because I was. But not for the reasons you think."

I was beginning to believe her, it was making sense, and my heart eased enormously as I began to realise that my friend had not betrayed me after all. Of course, simultaneously I had to begin to acknowledge that I had grievously misjudged her, and bear the pain of that. And the repercussions of that.

"I picked up on your guilt when I came back," I told her. "Your face gave it away. And Chris told me you had made a pass at him, and I believed him. I didn't believe him immediately," I rushed to say. "I told him you'd never do that to me, nor to Peter. But he insisted, and I trusted him too and believed him too. And when I rang you, you admitted it. Or seemed to."

She shook her head, and sat down again. "We were at cross-purposes." She shook her head. "Chris said *I* made a pass at him?" she repeated. "Why on earth would he say that?"

"That's a long story," I told her. "Same long story as the lies he told you about me, like saying I was having hallucinations. Which are also not true. Have you got some time?"

She glanced at her watch. "I have an hour before I have to collect Haley. Come into the kitchen and I'll put the kettle on."

I rejoiced at that sign of her increasing favour, even as I noted the remaining distance and formality in her voice.

I looked around me as I went into the kitchen. "No Jack?"

"He's at a friend's," she said shortly.

This was not, it appeared, the time to be asking about her children. Much though I longed to hear how they were getting on.

She put the kettle on and made a pot of strong coffee which she placed on the table with a yellow earthenware plate of gourmet dark-chocolate biscuits.

"Okay," she said, pouring two mugs of coffee, "tell me."

And I did tell her. I told her the whole sad sorry story. I told it succinctly and unemotionally, but even so her face was a picture of horror and pity as I spoke.

"That is *awful*," she said when I had finished. "You wouldn't think that such – such *evil* exists."

"Is he evil?" I asked. "Or is he only hurting, hurting so badly that he'll do anything to stop the pain, and the peculiarity of the disorder is that stopping his pain causes other people's?"

"I can't believe you're making excuses for him."

"I'm not. I'm not saying that he's *not* evil. I'm asking the question, not answering it. I've no idea of the answer. But I do suspect that it's not enough to just say that he's evil and let that be the answer. That's too easy. It stops us searching for answers. It makes the perpetrators a nice handy *Other*, rather than just a hurting *Us*, and that divorces us from having to possibly identify with them. It stops us having to wonder if we, too, would be like that if we had suffered the same circumstances."

"Yes, but – " she stopped abruptly and looked at her watch. "It's time to go and collect Haley from school, and then Jack from his friend's."

She stood and I took the proffered cue and stood too, awkward and embarrassed, not knowing what to do, as she swiftly cleared the table. She picked up her bag and fished her keys out of it, and began leading the way out of the kitchen. I trailed after her.

Once out on the path we hovered.

I said, "Can I come with you to collect Haley? And Jack? I've missed them so. I'd love to see them."

In my mind I could picture Haley's face when she saw me, lighting up, running towards me, perhaps in soft focus and slow motion, exactly like the ending of every feel-good Hollywood film. We could even manage a cringe-making moral-of-the-story speech about trusting your friends, perhaps.

But Gaby's expression tightened. No," she said abruptly. "Sally, you have hurt us all so badly. Our whole family. Never mind what your abrupt cutting me off did to me, who thought you were my friend, who thought nothing could come between us that we wouldn't sort out. Actually," she corrected herself, "*do* mind that, but that's a discussion for another time. But have you any idea what it has been like for me, trying to explain to a weeping Haley why you don't see her any more? Trying to explain that you do love her, it was just me you didn't love?"

"I'm so sorry," I whispered, crying for the hurt I had inflicted on that precious little girl.

"Can you imagine," Gaby continued, her tone hard with remembered pain, "how awful it was trying to let her down gently when she somehow became convinced you would turn up for her birthday?"

I was shaking my head in pain at hearing all this.

Gaby continued implacably, "And how much it hurt, Sally, when I had to witness her face light up every single time the doorbell rang at her party . . . and watch her repeated disappointment each time it was one or other of her guests, but not you. And watching the brave effort she put on, so young," said Gaby with a catch in her voice at the memory, "to welcome the guest warmly, even though she was near tears."

"I'm so sorry," I repeated uselessly.

"And poor Peter, the helpless pain on his face as he saw his daughter – and you know how he feels about her – going through that without him being able to protect her. You did that to us, Sally. Yes, I now understand a little about why, and I can feel for you too. But you did that to our family, hurt my children so badly. And I'm not going to let you just waltz back into their lives and risk that happening again."

"It won't happen again," I said weakly, hurting at the images of Haley she was describing. My beloved Haley, hurting because of me. "I swear it won't."

"And not just Haley." She glanced at her watch. "What about me? Did I not deserve better? It was bad enough when I thought that you were angry because of what I had done – even though I hadn't done much, just been there when Chris was sharing these ideas. But now to find out that you trusted me so little that you believed I made a pass at him. To discover that you thought so little of me that you believed I would betray both Peter and you like that . . ." She shook her head at the enormity of it all. "I can't take that on board. I really can't. That has hurt me dreadfully, and I'm going to have to spend some time getting my head around it."

"I didn't believe you would do it," I protested. "I told Chris straight that you wouldn't do that."

"You may have done, but you were quick enough to come around to the possibility so that you had to ring me to check on me. And to take what I had said as proof. That all doesn't show much – *any!* – trust in me." She stifled a sob and put the back of her hand to her mouth. "Look, I have to go. I really, really don't know where we go from here. On the one hand we were all victims of that man and it would be a victory over him if we could resume our friendship. But on the other – you've hurt us dreadfully, Sally, all of us, and I'm not sure the friendship can survive that. I'll need to think about it, and talk to Peter about it. I'll ring you."

"I'm staying at *Svelte* gym – the number's in the phone book," I told her.

"Okay," she acknowledged. "It could be weeks, it could even be a couple of months. And it might be to tell you that I – we – have decided not to try to resume the friendship. But I *will* ring you."

And with that she turned away and made her way the short distance to her car. I stood there and watched her as she got in and drove away. All without looking at me or acknowledging me once. But I did see her lift one hand to wipe her eyes.

I stood there, irresolute. Maybe my relationship with the whole family was irreparably damaged, another victim of Chris's illness. Collateral damage. Some things couldn't be fixed. Eggs couldn't be unscrambled.

Feeling heart-sore I got into my own car and drove home.

Chapter 36

"Well?" asked David that evening as we sat together over dinner.

"Your hat is safe. She didn't do it." I related what I now knew of what had actually happened. "You know, I've been thinking about it, and I remember when I said I'd ring her, Chris tried to talk me out of it by saying it would threaten the trust in our relationship, and that there was no point anyway because she would more than likely lie and deny she had made a pass at him."

"Right . . ." said David, getting it immediately.

"Yes," I confirmed, "he was setting it up for her denying making this pass. But he was very lucky – "

"The luck of the devil," David interjected.

I nodded agreement as I continued, "The way the conversation went, it sounded as if she was admitting what he had accused her of. And I remember now," I said slowly, "how relieved he looked when I came off the phone. That was the great gamble for him, what he couldn't control – whatever Gaby might have said."

"But why did he phone her in the first place? Just more game-playing? More attention-seeking?"

"Maybe. Or possibly he was trying to deflect suspicion. I had acted crazily at that dinner party at Gaby and Peter's, and he knew they were concerned. He probably anticipated their approaching him about my mental health – or approaching me."

"Pre-emptive action?"

"Exactly."

"And is it all sorted between you and Gaby now?" David asked then.

I laughed hollowly. "Far from it!" I related what had happened, and then continued, "And I can't blame her. I really can't. Of *course*, she feels dreadful about her family having been hurt. Of course, she does. And I feel terrible now."

"In what way?"

"Well, I'm so ashamed of myself. She was right – I didn't trust her enough. That's all it would have taken. Trust. So much would have changed if I had trusted her. If I *knew* that she wouldn't have done that, then by definition I would have known that Chris was lying. And I could have got myself out of that awful situation much sooner."

"Don't be so hard on yourself," said David. "It's pretty clear that he's an expert at deception – he would fool anybody."

"But I didn't believe him until Gaby – as I thought – admitted it," I said again. "I had to cling to that above all. And as well, I so wanted to believe him. I was so sure that this was *it*, that my search for a life partner and the life of my dreams was over. I couldn't afford not to trust him."

"Hm," said David sadly, "it's hard, isn't it? When you're single and you don't want to be."

"Yes," I said, my curiosity about David almost – not quite, but almost – replacing my own misery.

In the two days I had been here, there had been neither sighting nor mention of any partner. Maybe he was being discreet because I was around.

"You're so good to be letting me stay with you," I told him. "I hope that my being here isn't . . . well . . . cramping your style in any way."

"No," he laughed easily, "you're not cramping my style. Don't worry about it!"

I was left to wonder with a rather unbecoming prurience about where his style was flowing uncramped. And with whom.

None of my business, I quickly acknowledged.

"Here," he said, changing the subject and reaching into a pocket and taking out a piece of paper, "I got this for you today – I said I would."

I took it and realised it contained a name and phone number. "That counsellor I was telling you about," he explained. "She comes highly recommended. A friend of mine went to her when his wife was diagnosed with terminal cancer, and she really helped him."

"Thanks for that," I said. "I'll ring her tomorrow."

The rest of the evening passed uneventfully. David and I chatted lightly, watched some television together, played some cards. It was so peaceful, so relaxing and so restorative.

* * *

First thing next morning I rang the counsellor, Bronagh O'Hara. I gulped when I heard the price – one hour of her time was over half of my weekly income from the Social Welfare. But still, it was going to be worth it. I needed to recover in order to move on, and everything that assisted that recovery was essential. So I made an appointment for the following week.

I then organised myself and went downstairs for a swim. I managed two lengths again, although I will admit to having to stop for a rest halfway through the second one. It was all progress though, and I was very proud of myself.

After lunch, which was eaten alone in the flat (David rang up to say he wasn't going to be there, that he had a business lunch) I went out.

I checked the car first for sabotage, but there was none that I could see. Was Chris watching me doing this checking? Was he, even now, getting a thrill from witnessing me factoring him and his actions into my plans?

I looked around me, but couldn't see him anywhere.

I drove the short distance to Dundrum centre, parked the car and joined the throng of shoppers and browsers.

I was a little overwhelmed by the sheer number of people. But that had been half the point in coming here – to get used to life again.

And then, in the bustling crowds I heard a voice right in my ear. "Hello, Sally," it said.

I took a sharp in-breath and turned around abruptly. There was a man walking quickly away. It could have been Chris, endeavouring to play mind games with me. Or I could have imagined the voice, and the man walking away could have been a total stranger.

A raging fury overtook me and my immediate reaction was to chase after him and confront him. I even took a step or two in his direction.

But just as quickly sense came too and cautioned me to do nothing. If it wasn't Chris, I would only be making a food of myself to accost this stranger. And if it was Chris, I would only be giving him what he wanted – a reaction.

I refused do that.

The only way to win is to refuse to play, I reminded myself.

And so with shaking heart and trembling limbs I just turned and walked on. I wouldn't tell David, I decided. He was concerned enough about the punctures incident . . . I didn't know how he would react to this.

I tried to put it behind me. Chris wouldn't win, I swore. I would still enjoy my trip around the shops.

I ended up going into a second-hand shop. I had never before frequented such an establishment, but it seemed sensible now. I still had very little money – just what was left over from the money David had given me after paying for the doctor. And I fully intended to put back the weight I had lost until I no longer looked like a famine victim, so, even if I had ample cash-flow I wouldn't spend a lot of money on clothes which might only fit me for a month or so.

In the event, I bought two pairs of jeans, a denim skirt, and several tops, and one scoop-necked purple velvet dress. Not the most stylish wardrobe in the world, but the new clothes meant an end to leggings!

When I got home I cheerfully threw those bedraggled and tattered items into the bin, and made a determined effort to allow my pleasure in my new clothes to overcome the residual upset about what had happened earlier.

Chris was not going to win, I swore to myself. He was *not*.

When David came up after work that evening I modelled my new clothes for him, as excited as if they were designer gear from the trendiest boutique.

"They're lovely," he said, but his voice was strained and he seemed distracted.

"Are you okay?" I asked, concerned. I sat down beside him on the sofa and turned to face him. "Is everything okay?"

He wearily wiped his eyes with his hand. "Just a long day, with all sorts of problems which needed sorting out, the computer playing up, stuff like that. Oh well," he smiled at me with an effort, "that's my job, after all. Now, what would you like for dinner?"

"Allow me," I said. "You sit there and relax. Would you like a glass of wine?"

"Actually, if you could get me a beer out of the fridge that would be heaven," he smiled at me. "And if you're offering to make dinner, then I gladly accept."

I got him a beer and turned to the dinner. And as I prepared the meal I was aware of two emotions.

The first was a sense of primeval pleasure at cooking for my man. No matter that he wasn't, technically, my man. For those brief moments I could pretend. I could pretend that we were an ordinary couple, tired after a long day, with me taking my turn to cook while he relaxed in front of the television with a beer.

But at the same time there was fear. What if I ruined this meal? I knew in theory that I had never ruined any meal, that it was Chris all along. But still . . . I had so much failure and doubt behind me. How would this one work?

But in the end the meal turned out to be delicious, and I was so proud of myself. And so relieved.

"That was delicious, thanks!" said David. "Well done!"

"You're welcome," I said, delighted with myself.

I wouldn't hear of him helping to clear up.

"No, you sit down," I insisted. "I'll do it."

It was just so glorious for me to be competent at something. And, also, it was great to be able to repay David, no matter in how small a way, for his kindness and hospitality.

In such drops of success and joy would I measure my healing and recovery.

Once I had tidied away David said to me, "Come here then," and he held out his arm indicating that I should sit with him.

I needed no second invitation, and I went to him and sat beside him on the sofa. He let his arm settle on my shoulders, around me, and I snuggled into him. I sat with my legs curled under me, my head resting against his chest, and I could hear his heartbeat. He was so warm, so sturdy, so safe. But – I discovered as I snuggled into him – also so exciting.

Down girl, I told myself.

But was it so surprising? I had been attracted to David ever since we met. And no matter that I had suppressed that desire once I realised he was gay, I knew now that my desire had been more dormant than extinct.

I itched to reach out and touch him. But I restrained myself. This was *so* not appropriate.

We watched television for the rest of that evening, but I couldn't really have told what was on . . . I was just so conscious of David's body right beside mine. So acutely aware of him, and my heart was beating faster, and I was so, *so* tempted to turn my head to him and kiss him. But, of course, I didn't.

And so we chastely went to our own rooms at the evening's end.

As we parted he said, "I'm meeting a few mates tomorrow evening for a few pints. Would you like to join us? You'd be more than welcome."

That sounded great, but it seemed to me that he was being good enough to put me up, without having to be joined at the hip with me.

So I quickly said, "No, no, I won't. But thanks anyway."

And I appreciated the fact he even managed to seem duly disappointed at my refusal.

* * *

The following week, after the first Social Welfare payment went through, I had my first appointment with Bronagh.

I went out to the car to find a printed flyer under the windscreen wiper.

New Dating Agency! read the headline. *Meet handsome men! Enjoy committed relationships! Abandon them on a whim! Believe lies about them! Pay the price!*

There was a 1550 premium rate phone number under it, but no address and no website.

Trembling, I folded the flyer and placed it in my bag. I was going to be late for my appointment if I didn't go now.

No reaction, I reminded myself. Give no reaction. But that was so difficult to do.

As I drove, I had an image of Chris sneaking into the *Svelte* carpark in the middle of the night to put intimidating notes on my car.

It was working. I was intimidated.

I *hated* the thoughts of him hanging around, knowing where I was living, what I was doing. But I wasn't going to react, I told myself grimly. If he wanted reaction, then by definition I was going to give him none. And thwarting his desire for reaction would be my victory.

I just wished it tasted sweeter.

Bronagh O'Hara proved to be a thin forty-ish redhead with sharp glasses and a sweet, confidence-inspiring manner. The first session was taken up with my telling her about my experiences with Chris.

After paying for the session I had some money left. And I had the exact home for that money. The hairdresser's.

I got them to dye my hair my own natural brown, and had them chop so much off that I ended up with a short softly-spiky gamine look. I couldn't believe it when I looked in the mirror – my eyes looked so big, my cheekbones so defined, my neck so long and elegant.

"Is that really me?" I kept saying, and the stylist laughed with delight and satisfaction.

When I went home that evening everybody's reaction was all I could have hoped for – Liz didn't recognise me and Steve whistled when he saw me.

And David – when David came upstairs after the day's work and saw me, he just stopped dead and looked at me with rich appreciation in his eyes.

"Wow!" he said, and again, "Wow! You look great, Sal. Classy haircut! It really suits you."

"Oh well," I joked, "when you look like me you need all the help you can get!"

His expression changed immediately, no longer open and appreciative, but serious now. "What on *earth* do you mean?"

"Oh, you know," I shrugged my shoulders, trying to laugh it off.

"No, Sally," he shook his head, "no, I don't know. Please explain."

This was embarrassing. I hadn't expected him to pick up so intently on a throwaway self-deprecating comment. And to judge by his expression, he wasn't going anywhere until he got an answer.

I took a deep breath. "It's nothing really. Just that I know I'm basically quite plain, and need good haircuts and make-up and so on to look halfway good."

"That's not true." He was staring at me in disbelief at what I was saying.

"Oh, it is. I know it is. I've always known it. And it's not just me – " I came to an abrupt halt. I had been going to tell him what Chris had said about me being so ugly. But no matter how comfortable I was with David, I couldn't begin to share that. The pain and the humiliation of it were still too strong. I could feel my face reddening with embarrassment at both the memory of the comments, and the strained silence which I had now created.

Eventually David broke the silence. He said softly, "You were going to say something about Chris, weren't you?"

I nodded as he continued, "He told you that you were very ugly, didn't he?"

I nodded again.

"And did you never stop to think," said David very, very gently, "that he picked up on your belief of that. That he used that information against you. Exactly the same way as he exploited picking up on Gaby's secret. Did that never occur to you?"

I shook my head, tears streaming silently down my cheeks. But, of course! It made so much sense. Of course, Chris had said it just to hurt me. But that didn't make it all any less true.

I tried to share that with David. "But it's true anyway. I knew it before he ever told me that."

"Oh, you silly goose," said David, and he came to me and gathered me in his arms, "of course, it's not true. Maybe it's not appropriate for me to be saying this, but you are beautiful, Sally. You really are. Will I tell you a secret?" he whispered into my ear. I nodded so he continued, his voice gentle and reassuring, "I always wondered why you wore so much make-up. I never thought you needed it. I've seen you in the pool without make-up, and I was always struck by your beauty. You are beautiful. Sally. You really are. You just have to let yourself believe it. Chris didn't pick up on your lack of beauty – he picked up on your *belief* about your lack of beauty."

"Really?" I whispered hopefully.

"Really, really! Even Darius thinks so!" said David with laughter in his voice. "And I think we all have to agree that he's a true connoisseur of women. He should know. You are beautiful, Sally. You just have to believe it. Okay?" He gave my shoulders a little shake, as if to bring me to my senses. "Now, go and wash that face – that beautiful face – and we'll get some dinner organised."

Chapter 37

Over the next two or three weeks we fell into a pattern.

David was invariably already gone when I got up –
a combination of him starting work early, and me, still
recovering, sleeping in quite late.

Each morning I would go downstairs and either
have a swim or do a workout. And slowly but consistently
I found my strength returning. I began to regain weight
and muscle, to appear less skeletal and emaciated.

Because I woke late and took my time, all that would
fill in the morning well. But the afternoons lagged. I
watched a lot of afternoon television. I frequented the
library so much that they knew my name.

It was some ways a lonely life. I was alone during
the day – apart from passing hellos with staff and
fellow-members of the gym – and I couldn't depend on
David to be there after work.

Not surprisingly, he had a wide circle of friends and
a healthy social life, so he was often out in the evenings.

He also belonged to an Aikido studio and trained there regularly.

He almost always invited me to go out with him – not to Aikido, obviously, and there were other, unspecified, occasions to which I was not invited.

But apart from that, he invited me to accompany him.

However, I always declined, not wishing to impose any more than I had to.

I was even going to stay in my bedroom one evening when he had guests over. But his shocked and indignant reaction disabused me of that idea fairly promptly. I ended up having a great time with his friends, and it was wonderful to just have simple ordinary fun.

And, although I looked discreetly, I could see nobody who seemed to be *with* David. How strange! There was a mystery there, and I longed to know what it was. But it was none of my business, after all. And my prurient interest was not fair recompense to him for all his kindness. So, with an effort I put aside my avid curiosity.

On those evenings when he was home we would play at housekeeping. I continued to cook dinner for him, and believe it or not the meals always worked out. I never over-salted them; I never added half a tin of curry powder; I never burned them. Funny that.

And on those evenings we would sit and chat over dinner, and afterwards we might play a board game, or cards, or watch telly together, curled up comfortably and platonically on the sofa together. He felt so nice to lean against, and if I was keenly aware of deep regret that this man could never be for me – well, that was my problem.

At least, I acknowledged joyfully, it seemed as if my capability to love and have a relationship was unimpaired. Maybe at some stage I would meet somebody else. It was possible.

And, ironically given his homosexuality, it was in spending this time with David that I truly learned the difference between a real loving relationship and Chris's cardboard version.

David had a wonderful sense of humour (whilst, come to think of it, Chris had no sense of humour at all), he was kind ('nuff said), and decent and genuine (again, 'nuff said).

But he wasn't perfect, which I appreciated. After my experience with Chris I was wary of anything which seemed over-perfect. David could be impatient, and sharp if people were delaying him or getting in his way.

But there was a huge difference between him and Chris – he was never insulting, nor demeaning. He could – and sometimes did – robustly share his annoyance. But he always managed to do without assaulting anybody's character.

And so it was a strange, nearly-alone time. But I cherished it. I recognised it very clearly for what it was – a healing time. It wouldn't be like this forever; I would be going out into the world soon, I knew. It was good to take this time to recuperate and regenerate. And it was very special to spend this time with myself, learning about my strengths and weaknesses, and enjoying my own company.

There were still nights when I sobbed myself to sleep, as quietly as I could. There were still days when everything seemed like far too much effort, even living.

But those times grew more and more infrequent. *I am recovering,* I told Chris defiantly in my imagination. *I am winning!*

The stalking seemed to have eased also, which was a relief. My car remained untouched, and on the rare occasions I went out, I was unmolested. Maybe he had got bored. Maybe he had found a new woman to prey upon. I would leave it a couple of months and try to find out somehow, in order to try to help her as I had promised Angela I would do.

But for now all seemed to be well.

Other things were going well too. I took David up on his suggestion of doing work in *Svelte*. Two or three hours was plenty; I tired quickly. But that work filled the time, gave me company in the form of my colleagues, and earned me some money. And it helped immeasurably in restoring my self-respect.

I wasn't doing anything too demanding, true, but I was doing it well. I never burned anything with the iron. I never forgot messages when I took a turn at Reception. I never used the wrong cleaners. All that I did, I did well, which restored my self-confidence no end.

Around this time also David and I began to go out together sometimes of an evening. Not on dates, of course not. But friends can go out together. We might go to the theatre, or to the cinema, or for a meal. And it turned out that David loved chick-flicks! The advantages to having a gay friend!

When we were out together I sometimes slipped my

arm through his strong one, just companionably, and as I did so I fantasised that we were a genuine couple out together for an evening. But each night the coach changed back to a pumpkin when he dropped a chaste kiss on my forehead and we went to our separate rooms. And I knew then that we were not a genuine couple, nor ever would be.

Gaby had still not phoned. I didn't feel up to phoning any of my other friends, and of course they could not phone me since nobody had my phone number. I made no effort to contact them.

I would, I told myself, but now was not the time. Likewise none of my family could phone me, and I did not yet feel up to phoning them.

However, one day about a week after that, so about a month after I had seen her, I answered the extension in the flat to hear a beloved familiar voice – Gaby!

"Hello, Sally," she said, and her voice was still wary, "I told you I would phone you. Peter and I have been talking together about all of this," – my heart nearly stopped beating as I waited for her verdict – "and we've realised that you were not to blame for what happened."

I let a breath of relief out of me.

Gaby continued, "Peter read up on that disorder you were telling me about – NPD – and he said you were in the hands of a master manipulator, and that it wasn't your fault that you believed him. And it's not likely to happen again, after all, so we're not risking hurt to everybody to have you come back to us."

"That's *wonderful*!" I whispered.

"So . . ." she took a deep breath, "we would like to

start again. Being friends again, I mean. And we'd like to invite you over for dinner next Friday evening. Would that suit?"

"Friday would be fantastic! What time?"

"Say around seven? And then you can see the children."

"That's great. That's wonderful. I'm so glad. That's brilliant. Thank you." I was gushing and I didn't care.

* * *

When Friday came I drove over to their house (checking the car before getting into it – it was fine). My heart was pounding and my hands were slippery on the steering wheel. How would the children react to me? Would Haley ever forgive me? How would Peter treat me? Would Gaby and I be able to relax in each other's company?

I rang their doorbell and waited, my throat dry, for a few minutes until I heard footsteps coming towards the door and Gaby's voice saying back into the house, ". . . wonder who this could be?"

When she opened the door she did so only a little and she grinned out at me, but she had her finger to her lips signifying that I should be silent.

"So, Haley," she continued her discussion over her shoulder, "do you remember I promised you a big surprise this evening? Well, here it is!"

And with that she flung open the door with a flourish and I was revealed.

Haley was standing in the hallway looking at me, and my heart sank at her blank expression. I was right

– she was too hurt and angry with me to come back to me. I had ruined it forever.

But Haley was looking puzzled now, her brow was furrowed, and she was saying incredulously, "Sally? Is that Sally?" and I remembered then how much I had physically changed – still much thinner than she had known me, and with completely different hair.

Gaby nodded her head, her face beaming, "Yes, Haley, it is!"

Haley's face cleared as her confusion was swept away and her whole face lit up as if fireworks were going on around her, and she said, "Sally! Sally, oh, oh, it's Sally!" and she ran the short distance towards me and flung herself into my arms nearly knocking me over.

She wrapped her legs around my waist and her strong determined arms around my neck and clung to me as if she was trying to burrow into me.

"Oh Sally," she kept saying. "Oh, Sally!"

And Jack too was running up on his short sturdy legs. "Sally! Sally!" and I lifted him – with difficulty – onto my hip and clutched him there and we were all laughing and crying together.

"Come in. Come in," laughed Gaby, as we both realised I was still standing at the top of the steps.

I made my way, waddling like a duck, with the two children wrapped around me, into the house.

"I'm sorry. I have to put you down," I said, and I lowered Jack and Haley to the ground. But I hunkered beside them and the hugs continued.

They were both talking excitedly to me, sharing with me news which I couldn't even interpret as they mangled words in their excitement and interrupted each other and spoke too quickly. But it didn't matter. All that mattered was that I was there with my arms around their narrow backs, hugging them and breathing in the sweet shampoo smell of their soft hair, into which I was dropping salty tears of joy.

Eventually they released me and I was able to stand and look at Gaby.

"Hi," I said shyly.

"Hi back," she said, and her face broke into a broad smile. "Come here," she commanded, and held out her arms.

I moved into her embrace and we hugged tight, and we were both talking at once. *"I'm sorry. I'm sorry,"* we were both saying. *"I've missed you so much. It's great to see you."*

After some endless time I became aware of a plaintive voice and an insistent hand tugging at my skirt.

"Sally," said Jack, "my daddy needs to say hello too."

Gaby and I released each other, both of us wiping our eyes, and I then turned towards the end of the hall where Peter was standing, benevolently watching this scene.

He came up to me and took me into his arms and gave me a full hug. If I had any doubt about the uniqueness of this occasion, this hug would have removed it. Peter and I had always been so formal before – a hand on an arm and a kiss on the cheek had previously been the height of our intimacy.

"Welcome back," he said.

Gaby then led the way into the kitchen. My rehabilitation was obviously complete.

I sat at the table, and Haley scrambled onto my knee. She kept looking at me and patting my hair and stroking my face, learning its contours again perhaps, or reassuring herself that I was real, that I was really there.

I was awed and humbled at her reaction to me. *I don't deserve this*, I thought. *I don't deserve this adoration and delight when I have treated you so badly.* And I was so grateful for her generosity of spirit that didn't seek to punish me, but simply welcomed me back into her life and her heart. And as I held her on my lap I kept grinning in delight at her, and dropped kisses on her head, even as Gaby and I chatted.

Conversation was deliberately light as Gaby finished preparing the meal and put it in the oven.

"There," she said, "that'll be an hour or so. Do you want to do bath and bed?"

"*Do* I?" I asked in exaggerated tones.

And Haley giggled and said, "Yes, yes, Sally, you do it!"

So we went upstairs and I relished again that experience which I thought had gone forever, which I had thought a permanent casualty of Chris: the fun and laughter of giggling and laughing with Jack and Haley as we did the bath-and-bed routine.

When I got downstairs Gaby and Peter were sitting at the kitchen table, each with a glass of red wine. I joined them and Peter poured me a glass. Conversation began casually, and awkwardly, but eventually we began to speak about what had happened.

"I'm sorry I doubted you," I said again.

"I've been reading up on NPD," said Peter, who always likes to be informed about stuff, "and it seems to me that they are master manipulators, and you have nothing to blame yourself for. We're only sorry that we didn't realise what was going on. But again, how could we?"

"And he seemed so nice," said Gaby. "Such a good listener."

"That's his stock in trade," I said sourly. "I know that now. Listening well so you will like him, and all the time picking up information about you, the better to exploit your weaknesses."

"I think that's how he knew my secret," said Gaby with a quick glance at Peter.

It had obviously been discussed between them, and I wondered if they had come to any better understanding of each other. I hoped they had. To have one good thing, no matter how small, come out of this nightmare would ease the pain a little.

"He was watching us interacting, and perhaps my face gave it away for a second, or maybe it was something I said joking which he realised wasn't a joke at all. He's very good at what he does," she said dryly.

"Isn't he though?" I agreed.

"And to think that the thing I really liked about him was how well he treated you!" she laughed sardonically.

"You did have doubts," I reminded her.

"Only about how quickly the relationship was progressing. But maybe it was more than that, maybe I did pick up that all wasn't well. As they say, hindsight is always twenty-twenty vision. As for him picking up on what I was feeling – sure, I was flattered by his attention, the way he listened so avidly. I probably did tell him more than I should have. He conned me too. I don't know if he was already sowing the seeds of his plan, or came up with it later, but whatever, it worked."

"In essence," I told them, "he figures out what you want, and gives it to you, and of course you fall for him, whether romantically or otherwise. But he only gives it temporarily, and you spend the rest of your time with him trying to get back to that perfect place."

Gaby shuddered. "Nightmare stuff," she said.

"It is. It was."

There was silence for a few moments and then Gaby asked, "Tell me, what do your parents think about what's happened to you?"

I said, "Ahh, yes, well . . ."

She said, "You mean they don't know? Well, the way you've described your mother you're probably right. Some things are better left on a need-to-know basis. What did she say about you living in *Svelte*? Not quite the image she'd appreciate, is it?"

"She doesn't know. I haven't been in touch with her for ages. We had a row when I wouldn't go to Laura's graduation. But how could I? And I a total wreck?"

"I see the dilemma. But still, she should know where you are. That's only fair."

"True," I admitted begrudgingly.

"Why don't you ring her? And your father," suggested Gaby. "Just give them your new contact details. That's all."

"Okay," I agreed despite myself, but even to my own ears I sounded unconvincing.

Gaby and Peter were being so good to forgive me what I had done to them. They had welcomed me into their house this evening. And they asked so little of me in return. How could I refuse them this? And really, it was so little after all. Just inform my mother and my father of my whereabouts and my contact details. Was it too much to ask? Not really.

"Okay," I said again, but with a lot more conviction this time, and obviously enough this time to convince them as they nodded their heads happily.

"Ready for dessert?" asked Gaby then, recognising that we had gone deep enough and far enough and emotional enough for one evening.

"Yes, please! I'm still trying to get back to my normal weight and for this short period of time I can eat what I like, and I'm enjoying it!"

Gaby smiled pityingly at me, that woman who eats what she wants all the time.

She produced a rich trifle and we all tucked in, chatting together as old friends do.

Later in the evening conversation moved on to questions about my future plans.

"I don't have a clue," I admitted. "I'm helping out in the gym, and David's being scrupulous about paying me. He's not being *quite* so scrupulous, however, about charging me rent for staying with him, or even letting me contribute. I should be moving into one of the staff bedsits soon, and that'll give me that much more independence, and I'll definitely pay rent then. I'll insist upon it. I'm going to start looking for a job in the next week or two. Something to do with finances so that I'm getting back into my old industry. Just a part-time job, maybe, or else something fairly undemanding."

"Well done!"

"Thanks. It's a step back into the workforce which will be good for me. Maybe in a few months I'll feel up to a full-time job. It's a case of getting my life back to where it was before, and that's the life I was bemoaning! Now it seems like some kind of dream, something to be accomplished. I'll never take the ordinary for granted ever again," I told them solemnly.

I saw them exchange a quick look, one of those whole conversations in a single glance which seem to come effortlessly to long-term couples, and then Peter gave a little nod at which Gaby turned to me.

"Sally, how about this for an idea? If you need somewhere to stay until you get back on your feet, why don't you stay here? We have the spare room, you know that, and we'd love to have you."

The offer took my breath away. It was so kind coming from a couple who had been so hurt by me, and it warmed me and solaced me. But there was something else too – a resistance to taking them up on it, a feeling that it wasn't right for me.

Before I could analyse it further I heard myself thanking them, but declining.

"I really appreciate it, but I'm fairly settled at the gym, and as I said I'll soon have my own bedsit and I'll be totally independent. But I'll come and see you all often, and stay here as often as you'll have me!"

The rest of the evening passed in catching up on their news, and it was warm and relaxing and fun, and I treasured every moment in the way you can only do when you've nearly lost it all.

Chapter 38

When I left there was a leaflet under my windscreen wipers. I lifted it out and read it as best I could by the street lights.

Car windscreen cleaning! it read. *Call us when your car windows are dirty. We'll help you out!*

I glanced around anxiously, but no nearby cars had anything under their wipers. That means nothing, I told myself. The other drivers might have taken theirs already. But I couldn't suppress the shiver which overcame me, nor could I stop myself from glancing anxiously around me and hurrying to unlock my car and get in. I still clutched the flyer. Maybe it was nothing. Maybe it was genuine.

But still . . . it was worth hanging onto. As part of the evidence for the prosecution in the murder trial, I thought grimly. It might be nothing to do with Chris – and this was part of the hell of it, that I ended up suspicious of everything in case it had something to do with him. He had, by default, innocent window-cleaning companies helping him in his campaign.

I seriously hoped that it was genuine. If it *was* Chris, that meant that he had followed me from *Svelte*, and that was a seriously scary prospect.

It probably was genuine. The other messages had had very clear links to Chris – this had nothing of the sort.

But yet . . . no other car had the leaflet, which was certainly interesting.

And why offer just a car window-washing service? Why not wash the whole car?

It niggled a little.

And now that I looked at it, I noted that it, in common with the dating-agency flyer, had no address of any kind, only a 1550 phone number.

But I soon made myself forget it. I drove home and let my thoughts wander back to the evening we had had. It felt so good, so incredibly good, to resume my friendship with Gaby and Peter, and Haley and Jack. It was perfect.

And how nice of them to offer to let me live with them.

I pondered, as I drove through the city streets, why I had been so reluctant to take them up on it.

And once I had peace to think about it I recognised why. I didn't want to leave David. I didn't want to miss seeing him every day, to miss knowing he was around, to miss our chats of an evening and our chaste cuddles on the sofa. I knew that I would have to move on in due course. The bedsit was going to be available in little over a week, and I was already dreading that, even though we would be still close neighbours, for a while at least. But I wanted to take every possible moment of living with him. Because soon there would be no more.

* * *

Next morning was Saturday. I *loved* Saturdays. David rarely worked, and we would often just potter around the flat in the morning, and again, I could fantasise that we were a real couple.

He usually went to the Aikido studio during some part of the day, but otherwise we might go together to the Blackrock Market, or into town to browse along Temple Bar.

We might take in a film at the Irish Film Institute and congratulate ourselves, laughing, at how cultural we were.

We once even bought green flat caps and took an open-top bus tour of Dublin with all the tourists, embarrassing ourselves hugely by putting on dreadful American accents and exclaiming loudly to each other, "Gee, honey, look at that. It's so quaint!" at every opportunity.

I don't think our fellow-travellers found it funny, but it gave us *hours* of amusement.

But this Saturday was to be interrupted by a phone call to David's extension as we were eating breakfast.

"Hi," he said cheerfully into the receiver, and then his face grew more serious, "Hm, hm. Okay. Right Steve, I'll be straight down. Thanks for letting me know."

He replaced the receiver and turned to me.

"Somebody's interfered with your car overnight. Steve noticed it on his way in this morning. Nothing too serious, he says, but still . . ." He sighed deeply. "Come on and we'll see what the story is," he said wearily.

We made our way downstairs. I was full of trepidation as to what we would find.

We went out to the carpark and discovered my car with red lipstick smeared all over its windows. Words were scrawled among the smears: *Whore*. And: *Bitch*.

"The *bastard!*" hissed David. "That's it. He's gone too far!"

"No, no," I pleaded. "No reaction, remember."

"We can't let him keep going like this," he said. "I take your point about not reacting, but really, Sally, how much more of this are we going to take?"

"If we react now we're just telling him that he just has to keep going and he'll eventually get a reaction," I countered.

"True. But what I've been concerned about is that if he's that desperate for a reaction, and isn't getting one, he'll increase the level of what he's doing in order to get one. What is it?" he asked as I gasped.

"I've just remembered. I found a flyer on my windscreen last night when I left Gaby's. It was an ad offering car window-cleaning services. It didn't seem to have any connection with any tricks of Chris's, but now of course . . ."

"Let's see it," he asked.

"It's in my bag, which is upstairs."

"Please go and get it."

I ran upstairs and got it, and I also brought down the

original flyer I had found, about the dating agency. When we compared them we could see the similarities – same font, same layout. And same 1550 phone number.

"No business like that would use a 1550 number," said David. "They wouldn't expect their customers to pay the premium rate. Let's see . . ." and he took his mobile out of his pocket and dialled it. He listened for a moment or two, and then grimaced with distaste and hung up.

"A sex line," he said tersely. "Very funny. Not." He muttered a curse under his breath then before turning to me. "Look, I have a confession to make. Not a bad one," he added hastily, "at least, nothing bad about me. You don't have to worry that I've got any guilty secrets."

For one bemused moment I thought he was suddenly and inopportunely about to talk about his homosexuality.

"But I *have* been keeping something from you," he continued. "I didn't want to worry you, but I think you need to know now. The thing is, there's been more going on than you realised. There's been a bouquet of flowers nearly every day, each paid for by cash to a different florist. I've told Liz to just keep the card and give it to me, and bin the flowers. I didn't even want you to know about them. But the cards are definitely from him. Come on till I show you."

He led the way back inside, and into his office. He rooted in a desk drawer and took out a selection of florists' cards.

"You can handle them," he said. "I've checked each time, and in each case the florist wrote them and Chris never handled them, so there's no fingerprint evidence."

I took them nervously and read some of them. *I'll never forget you,* said one. *Please come back to me. I need you,* read another. *You'll never meet anybody who knows you like I do,* read a third. *I'm the one for you,* read another, and I screwed up my face and abandoned reading the rest of them.

I shook my head in revulsion and despair as I placed them back down.

"There's more," David told me. "It may not be related, but it's an amazing coincidence if it isn't. Ever since you came here I have been inundated by spam on the company's e-mail account, and we've been getting tons of viruses. I've had our computer guys practically living here. It's beyond a joke."

"It's no coincidence," I said dully. "He's a computer security consultant. He knows all about all these sorts of things. He can't really get to me here, so he's getting to you. And I might as well admit, there has been at least one incident which I haven't told you about because I didn't want to worry you. Apart from the dating agency flyer, I mean." I told him about hearing my name in the crowd in Dundrum.

"So," he sighed, "there's been a lot more going on than either of us realised. I'm calling the Guards, Sally, about the damage to your car. And everything else."

"Okay," I said, less an agreement than an acknowledgment of what he was saying – I could see that he wasn't to be deflected from this decision.

An hour or so later – my lipstick-smeared car not being deemed an emergency – the gardai turned up. One of them was the young man we had met at the

Garda station. He was enthusiastic and keen, friendly and officious.

The older one wore an expression of someone who had seen literally everything, who could be surprised by nothing, and from whom all illusions he had ever had about humanity had been stripped away, leaving just a weary and finely honed cynicism.

They looked at my car and shook their heads, wrote the details into their notebooks, listened to the stories about computer viruses and strange flyers and floral bouquets, and wrote them down too, but could do no more.

"But we *know* who's doing it," we insisted.

"Have you proof?" they asked kindly, clearly understanding our dilemma.

But they were constrained by issues such as due process, and the right to the presumption of innocence until proven otherwise, and civil liberties applying to Chris Malley just as much as everybody else.

And we had to admit that, no, we had no proof.

"Except the flyers," I suggested. "They might have fingerprints on them."

"They probably won't, if he has any sense. But even so, that isn't any use to us. We'd never be able to justify the resources to check the fingerprints on it, and take the fingerprints of all those who might have touched it, for elimination. Not for a bit of petty vandalism like this. And the person you're thinking of probably wouldn't be on our fingerprint database anyway, would he?"

"Probably not," I admitted.

That, then, seemed to be that.

Just before they left, however, the older, disillusioned

garda touched David lightly on the sleeve and with an almost-imperceptible jerk of the head eased him aside, away from me and his young colleague.

He spoke urgently and at some length into David's ear, and David was nodding understanding and – perhaps – agreement.

They returned to us and the garda said, "I'd suggest you take a photograph or two of the car. Just in case. On its own it means nothing, but it's better to have it than not. And then just wash it off."

"Thanks, Sergeant," said David.

We watched them leave and then turned back to my poor car.

"Will you get soapy water and cloths from the kitchen?" said David. "I'll just run upstairs and get my camera."

"Okay," I agreed.

Once he had taken photos from every angle we began to wash off the lipstick.

I waited until we were nearly finished before asking, "What did the Guard say to you?"

David paused in his washing to speak to me, and I paused to listen. "He told me that while he understood our frustration, there was nothing more they could do. He told me that we were on no account to take the law into our own hands, that civilisation depended on due process and the rule of law. However," and he grinned, "he acknowledged that if – by any chance – somebody *were* to have a quiet word in the stalker's ear, that they, the Guards, would be equally helpless to prove anything against *them* unless they were stupid enough to do it in front of witnesses. Indeed, he told me, even if they did do it in front of witnesses, there couldn't be a court case because giving friendly warnings against possible dangers wasn't a crime in this State, last he heard. But of course he would never, ever condone citizens doing it for themselves." And David winked at me.

"But Chris is living for reaction," I warned, worried. "We're only encouraging him if we respond to this. It's what he wants."

"Well," said David grimly, "I think it's time to give Chris Malley exactly what he wants. If he wants reaction, let's give it to him. Lots of reaction. More reaction than he ever expected. Enough to keep him going for a lifetime. Now, do you mind finishing here? I've a few phone calls to make."

And he strode off, leaving me standing staring after him in trepidation. And admiration.

Once I finished washing the car I replaced the washing paraphernalia and went upstairs to him.

He was sitting cross-legged on one of the sofas, his eyes closed and his hands resting on his thighs, palms upwards.

I stood and watched him and I was pierced with the knowledge of how dear he was to me. I loved him. He was infinitely precious to me.

Oh well, I consoled myself, it looked as if we would always be friends. He would always be part of my life. And if I wanted more, well, that was my problem. I would just have to get over it.

"Hi," he said into the silence, but without opening his eyes. "I should tell you that I'll be out this evening."

"Grand," I said. "Not that you're answerable to me for your comings and goings."

"True. But it's only manners when we're living together. And I think you'll be interested in why I'm going out."

"You're going to see Chris."

"Yes. Me and a few friends. We're going to have a word with him. I'm not looking forward to it. It's not my style to intimidate people. I'm much more the sort of man who likes to talk quietly but carry a big stick."

"I know."

"But that only works if sometimes you demonstrate the big stick, and are even," he said heavily, "prepared to use it."

He opened his eyes and looked at me. "And I am prepared to use it, Sally. This man has messed you around big time, and is still messing you around. That would be enough by itself to start waving big sticks. And now he's messing me around too, and threatening my business with his computer viruses and his tricks. I didn't tell you before, but he e-mailed everybody on our database saying that we were closing down. It took me and Liz all day to contact everybody and reassure them that we weren't."

"That's *awful!* I'm so sorry that I've brought this on you."

"It's not your fault. But it's up to me to do something about it. This is my business," he said heavily, "over which Darius and I have sweated blood and tears for seven years. My business which gives jobs to a reasonable number of people, which provides an excellent product to keep people fit and healthy. And he's threatening it out of pique because I've given you shelter?" David shook his head in incomprehension and, I noted, determination. "He's not getting away with it any more."

"Thank you," I said simply. "Thank you."

He opened his eyes then, swung his feet to the ground and stood up. "Come here to me," he half-asked, half-demanded. "Come here," and he held his arms open and I crossed to him and went into his strong and embracing arms.

We held each other for a while and I leaned my head against his chest and listened to his heartbeat. It was beating quickly – nerves because of this evening's endeavour, I concluded.

We stood in silence, rocking slightly, and I tried to drink in the sensation of it all, to burn it into my cells and my memory banks so that when time had passed and David and I were just ordinary friends again, I would be able to recall the sensation of his strong arms holding me tight, and the heat of his body and the power of his beating heart and his warm breath caressing the top of my head.

Eventually he pulled away – he had to, because I never would. We'd be there yet if it were up to me.

"I'm going downstairs for a workout," he told me, "and a swim. And then I think I'll go over to the studio for some Aikido. I probably won't be back until after we have . . . er . . . spoken to Chris." He disappeared into his bedroom and reappeared with his sports bag.

"See you later," he said, dropping a kiss on my cheek, and then leaving.

Chapter 39

I looked after the closed door and wondered what to do with the rest of the day. It would be a long day, just waiting for the evening. With a groan I remembered my promise to Gaby, that I would phone my mother. Well, I had nothing else to do, and it would get it over with.

I lifted the phone and got an outside line, and then dialled the familiar number. But I only let it ring for one or two seconds before I replaced the handset. This wasn't a conversation to be having over the phone.

I would call around to her house, I decided.

Accordingly I grabbed my bag and went downstairs.

As I passed reception I saw Liz give a guilty start when she noticed me, at which, of course, I looked more closely at what she was doing. Which was stuffing a big bouquet of flowers into a plastic bin bag. That's the last one of those, I told myself. I hope.

When I got into the car I checked the tyres for nails

and other booby traps. All looked safe. That might be the last time I had to do that.

I drove around to my mother's house. Not the one she and I had originally lived in, nor even the one we had moved to when she had married Barry. Oh no. This was the executive house, bigger than they needed, in a prestigious address. My mother and stepfather were upwardly mobile people, and their residence reflected that. My mother now belonged to the right bridge clubs, the right tennis club and the right charity. If I sound bitchy it's because I am. Sorry. I tried to pull myself together – this wasn't the attitude to bring with me to a reconciliation, no matter how superficial.

I pulled up outside the house and got out. I walked resolutely up the driveway and rang the doorbell. After a couple of minutes I heard footsteps and the door opened. And there stood my mother. Looking a decade younger than her fifty-one years, slender, beautifully coiffed and impeccably dressed.

"Sally!" she said in surprise. "I wasn't expecting you. Come in, do."

She led the way into the immaculate kitchen, put on the kettle and began gathering the other accoutrements of tea-making. The fancy biscuits and the good china, I noted.

"You've lost weight," she observed. "It suits you."

She belongs to the Wallis Simpson school of ideal figures.

"And you've changed your hair – I like it. I didn't like to say it at the time, but I never liked the blonde – so common."

"How are you, Mum?" I asked, feeling that familiar feeling rising in my stomach – that acidic, panicking frustration and rage which must *absolutely* be suppressed and held down lest all hell break loose. "And how's Barry?"

"Oh, we're fine," she said, and as she completed her preparations she regaled me with how well she was doing in the bridge club and the tennis club, and Barry's doings in the golf club.

"And Laura and Eva?" I asked when she dried up on that subject.

She sat down with me and poured tea. "They're great. Laura's graduation went well," she said pointedly. "We had a great time. We were so proud of her."

"Were you proud of me?" I said before I knew I was going to say it.

She looked at me in surprise, the bone-china cup and her perfectly manicured fingers paused in mid-air. "Whatever do you mean?"

"When I graduated, were you proud of me?"

"Well, of course I was," she said brusquely.

"It's just that you never said you were. Or gave that appearance."

She gave a big sigh and put down her cup. "Look, Sally, is this more of the old 'you never loved me' song? I should warn you that I'm pretty tired of it by now."

I could feel stress and upset rising, the acidic flavour of disapproval.

"Yes, the timing of your birth was unfortunate – nobody would ever argue that that was the optimum situation. But we did the best we could, your father and

I. We both love you very much," she said, but she sounded irritated rather than loving, and the words were therefore hollow to me. "Barry is very fond of you . . . despite your best efforts I might add. You were awful to him when we married with your little chip on your shoulder, and I think that all credit for such a relationship as you do have, goes to him. He tried very hard with you. He was very good to you."

"I never said he wasn't," I protested. "I've no problem with Barry, he doesn't owe me anything, and you're right, he has given me lots."

She carried on despite my interjection, "And your father loves you. There's many the eighteen-year-old boy who would have totally run away from that situation, but he stuck by me, by us. From your earliest days he was there for you as much as he could be, financially supported you as much as he could. He and I could never have lasted together, we were only teenagers, but he's a very good man, Sally, and I won't hear a word against him."

"I *know*," I said anguished. "He's been very good to me too. But even the way you say that . . . as if I should be grateful that he hung around, as if he did me a favour by doing so. Surely that was my birthright? And even though other teenage fathers deny their children their birthright, that doesn't make it any less a right rather than a gift. Why should I have to be grateful to him for that?"

She glared icily at me.

"Some people are never grateful for anything," she said, and continued, "Laura and Eva love you, and they have, I might say, young lady, been very hurt by your neglect of them these past months. Not everything's about you, you know. Your sisters have feelings too."

"How did this get to being about me being in the wrong?" I asked, impassioned. "I'm sorry that I was mean to Barry when you married, but did nobody ever stop to think that that is because I was hurting? I wasn't trying to be nasty. I was in pain."

"Oh, for heaven's sakes! More people should be in such pain, to have a kind decent man agree to take them on! To be able to have a traditional family. You'll forgive me," she said sarcastically, "if I don't have too much sympathy with that."

"I always felt like an outsider, and that hurt," I said, my voice breaking. "That still hurts. Look, even now," I said bitterly, "you've put out the best china and the posh biscuits, whereas I know Laura and Eva would get the plain family mugs and digestives – because they're family, and you're treating me like a guest!"

She stared at me derisively. "Let me get this right?" she asked slowly. "You are complaining because I am treating you *too* well? Because I am honouring you with good china?" She shook her head in despair. "There is absolutely no pleasing you," she said dismissively, "and I don't know why I even try."

"Can you not see any of my point of view?" I pleaded. "See how I always felt that I was a burden, my very existence a problem which had to be dealt with, whereas Laura and Eva were treated like treasured gifts?"

"You have had a chip on your shoulder from the day you were born," she said firmly, obviously not going to accept any of what I said lest she have to examine her own behaviour, lest she might have to admit to being in any way less than perfect, "and I really am not going to play your games, Sally. I'm not going to buy into this 'poor me' role you're playing. You *are* loved," she said crossly, "and you *are* a member of this family no matter what you decide to think. Any lack of love or belonging or whatever, is only in your imagination."

"Right," I said sadly. We were getting nowhere near an understanding, we had never done so, and were unlikely to do so in the future.

I had honoured my promise to Gaby, but in this at least there was going to be no happy ending. It would have been nice if my mother had acknowledged any of my pain and hurt, and had even acknowledged that it was possible she could have made mistakes – that's all it would have taken. But it was not to be. We would carry on, awkwardly colliding against each other whenever we unavoidably met. Which hopefully wouldn't be too often.

She hadn't even regretted my months-long absence. She obviously hadn't tried to phone me in all those months. Of course, she would say that that was because I had cut off communications when I refused to go to Laura's graduation. There's an answer for everything for her.

Or maybe she's right. Maybe it is all my imagination, product of the chip on the shoulder with which I was born like a caul or bright red strawberry birthmark.

"I've moved," I told her. "I'm not reachable at my old mobile number, and I don't have a new mobile yet – I'll let you know when I do. In the meantime, here's the number of where I'm staying for the moment," and I gave her a piece of paper on which I had written *Svelte's* phone number. "Just ask for me. If you ring."

"Okay," she said, placing the piece of paper beside her on the table. "I'll write this into the address book later. That explains something, though. Laura was saying she was trying to ring you but couldn't get through. She was quite concerned about you, because none of us knew where you were and couldn't contact you, but I remember telling her that I was sure you were fine. And wasn't I right?" she asked, beaming at me.

"I'd better go," I said abruptly, thinking that if I stayed I would either burst into tears or kill her, and I didn't know which would be worse.

"Going so soon?" she asked surprised. "Fair enough. I know you young ones, always so busy! Thanks for dropping by. I'll tell Barry you were asking after him."

She walked with me to the door and gracefully proffered her cheek for me to kiss. I obliged. And we parted. At least we had re-established diplomatic relations, I thought. At least there was that. No matter how shallow and tense those relations, at least they were there.

Chapter 40

I drove back to *Svelte* and went up to the flat.

From there I phoned Laura on her mobile.

"Laura, hi, it's me."

"Sally!" she shrieked. "Sally, how *are* you? It's *great* to hear from you! I've been trying to reach you for *ages*. Are you okay? Can we meet? I've loads to tell you, and I want to hear your news too."

She would too, I knew. Laura always had plenty to say, but she was one of those rare talkative people who would ask questions too, and – get this! – actually listen to the answers.

I laughed suddenly – the age gap between Laura and me might have been too great, and the jealousy too deep, for us to have any relationship when we were children together. But maybe we could forge a new relationship now that we were adults.

"Can we meet now?" I asked hopefully. It was still

only lunch-time, there were hours of the day to fill yet
before David came back.

"I can't," she said regretfully. "I'm working. That's
part of what I want to tell you about. It's so exciting!
What about this evening? Around ten? That too late for
you?"

"Can't do this evening," I said, equally regretfully. I
needed to see David, to hear how his adventure had
gone. Actually, I just needed to see David, to be with him,
to breathe the same air as he breathed.

It transpired that Sunday didn't suit Laura either;
she was free on Monday but that probably wouldn't suit
me. Oh, it would? *Fabulous!* We arranged to meet on
Monday for a long sisterly (her words!) chat.

"How's Eva?" I asked.

"Oh," she said dismissively, "Eva! Loving college, not
studying, breaking hearts. She's so like Mum – superficial
and, well, I'm sorry to say it, emotionally cold."

I gasped as her words hit me. Laura might have
been sorry to say it but I was totally delighted to hear it.
Somebody else who said my mother was emotionally
cold! It wasn't my imagination. It wasn't some handy (for
her) chip on my shoulder, which could conveniently
explain away any doubts I had as being my own problem.
There was a sudden lightness on my shoulders as that
burden eased.

At last I knew it wasn't my imagination. I knew now
that what I was experiencing as reality *was* reality.

And another thought hit me: that in a way my mother
had always done to a small extent what Chris had done to
extremes: denied my reality of what I experienced. No

wonder he had found it so easy. I had been raised to believe that other people's perceptions were more valid than my own reality.

Amid mutual virtual kisses and real good wishes, and expressions of looking forward to Monday, Laura and I hung up. Well, I was on a roll now. I might as well keep going.

I phoned Carla who expressed herself delighted to hear from me; she had been thinking so much about me, really wanted to catch up with me. I arranged to see her and the twins on Tuesday. I then phoned Sandra who shrieked with excitement at hearing from me, apologised profusely for not having been in touch. She had meant to but it was just so busy, but listen, what was I doing next Saturday night? Herself and a bunch of friends from work were going out on the town, would I come? I would? That was great!

I next phoned Jan and left a message on her answering machine, and then I went downstairs and, with Liz's help and permission, sent an e-mail to Majella in New Zealand.

Friends are too precious to let drop, I realised. I wasn't going to lose these people again.

In this way the afternoon passed and it was soon early evening. The silence was total up there in that flat, and I sat and waited. And I thought about things, and a realisation came to me.

I texted David. *Please come and see me before you leave. I need to speak to you first.*

He texted back a succinct: *Will do.*

* * *

Towards eight o'clock I heard footsteps on the stairs, the door opened and David came in. His wet hair suggested that he was freshly showered, and his grim expression suggested a distaste for the encounter to come.

"Hi," he said tersely, "you wanted to see me."

"I did. David, I've been thinking. And I have to come with you this evening."

"No way. It won't be pretty and I don't want you exposed to that." He was adamant.

"Please let me come," I pleaded, and when I saw his expression remain obdurate, I changed tack, "Okay. But please just listen to me. Once you've heard what I have to say you might agree to let me come. And in return," I offered hurriedly as I saw him begin to shake his head in refusal, "I promise that if you genuinely listen to me, and you still think I shouldn't go, then I won't argue any more."

"Okay," he acquiesced at that, and I knew him well enough to know that he was thinking he would listen in order to humour me, and *then* say no. So be it. It was up to me to convince him otherwise.

"David," I said, and took a deep breath, marshalling my arguments. "I have spent the last months terrified of Chris, and I realise that I still am scared of him. But if I can come with you, and see him cowed and down, it will free me from that. In my mind – I know it's not rational – but in my mind he's this huge, powerful bogeyman. He dominated me for so long. I need to see him brought down to size before I can move on."

I could see the conflict in David's expression. He still

wanted to shield me from what promised to be an unpleasant experience, but he was seeing the sense of what I was saying.

"It would be so good for me," I pressed home my advantage. "It really would."

David's expression was inscrutable as he stared intently at me. After a moment or two he said reluctantly, "Okay. I don't like it. Not one bit. But you can come."

"Great! Thanks David. I really, really appreciate that."

"Hmm," he said dubiously. "Okay, if you're coming, then come."

I put on my jacket, which I had to hand. "I'm ready," I replied.

"Let's go then."

He led the way downstairs to the lobby. Five well-built men were waiting for us there.

"This is Sally, everybody," David told them, and to me, nodding at each in turn, "Ger, Sean, Ronan, Brian, Philip."

"Hi," I said to each, and, "Thanks."

They nodded their acknowledgments.

"Okay, guys," said David. "The plan has changed a little. Sally's coming with us."

I saw them exchanging glances, but nobody questioned it.

"Sure, David," they told him.

We split up into two cars, David's and Ronan's. Ronan would follow us to Chris's house.

Chapter 41

We drove in silence. There was a tension in the car. Not fear exactly, but something close. Nervousness maybe.

We parked down from his house and walked back to it. I was aware of my heart beating strongly in my chest. Despite the presence of these six strong men I was aware of fear and trepidation. Whatever happened, it was going to be confrontational and unpleasant.

But it would end with Chris cowed, Chris too scared to come near me again. And me free of my fear of him.

Lights were on inside the house, which was good. That had been the flaw in the plan – what if he was out? But he wasn't.

We walked quietly up the short path.

"Sally, you stand over there," David told me, pointing off towards one side. I couldn't see his expression in the dim light, but his voice didn't brook argument and I complied.

The others ranged themselves around him, and he rang the doorbell.

A moment or two later it opened, and Chris stood there.

From the light spilling out of the hall I could see his eyes widening with shock and, yes, fear when he saw the men standing there.

"What? What's going on?" he asked, looking from one to the other of them, alarm in his voice.

"We've come to tell you to leave Sally Cronin alone," David said. His voice was stern, with no warmth in it whatsoever, and I, for one, wouldn't have argued with him.

"Sally Cronin? What about her?" Chris said, playing for time.

David took a small, menacing, step forward, and on this cue his friends did too. Chris took a small, cautionary step backwards.

"You – are – to – leave- Sally – Cronin – alone," said David, enunciating each word separately. "Do you understand?"

"But I never went near her!" Chris protested, the epitome of innocence.

Anybody overhearing this conversation would have been convinced of his blamelessness.

But not David.

"Malley, don't give me that crap. I'm not interested in discussing it with you. I don't want to hear your excuses, or your denials, or anything.

"Look – " he began, but just then the sitting-room door opened.

A young woman stepped into the hall. She was plump, bespectacled, barely into her twenties it looked like.

"Chris, what's going on? Who's this?"

He turned to her. "Why don't you mind your own business?" he said rudely. "Go back into the sitting-room. I'll be in when I'm good and ready."

She gave him an apprehensive look and turned away.

My heart turned over with pity for her.

I pushed forward, up beside the men.

I called her, "Hey!"

She stopped, and turned towards me.

"*Bri-dget*," Chris said, drawing the syllables out in a warning, and immediately she turned back and opened the sitting-room door.

"*Bridget! Listen to me!*" I shouted, even as she went into the room and was closing the door behind her. "*Some day you'll need my help! Sally at Svelte gym, remember that! The number's in the book. Ring me. I can help you!*"

I had no idea if she heard me, or if she would pay me any attention even if she had. God knows what Chris had told her about me in order to garner her sympathy, and to undermine any credibility I might have.

"Nice try," sneered Chris to me, conjuring up some bravado from somewhere.

"Right, that's it," said David. "Sally," he said, hugely irritated, "go over there as I asked you."

Chastened, I stepped back.

As I did so, David stepped right forward, up onto the porch, and stood very close to Chris. Chris, again, took a step backwards.

"Malley, I'm not listening to any more of your crap. You're to stop messing around with Sally. Or else we will make you very sorry that you didn't. Do you understand?"

Chris nodded, completely deflated now that David was so close to him, looming over him so threateningly.

"Good. Because it's important for your safety and well-being that you hear this. *Leave – Sally – Alone*," David enunciated carefully. "*Keep – Well – Away – From – Her.* Or the boys and I will be back, and we will hurt you. I mean it."

He certainly sounded like he meant it, and to judge by Chris's frightened and trapped expression, he also believed it all too well.

"You had better hope that Sally never, *ever* gets a genuine puncture," David went on. "You had better pray that no genuine admirer ever sends her flowers anonymously. Because we won't be giving you the benefit of the doubt, Chris. We really won't. We'll be back at the slightest excuse. In fact," he continued, anger in his voice, "I'm really hoping that you, or somebody else, gives us that excuse. After what you've done to Sally, and what you've tried to do to my business, it would give me the greatest of pleasure to come back here."

Chris was nodding pathetically at this stage.

"And one last thing. We called the guards after this morning's incident. They're disgusted at what you've been doing, and frustrated that they can't do anything about it. So they've made it clear that if anything does happen to you, they won't be looking too hard for any culprit."

That was stretching what the garda had said a *lot*. But no matter – it was clear, from the hopeless expression on Chris's face, that he believed it. Which was good for us. The more he believed David could, and would, claim retribution for anything that happened to me, the safer I would be.

"So . . . what's your decision?" David asked interestedly, as though he didn't care either way, but was curious to find out. "Are you going to leave Sally alone, or am I going to have the pleasure of smashing your face?"

"I'll leave her alone. I swear it."

David looked appraisingly at him for a moment or two.

"Fine," he said, disappointment in his voice. "Pity. We'll be off, so. But we'll be back if necessary. Come on, Sally, guys."

He turned and walked away, and we followed him.

There was silence from behind us for some long seconds, and then we heard the door close.

* * *

I don't know about the people in Ronan's car, but the four of us in David's car were all subdued, and the journey home was made in near silence.

At one point David cleared his throat and asked, "Did I sound convincing? When I said I was dying for the excuse to beat him up, did he believe me?"

We assured him that he had sounded convincing, that we had believed him ourselves. And Chris, we were certain, had believed him totally.

"Good," muttered David wearily, and said no more.

Just before we parted company with the five men in *Svelte's* carpark, David said, "Thanks, lads. I owe you one."

"Sure thing," they answered, and, "No problem."

"Anyone for a drink?" asked one of them, and most of the others were on for it.

"Not me, I'm afraid," said David. "I'm whacked. Catch you next week, though. We'll have a few drinks then."

We made our way upstairs to the flat.

"Would you like a glass of wine?" David asked me.

"Yes, please."

He opened a bottle of white wine, and we sat together on one of the sofas, the bottle of wine and our two glasses on the table in front of us. I was conscious of a deep weariness, but also a huge relief.

"Thank you for that," I told him. "I can move on with my life now."

"Yes," said David, "you can. I'm glad I helped you be able to do that." And not surprisingly there was satisfaction in his tone, at the help he had been able to give me. But there was some sadness too.

"You'll be moving away from me," he said. "I'll miss you."

"I'll miss you too," I said. "I've really enjoyed living with you. But it won't be for a while, and I'll only be going as far as the bed-sit in the first instance. I don't even have a proper job yet, no way of getting my own place for ages. It'll be a while yet," I said again, feeling great relief at that realisation.

"Yes," he said, relief in his own voice, "it'll be a while yet."

He's so nice, I found myself thinking, and I wondered yet again why he had no lover, or none that I could see. He was so handsome, so nice, such a great person, you'd think the guys would be queuing up. Maybe he's just over a break-up, I thought. And I knew that I would never ask him. For all that we had shared, all that we were to each other, he had never spoken to me of his homosexuality, and I honoured that. It was none of my business after all.

David closed his eyes and sipped his wine, and I respected his silence.

Eventually he said, "It wasn't easy."

"No," I said, encouragingly.

"I felt like a bully myself. Even though I knew he deserved it, and I knew it was the only way, it was still tough."

"Thank you again for doing it."

He made a don't-mention-it dismissive gesture.

Then he opened his eyes and looked at me. He sat forward and placed his almost-untouched wine glass on the coffee table.

"Do you know what? One of the perks of living above the shop is that occasionally I go down to the pool for a swim late at night. And tonight is one of those nights. Care to join me?"

"Sure," I said, "I'd love to." A midnight swim sounded luscious. And we would have the pool to ourselves.

"Come on then," he said. "Let's do it before we drink any more wine. We can finish the bottle when we come back."

Chapter 42

Accordingly we went to our respective rooms to get our swimsuits and towels, and met again in the sitting-room.

"Hush," whispered David into my ear, his breath warm against me, "we have to be quiet in case anybody hears us."

"Who could possibly hear us?" I whispered back. "The place is no doubt empty." It was Saturday night – Darius and the other residential staff would be all out having a life.

"You never know," he said mock-solemnly, and we both burst out laughing. So we whispered and giggled together as we sneaked our way down the stairs, laughingly telling each other to hush. Probably making even more noise than normal.

But yet, sometimes it's much more fun to feel you're getting away with something you shouldn't do, even when you have to pretend. Besides, whispering meant

I had to stay physically close to him, and I wasn't arguing about that.

David unlocked the office door and went in to get the key to the swimming-pool section, and then quietly he unlocked the door to that and led the way in.

"The lights in the changing room are just inside the door. I'll see you in the pool," he whispered, and disappeared into the Men's changing room. I went into the Ladies' and fumbled for the light switch and switched it on, blinking in the sudden brightness. The room was spooky in its quietness and emptiness. I had stopped giggling now, the silence was a little oppressive. I quickly stripped and put on my swimsuit and cap and went to the pool area.

The pool was lit by a mixture of the blue-tinted moonlight and the yellow-orange street-lights. The water was totally calm and very enticing.

"It's nice, isn't it?" whispered David from behind me.

He put a hand on each of my shoulders and I could feel his body heat behind me. I wanted, I so badly wanted, to lean back that fraction so that our bodies were touching, but with a massive amount of self-control I managed to restrain myself.

"It's so quiet," he continued. "I love it like this. Come on."

He led the way to the edge of the pool and then he dived elegantly, scarcely rippling the water. I watched entranced as he glided under the water – smooth and flexible, elegant and strong – and then surfaced. He shook his head to clear his eyes and ears of water. In the semi-darkness his skin-tone gleamed.

"Come in," he called in a whisper. "The water's lovely."

I didn't feel confident enough to dive in, but I went to the ladder and climbed into the pool. The water was warm and embracing, and I struck out, my arms and legs moving smoothly, enjoying that indefinable pleasure of swimming, of moving through this alien environment.

And, much as I enjoyed swimming usually, tonight was magic. Tonight was special. I was at last free from the fear of Chris and what he might do.

I was very aware of the silence, the muted light, the space and privacy we had. And above all, I was so aware of David's presence. I couldn't see him, and as I swam I didn't look for him.

It was enough to know that he was there and I was there. My body was all but vibrating with responsiveness towards him.

Get over it, I told myself crossly. It's going to go nowhere, going to do you no good. But it was hard to get over it right now this minute when the atmosphere was so redolent with possibility (no matter how false), and the sensuality of the warm water's touch, and the almost-imperceptible sound of little wavelets gently lapping against the edge of the pool as we swam.

I'll get over it tomorrow, I promised myself. I'm not going to be a pathetic cliché, in love with a man who can never love me back. At least, who can never love me in the way I want and need to be loved. I'll get over it tomorrow, but for tonight I'm going to enjoy and treasure this experience.

Speaking of which, where was he? I stopped swimming and turned around, treading water. He was nowhere to be seen but then – I was vaguely aware of a dark shadow under me and in the same instant I was pulled underwater. I sank down, but I was released immediately and I burst to the surface. David surfaced beside me, laughing.

"Got you," he laughed. "Got you!"

I glared at him, but realised that I could get a sulk on, or see the funny side of it, and I chose the funny side.

"I'll get you!" I mock-threatened and I launched myself at him, grabbing hold of his shoulders and pushing. Of course, I got nowhere. I was still out of my depth and so had no purchase, whereas he was – I now realised – within his depth and able to brace himself.

But I kept pushing, the pleasure of having my hands on his naked shoulders was too much to give up. And then somehow, I had stopped pushing him, and I had eased my hands down a little, over the arc of his shoulders and onto his muscular upper arms. His skin was smooth and warm, strong in its masculine curves. I longed to place my mouth there.

I held on tight to his arms as they were the only thing supporting me, and I stopped kicking my legs, which caused them to sink until our bodies were softly length-to-length in the water, separated only by tiny strips of cloth.

I looked into his eyes, wary of seeing scorn there at my blatancy. But instead, in his eyes, in his expression, in the soft half-light, I could see an intensity of expression. I couldn't read it, but I was impelled by it, impelled to gaze into that expression, into those eyes.

Then, just then, I felt his two hands on my waist, and

he pulled me tighter against him. And he bent his head towards me, and beyond conscious thought I lifted my own head to meet his, and our mouths met.

He moved his lips on mine, and I opened my mouth for him and soon we were kissing deep and plundering and exploring. And it was everything I could possibly have imagined his kisses to be. I put my arms around his neck and clung to him and pulled myself closer still as we kissed, and he responded by lowering his hands to my bottom and cupping me there and pulling me even closer if that were possible. And in the water, against my tummy, I could clearly feel him hard against me.

We kissed for some unknowable time, and neither of us made a move towards doing anything else. It was enough, for me at least, to just kiss him as I had longed to do for so long, to feel his body against mine, his mouth moving against mine, his strong hands holding me tightly.

And then some sort of sense began to percolate. What on *earth* was I doing? This was *David* to whom I was clinging, against whom I was – I now realised – rubbing my body as I groaned at his kisses. This was David whose head I was caressing as I clung him to me. What had I been thinking? The answer was, of course, that I hadn't been thinking at all. But now . . . now that I *was* thinking . . .

I pulled away a little. "I didn't realise you were bi," I said.

He accepted gracefully the loss of my mouth to him, and dropped his own mouth to nuzzle my neck. I couldn't help it, I gasped aloud, and I could feel him leap in response against my stomach. Despite myself I arched my neck to offer him more accessibility, of which he took full advantage.

"You didn't realise I was by what?" he asked, mumbling a little as he continued to nuzzle. He sounded a little puzzled but not overly curious, concentrating elsewhere as he was.

I took me a moment or two to answer, seeing as I couldn't marshal my thoughts with what he was doing to me.

"Bisexual," I managed to say eventually.

That got his attention all right.

He abruptly stopped what he was doing and pulled back a little, still holding onto me, and looked at me.

"I'm not bisexual," he said, half-puzzled, half-amused. "Why should you think I am?"

"Because you're kissing me."

"I'm sorry," he said. "I must be very stupid. Why would kissing you make me bisexual?"

"Simply because you *are* kissing me." Why did he need this spelt out? "I'm confused now."

"So am I," he laughed.

"Look," I said, determined to sort this out, "let's start at the beginning. Why are you kissing me?"

He shook his head in bewilderment. "I'm kissing you because you're a beautiful woman. Because I've desired you for a long, long time. Because we've been getting emotionally close. It seemed the right time. You didn't seem averse to it. All of the above."

"You've desired me for a long time? Even though I'm a woman?"

"Precisely because you're a woman," he said laughing, but a little uncertainly. "Look, Sally, I've an awful feeling that we're at cross-purposes here. You seem to be assuming some knowledge I don't have. Please explain, in words of one syllable spoken slowly, what you're on about. From the beginning."

"Okay." I took a deep breath. "It just seems to me to be very surprising that you're kissing me even though you're gay."

He went very, very still.

"I'm not gay," he said slowly. "Who told you I was gay?"

"Well . . . I just knew . . . I mean," I laughed nervously, "everybody knows."

"Not everybody. Not me for example. Who told you I was gay?" he asked again.

I thought back. When exactly had I heard it first?

Then I remembered. "The women in the changing rooms! One of them said you were cute, and another one, she seems to be the leader of that clique, laughed at her and said you were gay, and the others all laughed along with her and agreed that, yes, you were."

"What woman is this?" His voice was severe.

"I don't know her name. She's tall, and slim, with long red hair."

"Maura Donohue!" he breathed. "The *bitch!*."

"Why . . . what?" It was beginning to percolate through, the fact that he was saying he wasn't gay!

"She made a pass at me," he explained, still holding me, "and I turned her down. Nicely, I thought. Explained that I didn't date our clients. Although I was glad of

461

that excuse, I wouldn't have gone near her anyway. But either she genuinely thought the only reason anybody would turn her down was because he was gay – or she wanted to ruin anybody else's chance with me. I'll have words with her," he promised, "just about the time I refund her membership fee."

I spared no sympathy for Maura Donohue, about to get her marching orders. I had other things to think of.

"Really? You're really not gay?" I asked.

"Definitely not!"

"But," I said, "one day I saw you eyeing up some man in the snack-bar."

"No! You couldn't have."

"I'm serious! You were seriously eyeing him up, David. I didn't imagine it. And you were distracted for the rest of the conversation with me, your eyes kept returning to him. I don't blame you," I added to be fair. "He *was* seriously delectable."

"Describe him," demanded David, "because I sure as hell don't remember eyeing up any man."

"He was a hunk," I said. "That really was his defining feature. I can't remember much else about him. I do remember thinking that he would have made Arnie Schwarzenegger jealous."

"A hunk?" said David, giving a very good impression of a man who was searching his memory banks. "It wasn't . . . I wonder could it have been Jack FitzMaurice?" he said then. "That was one man who would definitely correspond to that description, and I was very interested in him all right," he said, "but again, not in a sexual way."

462

"No?"

"No. I was interested because he was bulking up way beyond what you would expect for his build and his training programme, and I was convinced – still am – that he was on steroids and God-knows-what-else. Darius and I didn't want stuff like that going on because it just gives the place a bad name. And I was watching him because I didn't really know what to do about it, didn't know how best to handle it."

"Ohhh," I breathed. It was plausible, wonderfully fabulously plausible.

"So, is that the sum of your 'evidence' for me being gay?" he asked. "And have I convinced you otherwise?"

"Essential oils in your bathroom? The fact that you like chick-flicks? The fact that you said it wasn't appropriate to tell me I was beautiful?" I hazarded, laughing now. *He isn't gay! He isn't gay!* my heart sang.

"Essential oils? To impress the women," he answered, equally laughing. "As for chick-flicks – I can't stand them. But I like *you*, and you wouldn't come out to anything else with me. I would have gone to wet-paint-watching if it meant being with you. And I didn't feel it was appropriate to tell you that you were beautiful when you were a guest in my home and I was honour-bound to treat you with respect."

My heart sang as he said that. He likes me! He likes me enough to go to chick-flicks and pretend to enjoy them!!

"So, seriously, Sally. Do you believe me that I'm not gay? Because I truly am as heterosexual as any man could be. As I was in the process of proving earlier."

"Maybe . . . maybe you could prove it again," I suggested. "Just so I can be sure."

He bent his head to kiss me, and this time I was able to give myself unreservedly up to the sensations. We kissed and sucked and his hands wandered over my skin and I glowed wherever he touched me, and I flayed my palm over his strong shoulders, and the shallow masculine curve of his pectoral muscles and brushed his nipple and he breathed in sharply.

We explored each other as if we were inventing this process, as indeed we were inventing what it would be like between us. We caressed each other where we chose, and the warm water caressed and embraced us. We floated together, and my thoughts floated as my body gave itself over to its sensations.

His breath was hot against my neck, and he was groaning and murmuring to me, and I arched myself against him and whimpered as he touched me as he pleased. I wrapped my legs around his waist and clung to his broad shoulders and nuzzled his ear and he muttered expletives of pleasure.

Until it became too much. And not enough, all at the same time. Until he clung to me and whispered, "Now?", and, there in that pool in which I had swum length after length, never dreaming of this moment, David Corrigan came into me, and I claimed him as he was claiming me.

Afterwards we drifted together, sated and exhausted, and he was idly caressing my stomach.

"You're so beautiful," he said, "and I've wanted you for so long. I hardly dared to dream this day would come."

"Why did you never ask me out?" I asked him. "If you liked me before? We could have been together for ages already."

"I know," he said sadly. "I so, so, wish I had. But I was struggling with my conscience. Darius does enough seducing the clients for both of us – it's a bit of a point of argument between us. He sees no harm in it, considers it at the same time a bit of a perk and another part of the service – Darius is pretty amoral – but I think it's very unprofessional. I wasn't lying to Maura Donohue when I said I didn't date clients. Because, I don't. And so I couldn't on the one hand complain about him doing this, and then turn around and get together with you. Not that what I had in mind for you was mere seduction, or a mere fling, but that was a subtle difference."

My heart was *singing* at hearing all this. It was like food and drink to me.

David continued, "I was getting my head around this, and I had planned to ask you out the very day that you told me, glowing with excitement, about meeting Chris. God, I should have got an Oscar for my acting when you told me that, having to pretend to be delighted for you. And at the time I was so grateful that you saved me from making a fool of myself. Now I wish we hadn't wasted all that time."

"And I could have avoided that whole experience with Chris." But I didn't want to dwell on that sad thought then, when I was so full of bliss, so I hurried on, "But we did find each other in the end. And that's all that matters now."

"Yes," he repeated, "we did find each other in the

end. And even though we have always been friends," he said smilingly, bending to kiss me again, "now we can be way, way, more than friends."

And that was exactly what I had in mind.

THE END

Published by poolbeg.com

Loving Lucy

TRACY CULLETON

'Ray could charm his way out of, through or around any situation. He certainly had always been able to get his way around me . . . until now.'

Although Tory is delighted that Ray is – at long last – showing an interest in their daughter Lucy, no amount of charm will convince her to allow him access until he's cleaned up his act.

But evidently Ray doesn't want to wait that long – soon afterwards, Tory gets a panic-stricken call from Lucy's childminder, Carol. Carol frantically relates how Ray has snatched Lucy from her, and worse, he's threatened he'll harm Lucy if Tory follows him.

Despite that warning, Tory feels compelled to find Lucy – but is she putting her little girl's life at risk by doing so? Would Ray really hurt their beautiful daughter? At least she's not alone in her search: Connor, Ray's ex-landlord, is clearly touched by her despair and offers to help get her daughter back.

But after being so cruelly betrayed already, how can she trust him? Is there some other motive behind his kindness?

And above all: will she find Lucy safely?

ISBN 1-84223-156-1

Published by **poolbeg.com**

Looking Good

TRACY CULLETON

*"I never forget that happiness is a
choice and that sometimes you have
to make that choice every day."*

But it's easy to be happy when you have no
problems. Grainne and Patrick are madly in love,
with successful careers, plenty of money, holidays
and romance. The only thing missing from their
lives is a baby, and for Grainne this is fast becoming
an obsession.

But on a cold November night on cold hard tiles,
Grainne's old life is suddenly and irrevocably ended
and a new uncertain one begins.

Now she has to question all she believes and trusts.
Now she has to begin again, to find resources she doesn't
know she has. Is her new life worth the
cost of everything they shared? Is it worth losing
Patrick for? Maybe it is.

Of one thing she is certain: the decisions she will
have to face will take all the courage she can grasp.

ISBN 1-84223-155-3